THE 2ND DEMON

TALES OF THE GRIMVOX

THE CHRONICLES OF JONATHAN STEEL
BOOK TEN

BRUCE HENNIGAN

MY BOOKS

Hope Again: A Lifetime Plan for Conquering Depression (with Mark Sutton)

The Homecoming Tree

Our Darkness, His Light

Shadow Merchant (A Jack Merchant Medical Mystery)

Just a Bite of Something Sweet: At Christmas

Death by Darwin (Jonathan Steel Prequel)

The 13th Demon: Altar of the Spiral Eye

The 12th Demon: Mark of the Wolf Dragon

The 11th Demon: The Ark of Chaos

The 10th Demon: Children of the Bloodstone

The 9th Demon: Time of the Cross

The 8th Demon: A Wicked Numinosity

The 7th Demon: The Pandora Stone

The 5th Demon: Demoneyes

The 4th Demon: Trial of the 3rd Demon

The 2nd Demon: Tales of the Grimvox

Can be found at hopeagainbooks.com

Contributed to:

Time Passages: Volume 1: A Collection of Diverse Short Stories

https://a.co/d/dBBnvaH

Copyright © 2024 by Bruce Hennigan

All rights reserved.

Print ISBN: 979-8-9871996-8-8

Ebook ISBN: 979-8-9871996-9-5

An imprint of 613media,LLC — Area613

Cover and layout design by ebooklaunch.com

All scripture quotes are from the NIV version.

No part of this book may be reproduced in any form or by any electronic or mechanical means, including information storage and retrieval systems, without written permission from the author, except for the use of brief quotations in a book review.

Websites:

hopeagainbooks.com

brucehennigan.com

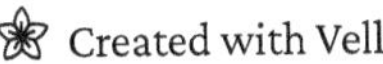 Created with Vellum

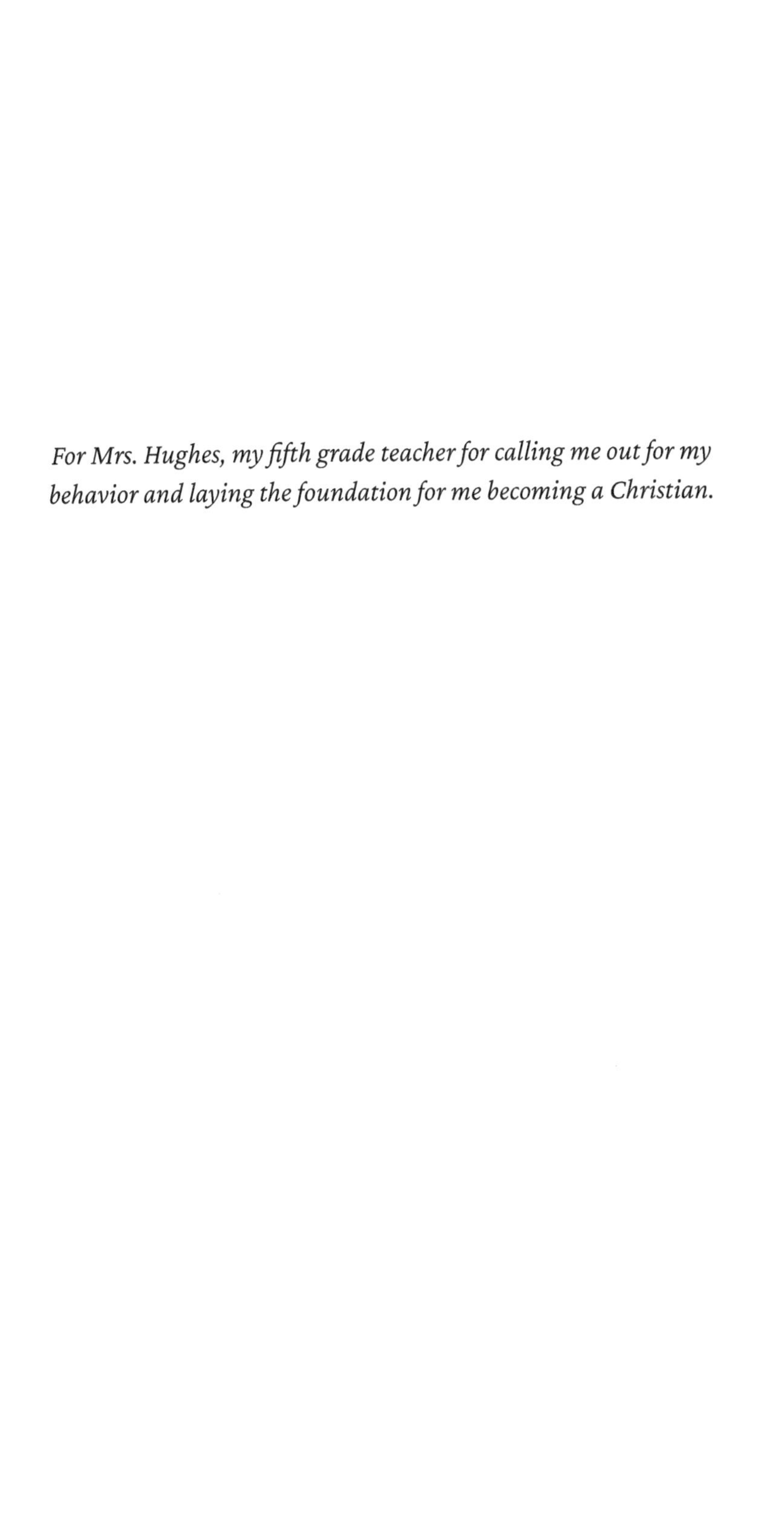

For Mrs. Hughes, my fifth grade teacher for calling me out for my behavior and laying the foundation for me becoming a Christian.

FOREWORD

This is the next to the last book in the series, "The Chronicles of Jonathan Steel". I have taken pains to make sure and summarize some past events. But understanding the unfolding story will require familiarity with the story up until now.

SPOILERS AHEAD!

The 13th Demon introduces Jonathan Steel, a man with no past. Steel helps Reverend Thomas Parker eliminate the demon from his church. In the process a physicist, Claire Knight loses her life protecting her son from Robert Ketrick, the man in league with the thirteenth demon. The demon escapes and Steel finds himself in custody of a surly teenager, Joshua Knight

The 12th demon introduces Steel's mentor, Dr. Cephas Lawrence, great uncle to Josh. Josh tries to help his girlfriend by infiltrating a vampire clan whose members are under the control of Rudolph Wulf and the 12th Demon. With the help of his new partner, Theo King, Steels tries to stop Wulf from unleashing an army of demon vampires on the world.

The 11th Demon finds Steel and company battling against an ancient demonic "council" warring with the Council of Darkness, the Vitreomancers. These humans with totally white eyes, are hatching a plan of world domination. The 11th demon, Mary Alba oversees a plan to assassinate an important government figure. Steel and company stop the assassination and defeat the eleventh demon.

The 10th Demon goes into nearby orbit to a space station constructed by Anthony Cobalt and his 10th demon. His plan is to use a coronal mass ejection from the sun to power an ancient artifact and open a doorway to another distant world. The book explores the UFO (UAP) phenomenon and asks the question, "Are We Alone?".

The 9th Demon influences the world's richest man to create a "time machine" and send a group of explorers back in time to record the last week of Jesus' life. In reality he has built a false Jerusalem and is planning on staging a fake version to disprove Jesus rose from the dead. Steel pursues his kidnapped partner, Theo King truly back in time to ancient Jerusalem and must stop the 9th demon from changing history.

The 8th Demon has created a virtual world hoping to pull humanity into a cybernetic interface that opens their minds to demon possession. Steel and company find themselves in Numinocity as they race against time to stop the 8th Demon from enslaving millions.

The 7th Demon and the 5th Demon books cover three demons: 7,6, and 5 known as the unholy triad. Each has a task only Steel can complete. They use Dr. Nigel Hampton to give Josh a fatal virus. Only by helping the demons can Steel save Josh's life. Steel races against time to save Josh and somehow, complete the tasks while making sure the demons do not succeed.

The 4th Demon book covers the 4th and 3rd demons. Steel is arrested for murder and Josh tries to enlist Ruth Martinez, an attorney with a past relationship to Steel to free him. In the process Steel is taken by an angel to the hideout of the two people who know about his past. He learns about his childhood and begins to recover his lost memories. In the past, he was accused of killing his mother and Yvonne Brown, an attorney, helped him escape conviction. However, they discover Steel has a brother, Jeremiah he never knew. Jeremiah worked with the 3rd demon to kill their mother. The 4th Demon in league with a powerful judge is determined to put Steel away. In a stirring and moving courtroom battle, the third and fourth demon are defeated and Steel is freed.

CHAPTER

ONE

R emote island
      Somewhere in the Caribbean

THE CRIMSON SNAKE touched the photograph of the young man with the fingers of her good hand. Well, it was her *only* hand. The young man had to be in his teens with long, braided black hair and deep brown skin to match his eyes. She studied the biography beneath the photograph. He is fifteen. Correction, he *was* fifteen. Until he died in the fiery crash of Swiss Flight number? She winced, realizing she could not remember the number of the Swiss flight she had sabotaged.

If the young man had lived, what would he be doing now? Playing video games? Texting his friends? Breathing. Living. Or worse, abused by his parents, his siblings, his relatives, as she had been. Pablo Jaurez, she mouthed the name silently.

"Pablo." She said out loud, allowing the feel of his name to cross her lips. "Am I supposed to say I'm sorry?" The memory of sitting with Max, Vivian, and Raven returned. Max had activated the nannomemes placed in Snake's tea and had threatened to use them to keep Snake in control. Then she had pointed to this very notebook.

Max placed the tablet back in her satchel. "This is my insurance policy, Snake. I don't trust you. No one should. You have done nothing to earn such trust. If you are truly repentant, then you may find redemption. Open the notebook."

Snake glared at Max hotly and opened the notebook. A plastic sleeve held laminated cards. She pulled one from the sleeve. A photograph of a young girl filled one side of the card. She turned the card over. "Melissa Graff? Do I know her?" She read the name at the top of the card. Below it, more text detailed biographical information about Melissa.

"How could you? She is dead. Perished in the crash of your Swiss flight." Max said. "There are 255 cards. The rest of the notebook has brief biographies of each victim. The laptop carries videos of those victims. These cards are basically flash cards. Vivian will return in two months. If you have memorized the biography of each of your victims and can give her those details based on the photograph alone, then you will have taken the first step on your journey to redemption."

ACCORDING TO MAX'S RECORDS, Pablo was fifteen years old and lived in Spain. His favorite sport, or course, was soccer. Although he loved to snow ski. No doubt, Pablo had been heading for Switzerland to ski when his trip came to a tragic end. Snake drew a deep breath as she looked into the boy's deep brown eyes. Each photograph included an extensive biography. Snake had not paid much attention to the details. Never get close to your victims! Pablo's bio included what, for Snake, would be an unusual notation.

"Favorite Bible verses? Really? Since when do fifteen-year-olds read the Bible?" She silently read through the paragraphs ending with the notation, Ephesians 6:10-20. "Armor? Swords? Shields? Makes more sense now. Pablo, you lived in a fantasy world complete with fantasy armor!"

Snake closed the notebook, and she was surprised by a tear trickling from her right eye. She touched the tear that ran down her cheek and withdrew it on the tip of her finger. She studied it like it was an alien insect. And she felt something. A deep touch of nausea. Or more like butterflies in her stomach! Guilt. She was feeling guilt. Not that she was unfamiliar with the sensation. Guilt had been a powerful motivator in her childhood. That and the need to avoid pain. Now, the guilt had a different shimmer to it. A vibration she had never associated with her victims. All two hundred and something victims.

"255." She said. "If only I had armor when I was growing up! Even a sword would have been nice!"

Snake stood up from the tiny dining table in her one-room hut and walked out underneath the star filled night sky. A cool breeze blew in from the ocean and she walked down to the beach. The odor of fish and salt water engulfed her. The breeze swirled around her mixing in the heady fragrance of the flowers blooming along the path.

On the far horizon, lights glittered from the distant shore. She had not set foot off the island for almost three months. As Max promised, food arrived on a regular basis. Zeta, as the young woman was known, arrived on a small boat with supplies. Zeta never spoke a word to Snake, unloading the wheeled supply cart on the tiny dock and taking the empty cart Snake had placed there.

It was close to midnight, and she really needed to get some sleep. Sleep, once a welcome escape, had become more elusive since she had studied the notebook and its 255 victims. Yes, not two hundred and *something*. They were more than just *something*. They were people. Her conscience was awakening. She did not like it. Something clattered up the walkway to the hut. She whirled, her senses alert. Instinct for survival kicked in.

Snake slowly made her way up the walkway and stopped beside the outside table. Sitting in the center of the table was a dark, egg-shaped object about a foot and a half tall. She glanced around at the clearing that circled the hut. Silence. No one moved in the darkness. Above her, a cone of light illuminated the table. A drone hovered over the table. It had delivered the strange object. What was it? More of Max's doings?

Snake sat at the table and regarded the object with wary eyes. Why was it here? She reached out and touched the pebbly surface with her finger, and an electric shock ran up her arm. Ozone tainted the air mixed with a hint of sulfur. She jerked her hand away, and the tingling sensation moved across her chest to her shoulder and down the stump of her missing arm. The tingling sensation became an itch and then a burning sensation. She stood up and her fell chair behind her. The tingling filled the empty air where her arm should have been. Her mouth fell open in astonishment as the tip of her stump swelled and shot outward in a flesh-colored spike that elongated and shaped itself into a forearm and a hand.

Snake held the new arm up to the cone of drone light. Was this really happening? She touched her face with her new hand and she felt the moisture of more tears as they flowed down her cheeks. She laughed and hugged herself with both arms. Both arms! She did not know how, but she did not question this miracle. Yes, it had to be a miracle. Or was it? Months ago, Max had activated the nannomemes, giving her the sensation the missing part of her arm had returned. Max could be playing games with her!

A pale, red light pulsed in the palm of her new hand. She stared at the tiny point of light. "What is this?"

"How does it feel to be whole again?"

Snake whirled. A man stood in the door to her hut. He wore a white, gauzy linen suit with a shirt open at the neck. As he moved into the scattered light from the drone, his turquoise eyes glittered.

Snake tensed. "Jonathan?"

The man froze. He cursed. "Why must I live in the shadow of my brother?"

Snake tensed. If only she had a weapon! "You're Jeremiah."

"That would be me." Jeremiah moved into the cone of light from the drone. His reddish blonde hair hung almost to his shoulders. His eyes now were hooded in shadow.

"How did you get here?" Snake said.

"I could say by boat. But Max has all approaches to this island under heavy surveillance. But she cannot keep me from teleporting." He smiled. "That's right! Beam me up, Scotty!"

Snake cursed. "No ride for me, then?"

"Not yet," Jeremiah said. "But there is hope. It depends on what happens in the next few minutes. Now, back to your new arm."

Snake looked at her new arm. "You did this?"

"Yes." He nodded. "Does it surprise you I can do miracles? I can, with the help the most powerful friend in the world." He grimaced. "Well, second most powerful."

"Friend? You're talking about one of Jonathan's demon adversaries, aren't you?"

"Sweetie, demons have never been a friend to my brother." He hissed.

Snake flexed her new hand and planted it seductively on her hip. She studied Jeremiah Stone. "Why are you here?"

"I wanted to make you an offer."

"Nothing is for free. I get it." She ran her new hand through her unruly curly hair. "What kind of offer?"

"To be whole again."

Snake looked at her hand. "To be whole, huh?" She glanced beyond him at the notebook sitting on the table in her hut. "I'm working on that."

"With one arm." Jeremiah said. He gestured over his shoulder with an index finger. The notebook flew through the air from within the hut and landed on the table beside the object. "Come on, Snake! You're not meant for this! Hunched over a notebook studying dead losers? You need to concentrate on the present. Now! Not that notebook."

Snake studied the pulsing red dot in her palm. "So, what is the catch?"

Jeremiah moved out of the cone of light and sat at the far side of the table. He brushed the notebook aside and put both arms on the table. He pointed at the object with a finger on each hand. "I need your help. That thing needs to be opened. In return, you get a new arm."

Snake glanced at the egg-shaped object on the table. "This is making no sense."

Jeremiah sighed and leaned back in the chair. He flicked the index finger of his right hand. Snake's arm disappeared. She gasped in panic as the flesh below her stump winked out of existence.

"Once you have been restored, it's hard to go back, isn't it?" Jeremiah said. He flicked his finger again and her arm was whole.

Snake reached forward with *both* arms and leaned on the table as her heart raced and her head grew woozy. It had been so long since she had actually felt her missing arm. "Why can't *you* open it?"

"Snake, Snake!" Jeremiah stood up and paced around the table. "Come on! Work with me here! Why so many questions?"

She turned and looked into those intense turquoise eyes. "You just took my arm away and then gave it back. I don't take lightly to being manipulated. Truth!"

Jeremiah's lips slowly turned up in a smile. He rubbed his jaw and walked away. "Truth! Truth can be cheap, Snake. Truth is what I make it." He paused and looked at her over his shoulder. "Okay, truth! I can't get the thing to open."

Snake smiled. "Bargain time, eh?"

"Bargain is you keep your arm. Only if you open it."

"Where did it come from?"

"I stole it." Jeremiah crossed his arms. "There, truth."

"From?"

"The Council of Darkness."

Snake drew a deep breath and sat in a chair before the strange object. "I hear there are powerful creatures on that council." At least, Jonathan Steel had said as much.

Jeremiah sat down opposite her with the object between them. "At one time, there were twelve powerful individuals on the Council of Darkness. Now, there are only two." He sighed and leaned back. "There are those who want to rebuild the Council, replenish its ranks with less powerful members than before. I am opposed to that and I have a better plan and it all hinges on this." He gestured to the object.

Snake studied the object. It was ovoid with a pebbly surface and tapered from a fat bottom to a small, rounded top. Odd looking runes covered the skin of the thing. "It looks like a deformed dinosaur egg."

Jeremiah shrugged. "Just as old as the dinosaurs."

"And all I have to do is open it? I don't see any seams. No magic red button to push. No latch."

"Opening it is simple. Put both hands on either side and it will open. Once your hands no longer touch it, you will have fulfilled the side of your agreement."

"And I can keep my arm?"

"Of course."

Snake studied her intact arm and flexed her fingers. She ran those fingers through her hair. She caressed her lips and touched her ears. No prosthetic had ever given her back the true sensation of her real arm. She glanced once at the notebook. Go back to that and she would lose an arm. She could always go back to the notebook after she opened this thing.

"Just sit down and touch it?"

"Yes."

"I'm going to regret this, aren't I?"

"You're going to regret rotting on this island, memorizing the lives of a bunch of dead people. Move on! Carpe diem!" Jeremiah's eyes gleamed.

Every alarm bell in her head signaled caution. She should NOT do this! Snake glanced at the notebook. Could she continue to wallow in guilt every day? She had done exactly what Max had required, and she had yet to feel even a smidgen of redemption. Only guilt. And Max could never give her back her real arm.

Snake gingerly reached forward toward the object. The red light pulsed more rapidly in her new hand. Both fingers of both hands touched the pebbly surface on either side of the object. The feeling of electricity ran up her arms again and this time, a seam opened in the object's front. Green light shot forth and bathed her face in oscillating waves. She gasped as something filled her vision. Something burrowed itself around her eyes and into her brain. She screamed in agony as the contents of the object filled her mind.

Jeremiah stood up and came around the table. He leaned over her paralyzed head and neck. His chilly breath caressed her cheek. "This is the Grimvox. It is the repository of all the deeds of every demon who has ever graced this ghastly mortal realm."

Snake could barely hear him as voices screeched and screamed in her mind. Images began to unfold and play like an old stuttering movie projector. Jeremiah walked to the other side of the table although she could not see him as her eyes were locked on the contents of the Grimvox.

"There is a rather portly old man, and when I say old, I mean really ancient. He was in charge of the Grimvox. The operation of this lovely arcane artifact requires a Keeper. Now the Tomemaster and I had lunch and he did not survive. He has passed on to his eternal judgment. Rather violently, I might add."

Jeremiah shrugged. "Unfortunately, the prior Keeper has also expired. Not my work, I must admit. Her mind gave out. You see, the Keeper's mind was insufficient, and I have the perfect opportunity to bring *my* Keeper to the Grimvox. Now, all those secrets are mine! I am the new Tomemaster and you, lovely Crimson Snake, are the new Keeper!"

Jeremiah pointed to the notebook. "Bad memories." He chuckled and pointed to the Grimvox. "Worse memories." He leaned across the table and touched her cheek, pulling away a tear moistened hand.

"In time, you will no longer weep. In time you will become one with the Grimvox. Your mind will preserve its energy and keep its precious memories from fading. But the only way those hands will release the Grimvox is in death. Sorry. I lied. It's what we do."

No! Snake tried to scream, but her mouth would not move. Her voice did not come. She was paralyzed just as she had paralyzed Inspector Goudreaux. All that goes around comes around, she thought weirdly. But the thoughts were fading into the miasma of demonic voices and images. She finally blinked and no more tears came from her eyes. Amid the swirling images, she found the face of Pablo from the notebook floating briefly into her awareness. Was he a demon? No! Pablo resided in her memory with the other 254 victims. She latched onto the memory of Pablo with every remaining fiber of her existence.

"There are more." She thought. "254 more. I need them." She fought for the memory of each of those dead. Like tiny life rings, they floated out of the madness and she flailed toward them, a woman drowning in a sea of evil.

"Pablo." She whispered.

TWO

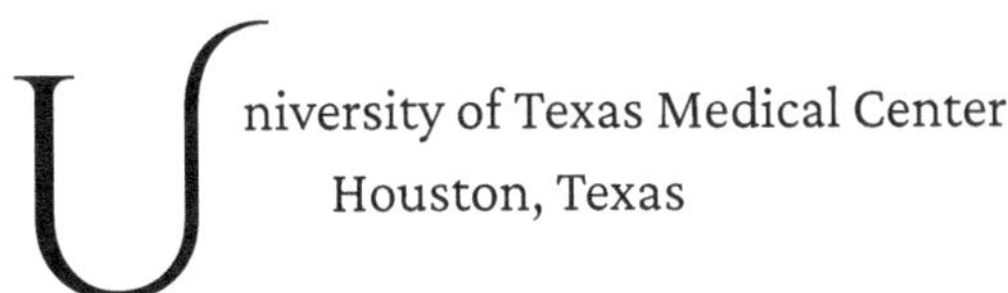

niversity of Texas Medical Center
Houston, Texas

"How much longer?" Jonathan Steel glared at Jose Salva, the nurse sitting behind his station. He seemed far too young to be a nurse!

"Mr. Steel, I will let you know something as soon as I know." Jose said firmly.

Steel drew a deep, calming breath. "Sorry. I'm just worried."

"I understand. Ms. Monarch will be fine. It's only been four hours and these procedures can take up to six hours. Dr. Mancini will let me know the minute they are finished."

Steel nodded and returned to his seat in the waiting area of the Epilepsy Monitoring Unit. He glanced over his shoulder at Olivia Monarch's room, where her mother, brother, and his adopted son, Joshua, were waiting. The room had closed in on him, so he had come out to the waiting area sitting at one end of the large open work area of the unit. Twelve rooms were situated around the periphery. At the opposite end of the working area was the observation room where technicians monitored patient's EEGs recorded every minute over 24 hours a day. The nurse's station sat in the center.

Steel glanced up at a television showing the national "corn hole" championship. Contestants threw small bags at slanted boards trying their best to hit the hole. He hoped and prayed the neurosurgeon working on Olivia would have better aim!

Olivia Monarch suffered from epilepsy after a stray bullet caused brain damage when she was a young girl. Steel's father, the Captain, had arranged for Olivia to undergo experimental brain surgery to ablate the seizure focus. A shadow fell over Steel and he looked over this shoulder at Olivia's mother, Dr. Monarch.

She settled into a chair next to him and sighed. "We just got an update. They're almost done."

Steel glared at Jose at the desk. Why hadn't he told him? Probably because he wasn't related to Olivia. "That's good."

Monarch pushed her long, dark hair behind her ears. Dark circles surrounded her eyes. "I know what you're thinking."

"You do?"

"Ironic that my daughter is having invasive brain surgery after what I did to you." Dr. Monarch had operated on Jonathan Steel in the past. She had implanted deep brain electrodes that controlled his memory. Recently, those electrodes had been removed by the angel, Alphus, freeing Steel's memory.

"Everything that goes around comes around." Steel mumbled. "I'm just glad something can be done to help Olivia."

"I guess it is fitting that my daughter suffered from a bullet meant for me because of my activities. In many ways, I am to blame." Monarch said hoarsely and leaned forward to rest her face in her hands.

Steel knew he should reach out to her, to comfort her, but his heart wasn't in it. She had brought a world of hurt down on his shoulders. But wouldn't he have done anything to save Joshua Knight? In fact, hadn't he performed evil deeds at the request of the fifth, sixth, and seventh demons to save his adopted son?

"I know how you feel," he said. "I'm not proud of what I did to save Josh. I understand that kind of desperation. I'm just hoping and praying Olivia will be healed."

Monarch turned her head and looked at him between her fingers. She nodded and sat back. "Thanks."

Steel's cell phone rang, and he answered it. "Hello."

"That was so sweet." A voice almost identical to his came over the speaker.

Steel sat up quickly. "You!"

"Yes, it's me. Your brother, Jeremiah."

"What do you want?" Steel hissed. Monarch stiffened beside him and he mouthed, "Jeremiah". She gritted her teeth and clenched her fists.

"Just to say I'm hoping for the best for your future daughter-in-law. And comforting Olivia's mother is a sign that maybe, just maybe, you're grown too soft." Jeremiah's voice dripped with honey.

"How do you know I'm with Dr. Monarch?"

"Security cameras. They're everywhere."

Steel glanced up at the television and spied a camera mounted in the ceiling's corner. "How?"

"Oh, come now, brother. Hacking into security cameras is a piece of cake! Let's see." Steel heard Jeremiah tapping on a keyboard. "Yes, they are still hard at work in the surgery suite.

Dr. Mancini is telling his aides they are almost done. Seems the procedure is a success."

"Why are you calling me?"

"Oh, you wound me, brother. I'm just very, very concerned." Jeremiah said sarcastically.

"Your only concern is yourself."

"Well, that's true. Now that your worrying about poor Olivia is about to end, I wanted to tell you that your season of rest will soon be over. My plans are about to be set in motion. Consider this a warning from someone who cares." The line went dead.

"Was that your brother?" Monarch asked.

"Yes! He's watching." He pointed to a security camera. It was now late February, and they hadn't heard a word from the demon forces since Christmas. Steel knew the quiet was too good to be true.

A woman in blue scrubs came through the door into the epilepsy monitoring unit. She pulled her mask off and removed her surgical hat. Her dark hair cascaded down around her face. They bolted to their feet. Dr. Mancini smiled at Monarch.

"Everything went well. The post procedure EEG shows no activity at the location of the ablated tissue. But we won't know for sure for a few days."

Monarch turned to Steel, and before he could react, she embraced him. She placed her face on his chest and sobbed. Steel tentatively wrapped his arms around this woman, who was once his bitter enemy. Steel nodded toward room six. "My son, Josh, is waiting with Olivia's brother."

As if he had heard, the door to the room opened and Joshua Knight looked out. His ginger hair was cut short and his eyes widened at the sight of Mancini. Olivia's brother, Steven followed. Josh hurried across the room and slid to a halt before them.

"How's Olivia? Is she okay? Did the surgery work?"

"Everything went according to plan, Josh. It's a waiting game now to see if the ablation worked." Mancini said.

Monarch pushed away and wiped the tears from her eyes. "Thank you, Dr. Mancini." She glanced at Steel awkwardly and sniffed. "I'll go wait in her room for her to return." She headed towards Olivia's room as her son, Steven put his arms over her shoulders.

Josh's breath came quickly. "I just want her to be okay. I've been in her room praying. I don't care if she has seizures. That changes nothing." He looked at Steel with desperation in his eyes. "She's going to be fine, right?"

Physical demonstrations of love were foreign to Steel. He had spent years in pursuit of his father and one of his operatives, Raven. Always he had arrived in time to save some of those his father had chosen to eliminate or "neutralize" as he put it. He did not know for years that his father's plan was to protect Steel from his evil brother. For the past few years, Steel had suffered from amnesia thanks to Dr. Monarch's implant, but all of that was behind him. An angel had removed the implant. Yes, an angel. And now Steel was working through his restored memories.

Throughout those memories, there was only one person to whom he had shown love and affection: his late mother. Steel thought of her gentle touch and her soft, calming words. Calm was what he needed after the call from Jeremiah. Steel knew what his mother would have done in this moment. Steel opened his arms toward Josh. "Bro, bring it in."

Josh fell into his embrace and Steel held him close. Memories of his mother's hugs surfaced. "Olivia is going to be fine. Dr. Mancini is the best at this."

Josh nodded, and then suddenly pushed away. His wet eyes

fixed on Steel's face. "Wait! Did you say, 'bro, bring it in'? Don't say that. It's too creepy."

Steel smiled. Josh smiled. It felt good.

The doors to the EMU opened. Two aides pushed a bed with a sheet covered figure. Olivia's eyes were closed, and a bandage covered her head. One aide opened the door to Olivia's room and pushed the bed inside. Josh glanced at Steel and nodded toward the door. Josh followed them into Olivia's room.

Steel backed away and stifled the emotion engulfing me. It had been much more tolerable when he hadn't given in to emotion. His phone rang, and he gladly slipped through the EMU doors and out into the hallway. Steel glanced up at a security camera and answered the call.

"Not now, Jeremiah! Leave us alone!"

"Who?" A familiar voice came over the speaker. Steel's heart almost stopped.

"Ruth?"

"Yeah, I was checking on Olivia. What's this about Jeremiah?" Ruth Martinez said. Over the past few months, Jonathan Steel and Ruth had grown close. After working with her at the request of her boss, attorney Grace Pennington, Steel's professional relationship had changed. Ruth had helped to get him out of jail in their recent encounter with the third and fourth demon. They had once been at each other's throat and had also once been at each other's heart. The hearts had won.

Steel glanced around the hallway and moved into an offset doorway, out of sight and sound of the nearest security camera. "He hacked the security cameras and called to brag he was about to bring havoc into our lives."

"I knew it had been too quiet." Ruth said.

"I will not let him ruin this day."

"How's Olivia?" Ruth Martinez asked. "Are you crying? Oh, baby! I wish I was there."

"I know." Steel said hoarsely. "I know you had business."

"Hey, it's okay. I've been praying for everyone. Now, how is she?" Ruth asked.

"Dr. Mancini said everything went well. She's back in her room. We won't know anything for a few days." Steel swiped at his eyes. "How was your meeting?"

"It went well. I was able to get all the licenses worked out. All the paperwork filed." Ruth paused. "And I have some good news."

"I could use some."

"I found a building for the office. It's on Louisiana Avenue, overlooking a bluff over the Red River. You can see all of downtown Shreveport and the parkway along the river." Ruth had decided to leave her law firm in Dallas, Texas, and start her own firm in Shreveport, Louisiana.

"So you are going through with this for sure?"

"Yes, Jonathan. I'm starting my practice next month. Yvonne and I will share an office on the first floor of the building. It's an old hardware store and the historical beauty of the building is worth saving."

"Wait a minute! You told me you were starting your own practice in Louisiana, but Yvonne? Yvonne Brown?" Yvonne and her associate, Sam, for years had protected Jonathan from a distance. Yvonne had defended him against the charge of murdering his own mother when he was fifteen. Recently, the two had been instrumental in restoring Jonathan's former life and helping him defeat the fourth and third demons.

"Yes!" Ruth said. "She agreed to be my associate. We have a steep learning curve since Louisiana law is so different from Texas law. And Yvonne has been out of the business for fifteen years. Sam has agreed to work part time as our investigator. But we will need someone full time."

Steel shook his head in amazement and glanced around the busy hallway. "I can't believe Yvonne is joining you. This is great!"

"We are taking on the tough cases, Jonathan. You know the people who really need help. And I've secured some business agreements that will keep us in the black. The upstairs level of the building is a wide open machinery shop. The building was built into a hill and the second floor was level with a street along the back, so all the metal working went on up there. It's been renovated into an open office plan. Even has a fitness area in the back. It's perfect for your office."

"My office?"

"Jonathan Steel. Private Investigator. Come on, baby, it's what you're good at. Once you get rid of these last two demons, what are you going to do?"

Steel looked down the empty hallway, his mouth suddenly dry. Things had been too quiet on the demon front for almost two months. "I hadn't really thought about it."

"Josh is going to Centenary College, right? He'll be living at the dorms in town. And then, he's off to law school. I know you don't need the money, since Dr. Lawrence left you a fortune. And Josh's needs are taken care of thanks to Cephas and your father. What are you going to do? Go sit on the dock at the lake house and fish?"

"I don't know, Ruth."

"Jonathan, you help people. It's in your DNA. It's what you do. All those years you thought you were a hired assassin, you were actually helping people targeted by your father and your brother. You're a good man. You help people in their time of need. That inspired me to open my practice. We could be partners."

Steel stopped breathing. He thought of the box sitting on the kitchen table at his lake house. He had picked up the ring just this morning. "Is that all we are?"

"Of course not." Ruth said. She was silent for a moment. "Jonathan, I love you. And you love me. We make a great team. But you mean far more to me than just a business partner. I, uh, I want more out of our relationship than that."

"Then I guess you'll have to marry me." Steel said. It just came out that way.

"What?" Ruth said in a gush.

"I have the ring at the house. This isn't exactly how I was going to propose."

Ruth giggled. She giggled some more. "Okay, you hold on to that ring. If you say yes to me, I'll say yes to you." Her voice had gotten husky and coarse. She sniffed.

"Right." Tears again. Was he really doing this? Could it really work out for once? The last two women he had loved had died. But this whole affair with the Council of Darkness would soon be over. "I'm sorry I blurted it out. I was going to wait until it was over."

"Until what was over?"

"The demons."

"Babe, I know what you've been through. I know what lies ahead. I'm there with you all the way. You don't have to do this alone. You have a family now. You have friends. I would love to be Josh's stepmother. I can help him with law school." She sniffed again. "Okay, let's do this. You go check on Olivia and Josh and Dr. Monarch. I'll be in Shreveport for a few more days signing leases and getting Yvonne's paperwork finished. When you get back to the lake house, you let me know. I want to be on the dock overlooking the lake at sunset. I want a fire in the dock fireplace and I want the most colorful sunset I've ever seen and I want you down on one knee proposing. Is that too much to ask?"

"No." Steel cleared my throat. "I love you, Ruth."

"Love you, too, my man of steel." The call ended.

Steel stepped out of the doorway, sliding his cell phone into his pocket, and the electric current hit him hard in the neck. He whirled and looked into the face of his almost mirror image: bright, turquoise eyes, chiseled cheekbones, aristocratic nose and long reddish blonde hair. Only the eyes that stared back at him were not filled with Steel's usual melancholy, but burned brightly with evil mischief. His last fragment of reality was the sight of his brother, Jeremiah Stone, holding the Taser as he fell into darkness.

THREE

Olivia opened both eyes, rimmed in purple. "How do you like my natural makeup?"

Josh sighed. For a moment Olivia's pale face and dark encircled eyes reminded him of his old girlfriend, Ila. He shook his head to chase away the painful memory. "You look beautiful. How do you feel?"

"Like the Battle of Gondor took place in my head."

Dr. Monarch stood at the edge of her bed and held her hand. "The doctor said everything went well."

Olivia nodded. "I don't feel any different."

Her brother Steven ran a hand through his long blonde hair and grinned. "You look better with no hair."

Olivia rolled her eyes and groaned. "That hurt." She blinked. "The eye rolling, not the remark." She pulled her hand from her mother's grip and weakly punched Steven in the stomach.

"Hey, sis, you look great!" Steven rubbed his stomach and Olivia's gaze shifted to his hands. Josh knew what she was thinking. When they first met, Steven's hands had been deformed from trauma. Somehow, during the encounter in Numinocity, Steven had been miraculously healed.

Olivia took one of Steven's hands. "Now we are both healed."

Jose, the nurse, stepped through the door and her concerned look focused on Josh. "Can I talk to you?"

Josh stood up. "Sure." He leaned over and kissed Olivia on the forehead. "I'll be right back."

Josh followed Jose out into the waiting room. He had been on duty for the past eight hours and had been so good to them. "What is it, Jose?"

Jose held up a cell phone. "Is this your father's phone?"

Josh took it. "Yes."

"I found it out in the hallway. On the floor."

Josh glanced at the closed doors leading out to the hallway. "Where is Jonathan?"

"That's just it." Jose sat before his computer monitors and played with the keyboard. "He got a phone call and went out into the hallway. I was watching on the monitors, you know, one of my jobs."

Josh leaned over Jose's shoulders and studied the security windows on the monitors. "Here, he's talking on the phone. And crying?"

"Yeah, bro, he does that a lot lately." Josh said.

"And then this."

Jonathan ended his phone call and suddenly stiffened, dropping his phone. He stood just inside an offset from the hallway. Someone moved behind him and wrapped Steel in his arms as the man collapsed. For a second, bright blue turquoise eyes focused on the security camera and then both men disappeared.

"What just happened?" Jose turned to look into Josh's eyes. "They just disappeared. Camera malfunction?"

Josh's heart sank, and he stumbled backward. "No! It can't be!"

Jose stood up and kept Josh from falling. "What's going on, Mr. Knight?"

Josh gripped the phone so tightly his hand hurt. "Jeremiah. It's Jeremiah. He's taken Jonathan."

~

DALLAS, Texas

"DID YOU CALL THE HOUSTON POLICE?" Jason Birdsong placed his pistol back in his shoulder holster. He looked out over the open road in front of the bodega.

"I started to, Jason. But they wouldn't believe me if I told them Jonathan's brother teleported him away from the hospital. Besides, he was kidnapped, and that falls under the FBI, right?" Josh said over the phone. "I know you're with Ross. I need your help."

"I'm in Dallas on a stakeout, Josh." Birdsong whispered.

"I told you to silence your cell." Birdsong glanced at Special FBI Agent Franklin Ross sitting behind the steering wheel. The man glared at Birdsong from behind his ever-present sunglasses.

"It's Josh. I had his contact on emergency mode." Birdsong said. "Besides, Carlos Canto hasn't come from the cafe yet." They sat in Ross' car across the street from the bodega.

Ross sighed and took his sunglasses off, and he glared at Birdsong. "If you are ever going to be an FBI agent, get your priorities straight."

"Jonathan Steel has been kidnapped by his brother." Birdsong said. "This is Josh. Doesn't this fall under FBI juris-diction?"

Ross shook his head. "Not our call. Tell Josh to contract the local police and they will get in touch with us through proper channels."

"What is Ross saying?" Josh said.

"Just a minute, Josh." Birdsong turned to face Ross. "I'd love to become an agent, Ross. This auxiliary training program is a good introduction. But I owe Jonathan my life. He is my brother."

"Not by blood."

"More than by blood." Birdsong's grandmother had pronounced them spiritual brothers after they first met in Arizona. "I'm going."

Ross glared at him. "You leave now, and you can forget any chance you may have with the FBI."

Ross' phone rang, and he pulled it from his pocket and stared at the screen. "Why is she calling me?"

"Who?"

Ross' jaw tightened. "Max."

Somewhere in Europe, Molly Alexandra Xavier oversaw a network of agents tasked with battling the evil empire of Satan. That was the best way Birdsong could describe her. Recently, Max, as she was called, had helped Jonathan Steel in his efforts to defeat the third and fourth demon. They had been members of a "Council of Darkness" and those demons were on Max's radar. Before Jason Birdsong had met Jonathan Steel in Arizona, Jonathan's mentor, Dr. Cephas Lawrence, had filled that role. Dr. Lawrence had perished in the confrontation with the tenth demon. And Jonathan's old partner, Theophilus Nosmo King, had been left behind in ancient Jerusalem during a time travel incident triggered by the ninth demon. As these thoughts went through Birdsong's mind, he marveled such things were truly happening. But he had long ago accepted the premise of an ancient spiritual warfare between God and Satan's minions. He had accepted the task of helping Jonathan Steel in that battle.

Ross answered the call. "Max?" He looked at Birdsong and then put the phone on speaker.

"Ross, I know you are there with Jason. I know that Josh is calling you about Jonathan Steel's abduction. And I know you are balking at helping," Max said.

"Max, I don't have time for a chitchat. We are in the middle of an operation."

Birdsong put his phone to his ear. "Just a minute, Josh. Max is calling on Ross' phone."

"Both of you need to come immediately to Lakeside, Louisiana. I will assemble a task force. Ross, you will get a call soon from your supervisor redirecting your efforts to my task force."

"Your task force?" Ross' face reddened. "Who put you in charge?"

"The Director." Max said coolly. "This matter is of national importance. Now, if you'll get Jason to hang up, I will contact Joshua Knight. I need to arrange his transportation from Houston to Lakeside. Good bye."

Ross shook his head and put a hand to his temple. "Getting a headache! A Jonathan Steel heartache! Another demon, right? Is that what this is all about?"

"Probably." Birdsong said. "Josh?"

"I heard, Jason. Max is calling me now." He ended the call.

Birdsong glanced over at the bodega where the drug cartel boss Ross had been stalking for weeks was about to be arrested in a sting operation.

"I won't be here for the biggest bust of my career." Ross

tossed his phone in the backseat and started the car. "Three hours to Lakeside. I hope you have a big bladder."

～

"MAX? JEREMIAH HAS TAKEN JONATHAN." Josh said as he paced in the hospital hallway.

"I know." Max's soft tones came over the phone. "Young man, I monitor everything that has to do with Jonathan. Just a short while ago, we intercepted a hijacking of the hospital security cameras and traced it back to an IP once used by Jeremiah Stone. Beta was able to look into the hospital security footage and saw Jonathan being taken by Jeremiah."

"He teleported him, Max." Josh said, his heart racing. "That's dangerous. It almost killed Theo." Theophilus Nosmo King had been Jonathan's first partner. He had once been kidnapped by a demon possessed person and the teleportation had caused him great harm.

"This is not the first time Jonathan has been teleported. He was taken by the angel Alphus to a safe house, remember? He has been through this once and survived. He'll have some side effects, but it's not the teleportation I'm worried about."

"Tell me about it." Josh ran a hand through his hair. "What will Jeremiah do to him?" The doors to the EMU opened and Dr. Monarch appeared. She gestured to Josh.

"Olivia wants to talk to you."

"Is that Dr. Monarch?" Max said.

"Yes."

"Listen to me very carefully, Josh. Do not tell Dr. Monarch or her son and daughter about this. Olivia is in a very delicate condition, having had this surgery and any stress could be dangerous." Max said.

A hand touched his shoulder, and he looked up into the eyes of Monarch. "What's wrong, Josh? What has happened?"

"Nothing." Josh's voice broke. "I'll be right there. Let me finish this phone call. I'm just updating, uh, Jason Birdsong."

Monarch nodded and went back into the EMU. "What do I need to do, Max?"

"I'm sending a driver to pick you up at the front of the hospital. He'll be there in five minutes. Say your goodbyes. He'll take you to a private jet at the airport and you'll be in Shreveport in an hour. Someone will meet you there and bring you to me."

"You're in Shreveport?"

"I'm in Lakeside. I was here on another personal matter when all of this happened, Josh." Max paused and sighed. "Cephas Lawrence's favorite motto was 'There are no coincidences', right? It is most fortuitous I am here with my task force for a different matter altogether. Now, I will have to switch gears to locating Jeremiah Stone. Go say your goodbyes. Now!" The line went dead.

Olivia's room was dark. Bright light bothered her eyes. Monarch motioned for Josh to come closer. "She is asleep. But she wants to talk to you. In private." Monarch glanced at her son. Steven shrugged.

"Fine by me, mate. Mom and I are going for coffee."

Monarch nodded as if this was a satisfactory conclusion to what was probably a minor disagreement settled before he came back into the room. Monarch frowned at him. "If anything happens, I'll have my phone. By the way, where is Jonathan?"

Josh swallowed hard. "The dude, uh, went for coffee, too. You might see him."

Monarch raised an eyebrow. "I thought he didn't like coffee."

"Coffee doesn't like him. Makes him irritable." Josh said.

Steven laughed. "Don't want an irritated Jonathan Steel around when we are trying to keep things quiet, right, mate?" He patted Josh's shoulder as they left the room.

Josh sat beside Olivia's bed. Brown elastic tape encircled her hairless head. He glanced up at the myriad of monitors, all showing heart rate, respiration, blood pressure, blood oxygen level and dozens of tracing lines of her EEG.

"They say I won't have any more seizures."

Josh jerked as Olivia turned her head to face him. "Don't move!"

"Silly, I have to move, don't I?" She licked her lips. "They said I could have some ice chips."

"Good." Josh nodded nervously.

"That would be your cue to get me some." Olivia whispered.

"Oh, right." Josh spooned some ice chips from her water pitcher into a small cup and handed it to her.

"You will have to spoon feed me, Josh," Olivia said holding up her hands which bore two I.V.s.

"Yeah, sure." He put a few small nuggets of ice in the spoon. His hand shook, but he kept the ice in the spoon until they reached Olivia's mouth. She took them in and smiled. "Much better." She mumbled.

"Sorry that I'm not very good at this," Josh said.

"Hey, you were pretty sick not long ago, and Faye took care of you. Just think of how you felt then."

The fifth, sixth, and seventh demons, along with Nigel Hampton, had infected Josh with a virus from which he had almost died. Nurse practitioner Faye Morgan had taken care of him. She had been instrumental in saving his life. And she had fallen in love with Jason Birdsong.

"She set a good example. Thanks for reminding me."

Olivia swallowed the ice and studied him with her black-rimmed eyes. "Josh, you know I love you, don't you?"

Josh set the cup down and leaned over the bed rail. "Of course. I love you, too."

"Then go do what you have to do." She whispered.

"What do you mean?"

"I know that look. I haven't seen a demon since I woke up and there should be a few haunting hospital personnel."

After her recent experience in Numinocity, the virtual reality created by the eighth demon, Olivia had developed the ability to see demons. All around her, demons possessing or oppressing humans were visible. She told Josh that at first, she considered it a curse. Then, after giving her life to Christ, she realized it could be an asset to help Jonathan Steel. Could it be the surgery had eliminated that gift? Josh had mixed feelings about that. Never seeing a demon again might be a good thing.

"Josh, I may not have seen a demon. But, before I woke up in recovery I had a dream. At first, I thought it was just the anesthesia wearing off and then I saw your face just now. In the dream, I had a visit from an angel named Alphus."

Josh's eyes widened. "Jonathan's guardian angel."

"Yes. He said Jonathan was in trouble and you would have to help him. So, go. I'm on the good side of things now. All I have to do is rest and get better." She put a hand through the bed railing. Josh took it in his own and avoided touching the intravenous line.

"Olivia, I can't tell you what is going on. I don't want you to worry."

"I know, babe. Mom and Steven will take good care of me.

The hard part is over. I owe so much to you and Jonathan. Go help him."

"What will you tell your mom?"

Olivia looked away and licked her lips. "Another demon is on the loose? That you left to protect me from getting involved? She'll buy that."

"I can't tell you what is going on, Olivia." He squeezed her hand slightly. "But I will do this to protect you, for sure." He pulled a necklace from within his shirt and held it before her. A tiny crimson jewel hung from the silver chain. "I want you to wear my father's gift to me, the bloodstone. It has protected me in the past and I will not worry if you have it hanging around your neck."

"Josh, you need that to protect you."

"Babe, I can't be here at a time when you are most vulnerable. For me, wear the bloodstone while I'm gone. Please."

Olivia reached out her bandaged hand. "I can't wear it now but I will wear it as soon as I can get these I.V.s out." He placed the necklace in her hand. Olivia motioned to him with her other hand. "Come here." Josh leaned closer. "I have dragon breath, but you're not leaving without a kiss."

He smiled. "You are amazing, Olivia." Josh kissed her dry lips and pulled back to study her pale face.

"I am aware of that, demon boy. Now go get 'em!"

FOUR

Steel awoke with every muscle in his body screaming in pain. He rolled onto his side and retched. He blinked away tears and stared around into total darkness. Was he blind? A faint green light came from behind him. He glanced upward and saw a barely lit 'EXIT' sign on the far wall. The cold concrete floor chilled his bare body. He wore only his underwear. He shivered and his hand brushed something on his breastbone. He touched the strange flat circular metal disc. The surface was smooth and the rim unbroken and when he tried to lift an edge away from his chest, a sudden shock burned his fingers. A bright light gushed into the room from behind him. He stumbled to his feet and squinted into the light.

"Finally awake, I see. Sorry for the disorientation and nausea. I understand you've teleported before." Jeremiah's face hid in shadow.

"By an angel. Not a demon." Steel said, holding up his hand to shield his eyes from the light. He lunged toward Jeremiah and pain lanced across his chest. He fell to his knees, gasping for breath.

"That little disc on your chest is more than a token of my caring nature, JJ. And don't remove it or it will stop your heart."

Steel looked up through tear-filled eyes as the pain lessened. "What do you want?"

"I'm glad you asked, brother." Jeremiah held up a tablet. "One press of this button and you will stop breathing. I don't relish the idea of CPR. Now, if you'll kindly follow me down the hall, I'll explain things."

Jeremiah stepped backwards into a hallway, and the light above illuminated his figure clad in a simple gray sweatshirt and jeans. Steel climbed painfully to his feet and stepped around his vomit. "Why am I almost naked?" He asked as he followed Jeremiah down a hallway with walls made of cinder blocks. The one light bulb outside his room cast shadows ahead of them as they left it behind.

"Humiliation, plain and simple." Jeremiah said over his shoulder. "You have nothing left to hide behind. Imagine if you will, that you suffer the same as your savior. Stripping a prisoner naked before nailing him to a cross equaled the greatest form of humiliation." He paused before a double door open into a darkened interior. He touched the tablet and a metal chair slid from the opening and stopped between them. "Actually, you messed up your clothes. Protein spill on aisle 33! Don't worry, I'll find you something to wear. Eventually. We look to be about the same size. Now, have a seat. Just a warning. It will be cold."

Steel settled into the chair and tried not to wince as the cold metal touched his bare skin. He placed his hands on the chair arms and metal brackets swung from beneath securing him to the chair.

"Just to make sure you don't try anything." Jeremiah

tapped the tablet, and the chair slid into the dark room beyond.

The chair smoothly slid forward and paused at the edge of a table. On the table before him, a pale yellow cone of light illuminated a strange, egg-shaped object. Steel gasped as he saw the Crimson Snake sitting on the other side of the table with her arms. Yes, *two* arms stretched out to touch the bottom of the strange object. A wavering sickly green light bathed her face. Empty eyes stared into an opening on the far side of the object.

"Snake! Why are you working with Jeremiah?" Steel growled. "He pay you enough?"

Jeremiah walked out of the shadows and stood behind Snake. The green light played across his face. "Oh, Snake has received her payment, all right." He reached down and stroked one of her arms. "I gave her a hand." The man giggled and moved to sit in a chair to Steel's left. He touched the tablet and the restraint on Steel's left arm released.

"Before you use your free arm to escape, just know your metal chair is attached to an electric current. Between the chair and the disc on your chest, I can end your life before you can draw your next final breath. Now, JJ, if I am not mistaken, your free hand is the same one that glows with holy light." Jeremiah said.

Steel glanced at his palm. It had not glowed since the trial of the third demon. "Yes. Why?"

Jeremiah steepled his fingers and sat back. "We are about to go on a journey. You see, once I realized who you really were, I often pretended to be you in order to misdirect those who were looking for you."

"Who is looking for me?"

"In time, my brother, in time." He smiled and took something from his jeans pocket. He held up the memory drive from their father, the Captain. "Recognize this?"

Steel nodded, gritting his teeth. "A memory card from my father."

"No, OUR father." Jeremiah said. "He is our father, much as I hate to admit it. I found it easily enough in your pocket."

"The Captain did not know you were still alive." Steel said.

"So he says. JJ, you don't know the entire story." He sat forward. "You don't know my story. You are only beginning to remember your own story. It is time we bring it all together."

Steel squeezed his free hand into a fist. If he tried anything, the shock could kill him. He glanced over at Snake. On the cheek away from Jeremiah, a tear slowly ran down. "Did she know what you were doing to her?"

Jeremiah glanced at Snake and hopped up. He leaned over her head and shook his head. "Poor baby! She agreed to this. But they never really understand what it does to their minds." He touched the tear with a finger and held it up before his eyes. "Tears of pain or tears of joy? Doesn't matter." He popped the wet finger in his mouth. He tilted his head as he looked Steel in the eyes. "This is the Grimvox."

Steel froze. His simmering anger gave way to an icy wave of fear. "I've heard of it. Satan's hard drive."

Jeremiah grinned. "Good one. I like that. Demonic deeds are stored here. Memories. Stories. Victories. All placed in crystalline storage. No one really knows how old it is. Theories are it was a piece of the heavenly realm tucked away beneath an appendage of one of the fallen angels. When they plummeted to earth, it survived and the energies of the divine realm still run through its interstices." Jeremiah came around the table and held up a finger. "Interstices? I like that word. Makes me sound smart, doesn't it? Anyway, it requires an organic interface, a human mind. And not just a brain, you see. A mind which implies the presence of a spirit, a soul. A chimpanzee would never work. The human soul provides the interface and the human mind processes the data streaming coming in from all around. It normally resides in the chamber of horrors where the Council of Darkness meets."

Jeremiah came around the table and squatted beside Steel. "Thanks to you, the Council is all but eradicated."

Steel's hand tightened in a fist and Jeremiah shook his head. "Don't even think about it." In a flash, Jeremiah stood and his hand hovered over the tablet. "One touch and you fry." Steel relaxed his fist. His heart sank. This was bad. This was worse than bad.

"Now, where was I?" Jeremiah sat in the chair. "Oh, yes. The Council. There are only two of us left. Good old number one, who is NOT our father, by the way, is so preoccupied with rebuilding the Council he did not notice my personal plan. You see, I want to be Number One. But right now we're number two." He held up two fingers in a victory sign. "And that is where you and your girlfriend, Snake, come in."

"She's not my girlfriend."

"Oh, I know." Jeremiah grinned and held up the tablet. On the screen a photograph of the kitchen table at Steel's house filled the screen. Jeremiah pointed to the box sitting on the table. Steel's heart sank.

"Engagement ring. My, how soft you have become. Remember this very important fact. I know your girlfriend. I know where to find her."

Steel lurched forward in the chair and a wave of electricity shot painfully through his body. His teeth chattered. His muscles stiffened, and he was gone.

CHAPTER

FIVE

"I didn't think it snowed in Louisiana." FBI Special Agent Franklin Ross blew smoke from his nostrils and wiped snowflakes from his nose. He wore his ever present khaki raincoat over a stained white shirt and red tie. Sunglasses hid his eyes. Snow fell from a leaden sky in large, lazy wet globs and covered the dead grass around the decimated cabin. A huge white Quonset hut like enclosure covered the entire foundation of what had once been a two-story cabin owned by Robert Ketrick. In the past, the cabin had been used as a focal point for the attempted assassination of the governor of Louisiana. All that remained was the foundation, the basement, and a fireplace.

"It even snows in Tucson. At least on the mountain." Jason Birdsong said. "I thought you had quit smoking?"

"I've quit more times than I can remember." Ross dropped the cigarette on the ground and stepped on it. "I only smoke a half a cigarette now. That's an improvement. Where's the kid?"

Birdsong glanced at his watch. "Coming from Houston. Should be here any moment."

A SUV emerged through snow topped pine trees and wound its way down a red clay driveway. It skidded to a stop in the snow and the passenger door flew open. Josh Knight hopped out and hurried across the snow-covered grass. He slid to a stop before Ross.

"Ross, have you found Jonathan yet?"

"Hello to you, too." Birdsong reached out and pulled Josh to him. Josh stiffened and then hugged Birdsong.

"Jason, I'm glad you're here." Josh pushed awkwardly away from Birdsong. He glared at Ross. "Dude, I asked you a question."

"You deserve answers." Ross said.

"You're not going to stonewall me?"

"You're not the same bratty teenager I first met in Lakeside." Ross said. "Besides, you've just been through an ordeal with Olivia." He paused and looked away. "How is she?"

"Recovering. And I should be in Houston with her instead of here." Josh said.

"But Jonathan is missing." Birdsong said with a heavy heart. "Again."

Josh nodded and wiped his nose. He looked beyond them at the large tent structure covering a large expanse of open ground. "Is she in there?"

"Don't know. We just got here." Birdsong said. "But if anyone has answers, it's her."

"That's why I'm here." Josh wore a black hoodie dotted with falling snow. He glanced over his shoulder. "Epsilon drove me up here from the airport."

A short, thick shouldered African American man climbed out of the SUV. He stood stiffly by the car. Josh shrugged.

"Wouldn't answer any questions."

"Epsilon?" Ross asked.

"One of Max's operatives." Birdsong said. "She loves the Greek alphabet."

Josh started toward the cabin enclosure. "What are we waiting for?" He stopped abruptly when the light of a red line appeared in front of him.

"I wouldn't cross that," Ross said. "According to my briefing, security is tight here. This area is under the control of a covert government agency." Ross said. "Gives me an ulcer just to think about it."

Josh backed away and the red line disappeared. He paced back and forth. "Come on, come on!"

Birdsong exhaled a steamy breath. "Josh, dude, relax. Remember. This is where Max's daughter died."

"Yes." Josh paused and sighed. "I wasn't physically here when it happened. I was in the woods down at the bluff overlooking the bayou."

Birdsong put a hand on the young man's shoulder. "And that is where Dude saved you?"

Josh nodded. "Yep. My guardian angel."

Ross belched and massaged his stomach. "After the attempt on the governor's life, they showed up and secured the site. It's not every day a microscopic black hole shows up on Earth and we are still around."

"Uncle Cephas said the black hole was used by the thirteenth demon to defeat the eleventh demon." Josh said. "And it also flattened most of the cabin."

"I thought we would get through a day without someone saying the D word!" Ross cleared his throat. He pulled another cigarette from his coat pocket and lit it up. "Something weird is going on here, according to my contacts. And, from what I understand, I am to give Max carte blanche. She has drones in the air, blocking any access to the site. And I understand the fabric is basically a huge Faraday cage that blocks all signals."

Birdsong studied the surroundings, always on the alert. He had been taking part in Ross' FBI parallel training program since Christmas and his senses always finely tuned. "That was the barn?"

Josh looked around the large man at the two-story barn in the distance. "Where the tripod and gun were found. I still think Vivian had something to do with this." It was from the barn the assassination was to have taken place.

"She claimed she was to be the patsy." Ross blew smoke from his nostrils. "Still galls me she got a deal and not the needle."

"She has tracked down ten families related to Raven's assassinations." Birdsong said. "What happens when that task is done?"

"That's up to Max. Again. She cut a deal with Interpol. That woman has incredible connections." Ross dropped his cigarette and ground it out. "Is there somewhere we can get in out of this snow? It's wet and cold."

The huge rectangular tent over the cabin footprint stretched over hundreds of feet, and a metal doorway opened. A young woman in a long, wool coat walked out. She wore a red knit cap over black hair and her faintly Oriental features were unreadable.

"Epsilon, you may go back to the airport." She said to the man by the SUV. Epsilon nodded, climbed into the SUV, and drove off in a cloud of fog and snow.

The young woman turned her attention to Josh. "I am Pi. Josh, Max wants to talk to you." She ignored Birdsong.

"Has she found Jonathan yet?" Josh's voice broke.

"You will have to ask her. Follow me."

Birdsong started after Josh and the woman put up her hand. "No one else. Just Joshua Knight."

THE FOUNDATION of the decimated cabin filled most of the interior. Scaffolding surrounded a large fireplace and what remained of a chimney at one end of the cabin. Bright lights illuminated gaping holes in the concrete foundation, revealing the basement prison in which Jonathan and Theo had been kept. Pi led Josh them around the foundation and the wall remaining around the stone fireplace. The smell of wet burned wood still lingered in the air, although it had been a long time since the encounter with the eleventh demon.

Max stood before the blackened fireplace. She wore a long, white wool coat that brushed the floor and had collected a rim of ashes. She turned to Josh. Tears stained her cheeks, and she wiped them away and adjusted her silver hair around her aristocratic face. "Josh, we finally meet in person."

Max stepped toward him and embraced him. The fragrance of lavender and roses tickled his nose. She pushed away. "I apologize for the emotional greeting. I am dealing with my own loss here." She gestured to the fireplace. "This is where Dr. Lawrence and my daughter stood against the eleventh demon. Or so Jonathan told me."

Josh swallowed back emotion. "I am so sorry. Uncle Cephas told us your story. The asylum. The priest. The exorcism gone bad."

Max focused her teary eyes on him. "Yes, I was convinced she had died as a young child and for decades, I blamed your great uncle for her death. I have more regrets than I have time in my life to deal with, Josh."

Josh cleared his throat. "Jonathan?"

Max nodded. "Yes, let us focus on the living and cling to fond memories of the departed. Come with me."

Max led Josh toward the back of the enclosure. Josh

glanced down into the depths of the dungeon basement and, for a moment, saw a flickering point of iridescent green light. He paused and a faint voice echoed in the back of his mind. "Find me!"

"Did you hear that?" He said.

Max paused. "No, Josh. What did you hear?"

"A voice. Maybe."

Max pulled her coat more tightly around her body. "There are unusual phenomena in this area after the use of a microscopic black hole. Many report seeing and hearing strange things. Our chief scientist believes this is because of residual energies imbedded in this place."

"Only one of several metaphysical phenomena we are investigating." Someone said behind Josh. He whirled. The woman approaching them wore a black turtleneck and slacks and a long, black lab coat. Her dark hair was tucked beneath a simple black pillbox hat. His ebony skin glistened in the sickly light through the tent fabric. She paused and extended a hand.

"Sister Mary Margaret."

Josh shook her hand. "Sister?"

"I'm the lead scientific investigator."

"A nun?"

"Yes, a nun, Josh. Not all the daughters of our Lord are cloistered in convents."

"Sister Mary Margaret's organization is tasked with investigating any supernatural events to assess the scientific, factual side of the event." Max said tersely.

"Yes, we are not amateurs, Joshua Knight." Sister Mary Margaret cut her eyes at Max.

Max cleared her throat. "I've partnered with this organization."

"We are, at times, lacking sufficient funds." Sister Mary

Margaret. "Unfortunately, there are times we rely on gifts from outside entities."

"Partners." Max said through a thin smile. "We have been investigating this phenomenon for a long while and we still do not understand what is happening."

Sister Mary Margaret sighed and pointed to the basement. "For instance, if you were to go into that basement, you would find yourself in another location."

"What?" Josh paused.

"You would be transported far away from here and not in a necessarily consistent fashion. One of our technicians ended up in Antarctica. Fortunately, during the summer and not too far from a base. He only lost his feet and hands to frostbite, but he lived. We have one technician who disappeared entirely. His body was found in orbit, spotted by the international space station. No one goes into the basement anymore." She took her cell phone from her pocket and touched the screen. The bright lights shining from the ceiling went out. The enclosure plunged into darkness. From the foundation of the cabin a green glow appeared out of the darkness. Josh walked to the edge of the foundation and looked down into the depths. The green glow undulated and moved with tiny waves and currents.

"I've seen something like this before." He turned and said to Sister Mary Margaret. "An energy pool in the baptistery in Lakeside. It was used by thirteenth demon."

"Who possessed a microscopic black hole." Sister Mary Margaret said. "The demon also used it to defeat the eleventh demon here in this cabin. We are still not sure if it took the black hole with it or if the object is somewhere below. In any event, the encounter with the eleventh demon that destroyed this cabin has left a significant residual of supernaturally maintained energy in this place." She tapped her phone and the lights came back on.

"Now you see why we keep our presence here a secret." Max said, cutting her eyes to Mary Margaret. "I was not informed at first. I had to learn of this after many inquiries."

"Pulling many strings." Sister Mary Margaret said. "One should be careful what strings one pulls on."

Josh swallowed hard. He tried to imagine an organization that had connections so strong they could silence the discovery of a body in orbit. Sister Mary Margaret pointed to the end of the basement extending beneath the fireplace. "We do not know what still lies at that end of the basement. We don't dare go there. Every probe we've sent has disappeared. Possibly on Jupiter for all we know."

Josh whistled. "My God!"

"Indeed." She said as she motioned to a tunnel leading out of the back of the tent. "The powers that be have decided Max has been allowed access to our investigation."

"Because we have need of a truly secure facility." Max said. "A giant Faraday cage, if you will. I have been meaning to visit."

"Your reluctance to come is not because of our secrecy, Max." Sister Mary Margaret's eyes burned with malice. She blinked and her features softened. "Instead, it was the inevitability of facing the truth about your daughter."

"Money speaks." Max said.

"Loudly, it seems." Sister Mary Margaret said. She led them down the dimly lit corridor and into a building behind the tent. "This is our permanent laboratory." She said. Behind windows, a dozen technicians in white one-piece suits bustled around counters and islands covered with scientific equipment.

"Are they all nuns?" Josh asked.

"They are all ordained into the ministry. Most of us in this room are from the Catholic faith. But we have others from other Christian denominations. We serve the same Savior, Josh."

Pi motioned to the right. "The conference room is over here." Josh flinched. He had forgotten she was with them.

Max lifted an eyebrow. "We have mutual enemies, Mary Margaret. It is time to put my loss behind me and move on with the search for the second and first demons."

Sister Mary Margaret crossed her arms. "Demons, per se, are not part of our primary interest. We keep our focus on phenomena in our space-time continuum. However, since we have been *asked* to help you, the facility is at your disposal. Now, if you will excuse me, I have work to do." She turned and joined the other technicians.

Pi led them into a spacious conference room. Monitors covered one wall above a console with several keyboards. A large table filled the center of the room. At one end, a couch and four comfortable chairs surrounded a table bearing a platter of fruit and pastries. Max motioned to a door on one wall. "Pi, Sister Mary Margaret is allowing us to bring Ross and Birdsong into this room only." Pi nodded, and Max motioned to a seat at the table.

"Josh, have a seat."

Pi opened a door in the conference side room. From a long, dark corridor, Ross and Jason came into the room. Max shrugged out of her coat and handed it to Pi. "No smoking, Ross. Have a seat and we will begin our search for Jonathan Steel."

Ross opened his mouth to speak and Jason shook his head. "Don't even try, Ross. You are way out of your league."

Ross removed his sunglasses and raised an eyebrow. "I would agree. I hope there's coffee?"

Max motioned to the table between the chairs. "Help yourself. I'm waiting for one more person before we review what we know about the disappearance of Jonathan Steel."

Birdsong poured a cup of coffee from the carafe and sat beside Josh. "Who are we waiting for?"

"Dr. Washington?" Josh asked. He didn't want to admit how desperately he wanted to see "Mama Liz" right now.

"Dr. Washington is back at her college teaching, but she assured me we could contact her by video chat. The problem, Josh, is every communication leaving this tent is subject to potential hostile surveillance, no matter my precautions." Max sat across from Josh.

A strident beeping came from the computers behind Max. She turned and tapped on a keyboard, and a video chat window appeared on the monitors. A woman with short, back hair stared back at them, her face twisted in anguish.

"Raven?" Max said.

"She's gone!" Raven said.

Max's face paled. "What?"

"Snake. She's gone."

Max swore out loud and Josh blushed at her words. "Tell me what you know."

Raven glanced at Josh and Jason. "Josh, Ross, Jason. No time for pleasantries. Jonathan is missing and now, so is Snake. Max had her safely tucked away on a secluded island for an extended period of, well, of rehabilitation?"

"Rehabilitation?" Ross snorted. "She's wanted in twelve countries! Do you realize how many laws you have broken by harboring the Crimson Snake?"

Max nodded. "One hundred and thirty-two. Bear with me, Agent Ross."

"Special Agent Ross." He growled.

"What happened?" Max turned to monitors again.

"I am opening a video from Max's surveillance drone." Raven said. "I take this facility is secure?"

Some color had returned to Max's face. "Yes. What do we have, Raven?"

Raven brought up a video feed on the monitors. The view was from high in the sky at night, most likely from a drone drifting slowly over the perimeter of a small island. On one side, an empty dock protruded into the turquoise waters illuminated by lights. In the center of the small island, a house sprawled over a large area spilling yellow light out into the surrounding palm trees. On the opposite side of the house from the dock, a deck sat lit by two pale lights. A table and several deck chairs covered the deck.

The drone drifted down toward the table. The Crimson Snake's carrot colored hair was unmistakable. She stood beside the table gazing out over the ocean. Suddenly, the point of view shifted, and the drone directed its cameras toward the horizon. Out of nowhere, a large, black drone materialized. The image abruptly ended.

"What was that?" Josh said. "Another drone?"

"It came out of nowhere." Birdsong said.

Max stood up and put a hand on her forehead. "He found her. That means he has the Snake."

"Who?" Ross said.

"Jeremiah." Max whispered.

"How do you know?"

Max glared at him. "That drone materialized out of thin air. It teleported, Ross! The only entity I know on earth that can do such a thing, such a supernatural thing, would be a demon. I have been searching for Jeremiah and his accomplice, the second demon, for weeks."

"He teleported Jonathan from the hospital in Houston." Josh said. "It's been hours."

Max looked back at him and then paced along the table. "Yes, I know, Josh. Raven, show them the security footage from the hospital."

Josh's heart raced as he watched Jonathan end his call and then the flash of the Taser. The evil grin on Jeremiah's face was the last thing they saw as both men disappeared.

Josh shot to his feet. "That's what happened to Theo. Just disappeared. Teleported! And Theo almost died!"

"I can assure you my sons are more robust than Theophilus Nosmo King." A man stood in the open doorway dressed in white linen pants and a black, full length fur coat. He took off his Panama hat and smoothed down his gray hair with the same hand holding his Meerschaum pipe. It was the Captain.

CHAPTER

SIX

Ross bolted up from his chair. "You invited the Captain?"

The Captain tossed his hat on the table. "Yes, Special Agent Ross. Max and are allies." He shrugged out of his coat and let it drape over the back of a chair. He wore a long sleeve white shirt and a bolo tie. "At the beach wedding of Cassandra and Montana, we made our peace."

"We agreed to exchange information. Everything I had on the first and second demon." Max looked like she had sucked on a lemon. "A necessary evil."

The Captain sat at the head of the table. "Josh, how is Olivia?"

Josh tensed. "It would seem the surgery worked. Thank you again for setting it up."

"You seem a little tense, son."

"One altruistic act doesn't undo years of evil." Josh said.

The Captain nodded. "I gave JJ a memory card containing videos I recorded shortly after the trial of the third demon. I told my life story, hoping one day JJ would understand why I made the decisions I had to make." He leaned forward and his intense turquoise eyes focused on Josh. "I don't believe he has watched the videos. If he had, he would have reached out to me."

"He hasn't watched them." Josh said. "He told me he wasn't going to watch them until he had sorted through his memories. Dude, the man just found out he had a brother who killed his mother!"

"And my wife" The Captain said, his eyes wide. He shook his head and massaged the bridge of his nose. He looked away from them and the room filled with an uncomfortable silent.

"I knew there was another child. I just thought he was dead. It wasn't until Josh was arrested for killing his mother and the trial I realized we had all been duped."

The Captain looked back at Josh with moist eyes. He lifted his pipe into view and massaged the its bowl. "Two figures are carved into my pipe. One is an angel. The other is a demon. I had no idea of another son until the trial. Since the day I made those videos, I have only had JJ's best interest at heart. This is a cruel and heartless world, Josh. You should know that! Only the strong will survive against the powers of darkness. I had to make JJ strong." He placed the pipe on the table before him so that the demon faced Josh. "Stronger than Jeremiah. My first act was to ensure JJ became a Christian and would never again be possessed by a demon. After that, his training was fairly standard. Now, let us discuss his kidnapping. I had JJ's phone analyzed."

"What?" Ross said. "The phone is in possession of the FBI."

"Yes, it is." The Captain didn't hesitate. "I have my contacts, Ross. I don't trust your agency's abilities or their devotion. The call that came from Jeremiah was from an untraceable burner phone. No help in locating where he took JJ."

Josh grit his teeth. "Will you stop calling him JJ? His name is Jonathan."

The Captain paused and nodded. "Of course, Josh. No disrespect intended. Remember, I have known my son much longer than anyone else in this room and for all those years we called him JJ."

The Captain picked up his pipe and tapped the mouth piece to his chin. "Jeremiah is possessed by the second demon, I believe. If that is so, then his demon is very powerful. Jeremiah could have teleported Jonathan to anywhere. But Jonathan would suffer if teleported over a long distance, as I understand he did when his guardian angel, Alphus, I believe is his name?" The Captain looked to Josh for confirmation as he sipped coffee.

"Yes." Josh said tersely.

"When Alphus transported him from Florida to Switzerland. I believe Jeremiah is after something. What, I do not know." He pointed the pipe stem at Josh. "This is not about revenge. Jeremiah wants something only Jonathan can give him. Since we have had no ransom demands, whatever Jeremiah wants is not in our power to grant. Only Jonathan can give him what he wants. Which would mean Jeremiah would want Jonathan in good health, both physically and mentally."

"Your suggesting Jeremiah has moved Jonathan over a shorter distance than Alphus did," Max said. "I had concluded as much, which is why I set up operations here in the United States. There is also the safety of this facility." She pointed to the canopy above them. "Because of Sister Mary Margaret's scientific inquiries, this entire area is basically a Faraday cage. Nothing can get in and nothing can get out unless I say so."

"I just walked in, Max." The Captains said.

"You were expected." Max hissed. "I instructed Pi to let you in when you arrived."

"I never told you I was coming."

"You didn't have to. I know you too well."

"Got it! Can you old people stopped trying to upstage each other? I'm tired of your enormous egos! We get it there isn't enough room in this tent for the Captain. Sister Mary Margaret, and Max!" Josh interrupted them.

That uncomfortable silence descended. Ross grinned. Birdsong cleared his throat. Josh's red face began to fade. "Sorry! I should be with Olivia, not having to track down the second demon. So, can we get on with this? I don't buy it that Jeremiah will not hurt Jonathan. Looked what he did to those people in Max's compound! The man's a psycho."

"I'm with the kid. Put up or shut up." Ross said.

The Captain glanced at Max and nodded. "Bottom line is, I do not know what Jeremiah is after, but I do not think he will kill his brother. Hurt him, yes. Torture him, probably."

"You have a lot of room to talk about torture." Raven said from her monitor. Everyone looked up at her.

"Hello, Raven, my dear." The Captain clinched the pipe in his mouth.

Raven's face reddened with anger. "Don't speak to me. You controlled my life for years. I did your dirty work. I know who you really are."

"Oh, enlighten me." The Captain said.

"Vivian told me she met you outside the Council of Darkness meeting place and you claimed to be in league with the first demon."

The Captain froze and his eyes widened. "What? She said it was me?"

"Don't act so surprised. You also gave her the mission of taking out the eighth demon when you met her in Austin." Raven said.

The Captain sat forward. "Now, that is true. But claiming

to be the first demon?" He touched the pipe stem to his chin, deep in thought. "Something is not right, Raven. Not right, indeed. While I am thinking about your claim, we need to look at a video. Max, may I send a video to your monitor?" He pulled a cell phone from his coat pocket.

Pi took the phone and returned to the computer table. In seconds, she had the video playing on the monitor. The images showed green leaves slowly pulling aside until the camera focused on Snake sitting at the table, as she had been in the previous video. Only this time, a dull green egg-shaped object sat in the middle of the table. And Snake had two hands on it. A green light emanated from the object onto her face. A figure walked into view of the camera.

"Jeremiah!" Josh stood up.

"Yes. Now watch." The Captain said.

Jeremiah touched Snake in the forehead and both of them, along with the object, disappeared.

Max turned abruptly and glared at the Captain. "You spied on my island?"

"My dear, you just saw the Crimson Snake, along with the Grimvox and Jeremiah, disappear. He has taken both of them from your island and all you can think of is your security measures?" The Captain said.

"I don't care, okay!" Josh slammed his fist on the table. "What is that thing?"

"That, my son, is known as the Grimvox. It is an arcane and evil object used to retain the memories of demonic powers. Jeremiah now has access to all those memories." The Captain's eyes burned with passion. "And if that is so, then the second demon has indeed turned away from the Council of Darkness. He has gone rogue, which should not be surprising based on his history."

"She had a new arm." Raven said from the monitor. "How is that possible?"

"Powers and principalities, Raven." The Captain sat back in his chair. "It is more than an illusion. Jeremiah no doubt, tempted the Crimson Snake with a restored arm. Once she accepted it, she sold her soul to the second demon and has now bonded with the Grimvox." He looked at Max. "I know you were hoping for her redemption, Max. But no one survives being bonded to the Grimvox. It will use up her life force and will destroy her mind. Once a human has bonded to the Grimvox, it is for the rest of their lives. If they are separated from the Grimvox, their mind will be scrambled, something Raven is familiar with."

"Thanks to this implant you shoved into my brain!" Raven tapped her head.

The Captain opened his mouth to speak and then sat back. "I should tell you something, my dear. When you came into my employ, you already had the implant. Dr. Sno placed it at the request of someone whose identity has always remained a mystery. It was only after seeing the effectiveness of his implant that I chose to have JJ receive one for his own protection." He paused and glanced at Josh. "Unfortunately, Dr. Sno was blind by the time I acquired Jonathan and I had to recruit Dr. Monarch to perform the surgery."

Raven seemed deep in thought. "Assuming you are telling the truth, then who hired Dr. Sno to operate on me?"

"I do not know, my dear."

"Stop calling me 'my dear'." Raven shouted.

"Raven, calm down." Max said, sitting back down. "This is all very confusing. We know that you and the woman known as Dr. Sno are working together and she is a Vitreomancer."

"Dr. Sno's wife. It is true that I infiltrated that organization to learn more about the whereabouts of Jeremiah. But I am hardly working with her."

"Jonathan told me about the Lion King theater. He told me you were there with Dr. Sno." Josh blinked. "I guess 'she' Sno, not 'he' Sno."

Confusion clouded the Captain's features. "What? I have never seen a production of 'The Lion King'."

"In London." Raven said. "When you hired me to kill Dr. Monarch."

The Captain grew very still and stared off into space. "It is true I hired you to shoot Dr. Monarch, not kill him. You do not remember those instructions now. But I was not at that theater."

"Jonathan said he confronted you and Dr. Sno on the London Eye after the failed assassination." Birdsong said.

"I have never ridden the London Eye." The Captain bolted up and, with trembling hands, picked up his pipe. "Could it be? My dear Lord, I hope not!"

"What is it?" Max asked.

"Could someone be passing themselves off as me? It would explain so much."

"Don't think you can get out of your past with such a cliché." Raven said.

"Let me guess," Ross chimed in. "You have an evil twin brother."

The Captain froze and glanced at Ross. "I am an only child. I have no brother."

"Jonathan thought he was an only child, too." Josh said.

The Captain ignored the remark and stared off into space. "This changes everything."

"What changes everything?" Max asked.

The Captain hurried back to his fur coat, hastily pulled it over his arms and shoulders. "I have to hurry. If what I think is true, then matters are for worse than I ever anticipated. I will be in touch." He disappeared down the dark corridor, leaving everyone speechless.

"What just happened?" Birdsong said.

"I don't know." Max whispered. "And I don't like NOT knowing."

"Forget about the Captain and Snake. Jonathan gets priority over Snake." Josh said.

"Josh is right. Focus on Jonathan Steel. If Jeremiah kidnapped Snake and this Grimvox, then most likely they are both in the same location." Ross said. "If this Jeremiah is behind all of this, he has a plan that involves both Jonathan and the Crimson Snake."

Max nodded. "One thing is for sure. Jeremiah has incredible resources for someone so young. The assault team that took out my people in Switzerland was only half of his forces. The other half assaulted the safe house." She shook her head and closed her eyes. "If only Yvonne had trusted me, I could have sent her a team."

"And they would all be dead." Birdsong said. "Where are Yvonne and Sam?"

"Yvonne has been working with Ruth Martinez on some personal matters. I contacted her, and she is meeting with Ruth to bring her up to speed on what has happened. Sam has moved back to his home in Austin. We must discover who or what is behind Jeremiah's forces. They have power and money."

"The Dark Council? The Vitreomancers?" Birdsong said.

Max paused and crossed her arms. She trembled quietly, as if a rat had run over her grave. "What if there is another faction at work? A faction with more money and power?"

"A third demonic council?" Josh asked. "Let's hope not!"

"No, Josh." Max stood up and paced along the other side of

the table. "We have tunnel vision. Demons everywhere. Easy to blame Satan."

"Finally, someone understands my skepticism," Ross said.

"And you, of all people, know just how wicked the human heart can be. We are the purveyors of original sin since our fall in the garden. Mankind can pull off the greatest evil without the help of a demon." Max paused. "The Penticle."

Ross laughed. "No! Not another conspiracy theory."

"You had a suspected member of the Penticle in your hands. You were investigating Dr. Faustus for financial malfeasance, and a member of the Council of Darkness killed him. Why would they kill the man?" Max said.

"So a human host of a demon on the Council could take that person's place." Josh said. "That was the entire purpose behind the triplets manipulating Jonathan."

"Okay, I'll concede there are powerful individuals with enough power, enough political pull, and enough information to blackmail others who could pull the strings behind the curtain." Ross said.

"Don't mix your metaphors." Max said.

"Whatever! I've been in the FBI for twenty years. I've seen no evidence of this Penticle you talk about. Nothing but urban legends."

"But what if it is true? And what if Jeremiah now has access to unlimited funds and unlimited political pull?" Max said.

"If he did, then why did he kidnap Jonathan? Why take Snake and this Grimace?" Birdsong said.

"Grimvox." Max corrected him. "Another good question." She shook her head and pounded a fist on her thigh. "So much confusion."

Pi touched Max on the shoulder. "I hate to interrupt, but he's here."

Max's flustered features, so foreign to Josh, spoke volumes

of how they all felt. Max nodded. "Ross, Pi will give you a copy of the video footage and how we obtained it. Perhaps you can have your resources clean up videos from the rest of the hospital grounds. The Captain is right about something. Jeremiah would not have teleported very far with an unconscious Jonathan. He most likely had a getaway vehicle stashed close to the hospital in Houston." Max motioned to Pi, and the young woman handed a memory card to Ross.

Ross' face betrayed his desire to say something profoundly sarcastic, but he held it back. "Good idea."

"Mr. Birdsong, can you assist Pi in rooting out any information about the Penticle?"

"I can."

"And I'll give you Sam's contact information. Check with him and see what he might know about this Penticle. He and Yvonne researched many such supposed organizations while they were protecting Jonathan. Raven, I suggest you contact Vivian and go to the island. See if there is anything there that might give us the least bit of indication where Jeremiah might have taken the Snake." Max stood up slowly and reached for her cane. She composed herself and turned her gaze on Josh. "Josh, you're with me."

CHAPTER

SEVEN

Max led Josh back to the laboratory. Sister Mary Margaret met them at the entry to the tunnel to the tent. "You did not tell me *he* would be here!"

"He is indispensable to our endeavors." Max said tersely.

"The man is a heretic!" Sister Mary Margaret fairly spat the words. "His presence on these grounds is an abomination to our Lord."

Max wiped a tired hand across her forehead. "Mary Margaret, he has received absolution and forgiveness."

"From a Protestant denomination. He is an outcast of the Church. And you will address me as Sister Mary Margaret."

Max stood her ground. "If I pull my funding now, over half of this equipment goes back to the owner, right?"

Sister Mary Margaret's face reddened. "Yes."

"This man has been involved in dozens of exorcisms and he may be the key to locating the Grimvox. You want to examine the Grimvox, don't you?"

Sister Mary Margaret's mouth twisted as she thought. "Unsanctioned exorcisms, Max." She looked away and sighed.

"Very well. You can escort him to the conference room. But keep him out of my laboratory." She whirled and went back to her technicians.

"What is this all about?" Josh asked.

Max ignored his question, and she stiffened. "A man from my past, Josh. Someone I thought was dead. I spoke to him by video chat just yesterday, and this is the first time I have seen him in decades. When Jonathan was kidnapped, I asked if he would come today. His insights into demonic behavior might help." She grabbed his hand and squeezed it in a rare show of emotion. "Pray I will keep my wits about me."

Hand in hand, they walked back through the tunnel to the ruined foundations of the cabin. At the fireplace, a man stood with his back to them. His hair was white, and he leaned on a cane. He turned and Josh gasped at the appearance of the man's neck and face. Scar tissue spread over his right cheek and into his hairline. A deformed nubbin was all that was left of his right ear. An ugly white scar ran through the scar tissue along the right side of his neck. He wore an ankle length black coat over a black turtleneck sweater and black pants. Max and Josh moved to join him near the fireplace.

"Father Caskey, thank you for coming." Max said.

"I am no longer a priest, my dear." He said hoarsely and his bright blue eyes focused on Josh. "You must be Joshua Knight."

"Yes."

Caskey extended a scarred, deformed right hand. Josh shook it and fought back a shiver at the touch of the dry, scaly skin. "You are my old friend's great nephew, right?"

"Yes." Josh's eyes widened. "Wait! You're the priest in the story about Molly."

Caskey paused and licked his lips. His gaze shifted to Max. "He told you, did he?"

"He told Jonathan and Jonathan told me," Josh said as he glanced at Max. "That means that you and Max."

"Were once in love. Yes, young man. At least in my mind. It was my undoing. And led to the death of a young girl." He reached out and touched Max's arm. "So, we thought."

Max's grip tightened on Josh's hand and he felt her tremble. She nodded. "From what I understand, Cephas was here with her when Mary, uh, disappeared. He made copious notes for Jonathan, and he claims Mary was pulled into a microscopic black hole."

"Uh, Max, Cephas made a video recounting the events." Josh said. "We can watch it if you want."

Max gasped and released Josh's hand. She stumbled and Caskey put out a hand to steady her and she stepped away from him. She reached out and Josh helped her steady her stance. Finally, her voice broke as she attempted to speak again. "I do not want to relive my daughter's last moments, Josh." She swallowed and fought for control. "I am visiting this place for the first time since I found out she was working with the eleventh demon for so many years."

Caskey looked down into the dark shadows of the basement. Josh thought he saw a flicker of green light, as if a firefly had crossed through the inky darkness. Caskey put out his right hand and closed his eyes. "Yes, I can feel evil here. Still here, Molly. It has not left this place. We are being observed. We need to speak elsewhere."

He opened his eyes and Max pointed down the tunnel. "Follow me." Josh followed them back down the tunnel and cast one last look deep into the eerie depths of the basement. *What* was watching them?

∽

Josh's growling stomach had alarmed them as they made their way back down the tunnel. Only instead of heading to the conference room, Max led them in the other direction into a small dining area. "What would you like to eat?" She asked Josh.

It was only then he realized how famished he was. "Burger?"

"Have a seat while I confer with the chef." Max headed through a back door into what appeared to be a kitchen area.

Josh raised an eyebrow. Max had thought of everything. "When you finish that burger, young man, I want you to tell me everything you can about the thirteenth demon's possession of your mind," Caskey said.

Josh shivered. "I'd rather not go there."

"If you want to help your father, I will need every bit of information you can supply, my good man," Caskey said. "Now, if I can find a fine cup of tea, it would be most welcome."

Pi appeared from the kitchen, bearing a plate with a hamburger.

"That was fast." Josh said.

"It was already prepared for some of the staff." She sat the plate before him.

"I don't want to take their food."

Max came from the kitchen bearing a tray with a teapot and cups. "I need you at your best, Josh. Everyone else has time. We do not. Now eat." She placed the tray on the table and Caskey smiled.

"You read my mind."

"I remembered your fondness for Earl Grey tea." Max poured tea into a cup. "Two lumps and a splash of milk, right?"

Caskey's eyes watered, and he nodded. "Yes, please."

Josh's mouth watered at the fragrance of the burger. He

paused, closed his eyes, and said a silent prayer for Jonathan Steel. Josh bit into the burger. It was wicked!

"How is it?" Max stirred her cup of tea.

"Very good." Josh mumbled through a full mouth.

"My personal chef goes with me everywhere. He produces a lovely hamburger. I thought it best to stay here in the secure confines of this room rather than risk going out where Jeremiah and his drones could overhear us." She sipped her tea.

"Now, young man, back to your demons." Caskey glanced at Max and then pointed his scarred finger across the table. "I have been absent from this entire affair because of shame and guilt. But when I saw Jonathan Steel's photograph on the news after the airplane disaster, I knew the demons were busy. It took me a while to piece together the events around this Council of Darkness, and that is when I contacted Molly."

"Please, James. Call me Max. Molly is quite dead." Max said.

"Very well." Caskey drew a deep breath and then sipped more tea. "Let me be blunt, Josh. You and those around you, specifically Jonathan Steel, have been very lucky. Or, I guess you might say blessed. You have handled these encounters with demons all wrong. You don't just command a demon to hell. Exorcism doesn't work that way."

"It worked well enough for us," Josh said as his face warmed.

"You were blessed. God was on your side or you would all be dead. How did you defeat the thirteenth demon?"

Josh swallowed hard. "Do I really have to talk about this?"

Caskey nodded. "Yes, young man. Let me explain something. Exorcising a demon is not like what you see in movies. You don't just command the demon to leave. Rather, the demon has occupied an individual because of being invited in. It is like a legal contract. Here's my body. We have an arrangement. Move in and live here. I'm ceding the deed of my house to you, mister demon. And always, always, there is a reason the person makes such an arrangement. Laddy, you must deal with the person's need that created such a situation before you can address the demon. It is only after the person has enough awareness of their situation to force them to change their mind that the demon can be removed."

Josh averted his gaze. Memories slid over his mind like sandpaper on an open wound. "My decisions cost my mother her life. I let the demon in to punish her."

"An act of very human rebellion, Josh." Caskey said quietly. "I understand human rebellion. My rebellion against the precepts I had accepted in my calling to serve God cost me my relationship with," he glanced at Max, "well, the woman you know as Max. And led to the corruption of her daughter by the eleventh demon."

Josh glanced at the aging man. His rheumy eyes glistened with moisture. "How do you live with the guilt?"

Caskey frowned and leaned back from the table. "That's the point, young lad. You live with it. Like living with a scar from being burned." He brushed the side of his neck. "I take that guilt and I reshape it into conviction to never let the circumstances that led to the decision behind my guilt happen again. I redeem the guilt. And so, my good lad, I cling to that guilt as a token of my willingness to let God teach me a better way. Did you ever make a failing grade?"

Josh snorted. "More than once."

"If you ignore the failure, it stays that way. If you examine the failure, learn from it, and vow to not fail again, it can become a stepping stone to success." Caskey chuckled. "Sorry. I sound like a health and wealth pastor in one of your evangelical churches."

Josh shrugged. "It's still the truth. One I have tried to learn to live with."

"Keep trying." Caskey said. "That is all any human can do. God takes our feeble attempts and honors them and heals our wounds. Rely on the Lord, Josh."

Josh nodded. "That is certainly something I have learned to do. And, bro, I had to learn the hard way."

"The hard way many times is the only way we learn valuable lessons, my boy." He rubbed his hands together. "If you are to truly face these demons, you can no longer rely solely on providential happenstance. God has sent his angels to take care of the demons you have faced so far, true?"

"Yes." Josh nodded. "Dude was one of them."

Caskey raised an eyebrow. "Dude?"

"That's the name I gave him."

"You have proven my point. In every encounter you and Jonathan have had with demons, the true defeat of those demons occurred at the hands of an angelic presence. It was never you or another human who successfully drove those demons out of their hosts." Caskey said. "My boy, is this not true?"

Josh ran through the list of demons in his mind. "I think you're right."

"But now, Josh, we are dealing with a demon who has possessed a member of your family. Jeremiah is Jonathan's brother, and dealing with this demon will be very personal." Caskey tilted his head. "I believe you had a spiritual encounter with another demonic being?"

"Pandora." Josh whispered.

"Tell me about it. Every detail." Caskey sipped more tea and leaned toward him, his bright blue eyes gleaming.

"Pandora had tried to take over my mind. But there was a moment when the real bad dude showed up. I found myself face to face with the strange apparition of a tall, elderly man with bright turquoise eyes, a chiseled face and a shock of short, white hair."

"Like Jonathan's eyes?" Max almost dropped her cup. "Was it the Captain?"

"No."

"No doubt this manifestation assumed such an appearance to evoke enough familiarity you would pay close attention to his requests, my boy," Caskey said, rubbing his chin. "A demon can assume any appearance it wants. Now, tell me more."

Josh shared the memory of the strange encounter with the man in the pith helmet.

∽

"Who are you?"

"I am the true spirit to which you have been speaking." The man said.

"Then you can go now." Josh said.

"Patience, Joshua Knight." A wicker chair with a wide up swept back that swelled into the shape of a cobra head appeared behind the man. The eyes and mouth were woven into the wicker and disappeared behind the man's figure as he sat in the chair. He crossed his legs and put the pith helmet on his knee. He snapped his fingers, and the hallway disappeared and a jungle setting surrounded them. He motioned to a stump. "Have a seat. So where to begin?" He massaged his mouth, and the sound of frogs and birds filled the air. "I don't want to give too much away. It is important that certain facts remain in the dark for you. Let's say it all began with your father, Arthur Knight."

Josh sat slowly on a stump and his hand closed on the shard of the bloodstone hanging on a chain around his neck. "My father? He's dead."

"Oh, that is what everyone wanted you to think. But he surprised us all. Clever man." The man shifted in the chair. "You see, he was chosen by Lucas long before you were born."

"The 'pale devil'." Josh said. "Worked with Vivian and the thirteenth demon."

"Let's just say that Lucas is far more than mere flesh and spirit. He is far more than the demonic spirits that inhabit his body for passing on to others. Although now, he is an outcast from his master. As you have surmised, Lucas had the vision of finding the genetic material that made the Nephilim a possibility. You mentioned the Bible. I'm sure you read about the Nephilim after the whole affair with the tenth demon. The men of old. The giants in the land. The 'sons of man' who had children with the daughters of Eve." The man tapped the helmet. "You know the Philistines were descendants of the Nephilim in that the same remnants of demonic powers sired their ancestors after everyone but Noah's family died in the flood. Goliath was a giant. Not quite as powerful as the original Nephilim or the children of the Bloodstone because of the diminished power of these demonic spirits."

The man leaned forward. "Lucas did not know about genes. He predates that knowledge, for he is very ancient. But once the knowledge surfaced, he went in search of the genetic material. He took your father to Patagonia. Did you know that?"

"No."

"He brought back samples of the Patagonian giants. Lucas approached your father not because of his knowledge, but because of your father's genes. Your father contains certain genetic material that was essential to the success of Lucas' plan. The children of the bloodstone came from thirteen different men. What Lucas never told your father is the other twelve men all perished. Died within weeks of passing on their altered genes to the mothers of the children of the bloodstone." The man leaned forward and his bright turquoise eyes gleamed. "And here is the secret only you now

know. Your father lived. He survived the procedure because of his own genetic material. Which he passed on to you, my dear boy."

Josh's heart raced. "What kind of genetic material?"

"In time, in time." The man sat back. "You're wondering why Hampton allowed you to suffer with this viral infection."

"He said to force my brain to change. Make me a petri dish."

"Yes, yes, to eliminate the hard-wired part of the brain that clings to God." The man waved his hand dismissively. "If that succeeds, icing on the cake." He smiled. "No, the real reason was to force your mind to awaken to new possibilities. Your mind and body, Josh. You have unlimited capacity for a level of intelligence known to only a few people in the world's history." The man nodded. "Yes, I must admit that exposure to extra dimensional spirits can do that. How do you think twelve simple men called by the Son changed the world?"

"The Holy Spirit." Josh said.

"Yes, yes! Now imagine what prolonged indwelling of any kind of spirit would do to a man."

"Besides leading him to death? Bro, your kind kills the host before the host even knows what is happening."

The man frowned. "Humans are fragile, I'll grant you that. The corrosive power of demonic possession is dangerous and ultimately deadly."

"Why are you telling me all of this?"

"You need to know that I and my demonic partner have had a very long time to think and plan this. We have ascended beyond the petty battles of the Council of Darkness or the Vitreomancers. We have had an endless view of mankind, and we are very patient. I am not like Pandora's spirit. She is a manifestation of the Elixir of Life passed down for thousands of years and is now in the possession of Hampton."

"What is the Elixir of Life?"

"DNA, viral agents, biochemical soup kept alive by my spirit,

protected from decay as through the centuries, knowledge and genetic material is incorporated into the fluid. Hampton thinks this Elixir of Life will grant immortality. It is merely a repository of arcane knowledge, a biological version of the Grimvox."

"The what?"

"Ask your 'Daddy' about his palm. He'll tell you all about it." The man put his feet down and leaned forward, playing with the pith helmet. *"Hampton is deceived. His Elixir of Life is actually the Elixir of Lies, my boy."*

"So, you're in the Elixir?"

"Part of me. However, my human part is very much alive, hidden away from the prying eyes of man." The man stood up. *"There is a spiritual battle coming and you and the man known as Jonathan Steel will be at the epicenter. What you have been through so far is nothing compared to what is coming. You will lose heart. You will be discouraged. You will possibly lose your faith. I tell you all of this because you are so important to my cause and you must endure to the end."*

"I will endure to the end, but I will never denounce my Savior." Josh stood up and walked slowly, haltingly toward the man. *"My God and my Savior have gotten me through this ordeal. Bro, you may have messed in your pants with this one. Revealing to me what is going on was not wise. I will never renounce my faith. I will never walk away from Jonathan Steel. And I will never serve you or Satan."*

The man put his helmet on his head and tapped it. "Excellent! My goal has been achieved. You are now prepared to deal with any type of demonic influence. After all, to prepare you for any eventuality was one of the most important reasons I have paid you these visits." His turquoise eyes glowed with mischief. *"You see, there are many demonic factions in this universe. As long as you are prepared for the faction that is coming for you, I can breathe*

easier. After all, the enemy of my enemy is my friend." He disap-
peared and Josh opened his eyes.

CASKEY SIGHED. "I am afraid that what you heard makes very little sense to me. This creature who spoke to you in your mind was most likely lying to you and seeding discord and doubt. I do not know who or what this creature is, but one thing is certain. This person seems to intimately know you and Jonathan."

"I thought it might be the Captain, but he denies his presence at many of these encounters." Josh said.

"It seems this creature, most likely the first demon as you lot would designate him, can assume multiple identities." Caskey tapped the table.

Josh lifted an eyebrow. "Are you the first demon?"

Caskey paused and his mouth fell open. "I acknowledge the creator and ruler of all reality is the triune God, specifically the Father and the son, Jesus Christ, and the Holy Spirit forever three and one, Josh. I acknowledge and openly submit myself totally to the triune God." He lifted his hands toward the ceiling. "I worship and humble myself before you."

The hair stood up on Josh's neck. "Okay."

Caskey wiped moisture from his eyes. "This is the test for any spirit. A demon will never acknowledge complete obedience and submission to Christ. He will unwillingly submit to Christ as we saw in Christ's encounters with demons. But they always beg to be left alone. They do not want to bask in the awesome majestic presence of the Son of God."

"Okay, dude, I accept you are not demon possessed by this first demon. I was only kidding."

"Never kid about such issues, my lad. This is very serious business."

"Do you think he was referring to the second demon when he said I must face these trials?" Josh said.

"Most likely. If this entity is indeed the first demon, he is the apex predator, only lower than Satan. It makes sense the only other remaining demon would have its own plan. And that plan seems to involve you and Jonathan Steel." He sipped more tea. "As to the claims about your genetic heritage from your father, I am woefully educated in that area. Perhaps consulting Sister Mary Margaret?" He smiled. Throughout the exchange, Max had sat silently sipping her tea. Caskey smiled at her. "My dear, I hope we are not boring you."

"Not at all. This information is important." She looked at Josh over the rim of her teacup. "You did not tell me of this encounter with this strange spirit."

"I haven't had a chance." Josh said. "I don't know what other make of what it said. Probably more lies."

Caskey placed his cup noisily in it saucer. "Now, Max, I was hoping we could have a few moments in private."

Max straightened. "If you have come here hoping to rekindle our relationship, I assure you there is nothing to talk about. I thought you died the day Mary died. I have put you in the past."

"Very well. I can assure you there are no feelings left for you except the guilt of giving myself to the power of the eleventh demon to win your affection." His hand shook as he lifted his teacup to his lips. "A priest must never surrender to the power of a demon to save someone as I learned the hard way, my dear." He placed both hands around the cup to stabilize it. He frowned. "My prayers dried up. My faith was dampened. In all ways, and in everything, the demon was there in the shadows.

Oppressing me, but not possessing me. I cannot tell you the freedom I experienced when the eleventh demon left this plane of existence on the day Mary sent it packing to Tartarus."

"At the cost of her life." Max said through tight lips.

Caskey glanced at her with moist eyes. "On that day, my dear, we were both freed. That was when I looked for evidence of what had happened. When I saw the image of Jonathan Steel on the news feed following the aircraft disaster, I knew he was somehow involved and that led me here. To you. To now." Caskey sat back. "I have no illusions of a relationship with you, Molly. That ship has sailed and sunk. I am here for one reason. I believe this young man is the key to defeating the Council of Darkness forever and he must be prepared."

"By a disavowed priest?" Max said.

"True, I was removed from the church. But since that time, I have been involved in dozens of exorcisms by faithful individuals not officially connected to the Catholic faith."

"Just how did you survive the fire?" Max said. "When I thought my daughter did not?"

Caskey sighed. "I awoke beneath dozens of collapsed hospital beds. The fire consumed most of the old asylum, but I survived. My dear, there were many days afterward I wished I had succumbed. I couldn't face the authorities. I had connections to a convent that took in troubled women. In the past, I had helped them out, and they agreed to nurse me back to health without contacting the authorities."

Caskey sat forward and fiddled with his empty teacup. "Unfortunately for me, they contacted the church authorities, and I had to face a tribunal. I was defrocked, thrown out, exiled. For years, I merely existed working at the convent as a janitor, until one day, I read a story in the newspaper about a father who had murdered his own children. The man claimed he was demon possessed. His sister was a nun at the convent and she asked me to talk to him. The church wanted nothing to do with the man, no matter what he claimed."

Caskey looked away, as if examining the distant past. "I met some fellow exorcists not officially associated with the church. They were drawn to the man's claims. By this time, he had been convicted of first-degree murder and was on death row. We attempted to exorcise the demon for weeks. Because of the heinous nature of his crime, his attempts at appeal were refused." Caskey cleared his throat and wiped moisture from his eyes. "A day before his execution, they allowed us to try one more time. Clearing the man's name was impossible. Only saving his soul."

Caskey paused, and a haunted look came over his face. "The man's eyes changed. Turned to pearly white. No pupils. His last words to us were of victory. Triumph over God. He laughed at us and said he was a Vitreomancer. I'd never heard that term. Then he said something I will never forget."

"What?" Josh said.

"We are the enemies of the Council of Darkness." Caskey whispered. "He was executed the next day."

Max's eyes softened and she poured more tea into his cup. She added two lumps of sugar and a splash of milk. After stirring the tea carefully, she handed the cup to Caskey. "Have some more tea, James."

He looked up at her and, for a moment, Josh saw the old affection fill the man's eyes. The fire of his love for Molly had never died. He took the cup. "Thank you, my dear." He sipped some tea and looked back at Josh. "After that, it no longer mattered if I was official or not. I set about helping exorcist teams to seek and defeat these heinous fiends. I learned all I could about these Vitreomancers and the Council of Darkness.

But there was precious little to learn. Now you know why I am here, Josh. This is the closest I have come to engaging these demons in decades. I want to help. I want to make sure your fate and that of your father, Jonathan Steel, are not what that poor man faced."

CHAPTER
EIGHT

Steel awoke in the room again. He rolled over onto his back and right into the mess he had left from before. This was beyond humiliation. He sat up and rubbed his chest where the disc had fried the skin around its edge.

The room was almost pitch black, and he stood up slowly, the stench of his excretions and body fluids filling his nostrils. In the dim, green light of the EXIT sign, he stepped carefully ahead, hands outstretched until he felt the rough surface of the cinderblock wall. He followed the wall around the small room and concluded it was about the size of a small one-car garage. He encountered nothing but blank walls until he reached the metal door. Its surface was smooth with no handle and no window. He sat slowly with his back against the door. What now? Why did Jeremiah need him to sift through their father's memories? Would the Grimvox somehow record those memories? Or perhaps enhance them?

When he had encountered Robert Ketrick in the man's library, Ketrick had somehow shared a memory from the past. He had relived the time when he was born and Ketrick and

Lucas had been there in Mexico. The shared memory was as real as one of his own.

Was this ability somehow linked to the Grimvox? A ghostly pale light erupted into the darkness. Steel gasped as a glowing ball of green light pulsated in the far corner of the room. His palm burned, and for the first time, it glowed in symphony with the pulsating cloud. A vague face appeared with limpid eyes and a mouth open in a silent scream. Man or woman, he could not tell. The face was vaguely familiar and suddenly a hand lurched out from the cloud of green light, almost reaching him.

"Help me." A wavering voice echoed in the room.

Just as suddenly as the phenomenon appeared, it winked out of existence. Darkness returned with just the afterimage of the cloud and the reaching hand remaining in his vision.

The door behind him flew open, and he fell back into the hall. Jeremiah held a flashlight, and he directed the beam into the room. Gray, stained cinder block walls gave no hint to the ghostly apparition of a few moments before.

"What happened in here?" Jeremiah glanced down at Steel.

Steel smiled and looked up at his brother. For once, the man had no idea what was going on in his own torture chamber. "I'll never tell." Steel hissed.

The tablet appeared from behind Jeremiah's back and pain flooded over Steel, sucking him down into his own green, nauseating oblivion.

STEEL WOKE up once again in the chair. On the table before him, the green light of the Grimvox played across Snake's empty features.

Jeremiah appeared behind Snake. "Near naked and tied to a

chair, you seem so hopeless, brother. Just give in and do as I ask."

"All I have to do is say one name." Steel growled.

Jeremiah smiled. "You want to say HIS name, don't you?"

"Yes." Steel noticed the tablet was on the table over three feet away from Jeremiah. Could he say the name of Jesus Christ before Jeremiah got to the tablet? Could he send the second demon to Tartarus?

"It won't work, you know." Jeremiah crossed his arms.

"Then let me try." Steel hissed.

"Look, brother. If you are so close to your Savior, then why is He allowing this to happen? Why hasn't he stopped me? Where are your precious guardian angels? Haven't seen one, have you?" Jeremiah gestured into the darkness. "Oh, precious angel? Are you here? Come and get me!" Jeremiah put his arms out and spun around, his gaze toward the invisible ceiling. He paused and shrugged. "Looks like you're on your own, brother."

Steel swallowed hard. Was the greenish cloud in his room an attempt by an angel to reach him? No. An angel would not call for help. "Go on. You're gloating so you might as well finish."

Jeremiah laughed and paced around the table back to his chair and the tablet. "JJ, you tried to kill me, remember?"

Steel raised an eyebrow. He was back in the alley fifteen years before. "Yes, I did."

"Someone stopped you."

"Kevin, my youth pastor."

Jeremiah moved to his side and squatted down until his face was even with Steel's. Steel stared into his intense turquoise eyes and noble face. It was like looking in a mirror.

"But the desire, the need to kill, hasn't stopped, has it? Granted, while you had amnesia, you couldn't recall my existence. But the hatred was always there. Simmering. Stoking. Burning. Where do you think your anger came from? Our subconscious may keep secrets, but it always whispers." He leaned closer, whispering. "Find him. You hate him. Kill him. That hate is still there, JJ. And as long as you harbor hatred toward me, you are powerless in my presence. Your angels will keep their distance. Your master has abandoned you because you have made yourself judge and executioner toward your own brother."

Jeremiah stood and put a hand to his chin. "No, wait. More than judge and executioner. When it comes to me, you want to be your own vengeful god." He leaned down again. "And as long as you play god, your supernatural connection is worthless. Want to know how to fix it?"

Steel's face burned with anger. "How?"

"Love me. Simple. Embrace me as your long, lost brother." He smiled.

"You killed our mother." Steel said.

The smile faded and Jeremiah stood up and backed away. He glanced at Snake's empty eyes and then stabbed the tablet.

STEEL HAD no idea of the passage of time. When he woke up the room had been cleaned and a small light in the ceiling gave dim illumination to the room. A tray of food with two bottled waters sat in the center of the room. His stomach growled and he knew for a fact he was dehydrated. For a fleeting moment he wondered if the food might be poisoned. Jeremiah could have killed him a dozen times over by now.

First rule of survival: survive. Take care of basic needs. Several slices of bread, along with slices of cheese, covered a paper plate. An apple sat beside the two water bottles. He slowly chewed the bread, followed by small bites of cheese. He sipped the water, resisting the urge to guzzle. His stomach tried to revolt, but he kept it down. It took a while, but he finished the plate and the two bottles of water.

Could he possibly love the monster that was his brother? The pale light appeared again in the room's corner. The blurred face wavered in the undulating light. Eyes filled with fear. Lips twisted in pain. "Help me." This time, the voice was distinctly feminine.

"Who are you?" He walked toward the light.

A hand appeared from the cloud of light. Polished fingernails and a gold ring. "Help." She said again. "Don't leave me." For a fleeting second, her face almost came into focus. Horror filled her eyes, and she looked behind her. "No, don't stop me! He can help!"

Another hand appeared from the mist and closed around the first person's head, jerking her back into the darkness. The light faded as the words echoed in the room.

Twice now, this person had asked for his help. Who was she? Where was she? And who had pulled her back?

Steel reached up with his glowing palm and felt the air where the apparition had appeared. His hand tingled. He sighed. If he escaped, then this person, whoever they were, would be at the mercy of something? Someone? He could not abandon her. For a moment, he felt the anger surge and then swallowed hard. How many times had he found himself in this dilemma? His personal need for vengeance warring against his need to help others in need. "My mission. I know." He said to the empty air.

The door opened, and Jeremiah studied him. Jeremiah wore a black turtleneck shirt and jeans. He held the tablet up. "Still fighting me?"

Steel shook his head. "No. I'll help you. I want to know more."

Jeremiah's eyebrows arched. "Really? Is this a trick?"

"No trick. But I'm tired of this stinking room. I want to clean up. I want clothes. I give you my word. I will help you."

Jeremiah studied him with eyes filled with suspicion. He turned aside and gestured across the hall. "A one bedroom prison cell with more amenities." The door opened with a press of a button on the tablet. "Shower and toilet. It's yours from now on. If you cooperate."

"Clothes?"

"I'll bring you a set of surgical scrubs." Jeremiah grinned. "And some bunny slippers."

Steel walked past him into the room, and the door closed behind him. Had he made a deal with the devil? Yes. He had done it before with the best of intentions of saving Josh. He would help the stranger from his cell. A small shower stood in the room's corner next to a toilet. A slab with a thin pad protruded from the opposite wall. All the comforts of home.

The water was ice cold, but he didn't care. As he scrubbed the stink from his body with a sponge and some kind of institutional soap, the thought came relentlessly. Was he really trying to help the woman in his cell? He had to admit he wanted to know more about Jeremiah. He wanted to access the memory card he had ignored since his father had given it to him. True, most of his memories had returned. But they were like jumbled up pieces of a jigsaw puzzle and he had no idea what the final picture looked like. As much as he hated to admit it, he wanted to know more.

CHAPTER

NINE

Jeremiah led Steel down the hallway to the double doors leading to the Grimvox room. He smelled better and the gray surgical scrubs were too large. But he felt better. Except for the bright pink bunny slippers on his feet. He settled into the metal chair and it slid through the open doors.

"Right this way. Your table is waiting." Jeremiah said.

Steel settled into the seat, placing his arms on the armrest. He tensed his muscles as the restraints snapped into place. When he relaxed, the restraints were loose around his wrists. The chair slid forward toward the table, hidden in darkness. He came to rest at the table's edge and the pale yellow light came on. He gasped at the sight before him.

Snake had been replaced by another woman. She was diminutive and her wide-open eyes stared into the Grimvox from a slack face. Her head was shaved and black netting covered her arms draped around the Grimvox.

"Ila?" He said. Ila had been Josh's girlfriend during the affair with the Rudolph Wulf and the twelfth demon. She had reunited with her mother. "I thought you went back to your mother."

"Oh, she did." Jeremiah said from behind him. "But in time, the vampire clan rebooted, so to speak and pulled her back in." Jeremiah leaned forward and whispered in his right ear. "Of course, I was the one who encouraged the clan to come back together. You see, the Grimvox is hard on its interfaces. I have more than one. If you give them a rest, they last longer."

Steel jerked in the chair and the disc tingled on his chest. "No!"

Jeremiah walked around the table and motioned into the darkness. A wheelchair bearing Snake appeared pushed by a white haired woman in a dark, gray robe. Her face was hidden in shadow.

"Nanny, time for Ila to be cleaned up and fed."

Nanny placed Snake at the table. "Of course." She glanced at Steel with pitch black eyes. "Cat got your tongue?"

Nanny disconnected a line from what appeared to be a feeding tube coming out of Snake's left nostril. She connected it to a similar tube in Ila's nostril. "Time for breakfast! Blue eggs and ham!"

Blue fluid filled the tube from a bag hanging at the back of Snake's wheelchair. Snake's empty eyes never fluttered and her face remained motionless and slack. Nanny leaned down and whispered in Ila's ear. "Time to change out, deary."

Ila pulled one hand from the Grimvox and Nanny placed Snake's good hand in the girl's grasp. Ila placed Snake's hand on the base of the Grimvox. Nanny nodded. "Now, the other hand."

Ila took her other hand away from the Grimvox and Nanny placed Snake's new hand on the base of the Grimvox. Ila's head slumped to her chest, her eyes closed. Nanny rolled Ila away in her own wheelchair and pushed Snake up to the table. "Let's get you decent, young woman." Nanny said to Ila as she transferred the feeding bag from Snake's chair. She wheeled her into darkness.

Jeremiah sat beside Steel. "See, I am not without compassion, brother. I make sure my keepers are cleaned and fed and rotated out on a twelve-hour basis. Keeps them from dying too soon. And splitting the spiritual feed coursing through their brains makes sure their brains are fresher. Better reception, you might say. Like defragmenting a hard drive."

Steel had finally gotten his anger under control. His breathing slowed. "And you wonder why someone would hate you."

Jeremiah lifted an eyebrow and his turquoise eyes gleamed in the green light from the Grimvox. "Oh, I know why people hate me. It is the currency of the damned, JJ. Your currency is love. But hate is ten times stronger." Jeremiah tapped on his ever-present tablet and turned it to face Steel. "See that graph? Studies have shown that one tragic moment needs thirty-three magic moments to undo the damage. Good does NOT always win out in the end. Statistics prove it. One angry outburst can snuff out dozens of smiles. Now, shall we begin?"

"Begin what?"

"The review of your memories, my memories, and the memories of our father." He held up the memory card. "You never looked at these recordings, did you? I haven't either. I wanted us to experience them together. Fresh. New." Jeremiah grinned. "And here is the beauty of this setup, JJ. The Grimvox will interface with any recorded memories taken from demons during the time of these events. It will mix them together and produce a real time approximation as if we were there, watching, listening." Jeremiah slid the memory chip into a slot on the tablet and placed the tablet at the base of the Grimvox. The tablet glowed as a green tinted energy field engulfed it. "I believe you have experienced this before. With my servant, Ketrick."

"Your servant?" Steel said. "He served the thirteenth demon, not you."

Jeremiah froze. Malice filled his eyes and, for a moment, Steel saw the demonic presence behind the façade of his brother. "Never speak that name!"

Steel raised an eyebrow in surprise. "Why are you afraid of thirteen?"

"I am not afraid!" Jeremiah's voice boomed with demonic power.

Steel smiled. "It's not fear? What is it? Did he take Ketrick away from you? Is that it? Let me guess. You started with Ketrick and while you were not looking, thirteen swooped in and took over. Thirteen told me he was the most powerful of all the demons."

The disc tingled on his chest as Jeremiah's finger hovered over the table. "Do not speak his name again!"

Steel nodded. "Got it. Can we get on with it?"

Jeremiah's breathing slowed, and the fire faded from his eyes. He nodded as control returned. "Now, JJ, this will be very simple. All you must do is place your hand on the Grimvox at the same time I do."

Jeremiah sat in his chair. "You know you want to. You want to know just as badly as I do. Don't you? One finger will suffice. Just one touch and all our father's secrets will be revealed." Jeremiah leaned toward him. "You can't resist it, can you? You chased his secrets for years. He erased your memory because of that. You want this so badly, JJ. Whatever secrets hide in those recordings were so bad, our father had surgery performed on your brain to make you forget. How can you not want to know?"

Steel glanced at the Grimvox. He wanted to know, yes. At

what price? As he watched the pulsating light around the tablet and the base of the Grimvox, his gaze shifted to Snake. For a fleeting second, her eyes left their focus on the Grimvox and focused on him. Snake blinked and then her gaze was back locked on the Grimvox. Jeremiah had not noticed. Perhaps he would not be alone in his battle against Jeremiah. Light glowed in the palm of his hand. The restraint released on his left arm and he reached out to the Grimvox and touched its pebbly surface.

CHAPTER

TEN

The ground undulated away from Steel like the waves of the ocean. He stood ankle deep in dead, brown grass. He looked around at a gray, featureless horizon. For a horrifying moment, he thought he was back in Numinocity. He tried to rub his eyes, but his hands would not move. He looked down at the gray scrubs he wore and to the pink bunny slippers on his feet. What had happened? He had been somewhere. The chair! Jeremiah! He had touched the Grimvox.

No matter how hard he tried, he could not move his arms and legs. From far away, across the uneven ground, something moved. Antenna appeared, followed by a red gleaming carapace of a millipede. Black legs flowed in synchronous motion as the thing came toward him. Its head was as big as a boulder. Jet-black eyes glittered as the creature paused before Steel. Its antenna touched his face, and he tried to scream.

"Welcome to the Antechamber. What secrets do you seek?" A hissing voice came from its mandibles.

85

Jeremiah appeared beside Steel. "We seek an audience with the Librarian."

The millipede shifted from right to left and for a fleeting second, one of its forelegs changed from a sleek, black, shiny surface to a red copper hue like Snake's artificial arm. Steel glanced at Jeremiah, but he did not seem to have seen the change. What did it mean?

The creature recoiled and hissed. "He is of the Other."

"He is here willingly. Now get with the program." Jeremiah shouted.

"Where is the Tomemaster? Only he can request an audience."

"I am the new Tomemaster." Jeremiah gestured with his hand and a green spike of electricity shot out engulfing the creature's antennae. It writhed in pain and hissed some more.

"I will let the Librarian deal with you." It said then turned and undulated over the brown grass hills. Steel floated after the creature. Jeremiah hovered at his side. Soon a black, stone wall appeared stretching from the ground into the heavens. Sitting before the wall sat a gleaming glass and chrome desk. The millipede shrunk in size and disappeared under the desk. Behind the desk, a figure looked up from a ledger. Her face was the texture of dried prunes and her skin a bile green. Bright yellow eyes gleamed with unholy light and purple hair hung listlessly to her shoulders. Skin barely covered her bones. She wore a high necked sweater made of snake skin. Thin, black lips parted and a forked tongue darted out.

"Who approaches the Librarian?"

Steel paused before the desk and Jeremiah joined him. He spoke something vile and desecrating in a language Steel could never understand. The Librarian hissed and scribbled something in the ledger with a gloved hand. "Your demon name is duly noted. Do you have the authorization form from the Tomemaster?"

Jeremiah laughed and rubbed his hands together. "About that? Let me see." He threw his hands apart and the air between them sizzled and popped. Something appeared in the air and fell onto the Librarian's desk. The hairless head rolled up to the Librarian's ledger. Dead, white eyes stared out into eternity.

"The former Tomemaster has given me his position." Jeremiah said. "Any further questions?"

The Librarian snorted and shoved the head away. It rolled off the end of the desk into the dead, brown grass and disappeared. "Fine. What is your request?"

"I bring a mortal for a review of matters that do not concern you." Jeremiah said curtly.

The Librarian regarded Steel with wide eyes. "He is of the Other. We do not allow him here."

"He is willing." Jeremiah said. "He comes here of his own accord." Jeremiah glanced at Steel and his eyes filled with the power of his demon. "He wants to know why mother had to die."

Steel tensed but could do nothing but hover up and down in helpless motion. "You can tell me that while my hands are around your throat!"

"Good!" The Librarian hissed. "He is willing to kill. Perhaps you have a point, my demon friend."

"Fine. Librarian, just know that I consent to being here, but if I object to anything I hear or see, all I have to do is speak His name and you will be undone."

The Librarian grunted and her forked tongue shot out at Steel. "Very well. I cannot refuse if you consent." She swiveled in the chair and stood up on spindly goat's legs with red hooves. From a receptacle on the desk, she withdrew a ring of huge, skeletal keys. Behind her, three doors appeared in the wall. "Where shall we start, my demon friend?"

Jeremiah's tongue ran over his lips as he thought. "Let's see. Me? Dad?" Jeremiah pointed at Steel. "Or, you? Where to begin?"

The Librarian held up the keyring. "Decide. I have things to do."

Steel hid his shock as one key suddenly glowed a red copper hue and then disappeared. Copper colored? Red? The Crimson Snake again? Was she trying to communicate with him? Was such a thing possible?

"What about Snake?" Steel asked.

"What?" Jeremiah said. "Snake? She is doomed, brother. Once she agreed to interface with the Grimvox, her fate was sealed. Why do you ask? Don't tell me you have feelings for her? She killed hundreds! She deserves her fate."

Steel nodded. "Just asking."

"Oh, I get it." Jeremiah chuckled. "You think you can save her?"

The Librarian laughed with him, and her forked tongue danced in the air before her face. She licked away tears from both eyes. "Save her? She is doomed, human mortal. She has chosen her fate."

"He can't help it." Jeremiah snapped his fingers and a business card appeared. "*A helper in the time of need.* His motto. He is burdened with glorious purpose, a self-proclaimed savior of the downtrodden and oppressed."

"Only if they are oppressed by the likes of you." Steel said quietly. "Can we get on with this? Start with our father. Chronologically, that would be best."

Jeremiah shrugged and the business card went up in

flames. He dusted his hands off and snapped another finger. The tablet appeared before him. "Very well. Let's access the memory card and see what our father has to reveal." He handed the memory card to the Librarian. "You can put away the keys for now and access these memories."

The Librarian's eyes widened. "Technology? Ah, our greatest tool." She smiled, and her forked tongue waggled in the air. "Perhaps you should share one of your memories first to make sure it will not drive this mortal insane."

Jeremiah blinked, and suddenly his eyes bulged with anger and fire. The second demon had taken over. "Great idea, Librarian. Before we descend into the mundane memories of humans, let's show JJ one of *my* oldest memories."

The Void

Aballon floated toward the singular point of light ahead. Others of his kind spun and screamed around him. Their pain filled the emptiness. Aballon finally approached the point of light and it coalesced into a strange, serpiginous form.

"Master?"

The serpent writhed in the Void's emptiness as his followers tumbled in chaos and confusion around them. "Yes."

"What is this form you have taken?"

The serpent's bright red eyes glittered. "I have a plan. All is not lost, Aballon."

Aballon assumed the form of a stick like figure. "This is less painful, master. Our brothers suffer from the wounds of battle. Can you not ease their pain?"

The serpent hissed. "Ah, yes, pain. A new and powerful sensa-

tion. They have chosen to follow me, Aballon, into this pain. Do you choose to follow me?"

"Yes, master." Where else could he go, Aballon thought? "You are beautiful and powerful? What is your plan?"

The serpent's body wound its way around Aballon's thin figure. "My plan is to destroy anything the Creator has made. He has taken our lives from us and cast us into this Void. But he has made a new universe with living creatures much lower and lesser than us."

Aballon could not see beyond the serpent's constricting coils. "This new universe, will we have access to it? Perhaps journeying there will ease our pain."

"If my plan succeeds, this universe will be mine. All I must do is to deceive the Creator's new creatures." The serpent hissed and his forked tongue touched Aballon's figure. He shuddered at the painful caress.

"Who are these creatures?"

"Two of them placed in a garden of perfection that should have belonged to us. And two trees the Creator has placed there." The serpent's long neck turned, and he looked behind him toward a pale light growing brighter as it grew closer.

"Two trees?"

"Yes, the tree of eternal life." The serpent hissed.

"We already have eternal life." Aballon said. "Now we are to spend it apart from the Creator."

"These creatures do not have eternal life. Yet. If they eat of that tree, then they will become like us." The serpent turned its gaze back onto Aballon. "The other is the tree of the knowledge of good and evil."

Aballon tensed and if he had lips, he would have smiled. "Knowledge. That is my strength. Was I not the one who planned the campaign against our enemy?"

The coils tightened and pain lanced throughout his body. "Yes, you were."

"Master, it was the best plan we could imagine." Aballon winced in pain. The serpent's coils tightened even more. How was he to pacify his master? "Knowledge, master. It is what all thinking creatures desire. If you tempt them with greater knowledge, will they not expect to be like the Creator?"

The serpent's eyes brightened, and the coils lessened. "Now, you are thinking like me, Aballon. You have arrived at my strategy. Perhaps knowledge is indeed your asset." The light behind the serpent had grown brighter and the new universe neared their edge of the Void. "Watch as I descend into this new universe and destroy the Creator's newest love. Knowledge will indeed by their downfall."

The serpent released Aballon and fell into the great light of the new universe. Pride blossomed in his chest. He and the master were on the same wavelength. Knowledge was power!

STEEL LURCHED as the memory dissipated like a mist in a hurricane. His head ached from the attempt to make sense of what he had seen. Like in the past, experiencing the Beyond taxed the human mind and, in time, memories faded.

"So you were Satan's what? War planner?"

"I was so much more. I should have been higher than number one. In time, JJ, I will ascend and replace number one. You will see. There are many such memories I will share when I deem it important. For now, your brother struggles to return."

Jeremiah's face slackened, and he was back. His wild eyes roved around him and focused on Steel. "What happened?"

"You don't know?" Steel said. "Your boss shared a memory.

Looks like I survived, though I'm having trouble recalling all the details."

"Shall we get on with it?" The Librarian rasped. "I have inventory to count."

"Yes." Jeremiah cleared his throat and tapped a finger on the tablet and the middle door opened. "Let's see what father has to tell us."

CHAPTER

ELEVEN

The bitterly cold wind cut through Yvonne Brown's coat and brought tears to her eyes, thrashing her salt and pepper hair around her face. Waves crashed against the end of the pier and she stepped back away from the freezing mist. Sam appeared at her side.

"When it's cold in Austin, it's really cold." He said. His sparse white hair blew in the breeze. "We shouldn't stay out here on the pier too long."

Yvonne shivered and studied her friend's wrinkled face. Sam had retired from the police when she first met him years before. He had aged under the stress and pressure from the time they had worked together. "I had to see it once more. This is where Jeremiah tried to kill us years ago."

"Yes, but this time, we stay out of the water." Sam took her by the arm. Sam had hidden Yvonne in the water under the pier while the assassins attacked his boat sent out onto the lake under its own power. "Let's go back into my house and have some coffee."

"I'm glad you still have your house."

"I rented it out. Can't give up my home, Yvonne." Sam said. "It's all I have left of my former life."

For years, she and Sam had traveled about the world hiding from Jeremiah Stone and trying to protect the man known as Jonathan Steel. Now that Jeremiah was out in the open, Sam had returned to his home at the request of Max. "Check out the local area for any sign of Jeremiah or Jonathan. Go back to JJ's home." She had told them.

Yvonne turned her back on the lake where fifteen years before Sam had incinerated his boat to make their would be assassins think they had succeeded. She looked down between the gaps in the slats across the pier at the cold water where she and Sam had hidden. "Are they here, yet?"

"Just arrived. Jason is making coffee. Ross is smoking on the front porch." Sam ran a hand through his white hair to smooth it back down. "He's probably quit a dozen times and started again. I know. I was right there with him. When I was on the force."

Sam led Yvonne through the back door into his house. The air was still cool and musty. Sam had only been back for a short while. Jason Birdsong poured a cup of coffee from a carafe and sniffed it.

"Kind of stale, Sam."

"Don't know how old it is. May be left over from the renter, or possibly from years ago." Sam shrugged. "We weren't very picky at the police station."

Birdsong took one sip and spit it into the sink. "You could use that to strip paint."

The front door opened and Ross stepped in, surrounded by a cloud of cigarette smoke. "Don't say it. Smoke has got to smell better than your house, Sam."

"I agree. Let's sit and talk." Sam motioned to his sofas. "My last renter moved out a year ago. Still a bit musty."

Yvonne settled into the same chair she had sat in so long ago when she coerced Sam to help her defend a young JJ against murder charges. A stain on the floor was probably from the same coffee spilled on that night. "What have you found out?"

Birdsong settled on a love seat next to Ross. His towering frame put the FBI agent to shame. "Nothing. No sign of Jeremiah Stone."

"We scoured the footage at the hospital in Houston. That one shot of Jonathan being pulled into the door frame and then just disappearing is the only footage with Jonathan or Jeremiah in it." Ross pulled out a cigarette from his rumpled raincoat and put it between his lips. His eyes widened. "I'm not going to light it, Yvonne."

"Thanks."

"What about footage in the garage or the receiving area?" Sam asked.

"Nil. Nada. Nothing." Birdsong said. "We know how they left."

"Yes, same way Jonathan came to find us." Yvonne said. "Alphus teleported him to my backyard in the mountains."

"Took him a few hours to recover." Sam said. He motioned to the coffee table. "Yvonne has some info."

Yvonne picked up her iPad and the pale light illuminated her face. "For years, Sam and I eluded the Council of Darkness while looking for Jeremiah. Never found any trace of him until we started looking back at events after Jonathan survived the Swiss air disaster."

She brought up an image on the screen. It showed a man boarding a flight. The man turned toward the camera and his turquoise eyes glittered. He winked. "A flight to London. This is not Jonathan. It's Jeremiah. They look enough alike you could mistake them for each other. We think Jeremiah was trying to keep someone from finding Jonathan."

"The Crimson Snake." Birdsong said. "According to Jonathan, she told him as much when she finally tracked him down on the train to London."

"Why would Jeremiah want to help Jonathan?" Ross said, the unlit cigarette wobbling between his lips.

"So he alone would have access to him?" Sam answered. "We didn't know Jeremiah had found out about Jonathan until he assaulted our mountain house. Seems he had been biding his time."

"We think his discovery of Jonathan at our safe house was a pure accident. His team was there to assault Max's compound which just happen to be on the other side of the ridge from the safe house."

"And you knew it was there?" Ross asked.

Yvonne glanced at Sam. "Yes. Close proximity to Max was always safer than being far away. We knew that Jonathan was working with Max and might show up so we were trying to remain vigilant. We had no idea the angel Alphus would bring Jonathan directly to us."

"This team that Jeremiah had," Birdsong leaned forward. "How did he put that together? Where did they come from?"

"That's the first prize question." Sam said. "Jeremiah had resources over the years. He used an assault team here at my house on the eve of Jonathan's trial. We were never able to determine how he found them, hired them, or whatever. I mean, how does a fifteen-year-old teenager put together an assault team?"

"I may have some new information on that." Yvonne turned the tablet back to face her. "I should have received some new information from our financial contact in Europe. Once we realized Jeremiah had been masquerading as

Jonathan we were able to pinpoint times and places where he might have accessed funds." She tapped on the screen. Her eyes widened and she smiled. "Gotcha!"

"What?" Birdsong asked.

"Links to several Swiss accounts, of course. Not surprising. Basil was able to track them back to several shell corporations." She tapped on the screen.

"Basil?" Sam straightened. "I thought he had been killed."

"Who's Basil?" Birdsong asked.

"Need to know only." Yvonne wagged a finger at him. "We keep our contacts very close, Jason. For your protection. And theirs." She returned to the screen and the name that popped up drove her heart into her throat. She stood up abruptly, her heart racing. "Oh my."

Sam stood up. "Oh my, what?"

She turned the screen to face them. "Basil tracked the money back to one person."

The name filled the screen: Saul Stone. Birdsong swore. "The Captain?"

Sam shook his head. "No way. Not possible. Why would the Captain fund our efforts to keep Jonathan hidden from the world and look for Jeremiah and yet, at the same time, pay Jeremiah to find Jonathan?"

"He's the patsy." Ross said, slipping his unlit cigarette back into his shirt pocket. "Remember how the Captain reacted when Raven claimed they had met? He denied it. More than once."

"Someone is trying to frame the Captain?" Birdsong said. "Why?"

"Why not?" Yvonne settled back into her chair. "Jonathan already hated his father. This way, if he ever found out, think of the sense of betrayal he would have. His own father would have chosen devotion to Jeremiah over Jonathan. Jonathan claimed his father had brain surgery performed to erase his memory. He also said the Captain had tortured him."

"Which the Captain had good reasons that, in some strange way, protected Jonathan." Sam said. "That's what he said in that video he recorded."

"What video?" Birdsong said.

"After the dismissal, the Captain recorded a video for his son with everything Jonathan would need to know if something happened to his father. He said he would have to train Jonathan to face any trials. Suggested he might have to use tools, like drugs or amnesia, to hide him from Jeremiah. Looks like that is exactly what he did. So it makes no sense he would be in cahoots with Jeremiah." Sam said.

"Cahoots?" Ross shook his head. "Haven't heard that word in a while. How does this help us find Jonathan?"

"It doesn't." Yvonne sat back down. She returned her attention to the tablet. "What is Jeremiah's motive? What does he want from Jonathan? No ransom. No demands. He wants something personal from his brother."

"Not a family reunion, I can tell you that," Birdsong hissed. "But what did Jonathan just acquire that he did not have before a few months ago?"

Yvonne glanced at Sam and nodded. "His memories."

"That video." Sam said at the same time.

Ross nodded. "Bingo. Both. Jeremiah wants something from Jonathan's past that has been hidden away for fifteen years. But what?"

Birdsong stood up. "Yvonne, Sam, do you have another copy of the video?"

Sam glanced at Yvonne, and she swallowed hard. "Yes. But it is deeply private. Things that Jonathan would want no one to hear."

Birdsong took the tablet from Yvonne and gently pulled to

her feet. He looked into her eyes. "Yvonne, I am not just Jonathan's partner or Ross' mentee. I am Jonathan's brother. His real brother, by my grandmother's proclamation. We share everything. Jonathan would want me to know."

"Are you sure, son?" Sam stepped up to Birdsong and put a hand on his arm. "He has had months to share it with you. Did he?"

Birdsong shook his head. "No. But he said one day he would. He said he was still processing his memories." Birdsong glanced over his shoulder at Ross. "I think it's time someone else processed those memories, too. Because doing so may be the only thing that will save Jonathan."

"Well, I have no interest in the sad father son story of Jonathan Steel." Ross stood up. "Birdsong, if there is any actionable intel, call me. I'm off to work on more established channels. Divide and conquer." He pulled out his cigarette. "And I need a smoke."

He walked out the door and Yvonne pointed to the kitchen. "Let's go to the table."

Jason Birdsong sat at the kitchen table beside Sam. "Ross is one strange dude." Sam said. "I know his type. Worked with them too long."

"No affection between him and Jonathan. They have a history. Jonathan broke his nose. More than once. And," Birdsong smiled. "He can't smoke in your house."

"Nicotine addiction is the worst." Sam said. He licked his lips. "I would kill for a good cigar at times. But enough of that. Let's get started."

Yvonne had placed her laptop in the center of the table. "What you will see, Jason, is the Captain seated at the desk in the judge's chambers. Meridian used a hidden camera to record all conversations."

"For what reason?"

"Blackmail, most likely." Sam hissed. "He was a piece of work all right. Got his just rewards." Judge Meridian died after his "hound from hell" ripped out his heart in his own courtroom.

Yvonne tapped the keyboard. "He will tell his story piece by piece. Jonathan now knows everything you're about to see and hear. We've heard it before."

"We were there." Sam pointed out. "Just out of camera range. It's time you see the Captain's story."

CHAPTER

TWELVE

Saul Stone held the meerschaum pipe up to his turquoise eyes and studied its carved surface. Someone had carved the white stone into the grimacing face of a demon. Its wide eyes glared out with undisguised menace. The thing's mouth opened in a leer, revealing fanged teeth. Along the sides of the bowl of the pipe, arcane symbols were etched into the white stone.

"Two hundred dollars, sir."

Stone glanced up at the pawnshop owner. "I'll give you one hundred fifty. Call it a discount for the military."

The man frowned and scratched at his head as he glanced at Stone's uniform. "That is too little, my friend. Even for the military."

Stone leaned across the glass counter and held the pipe close to the man's face. "You are not my friend. And, this pipe is stolen. Shall I contact the police?"

The man behind the counter shook his head. "Please, sir, no. But I must get more than I paid for it. One seventy-five?"

"One sixty."

The man rubbed his jaw, his eyes averted, and Stone knew he had won. "Very well."

Stone pulled the money from his pocket and placed it on the counter. The man snatched the bills up and began counting.

"Wait! Don't sell him that pipe!"

Stone turned as a woman came through the pawnshop door. She was slightly taller than he, with reddish blonde hair pulled back in a ponytail. Her face was flushed with excitement. Her jade green eyes glittered with intensity.

"Too late, whoever you are." Stone pushed the pipe into his pants pocket.

The woman paused at the counter and glanced at the owner. "You said you would save it for me until I could get the money."

"He had the cash right now. I couldn't wait for you." The man shrugged. "Sorry, ma'am. Business is business."

The woman turned her gaze on Stone and he realized if looks could kill, he would be dead. She was breathing heavily. "You don't understand. That pipe was stolen from one of my friends. It is a valuable historical artifact, and I must have it back."

Stone raised an eyebrow and smiled. "Historical artifact?"

Her eyes danced with anger. "Oh, what would you know about history? You soldiers are all alike. If it doesn't salute, shoot it. Or put pot in your pipe and smoke it."

Stone smiled and pulled the pipe back out of his pocket. He held it up to the sunlight streaming in through the dirty pawnshop window. "I venture to guess that this pipe was German, and they made the bowl from clay. The German word means 'sea foam'. If you look, they made the stem from amber, not wood. So, this pipe probably dates from the 19th century."

The woman's mouth fell open. "You are correct."

"Of course I am. I do not put marijuana into my pipes. I use the finest tobacco products. And, a pipe of this quality is not for smoking, anyway. I would display it with my other pipes."

The woman closed her mouth and looked away. "So, you know what you're buying? That doesn't change the fact that this pipe was stolen."

"Did you file a police report?" Stone asked.

The woman looked back at him. "No."

"As I guessed. Your friend probably came by this pipe illicitly. More than likely, this pipe belongs in a museum somewhere in Germany or Turkey. Am I correct?"

The woman glared at him defiantly. "A soldier stole it from a museum in Europe on his way to Vietnam. When he died, they returned his effects to my friend. But before she could have the pipe appraised and registered, someone stole the soldier's chest with all his effects."

Stone stepped closer to her so he could get a better look at her eyes. They were captivating. "And now, if the pipe were to surface without the proper chain of custody, it would be returned to the museum, correct?"

"Yes."

Stone cocked his head and lifted the pipe into view. "Why would you not want it to be returned to its museum? You seem to be one of those fiery, righteous women who would champion lost causes."

The woman stepped back, and her face reddened with anger. "You don't know me, sir. And, the museum is in East Germany. The Communists would, no doubt, lock it away in the cellar with all the Bibles and statues and other fine art. It deserves to be seen."

Stone shrugged. "The iron curtain is rusting. Soon, the wall will come down. Reagan will see to it. Besides, what does your friend plan to do with it?"

"Donate it to a local museum in exchange for access to the rare documents library."

Stone blinked. "Now, I didn't see that coming. Perhaps you could pick one of my other pipes that would please the curator of the local museum."

The woman laughed. "Are you asking me up to your apartment to see your pipe collection?"

Stone pocketed the pipe. "No. I'm asking you to my *manor* to see my pipe collection. You see, I am not your typical soldier boy. I was once a professor at the university. And, I promise you that your visit would be of purely academic interest. If you see another pipe that would satisfy your needs, I will consider donating it to the museum in your 'friend's' name."

The woman nodded and extended a hand. "Christine Green, graduate student in ancient history."

He smiled as he enveloped her hand in his own. "Saul Stone."

CHRISTINE FELT like her heart would burst. It was pounding with excitement and amazement. She glanced at the huge room filled with historical items. "I can't believe you own all of this."

Stone walked across the room to a wall covered with shallow glass cases filled with meerschaum pipes. "My father is an avid collector of artifacts. He has loaned out his collections to museums all over the country."

Christine paused in front of a glass case filled with golden medallions. "I recognize these medallions. They're from Mexico. They're Aztec gold."

Stone nodded. "Rare items that they are. The Spanish conquered Mexico searching for gold that was rare, not abundant."

Christine tried to catch her breath. "I am very interested in the Aztec era. It is the subject of my thesis."

"And it is why you need access to the rare document section of the museum."

"Yes." She paled and glanced up into Stone's haunting turquoise eyes. They were impossibly beautiful like flakes of turquoise stone imbedded in the carven image of a Greek god. "I mean--"

"Your friend?"

Christine smiled. "There is no friend. But you knew that."

"And the soldier?"

Christine drew a deep breath and felt the old pain deepen. "My brother. He was brilliant and headed for a career in medicine when he got drafted. He died in the jungles."

"Funny, I lost my father to the jungles."

"I'm sorry." She said. "What happened to him?"

"Oh, he is alive. Just obsessed with the Amazon." He tapped the pipe stem to his head. "Lost in the jungle of his own insanity. My mother lives here in the manor."

Christine stepped back and raised an eyebrow. "You live with your mother?"

Stone gestured around the mansion. "If you could live here, wouldn't you?"

"I would live here with my mother or my father, if I had one. I'm adopted. I tracked down my biological brother a few years back." She paused and pain filled her eyes.

"Did your brother die in battle?"

Christine shook her head and sat on a sofa in the library. "No, he died in India. He became fascinated with an artifact. A statue with a spiral around one eye. He thought it was a talisman for a demon." She looked up at Stone. "My real parents died when we were toddlers. Ben was obsessed with learning how they died. The obsession started when he was a teenager."

She looked around at the artifacts. "He would have loved seeing this room and all its artifacts and old books. He believed there was an ancient evil that was unleashed on the world by my biological parents."

"Why did he think that?"

"Because my biological parents died in a satanic ritual that went wrong. They were Satan worshippers. It took Ben three or four years to dig up the truth about them."

"And this artifact you search for?"

Christine stood up. "I will find the thing that killed him."

"Thing?"

"A demon. Called himself the thirteenth demon. I've been doing research on the history of this demon. He originated in Mexico."

"Thus your fascination with the Aztecs?" Stone said.

"You're unfazed by my talk of demons."

"Look around you. My father is fascinated by ancient legends as well. I've heard this kind of talk my entire life. It's all a bunch of baloney."

"Tell that to my brother." Christine tensed.

"I'm sorry. I don't mean to be insensitive. You can't spend your life chasing ghosts and ghoulies and things that go bump in the night." He paused. "But you can spend your life looking for ancient historical facts that subsequently develop into legends. I think you're very brave to keep looking."

"And if I discover this demon is real?"

"Then you'll win a Nobel Peace Prize for proving the supernatural is real."

"I believe it is real." She said.

Stone nodded. He pointed to dark double doors at one side of the library. "My father allowed me to go into that room only once in my life. There is a spiral staircase that descends to an altar. Who knows where it came from? Right now, my father has shelves around that chamber. Know what is on them?"

"What?"

"Arcane artifacts from the most vile and despicable practices in the history of man. Demonic talismans, voodoo dolls, human skulls pierced with gold rods. My father tried to understand the nature of the evil that led this world into the depths of World War II. He tried to understand how man could be so depraved to kill millions in the ovens of Auschwitz or burn pregnant women alive in China."

Christine felt a cold chill pass over her. "But man is depraved because he is fallen. Man turned away from God."

Stone regarded her with those intense eyes. "You believe in the supernatural?"

"I am a Christian." She whispered, barely catching her breath.

Stone stepped closer to her. "Then you would understand that when a man dabbles in the occult, he is drawn to its power, deceived by the sly workings of Lucifer. That man falls into a deadly spiral that leads downward to his demise. Your brother, for instance. What happened?"

Christine's mouth was so dry she could hardly talk. "The shaman he was working with said my brother called forth a demon. It was an occult ceremony that was supposed to be very scientific. But things got out of hand. The demon possessed another shaman in the room. At least, that is what the first shaman claims. He alone escaped. There were six people in that chamber and when the authorities arrived, they found the people present at the ceremony were dead. It had ripped their hearts from their chests like an arcane Aztec ritual. Blood was an inch deep on the floor. My brother was dead."

"Christine, I am so sorry. I am a man of science in my role with the military."

"Science?"

"I am with the biological warfare division."

Christine gasped and put a hand to her mouth. He shook his head.

"Not offense. Defense. We work on ways to combat genetically altered biological agents. Cutting edge gene research. Trust me, I've seen horror, and it is always at the hands of man."

"You just proved my case. Man is broken. God is not."

Stone nodded and his hand drifted up and touched her chin. "Maybe you could convince me."

"Missionary dating?" She laughed. "Been there, done that. Didn't work then."

Stone shrugged. "Might work now. I'm willing to give it a chance." Slowly, his right hand moved across her cheek, gently caressing her soft skin. She closed her eyes, and a tear trickled down her cheek. He wiped it away with the back of his hand, leaned closer and pressed his lips to hers.

CHAPTER

THIRTEEN

"We have two embryos left."

Christine massaged her abdomen and looked up at Dr. Brenda Fields. "I don't know, Dr. Fields. I've lost two babies already. I'm not sure I want to keep trying."

"Of course, we will keep trying." She felt her husband's hand on her shoulder and wanted to rip away from it. Christine turned and glared at him.

"They may call you the Captain, but this is my choice."

His turquoise eyes glowed with anger. "It's *our* choice, Christine. We must try one more time."

She shrugged off his hand, and Dr. Fields turned to the door of the examining room. "Why don't I give the two of you some time alone?" She left.

Her husband, "the Captain," came around and sat in the chair. Christine gripped the open backed gown to her and tried to shrink into the table. "Honey, I'm sorry I was so abrupt." He whispered. "This has been so hard on you."

Christine tried to tear her gaze away from those hauntingly

beautiful eyes. "We've been trying for ten years. I don't know if I can take this disappointment again."

The Captain nodded. "Then we adopt."

Christian flinched. "No! You know what my past was like."

"We will be much better parents than your foster parents."

Christine looked away, and her memory was awash in pain and disappointment. Her foster parents had been interested only in the money. She had escaped from them when she was sixteen and passed herself off as an adult while attending college. "I know. We are not them. It's just the children are so traumatized. I'm just as broken." She stifled a sob. In the years since they had married, she went back to school and got a degree in counseling and occupational therapy. Her day job kept her occupied with traumatized children in the psychiatric ward at the hospital.

The Captain stood up and came to her. He put his hands gently on her shoulders. "Christine, I promised to love you no matter what. It is a pledge I will never break. If you do not want to have children or adopt, then we will live with that."

Christine wiped at her nose. "If we went ahead with the implantation, it would delay our trip to Mexico. I really want to see those ruins." She looked back at him. "I know I gave up my fascination with ancient history, but this new discovery has reawakened my desire. I've been at my new job for six years now. I want to revisit my old obsession with archeology."

"I have already checked things out. There is an excellent physician in Mexico City who has agreed to watch over you. His reputation is flawless." He rubbed her shoulders. "But the decision is yours."

Christine nodded. "I want to go to Mexico City." She drew a deep breath and massaged her abdomen once more. "And I want a child. I'll give it one more try. If that doesn't work, I'm done."

The Captain squeezed her shoulders. "Thank you, Christine. I love you."

She looked up into his intense turquoise eyes. It was difficult to lie to him. But agreeing to try again would divert his attention from the real reason for going to Mexico. The latest discovery tied into her theories about a certain demon with a spiral around its eye. She put on a false smile. "I love you, too."

STONE PACED AROUND the manor library. How could he stop Christine from her foolish desire to go to Mexico City to see the archeological dig? He did not want his son to be born in Mexico. He would still be an American citizen. But what if something went wrong? True, Santiago was the best doctor money could buy in Mexico City. Christine had agreed to undergo the embryo implantation in two weeks. Then, they would make sure the implantation took and if so, he would keep his promise and take her to Mexico City for the duration of the pregnancy. Dangerous and foolish, he thought.

"There are alternatives." Someone said. Stone whirled and looked around the library. It was empty.

"Who said that?"

"I did." He spun around and the dark double doors, sealed since his father's death, gaped open. "Come downstairs. I have something to show you." The voice echoed from the open doors.

The hair stood on the back of Stone's neck. Carefully, he entered the chamber beyond the doors. A spiral staircase led down into the depths of the lower chamber where they had found the bodies. Around the periphery of the room were the shelves with the genuine, evil artifacts collected by his father.

He swallowed back bile as nausea hit him. He took a few tentative steps down the spiral staircase.

"Come, come. Time is precious."

In the center of the room sitting cross legged on a five sided raised stone was a near naked man with totally white skin. His hairless body gleamed in the light from five candles guttering at each corner of the platform.

"Who are you?"

"My name is Lucas." The man's red tongue ran over his lips. His red eyes glowed in the candle light. Stone squinted at the sight of dozens of tattoos covering the man's body. Were they moving?

"How did you get in here?"

Lucas gestured over his shoulder. "Five doors leading to five mysterious destinations. Surely you have wondered what lay beyond the doors."

Stone slumped onto the bottom stair. "My father died down here. We thought someone came through the door but his death was a suicide." A murder suicide, he thought.

"I can assure you anyone found on the other side of one of these doors would have no interest in your father." Lucas smiled. "At least not then. Times change and we are in need of your services."

"We?"

"You must have a son." Lucas said.

"What are you talking about? Who is 'we'?"

Lucas gestured, and one door opened onto an office. At a desk, a man sat with his back to the door. Beyond the man, the Eiffel Tower could be clearly seen through the windows. The door slid shut. "We know what you crave, Saul Stone."

Stone rubbed his eyes and shook his head in confusion. "I want to have a son. You've already said that."

"No, you want power." Lucas hissed. "Unlimited power. All

men crave such. You are no exception, and the power of the five individuals behind these doors can be yours."

"Five individuals? Power?" Stone stood up slowly. "Urban legends. Conspiracy theories."

"No, it is reality. Five human beings who control the world." Lucas put his hands on his knees. "But they are immune to the control of my associates and we long to place someone in one of those offices who will help steer the world in a certain direction."

Stone squinted at Lucas. "Your tattoos are moving. Did I ingest some kind of hallucinogen?"

"This is all very real, Saul. You must have a son. That son will inherit power and knowledge. You must prepare him. You must raise him up to be a man of ambition."

"Why me?" Stone said.

"Your father prepared the way for you. He raised you to one day walk through one of those doors."

"And he died here in this chamber." Stone said.

"Saul Stone, your father's death was part of a plan that is now unfolding. Do you want a son?"

"Yes. We have tried and tried. In two weeks, Christine will undergo embryo implantation."

Lucas reached behind him and retrieved something. He held up his hand and from his fingers, a red stone pulsed with inner light.

"This stone contains a very special property. If you place it under your pillow while you and your wife try to conceive, you will be quite successful."

Stone laughed. "A magic stone? Looks like blood."

"Have you ever heard of the thirteenth demon?" Lucas' face reddened from the light of the stone.

Stone flinched. "Where did you hear that name?"

"Your wife's brother died at the hands of the thirteenth

demon. You may not believe in these supernatural creatures, but they can influence human beings. Just read the Bible about the Nephilim, children sired by men controlled by demons." He held up the stone. "This stone contains supernatural power. It will guarantee you will have a child. And that child will be special."

Stone closed his eyes and swore. When he opened them, Lucas was gone. He searched the room. Where had he gone? He tried each door. They wouldn't open. When he turned to go back up the stairs, he saw the glowing stone sitting on the edge of the altar. He wiped sweat from his upper lip. He paced. He paused. The Captain glared at the stone.

"This is insane." He grabbed the stone, and everything changed. Power surged up his arm and jolted across his chest. It poured itself into his heart and coursed along his arteries. It ignited his brain, and he moaned in pleasure. What was this? Who was this?

"Well, hello there." He said to himself. "Let's go make a baby!"

THE GREEN LIGHT faded around Steel. He sat dumbfounded at the table, not at the Librarian's desk. He glanced across the table at the Crimson Snake. For a second, her gaze shifted from the Grimvox to his face and then back again. He glanced at Jeremiah's empty seat. Where had he gone?

"He's shocked by this revelation." Nanny appeared from the shadows. Earlier when she had taken Ila away, Steel had not paid much attention to her. Now, her dark eyes glittered with the hunger and malice of a ravenous shark. Her white hair was pulled back into a bun so tightly, every wrinkle in her aged face had disappeared. She wore a high neck blouse with a pin at the throat. The red face of a demon leered back at him.

"Who are you?"

"I am the Nanny as Jeremiah said earlier. Pay attention!" She said with a voice that sounded like wet gravel grinding under car wheels. "I raised Jeremiah."

"You know about the bloodstone and our father?"

"I know many things, JJ."

"I'm not JJ. I am Jonathan Steel."

She held up Jeremiah's tablet. "You reek."

Steel only then realized his pants were soaked. "What?"

"Some shared experience startled both of you. You tried to tear away from the Grimvox and Jeremiah had to shock you. I am afraid you lost control of your bladder."

Steel blinked. "I don't remember that."

"A side effect of the medallion on your chest. Retrograde amnesia. Something you should be intimately familiar with." She smiled exposing brown teeth. Steel's chair slid back abruptly into the hallway and Nanny followed allowing the door to slide shut on Snake and the Grimvox. She tapped the tablet and his restraints released.

"Don't try anything, JJ. Jeremiah still has the settings quite high. Now, get up and head to your chamber."

Steel stood up slowly, uncomfortable with his situation. She pointed to the hallway opposite from the direction of his cell. He preceded her. They passed several packing boxes along the hallway visible only by faint green exit signs.

"Stop." she said behind him. The door to a different room clicked open. "Clean yourself up and eat. I do not know when Jeremiah will get back to you."

Steel glanced over his shoulder at her. "What time is it?"

"Sorry, but it is important we keep you disoriented, JJ. Inside. Now." She held up an arthritic hand and a crooked finger danced above the tablet's screen. Steel walked into the room, and the door clicked shut behind him.

The room was larger than the prior one, with a bunk bed on one wall. On the other was a small sink and a doorway that opened into a small bathroom with a commode and a shower. A tray bearing a sandwich, an apple, and a bottle of water sat on his bed. He grabbed the sandwich and wolfed it down. He needed sustenance to survive. He finished the apple and guzzled the water. Only then did he strip away his nasty scrubs and toss them into a trashcan by the sink.

Before stepping into the shower, he ran through a series of basic exercises: pushups, jumping jacks, sit-ups on the cold concrete floor. By the time he finished he was soaked in sweat. He stepped into the shower and turned on the freezing cold water. No hot water! A dried bar of soap provided scrubbing power. His hands passed over his stubble of a beard. Despite the cold water, he felt invigorated and clean.

No towels, though. He squeegeed off as much water as possible. A simple wooden chair sat next to the sink. He would have to drip dry before putting his clothes on.

"Sorry, I don't have towels."

Steel jerked at the sound of the voice. Jeremiah sat on the bed. His tablet lay on the covers beside him. Steel studied the man's face, hidden in shadow, and sat in the chair. "I'll dry out."

"Sorry for bailing on you. Didn't expect that." Jeremiah whispered.

"Just what didn't you expect?"

"The bloodstone. That means we were conceived through the influence of a demon."

"You shouldn't have a problem with that." Steel said.

Jeremiah's eyes glittered in the light from the exit sign. "I have had a demon with me since I was very young. You'll see. You can identify. You were demon possessed."

"For a short period, yes." Steel tried to repress the memory of the courtroom and the emergence of the third demon from his very soul. "But, Jeremiah, there is a problem with our father's claims."

"Yes, I know."

"We are not Nephilim. We are ordinary human beings. I should know. I've met the Nephilim." Arthur Knight's daughter, Vega, was the product of demonic influence during her conception and she was a giantess. He paused, wondering just where she had ended up. Anthony Cobalt and the tenth demon had opened a portal to another world. Vega and her friends went through the portal accompanied by their new guardian, Renee Miller. Did Jeremiah know this?

Jeremiah stood up and paced. "Maybe we are something greater than the Nephilim."

"Didn't you hear what he said? Our parents were going through in vitro fertilization. No guarantee we were conceived under the influence of a demon."

Jeremiah paused. "It doesn't matter. Demons have been a part of our history from the moment of our conception. Why do you deny it, brother? You have been possessed by a demon. You know the allure of their power. Eternal power beyond anything we can imagine."

"Maybe that is what drove our father to become who he is." Steel hissed. "A hateful, selfish person obsessed with power over human beings." Steel paused and studied Jeremiah. "Why was he looking for you?"

"What?" Jeremiah said.

"I remember now. The interrogation on the ship. Daniel Brown, or Toady as he was known, asked me if I had found you. Our father was looking for you!"

"After the trial, he never stopped looking for me. Why? Perhaps to tap into my power?"

"Or to kill you for murdering our mother." Steel said.

Jeremiah froze and his features twisted in anger. His eyes glowed with unholy light. "You think you know the truth, human scum!" His demon voice echoed through the room. "My host knows the truth about your mother and he will never reveal it." Suddenly Jeremiah's face was close to his. His breath stank of sulphur and smoke. "You will die before he tells you the truth."

Steel's anger surged and he head butted Jeremiah. The man fell backwards and the tablet lay unprotected on the bed. Steel hurtled across the room. Jeremiah arose from the floor and moving with inhuman speed beat him to the bed. His finger stabbed the button. Pain lanced across Steel's chest and he was gone. Again.

FOURTEEN

Josh floated through the darkness toward a swirling whirlpool of light. Bright colors burst forth, moved in a psychedelic vortex. He fell into the center, his head spinning and the colored lights swallowed him.

When he emerged on the other side, he floated in a vast charcoal tinted void. Things floated in the distance, throwing off glints of silver and gray. He slowly turned until his vision focused on someone nearby. Red hair exploded from her head and the Crimson Snake rotated slowly, not ten meters away. She had two arms, and both were normal, no prosthetic! Eyes closed in pain, she trembled as she slowly spun.

"Snake? Where is Jonathan? Tell me!" Josh screamed. But his voice only carried a few inches and died in muted silence.

Suddenly, her eyes opened, and it was as if he were inside her head. He looked out through her eyes as something emerged from the void.

A frog in a blender. A blender filled with green water and swirling spirits. Snake could not make sense of her surroundings. Green fire coursed through her mind in rivulets of insanity. Gibbering demons tumbled and gyred along the sulci and gyri of her brain. Ahead in the stream a face. Dark hair. Young man. Pablo!

"Pablo!" *she screamed, and he receded, washed along by the eddies and currents of demonic deeds.*

"Moh, look, it's her." *A voice screeched behind her.*

Snake spun somehow. Three demon spirits floated before her. Their attention calmed the surrounding streams, gave her something to concentrate on. Where had Pablo gone?

'Moh' assumed a humanoid shape with long, rat ears and two teeth protruding from thin lips. Tiny, black, beady eyes surveyed her. Moh wore a tattered one-piece pair of coveralls with the words "Grady's Shop" *on the upper pocket. The sight of that name chilled her.*

"No! Not this! Please?"

"Lair, it is her." *Moh said around his sharp teeth. Lair stood beside Moh in a similar coverall. Squatty and fat with a toad face, Lair licked his lipless mouth with a long, green tongue. Bulbous eyes glistened at her. The tongue cleaned his eyes.*

"She remembers us," *Kurl said as he emerged from behind them. Kurl's fat, newt figure bulged through the coverall's seams. His pale, wet face bore his large, black eyes and flat nostrils. Fimbria hung from the sides of his head like dead sea anemones.*

Snake tried to turn away from them. Any other horror was preferable to them. She felt Moh's thin, wet, ratty fingers on her face as he floated closer. "You remember us, don't you, sweetheart?"

"Get away from me, you monsters." *She hissed.*

"Honey, we weren't the monsters." *Lair's tongue flicked out to caress her cheek.* "It was our hosts. Your three brothers."

"They weren't my brothers!" Snake shook the wet drops from her face. "They were co-workers in my father's shop."

"We know." Kurl burbled and giggled. "We had so much fun with them. Would you like to see their eternally tortured souls? We can show them to you." Kurl lifted a segmented hand with flat, fleshy appendages and motioned over his shoulders. "Just across the Void. Keepers can see anything, sweetie."

Snake began to sob. "Please, leave me alone. Just leave me alone."

"Don't you want to remember how much fun you had with the three stooges?" Moh said.

"Yeah, until you killed them." Lair's tongue hung from his lipless mouth. "Nice touch with the nail gun."

"And the hydraulic lift." Kurl giggled again.

"Someone help me!" She screamed.

A dark shadow eclipsed the ever-present green light as something floated over their heads. She looked up into the face of Pablo. The three demonic stooges screeched in horror. Their eyes widened, and they swam away from Snake into the surrounding chaos.

"Pablo?" she said.

The dark figure settled before her. The facial features blurred. "I am not Pablo." A gentle voice said. "But I will do my best to protect you in this realm. Your work is not yet done."

Snake blinked in confusion as the figure faded away. "Wait! Who are you? What are you?"

The green swirling currents resumed around her body, and she searched in vain for the disappearing figure. Pablo! She had to hang onto the memory of Pablo. And others? Yes, Melissa. That was one of the names. Melissa's photo floated to the surface of the green stream around her feet. She would remember Melissa and Pablo. And there were others. Buoys in the stream. Anchors in the water.

"I'm so sorry." She whispered. "I am so sorry."

Tears filled her eyes. Tears! Guilt and regret gripped her heart. The movement in the eddies of the Void slowed and stopped. What was happening? A figure emerged from the dark shadows. A familiar young face with ginger hair. Josh Knight materialized before her, his eyes wide in shock.

"Josh!" Snake screamed but nothing came from her lips. "Help me!" She tried again. Josh blinked and was gone.

JOSH LURCHED awake and sat bolt upright in his bed. Where was he? He glanced around at the small enclosure housing his twin bed. Max had converted empty space in the barn to rooms. Safer that way, she had said. The entire area was under her extended "Faraday Cage" to protect them from Jeremiah and his prying eyes. Josh rubbed his eyes and blinked to remove the image of the Void from his mind. What was the Void? And how did he see Snake there?

Josh stumbled out of his bed and grabbed jeans and a sweatshirt. He slid his feet into sneakers and hurried from his room, across the snow-covered ground to the door into the giant tent like enclosure. A guard stopped him, his eyes filled with suspicion. He took one look at Josh and ushered him through.

Josh ignored the green waves of energy lapping against the edge of the cabin basement and hurried through the tunnel into the conference room.

"Max! Max!" He shouted.

Max sat at the table sipping a cup of tea. Dark circles rimmed her eyes. "Josh?"

"I had a dream." He gasped as he collapsed at the table. "I saw Snake in something called the Void."

Max let her cup clatter onto a saucer. James Caskey emerged from the kitchen at the end. "Did you say the Void?"

Max glanced at him and patted the seat next to her. "Sit James." She turned back to Josh. "Tell me everything."

Josh swallowed hard and paused. "Have you been awake all night?"

"Do I look that bad?" She said and straightened to her regal posture. "The Void?"

Josh told them his dream. Caskey put a hand on Max's shoulder. "Could it be?"

"This Void you speak of," Max sipped more tea. "Mention of it has occurred in many of the arcane writings of the past. Think of it as the in between world, the chasm."

"Chasm?"

"Yes, chasm." Caskey put a steaming cup of coffee before him. "Jesus tells the story of the beggar and the rich ruler. The beggar eats scraps from the rich man's table and both of them die. The ruler is tormented in eternal punishment but can see across this chasm at the beggar." He paused and searched the conference room. "Max, surely there is a Bible nearby."

Max tapped on her cell phone and handed it to Caskey. "There's an app for that."

Caskey took the phone and nodded. "Of course. Now let me find it. Ah, here it is." He pointed to the phone. "I'll read the scripture for you."

"There was a rich man who was dressed in purple and fine linen and lived in luxury every day. At his gate was laid a beggar named Lazarus, covered with sores and longing to eat what fell from the rich man's table. Even the dogs came and licked his sores. The time came when the beggar died and the angels carried him to Abraham's side. The rich man also died and was buried. In Hades, where he was in torment, he looked up and saw Abraham

far away, with Lazarus by his side. So he called to him, 'Father Abraham, have pity on me and send Lazarus to dip the tip of his finger in water and cool my tongue, because I am in agony in this fire.'

"But Abraham replied, 'Son, remember that in your lifetime you received your good things, while Lazarus received bad things, but now he is comforted here and you are in agony. And besides all this, between us and you a great chasm has been set in place, so that those who want to go from here to you cannot, nor can anyone cross over from there to us.'

"He answered, 'Then I beg you, father, send Lazarus to my family, for I have five brothers. Let him warn them, so that they will not also come to this place of torment.'

"Abraham replied, 'They have Moses and the Prophets; let them listen to them.'

"'No, father Abraham,' he said, 'but if someone from the dead goes to them, they will repent.'

"He said to him, 'If they do not listen to Moses and the Prophets, they will not be convinced even if someone rises from the dead.'"

"This great chasm, then, is the Void?" Josh said.

"Most likely."

"Why is Snake in the Void?"

Max sipped more tea. "Jeremiah kidnapped Snake, and we saw the Grimvox in her presence." She almost dropped the cup again and looked at Caskey with a gasp. "Could it be she has become their, what is it called?"

"Keeper." Caskey whispered.

"What is that?" Josh asked.

"Legend holds the Grimvox requires a human interface, so to speak, laddy. The Grimvox stores memories but a human brain must interpret them." Caskey put a hand on Max's arm.

"If this is true, then the Crimson Snake is lost. Once a human is tethered to the Grimvox, legend says they can never escape."

Josh sat back. "But what about this Pablo?"

"One victim of the Swiss flight disaster. He is in the photo album." Max said. "I instructed Snake to memorize each name and face." She looked at Caskey. "James, is it possible her memories are keeping her connected to reality?"

"If she feels guilt and regret, Max, then perhaps those memories will be her salvation."

"And, Jonathan's!" Josh said excitedly. "If Snake retains herself, then he's not alone."

Caskey put a hand on Josh's arm. "You must tell me more about these visions you have experienced. Perhaps while we discuss the process of exorcism?"

Josh glanced at Caskey and shook his head. "I'm not here to learn about exorcism. I'm here to find Jonathan!"

"And while we wait for more information on Jonathan Steel, I want to instruct you in the proper manner of dealing with demons." Caskey said.

"I know how to deal with demons!" Josh blurted out.

"How prepared were you when the thirteenth demon possessed you?"

Josh opened his mouth, and his face warmed with anger. "I've encountered more demons since then."

"And each time, as I mentioned, has been fortuitous for you and Jonathan, thanks to intervening angelic activity." Caskey leaned toward him. "Young man, I sense you are wise beyond your years. Already, a demonic being has shown you are special in some way. It is obvious to me, young man, they are targeting you for a reason we have yet to ascertain. You must admit to yourself further instruction will help you avoid the next 'Pandora' influence. Am I wrong?"

Josh looked away and blinked away tears of anger. "Okay,

I'll admit I can learn more. But right now, my concern is for Jonathan."

"Who is in the clutches of the second demon." Max said. "I agree with James. When we find Jeremiah, Jonathan will need all the help he can get. Being more prepared to face the second most powerful demon on the planet can't be a waste of time."

Josh looked back at her and nodded. "Fine! Let's get started so I can get on with this, bro."

Caskey stood up and gripped his cane. "Come to the kitchen and have some pancakes. Then, young man, you an I will take a walk to the barn. No time like the present."

Josh followed him across the conference room and cast one glance at Max, huddled over the table. He hoped he wasn't wasting his time. His stomach growled craving those pancakes.

GAMMA APPEARED FROM THE TUNNEL. "Max, Ruth Martinez is here."

Max drew a deep breath and sought deep within her for more strength. In the past hours and days, her seeming unrelenting strength waned. Seeing James again had drained some of her resolve. She stood shakily and straightened as Ruth Martinez appeared from the tunnel.

Ruth hurried into the conference room and dropped an overnight bag on the floor. Her short, dark hair was frazzled and dotted with snow. The cold had reddened her cheeks and her eyes widened at the sight of Max. "Max? Oh, my God!" Before Max could react, Ruth grabbed her in an embrace. The woman's body shook with her sobs. Max looked over Ruth's shoulder at Gamma.

"Gamma, would you be so kind as to bring a bottle of water for Ruth and some tissues?"

Gamma nodded and disappeared into the kitchen. Max gently pushed Ruth away and motioned to a seat.

"Ruth, sit, please."

Ruth wiped at the tears on her face and slowly sat in a chair. "I'm so sorry. I'm shocked about Jonathan. I was just talking to him on his phone when he said Jeremiah had called and threatened him. And now, he's gone."

Gamma placed a bottled water on the table and a box of tissues. Max pulled a tissue from the box and offered it to Ruth. Ruth wiped her face with the tissue and drew a deep breath. "Sorry for the crying. I held it in since yesterday. And when? You called this morning and asked me to come here. I was hoping there wasn't bad news."

"Ruth, we have learned nothing new." Max opened the bottle of water and had it to Ruth. She sipped water. "I am worried you might be in danger."

Ruth Martinez paused, her eyes wide. "I am in danger? Of course, I am in danger. I'm in love with Jonathan Steel. Anyone who threatens him threatens me. But I will NOT be intimidated."

"No, you will not." Max smiled. "Jonathan is a blessed man."

Ruth lowered the bottle. "You are right, Max. More blessed than he is willing to admit. Just tell me you're closer to finding Jonathan."

Max shook her head. "Nothing so far. I've reached out to every connection I can think of, my dear."

Ruth looked around the conference room at the empty table. "Where's Jason?"

"He went with Yvonne and Sam to check out any connection with the manor in Austin."

"Where's Josh?"

"He's with Father Caskey." Max fidgeted with her hands. "I'm worried about the boy."

"I am, too. What can I do?"

"We have some rooms here under the safety of the Faraday cage, if you wouldn't mind staying in a converted barn. They're no better than college dorm rooms, but you will be safe for now. I've placed this entire complex under an electronic shield, so to speak."

"I don't suppose you've heard from Yvonne or Sam, either?"

"No. Yvonne said she would contact you as soon as they had any useful information. Ruth, we must trust that Jonathan's friends are doing all they can to find him."

Ruth nodded. "Friends and family. Something Jonathan never thought he would have."

"Well, my dear, I can tell you one thing. The only person we should really feel sorry for is Jeremiah Stone. We both know what Jonathan is capable of," Max said. "He's been in much worse circumstances."

Ruth patted her hand. "More importantly, we know Who is protecting him."

Max sighed and ran her free hand through her white hair. "I wish I had your faith."

"It was a hard time coming. I first met Jonathan when I had to defend Dr. Frank Miller for murder. Let me tell you he was one cold, hard man, obsessed with finding the thirteenth demon."

Max smiled. "I've never heard that story. Please. Tell me more."

Ruth shook her head. "I was up for the next full partner at Grace Pennington's law firm when Dr. Frank Miller was arrested for murdering his boss at the Darwyn Paleontology Institute. Grace pitted me against another junior partner in the trial. Jonathan showed up out of the blue looking for an artifact Grace's husband owned giving information about the thirteenth demon." She looked away. "I thought they were all nuts. I mean, demons? Really? But then I thought about Reginald Drake, a serial killer I had inadvertently allowed to escape prosecution. The man was demon possessed, if anyone ever was."

Ruth sipped more water. "Grace hired Jonathan to help with the investigation. A renegade robotic dinosaur almost killed me. Jonathan saved me more than once and there was something there. A spark. But he was so impenetrable, enigmatic, closed! Dr. Miller was exonerated when I exposed the actual killer in a very dramatic, and I have to admit, bloody finale in the courtroom."

Ruth smiled. "He called me again more than once since then and I noticed he had softened. God was polishing away his rough edges. Over the past few months, that spark of love has grown." Ruth put a hand on Max's hand. "He has lost so much in his life. But this is real, Max. I don't want to lose him. Ever."

Max gripped her hand. "You will not, Ruth. I will do everything in my power to find Jonathan. Now, there is something you can do."

"Anything. Just name it."

"Jeremiah Stone has had enormous resources available to him. He amassed a small mercenary army, for instance. There must be a money trail somewhere. He can't have done what he did in Europe without legal ramifications. With your legal expertise and contacts, perhaps you can find out any information that might give us an idea of where he is and who his contacts might be. Is that possible?

Ruth wiped tears from her cheek and sat up. "Absolutely. I will need access to the internet and a place to work."

Max motioned to the monitors on the wall behind her. "We have that, my dear. Yvonne has already discovered some connections with offshore accounts and has sent those findings to us. So far, she has traced some offshore accounts to the Captain."

"The Captain? He's funding Jeremiah?" Ruth said.

"The Captain was here and denied any involvement. It is possible someone is framing him and making it look as if he is responsible." Max said. "I know that is hard to believe. The man is evil."

"I want to look at that information myself." Ruth said.

"Exactly what I had in mind. So, before you start, how about some breakfast?"

"I'll have pancakes, scrambled eggs, bacon, and lots of coffee." Ruth stood up and moved toward the computer table at the side of the conference room. "I haven't eaten since yesterday morning."

Max smiled to herself. "Ruth, you got it."

CHAPTER

FIFTEEN

"Father James, all of this is very fascinating. But why are you teaching me how to exorcise a demon?" Josh said. The pancakes had been wonderful. But he had slammed them down too quickly. They felt like a rock in his stomach.

Caskey leaned on his walking stick and watched the tip sink into the snow covered ground behind the cabin. "Let's get inside where it is warm, my boy. This cold soaks into my joints."

They walked to the barn and into the open first level. The stalls had been enclosed both on the first and second level for bedrooms. Steam blossomed from their mouths in the cold air. Caskey pointed to a room in the corner, converted into a "break" room. Josh opened the door to welcome warm air and the smell of coffee. Caskey settled into a comfortable chair. "Now, how about a cup of coffee? Two lumps and a splash of milk, please."

Josh sighed in exasperation and fixed the coffee. Caskey

took the cup in his deformed hand and sipped. "Ah, caffeine. My only vice. Sit. We have much to discuss."

"Might as well." Josh plopped into a chair opposite to the priest. "Hurry up and wait!"

Caskey chuckled. "The impatience of youth. Son, you must give Jonathan Steel some credit. He will find a way to overcome his brother, don't you think?"

"Yes. You're right." Josh fidgeted and his cell phone rang. He jerked it from his jean's pocket and looked at the caller ID. "It's Olivia."

"I'll leave if you wish privacy." Caskey said.

Josh shook his head. "Hello."

"Josh? It's Olivia."

Josh smiled. "You sound stronger."

"I've been up and walking around. So far, no seizures. Any word on Jonathan?"

"Not yet." Josh ran a hand through his hair. "Hey, don't be in a hurry to leave the hospital. At least there, you will be safe."

"I don't know, babe." Olivia said. "That didn't help Jonathan. Anyway, they're going to keep me one more night and then I'll go home with Mom and Steven."

"Great!" Josh sat forward and glanced at Caskey. "Hey, babe, I love you. Get well soon."

"I will. And by the way, no sightings yet," Olivia said. "Bye."

Josh looked at the cell phone screen. "She's doing well."

"Sightings?" Caskey asked.

Josh slid the phone in to his pocket. "Olivia can, uh, see demons."

Caskey's eyes widened, and he sat up. "See demons?"

"Yeah. She sees them in their, I guess, native form. All kinds of weird creatures wrapped around their hosts."

Caskey sat his cup on a table beside the chair. "I have heard of such gifts. In all my dealings with demons, I have never met someone who could actually see them. Imagine what an asset that would be during an exorcism."

"No!" Josh put up a hand. "You are NOT recruiting my girlfriend to help with your exorcisms. Besides, since her surgery, she's seen nothing. Her 'gift' is gone."

Caskey sat back and sighed. "Very well. No doubt part of her brain has been altered. She may never have this gift again."

"Can we get on with the exorcism stuff?" Josh slumped back in his chair.

Caskey retrieved his cup and sipped coffee. "You have been blessed so far in your encounters with other demons, as I said. This encounter you had with the man in the pith helmet is a very dangerous situation. Even if you are a believer, once a demon has gotten into your mind, the pathway is still open. It is difficult to close. I must teach you so you can guard your heart and your mind. There are very specific tasks to be followed during an exorcism. The Catholic church has engaged demons for centuries. There are specific prayers which are needed to control and entice a demon to present itself."

"Present itself?"

"Yes, demons are a manifestation of their master, who is the father of lies. You cannot believe anything the host says. The demon will lie and deceive you throughout the procedure. Such is their nature."

Josh sat forward. "Okay, I'm familiar with their lies. I've heard them before. Anthony Cobalt lied to his followers. He never told them he was planning on killing them during the solar mass ejection."

"Precisely." Caskey paused. "Solar mass ejection? Never mind. We do not have time for you to tell me that tale."

"Bro, that's what I've been saying. Time is not on our side."

"But God is." Caskey placed his cup on the table and sat

forward. He rubbed his hands together. "But the problem with demon possession is teasing out the reason the host has allowed the possession to occur."

"They invited it in." Josh said. "I know that much. I did that with the thirteenth demon."

"Yes. As I said, inviting a demon in is tantamount to signing a legal contract. Here's my empty soul. Fill it. Once they move in, the only way to get them to move out is for the host to invoke the reversal of the contract, so to speak. That requires recognizing the defiant, sinful behavior toward God that must be confessed. Here is where the demon has its greatest ally. Pride, Josh. I took part in an exorcism once that took six weeks. The team thought the exorcism was over and then the woman returned, claiming possession again. Turns out she had placed a 'hex' or a 'curse' on her ex-husband and failed to tell us such a thing. Until she forgave her husband, the demon still had custody."

"Hidden sins. I get it." Josh said. "I've had my fair share of them. Still have them."

"But you have surrendered your life to Jesus Christ. The holy spirit dwells within. Where the holy spirit dwells, demons cannot reside."

"But you said a demon still oppresses you."

Caskey froze, and his mouth fell open. He slowly nodded his head. "Once you have allowed a demon to influence you, even if you have the holy spirit, such actions can have a greater influence than God. Because you have chosen such! And once a demon gains the smallest foothold, even though it cannot possess, it can hover nearby, waiting for every little failing, every small sin to destroy the joy of your relationship with God. It is like trying to hear the small, whispering voice of God during a heavy metal concert." Caskey drew a deep breath. "One day, I will no longer be a prisoner in this deformed physical body, which is a target for the demon. I will be reunited in full with my Savior."

"Damaged goods because you sided with a demon?" Josh said. "Jonathan did that to save me."

"Ah, I'd like to hear more about that, in time. But I would imagine, knowing what I have learned about your father, his motives were always hidden from the demons. He had a plan, did he not? Wasn't his agreement to aid the demons, also a hidden agenda to free you?"

"Yes."

"My failings were purely selfish. I wanted the love of Max, and I was willing to do anything to have it. No hidden motives there, young man, when it came to the affairs of my heart." He relaxed in his chair.

"You said there was a team?"

"Yes, my son. A team of professionals carries exorcisms out. Priests, of course, in addition to a physician trained in psychiatry and ordained members of the team capable of restraining the host if needed."

"Why a psychiatrist?"

"Most alleged cases of possession turn out to be psychiatric in nature. The truth, Josh, is there are very few actual possessions. In the decades since I left the church, I have been involved in only a dozen or so such cases. Demons are far more subtle in their suppression of their hosts. Manifestations of overt possession are few and far between. Remember, the demon's greatest tool is apathy."

Josh suddenly sat forward, an idea forming. "Father Caskey, don't you think the best way to familiarize me with exorcisms is to see one?"

Caskey froze and something dark and haunting fell over his face. "I cannot speak of these things, Josh. Confidentiality is paramount between a person and their priest!"

"I'll sign an NDA. I'll do anything. You said you wanted to protect me from another demonic influence like Pandora. If so, then bring me in and let me witness a team at work."

Caskey sat forward and his face paled. "I am not welcome on exorcisms right now."

"You said you had been involved in a dozen or so exorcisms. Those had to be since you were exiled." Josh said.

Caskey drew a deep breath. "It is true I have been allowed to consult on some exorcisms. But I am not welcome in conventional exorcisms conducted by the church."

"But there are other types, right? You said so."

Caskey stood up and wobbled around the chair. "Josh, what you are asking is almost impossible."

Josh stood up. "Father Caskey, James, my father is missing. Who knows what I will face when we finally find him. Prepare me. Teach me. Let me experience an encounter with a demon in the right way. You told me I had to learn this. Now show me."

Caskey rubbed his hand across his forehead. "The reasons I was in this area is there is a local group with whom I have worked. I understand they are involved in an exorcism. I was hoping they might allow me to observe." He sat back down. "Perhaps I can talk them into letting you sit in." He poked a gnarled finger at Josh. "But, it will be dangerous for you and the group. You will have to do everything they tell you. To the letter!"

Josh smiled. His plan was going to work! "I'm willing. Let's go."

"I will need to make a contact. It will take time. Most likely we can go tomorrow or the next day." Caskey said.

"What? Time is wasting, James."

"Josh!" Caskey raised his voice. "Max and the authorities are doing everything they can to find Jonathan. There is nothing more you can do right now." He stood up slowly. "So you have some homework."

"Homework?"

"Yes. For the rest of today I want you to do a Bible study on demons. Read every passage in the Bible mentioning demons. Once I have established where and when this local team meets, we will go. I promise you. But, it will not be today."

Josh sighed. "Fine! I'll be in my stall." He stormed off towards his tiny bedroom.

"Josh," Caskey said. "The first rule of any encounter in an exorcism is patience. Sometimes these things take weeks or even months. Haste is the demon's tool. Don't be in a hurry. Read your Bible. Confess your sins. And, pray."

Josh nodded, calming his racing heart. "I'm a teenager. Patience is not one of my virtues."

CHAPTER

SIXTEEN

After his second shower, Steel put on the clean scrubs and sat on the edge of the bed. Lucas had been involved with his father? The red stone had to be a fragment of the bloodstone. According to Arthur Knight, the bloodstone influenced the conception of his daughter Vega. Vega was a Nephilim along with the other children sired at the bidding of Anthony Cobalt and the tenth demon. Lucas had been a part of that process, according to Knight. But neither he nor Jeremiah were Nephilim. No attributes of the giantism of the children of the bloodstone. Maybe he and Jeremiah were ordinary humans from the in vitro procedure their mother had gone through.

"It had to be," he said to the empty room. "I am not the product of demon conception."

He paced around the room and paused at the door. Could he escape? Did he want to escape? The Grimvox held information he desperately wanted to have. And if he had watched his father's videos before now, he wouldn't be in this position.

The faint green glow started in the wall above the door and the familiar voice echoed in the room.

"Find me. Help me." The woman's voice pleaded. A hand appeared from the green cloud of light. Steel felt the warmth in the palm of his left hand and he studied the faint white pinpoint of light. He reached toward the hand and as his finger touched those of the ghost like hand the mist abruptly disappeared.

"No, don't pull me away." A woman's voice pleaded. The room was dark once again.

Steel collapsed onto the cot, his mind whirling. Who was this woman? And who kept pulling her back into, what? What was going on? Once again, he had been placed in an impossible situation. He closed his eyes in prayer and drifted off in sleep.

The opening door woke him up. Jeremiah stood in the door's frame. His eyes were rimmed in darkness.

Steel sat up. "What time is it?"

"Doesn't matter." Jeremiah said.

"You haven't slept much, have you?"

"No. Let's go." He held up the tablet. "Don't try anything."

Steel stood up and crossed his arms. "No more tablet. I'm just as curious now as you are. I'm seeing this thing to the end."

Jeremiah's finger hovered over the tablet. "I don't trust you."

"You shouldn't trust me any more than I trust you, brother." Steel walked across the room. Jeremiah stepped back into the hallway. "My word is good. You know that. I promise I will not try to escape. In return, we will watch the rest of our father's video."

"That's not the endgame, JJ."

"What is?"

"Shared memories. I give you mine. You give me yours. Without question or restraint. Agreed?"

Steel drew a deep breath. Jeremiah wanted a specific memory from Steel's past. Just what memory he did not know. Now he had a chance to understand his brother and find out more about his father's past. And he had the woman in the mist to consider.

"I'll think on it."

Jeremiah pursed his lips and nodded. "Good enough." He tapped the tablet and Steel felt the metal disc loosen on his chest. It tumbled to the floor.

"Let's finish this." Jeremiah turned and led them down the hallway. Steel picked up the disc and slid it into a pocket of his scrubs.

SEVENTEEN

"Everything looks to be in order." The doctor said crisply. "The baby is very healthy and right on target for the delivery date."

The Captain squeezed her hand. She smiled. "Thank you, Dr. Santiago. I just seem to have gained so much weight. And it's all baby. I just wanted to be sure. I've read about polyhydramnios, you know, too much amniotic fluid and that comes when there is an abnormality of the baby."

Santiago shook his head. "Don't be silly. There is no evidence of polyhydramnios, Christine. You are spending too much time on the internet. Your weight gain is not endangering you or the baby, and you will lose it once the baby is born."

"Is she still due in two weeks?" The Captain said.

"Yes. I will be out of town next week. I am vacationing in Tahiti. My wife insisted. I understand you have a midwife in the hacienda?"

"Just in case." The Captain said. "I have planned for all eventualities."

"Then there should be no worries. I will be back with a rested mind and spirit, Christine, to deliver your son." Santiago nodded his head.

Stone walked Santiago out of the room. "Doctor, I need to know something."

"Yes, Captain."

"There was a night two weeks before the implantation. I don't remember what happened, but Christine was quite emphatic that I was very amorous." He paused. "In fact, I remember nothing about that night."

"What is your point, Captain?"

"What would happen if she was already pregnant when you implanted the embryos?"

Santiago massaged his goatee. "An interesting conundrum. I supposed you would be the father of fraternal twins. Maybe even triplets. But, Captain, the two of you have tried many times. It is very unlikely a pregnancy was present. Do not worry. All is going according to plan."

A JERK PULLED AT STEEL, and the memories swirled, changing the point of view. The nauseating evil of Robert Ketrick's soul penetrated to his core, and he fought down panic. He had relived this memory once before at Ketrick's house. He did not want to witness it again. But he had no choice. The Grimvox had taken over, filling in the gaps in the Captain's story.

Night had fallen, and the courtyard was lit with many torches by the time Bobby Ketrick arrived at the museum hacienda. Servants were bustling around the courtyard and up and down the stairs to

the second floor entrance of the house. Bobby hurried into the main courtyard. The air was hot and muggy and smelled of antiseptic and sweat. A scream echoed down from the second floor. Bobby stopped a short woman hurrying by with a pan of water.

"Maria, what is happening?"

Maria's eyes were wide with fear. "It is the mistress of the house. She is having the baby."

Bobby watched her hurry away and looked up at the balcony. The Captain stood there, minus his hat. Sweat soaked his shirt. "Bobby! Good, you're back. Watch for Dr. Santiago. I was hoping we could get back to the States, but Christine is in labor."

Another scream cut through the air, and Bobby flinched. He thought about the stone disk. He pictured the pregnant mother giving birth to a full-grown man capable of hacking his sister to death. Why did he think such things at a time like this? He liked Christine. She had been kind to him over the last few months when most of the adults at the museum ignored him. She had seen his potential and had asked him to help find the disk of Coatlicue, the mother of the woman on the stone. Where had that mother's compassion gone? How could a mother sit by and watch as her daughter was killed?

"Am I interrupting something?"

Bobby turned, and the tattooed man stood in the open archway leading into the courtyard. "No. My teacher is having her baby. She may be in trouble."

Bobby watched the man's face flush with crimson. For a second, a smile played across his lips. Bobby studied the man's red eyes and felt a shiver course over him. For a second, he felt a sense of dread at the man's presence.

"Bobby, who is this gentleman?" The Captain was suddenly behind him. Bobby whirled. The Captain held a bloody blanket to his chest. The head of a baby lolled against his bloody chest.

"Is that your baby?" Bobby asked.

The Captain looked down at the child and blinked. "Yes. His name is John."

Bobby leaned forward and watched the newborn child squirm in his father's grasp. For a fleeting second, the baby's eyes flew open, and the startling color of turquoise gleamed in the torchlight. The Captain looked over Bobby's shoulder.

"I asked you who that man was. He's not Doctor Santiago."

"Just someone I met at the dig."

The tattooed man smiled and exposed his white teeth and red gums. "My name is Lucas."

The Captain was silent for a moment, and his greenish-blue eyes stayed riveted on the tattooed man. "I don't want you to have anything to do with him, Bobby."

Bobby nodded. "Of course, Captain. I'll show him out." Above them, another scream pierced the night. The Captain grabbed Bobby's arm and turned him back. He thrust the baby into his arms.

"Here. Hold him until Consuela comes for him. My wife needs me." The Captain hurried away and disappeared up the stairs.

"What a beautiful child." Lucas smiled.

"I think you need to go," Bobby said. He glanced at the squirming baby in his arms.

"I will go. In a moment. But first, I must tell you more about the child you hold in your hands." Lucas leaned forward, and a finger strayed toward the baby. He paused just before touching the baby's forehead. "Your destiny and his are connected. But it would seem that destiny may have given you an unprecedented opportunity." Lucas walked across the courtyard to the fountain. "Come. Follow me."

Bobby glanced at the baby and hurried after the man. "What are you talking about?"

Lucas sat on the edge of the fountain. "Pick the baby up by the leg."

Bobby frowned. "Why?"

"Trust me."

Bobby blinked as something swelled within him, a heat that burned its way to his fingertips. He reached down and took the baby's right leg in his hand and gently lifted the baby into the air. The baby's blanket fluttered to the ground.

"Good. Now lift him up in the air." Lucas's voice grew hoarse.

Bobby lifted the naked baby until his face was level with his, his arms and left leg dangling. The baby ceased his squirming, and for a second, his eyes flickered open as if to study Bobby.

"Now, drop him in the water."

Bobby looked at him. "In the fountain?"

"Yes. One quick release, and your future will be secure. Just like you dropped the scorpion."

Bobby blinked. That morning, he had dropped a scorpion on Consuela, the girl he hated so much. He could still remember her screams. "How did you know?"

The tattooed man stood up and drew very close, and his eyes gleamed in the scant light. "I know everything about you, Robert. It is a matter of record that your mother committed suicide. But the truth is, you were playing with the gun and it accidentally went off and she died. You wanted the gun to kill your father. He's the one who deserved to die, right?"

Bobby trembled, and his grip weakened on the baby's leg. "No one knows that."

"I told you I have had an eye on you for some time. And now, if you listen carefully to my advice, I will complete your training."

Bobby felt the heat intensify and felt his mind blur. An inexorable force seized his mind, and he lifted the baby higher as he reached over the edge of the fountain.

"Good. Now, just relax your grip. One simple movement, and your adversary is gone. And all you have to do is blame it on Consuela."

"Son of the devil! What are you doing?" Bobby whirled, and Consuela appeared out of the darkness. Huge, red welts covered her face from the scorpion stings. She snared the baby from Bobby's grasp and pulled him to her chest.

The Captain appeared on the upper level. "What is happening?"

Consuela retrieved the blanket and wrapped it around the baby. "Bobby was going to drown the baby."

The Captain glared down at Bobby. "Is this true?"

"I don't know, sir. I just lost my mind, I guess." Bobby fumbled for words. He watched the man's face redden with anger.

The Captain glanced at Lucas. "Take your friend and get off my property. Now."

"But sir... "

"Now. Pack up your things, and have your friend drop you off at the airport. You can catch the first flight out in the morning. I don't want you around my son another moment." He motioned to Consuela, and she hurried up the stairs.

EIGHTEEN

S teel lurched, trying to pull his hand from the Grimvox as the memory died away. But there was no respite. Immediately, he found his attention drawn to the room where his mother had just given birth to him.

CHRISTINE SCREAMED FOR HER HUSBAND. The Captain threw open the bedroom door. Christine had never felt such pain. Delivering their son had been horribly painful. With only Consuela to help her with breathing and with Santiago still out of town, she had done so without pain medication. But the pain that she was feeling now was ten times worse.

"What is happening?" The Captain said to Consuela.

"Sir, there is another baby!"

"What?"

Christine panted, trying her best to control the pain. "I knew I was too large for my dates. That Santiago is a quack!" She screamed as the labor pain ripped through her.

"It is a breech birth." Consuela said. "I will try to turn the baby."

Consuela climbed up onto the bed and began massaging Christine's abdomen. "In between contractions, I will turn it. You must control your breathing."

"I'll call an ambulance." The Captain said.

"There is no time!" Consuela said. She began to push and shove on Christine's abdomen and Christine screamed in pain.

"Contraction?"

"No! It hurts. Something is wrong!"

"There!" Consuela slid off the bed. "It is turned. The head is crowning. Now push!"

Christine grunted as she bore down with as much strength as she had left. Blood suddenly poured across her legs.

"Placenta has separated!" Consuela shouted. "We must get this baby out now so I can remove the placenta and stop the bleeding. Captain, call that ambulance."

Christine grew weary and felt like she was sinking far down into a dark, cold well. She heard a baby cry? Maybe? Who was the man standing in the door? Was he wearing a pith helmet? And next to him, a man? Was it Santiago?

The Captain was screaming at the man. There was a baby. Quiet now. No crying. She was sinking faster and deeper. The Captain ran out the door. Sirens? Maybe coming for her?

STONE'S HEAD pounded from his elevated blood pressure. Outside in the courtyard in Mexico, that young brat, Ketrick, and that strange man Lucas had almost killed his son. He had taken his son back to one of the midwifes when he had heard the second scream. Now who should appear but his father? For a second, he thought there had been a second man bearing a striking resemblance to Nigel Hampton. But his father was alone. He held the screaming baby and glared at his father.

"You're supposed to be dead."

"Well, reports of my demise were obviously mistaken." He looked over his shoulder and Dr. Santiago stepped from the shadows.

"Why didn't you tell me there were twins?" The Captain screamed at Santiago, who had obviously never gone to Tahiti.

The elder Stone merely shrugged, wearing his every present pith helmet. "Would it have changed anything? You have a healthy son. This one belongs to us."

"Us?"

Behind him, blood pooled on the floor and his wife was gasping for breath. When would the ambulance arrive?

"If you want your wife to live, give me the baby." Dr. Santiago said.

Stone tuned to his wife, and Consuela was trying her best to stop the bleeding. He heard approaching sirens. A hand rested on his shoulder.

"Your wife will live, son." He whirled on his father. "But this child is ours."

Stone stumbled back. "No! This can't be happening."

"It is. Save your wife." His father walked out of the room, followed by Dr. Santiago carrying his other son.

CHAPTER

NINETEEN

"Christine?"

She opened her eyes with great effort. It took all her energy. She was in her bedroom. At the hacienda. "Where am I?"

The Captain held something in his arms. "Home. You've been out for two days. We gave you blood. Here's our son." He turned the bundle toward her. The baby's bright, turquoise eyes almost gleamed. She reached for the baby.

"John?" She took the wiggling bundle and held it to her chest. "Is he okay?"

"He's perfect." The Captain said.

Christine froze. "What about the other baby?"

The Captain merely stood there quietly, his gaze shifting away from her. "What baby?"

"I had another baby!" Christine said. John cried, and it startled her.

"Christine, there was no other baby. You lost blood from a separated placenta." The Captain looked back at her.

"No, Consuela was here. She delivered the baby. I heard him cry."

The Captain took the crying baby from her and had to pull him from her grasp. "You were delusional, Christine. Maria will take care of John until you are stronger."

Christine tried to sit up, and the dizziness took her. She collapsed on the bed. "No! I had another baby! I know I did!"

A strange woman appeared behind the Captain and took the baby. "Who is Maria? Where is Consuela?"

The Captain glanced back at her. "Consuela is no longer with us. Maria will take care of John for now. When you are stronger, we are returning to the states. Now, sleep."

They left her alone in the room, and all she had the strength to do was cry.

CHRISTINE TOOK off her glasses and rubbed her eyes. She glanced at her watch. It was ten o'clock!

"Mom, when are you going to come and read me a story?"

Christine sighed and turned to face her seven-year-old son, a book clutched in his hand. "JJ, I'm coming now."

"You've been stuck on that computer all night." He said. His gleaming turquoise eyes almost glowed in the dim light of her office. "Father is asleep in the library, and Hobbs is too old to play hide and seek. You promised we could play before I went to bed."

JJ wore his Star Wars pajamas and his reddish blonde hair was stuck to his head. "Who gave you a bath?"

"I did. Maria is drunk again."

Christine stiffened. She had tried to fire Maria many times, but the Captain always stopped her. "Maria has problems sleeping, honey." Christine put a hand on her son's head. "You still have shampoo in your hair!"

"You were too busy." He said sadly.

Christine fell to her knees and hugged her son to her. "I'm so sorry, JJ. I should have played with you earlier."

He glanced over her shoulder at her computer monitor. "What is that, Mom?"

Christine glanced over her shoulder, and her heart sank. She put a false smile on her face. "That is called an ultrasound. It's a picture of you when you were in my tummy." She avoided his eyes.

"Mommy, I was not in your tummy!" JJ said. He pulled her face back to look into her eyes. "I was in your you-truss."

Christine raised an eyebrow. "And just where did you learn that?"

"Clay told me that a seed is planted in a woman's you-truss and it grows into a baby. If I was in your tummy, you would have to digest me."

Christine had to smile. "You are one smart young man, JJ. Now, why don't you go run a small tub of warm water so I can rinse that shampoo out of your hair and then I will read you that book."

JJ shrugged. "Okay. I don't mind playing with my boats again tonight." He ran out of the room after thrusting the book into her hands. It was a book about the body that the Captain had bought for JJ. Did this book talk about her uterus? She turned back to the ultrasound image on the monitor.

"Now, Dr. Santiago, wherever you are, these are images pulled from my medical records." She started scrolling through the images. A few carefully placed bribes to the doctor who had taken Santiago's place had produced a DVD with her ultrasound studies. One image came up on the screen. Even with no expertise in interpreting ultrasound, there was no doubt what she was looking at. It was a three-dimensional image of a baby's face with the eyes, nose, and lips perfectly outlined. The problem was, there was a second face right by the first one! Dr. Santiago never told her she had carried twins!

"What are you looking at?"

Christine closed the window and turned to see her husband standing in the doorway. How long had he been standing there? "Just looking at some material for my lecture. I have to go wash the shampoo out of JJ's hair. He said Maria was drunk, Saul. Drunk!"

Stone sighed. "I guess I'll have to get Hobbs to let her go." He paused as he turned and glanced once more over her shoulder at the computer screen, then walked away.

"Stillborn?" Christine shouted. Hobbs and Gracey, the two servants in the living room, scurried from sight as Christine stormed over to her husband. The Captain sat quietly in his big wicker chair.

"I didn't think you could stand the strain of knowing that at the time, Christine. You had lost a lot of blood and you were almost dead." The Captain said as he puffed on his pipe.

"When were you going to tell me that JJ had a brother? Or was it a sister?"

"Fraternal twin." The Captain said.

Christine paused. "What? Two embryos were implanted. They were two different children?"

The Captain stood up and approached her slowly. "Christine, I am truly sorry. I never told you. I was trying to spare you unnecessary pain. We had already lost two other children with the miscarriages." He put a hand on her arm, and she jerked it away.

"You made me see your Dr. Santiago who has disappeared off the face of the earth. He had ultrasounds that showed I was having twins." She said.

The Captain raised an eyebrow and nodded. "So I discovered after the fact. When Santiago failed to return after we came back to the states, I obtained the medical records. He said in his notes you were having twins. Two separate gestational sacs. Fraternal twins. Not identical twins. Why he never told us is a mystery to me."

Christine clenched her fists and glared at him. "You are lying to me. You knew. You and your precious projects and secrets. Am I one of your test subjects?"

"Christine, I would never experiment on a loved one. What would make you think such a thing?" The Captain tapped his pipe on a nearby bowl and emptied the ashes.

"Your father? Are you carrying on his footsteps?"

The Captain whirled. "No! I am not like my father!"

Christine glared at him and slowly advanced on him. "Then who was the other man at JJ's birth?"

The Captain froze. "What did you say?"

"I saw him at my delivery. He looked familiar."

The Captain tore his gaze away from her and walked to the library. "There was another person in the room, Christine. An associate of Dr. Santiago's. He came at the last minute to check on you. When the baby stopped breathing, he took him and tried to resuscitate him. Without success, I might add. With the placental abruption, the baby perished. The man is, uh, a geneticist. I wanted to check the deceased baby's genes for genetic abnormalities."

Christine felt weak and she collapsed slowly into a chair. "Genetic abnormalities?"

"You mentioned my father. His mental problems were inherited. It is true you should be wary of me. I might develop similar tendencies over time. It is one reason I do the research I do. It is one reason I travel around the world investigating these genetic diseases." The Captain came over and sat tentatively beside her. "Christine, I only had your best interest at heart. And I didn't want JJ to find out he had a dead brother. No need to burden him with that gruesome news. We have a healthy son. We anticipated only one son. We should focus on JJ and put this unfortunate circumstance behind us."

Christine leaned away from him. "I don't know. I need some time to think and I might go visit my friend in Pittsburg. Next week is Christmas break. I'll take JJ with me. Take him skiing on Seven Hills."

The Captain nodded slowly. "That would be acceptable. I'm heading to South America tomorrow. We both need time to regroup."

Christine stood up slowly and refused to look at him. "You already have all the time in the world."

THE SCENE FADED into the dark shadows of the Grimvox chamber. Steel pulled his hand away from the pebbly surface of the macabre device. Jeremiah sat silently to his left, his eyes moist.

"Now you see why I wanted to do this, JJ. You were the privileged one. You ended up with a mother and a father and I had Nanny." He hissed.

"I had no idea, Jeremiah, until you killed our mother." Steel said.

Jeremiah's gaze shifted from the Grimvox to Steel. "Well, I'll let you in on some news, brother! I didn't kill our mother. I couldn't! I was supposed to. It was my final exam, you might say, and I couldn't do it." Suddenly, his features twisted and a different tone issued from his lips.

"Ignore that remark." Jeremiah's eyes filled with fire. "He is babbling."

A chill ran down Steel's spine. "What did he mean by that?"

"Knowledge is priceless, JJ." The second demon chuckled. "I will choose which knowledge he gives you from now on. In fact, I'll let you in on a little wisdom right now. How about sharing another of my memories?"

The room swam dizzily and Steel was somewhere else.

Jerusalem

"You!" King Solomon screamed as he sat in the shade of a sycamore tree on the Mount of Olives.

Ablon bowed his head in deference as he approached the king. "My king, why are you so troubled?"

Solomon wore a gold laced robe. His crown glittered upon his head as sunlight filtered through the limbs of the tree. As regal a figure as he commanded, his face betrayed the brokenness of his heart. "My God has just spoken to me!"

"All is well then, my king." Ablon's heart raced. How could this happen?

"No, it is not well!" Solomon paced and pointed into the distance. "What do you see?"

"The shrine to Ashtoreth you had constructed for one of your wives. A most wise move I had, to remind you to reach out to Egypt and ask for his daughter's hand in marriage. Such moves have guaranteed your kingdom will grow and prosper as it has done now for years." Ablon stepped closer, his robes whispering in the

grass. "Have I not told you how wise you are? How your knowledge has made you the greatest king who has ever reigned?"

"Ashtoreth! Molech! These pagan gods are an abomination to the Lord God Jehovah! Why didn't I realize that?" Solomon paused and glared at Ablon. "Because I listened to such as you. Knowledge is power, you told me. Celebrate the wisdom God has given you, you said."

"My king, you have built the greatest temple man will ever know. You have brought the Ark of the Covenant into its holiest place. The queen of Sheba visited you and fell at your feet. Your mighty kingdom stretches to the north, south, east and west! You know so much about animals, plants, silver, gold, the land itself. Your knowledge is unequaled by any man on earth! Everyone speaks of the unlimited wisdom of Solomon." Ablon stepped closer, his voice taking on a comforting nature. "Now your God is angry with you. Why shouldn't he be? You are almost as wise as a god, Solomon."

"How dare you blaspheme the name of Jehovah God!" Solomon towered over the court adviser. "I am a mere mortal. All is vanity. All is death and dust. I cannot turn away the worm that awaits my last breath! I cannot keep age at bay! All my knowledge and wisdom is dust on the wind!"

"My king, your writings are very powerful. They will be cherished by mankind for thousands of years! Your influence will extend well beyond your earthly demise." Ablon bowed his head again.

"Then, oh wise one, what should I do when God raises up a king to oppose me? Who will God strengthen then? Me? I think not." Solomon turned away and shook the tree with trembling hands. Leaves fell lazily around him.

"What did your god tell you? Perhaps I can help you understand it better." Ablon wrung his hands.

Solomon turned from the tree and his face glistened with tears,

"Since this is your attitude and you have not kept my covenant and my decrees, which I commanded you, I will most certainly tear the kingdom away from you and give it to one of your subordinates. Nevertheless, for the sake of David, your father, I will not do it during your lifetime. I will tear it out of the hand of your son. Yet I will not tear the whole kingdom from him, but will give him one tribe for the sake of David, my servant, and for the sake of Jerusalem, which I have chosen." Solomon sat on the bench beneath the tree and put his face in his hands. *"All is lost, Ablon. Because I listened to your 'knowledge' and turned my back on God's wisdom."*

Ablon hid his smile. Here before him was the final destruction of the Creator's greatest living king. And all he had to do was dangle forbidden knowledge before his vanity. "Then, my king, your kingdom is truly lost. Perhaps you have gone too far in seeking knowledge."

Solomon glared at Ablon and bolted to his feet. "You spin your words and your affirmations at me like sweet candy, Ablon. I never should have listened to you. Political alliances were the guise for pagan infiltration into my kingdom. Visitors from foreign kingdoms were exploiting my vanity. I am anything but the wisest man on earth for not seeing you for the evil spirit you are. I will have you beheaded at dawn, Ablon. Guards!"

From nearby, the king's guardians appeared, bearing their spears and swords. Ablon felt his human host recoil in fear. Hosts never realized what they had asked for. They were never wise in their search for knowledge. He shrugged. "I have succeeded, my king, in making you the most powerful man on earth. For that, I am willing to accept punishment. Do not forget what you have learned."

Solomon frowned. "Of making many books there is no end, and much study wearies the body, Ablon. Now all has been heard and said of this matter." He pointed a finger at Ablon as the guards *seized him. "And here is the conclusion of the matter of what I have forgotten: Fear God and keep his commandments, for this is the duty of all mankind. For God will bring every deed into judgment, including every hidden thing, whether it is good or evil." He moved closer to Ablon. "And now, you must face that judgment while I must seek forgiveness from God."*

STEEL'S VISION cleared and he looked around. The chamber was empty except for the wide open eyes of Snake, tethered to the monstrous device before her. The vision of Solomon's fate still resonated in his mind. Knowledge without wisdom was dust in the wind. Did he seek only knowledge about his brother and his father? Or would he temper that knowledge with wisdom?

He waited for a moment or two and then stood up. Nanny did not show up. Jeremiah didn't return. He touched the metal disc still in his pocket. Could he just walk away? Would it be that simple?

But he was getting some answers to questions he never knew he had. And Jeremiah was slipping. He blinked and tore his gaze away from Snake. Jeremiah was hurting. And if he hadn't killed their mother, who had?

He made his way into the hallway and back to the door to his room. With a touch, the door swung open and he returned to his prison, the price he was willing to pay for the information he would learn.

CHAPTER

TWENTY

Caskey waited for Josh when he emerged from his bedroom the next morning. He stood next to the sink and barn's kitchenette.

"Tea?" Caskey said.

"I prefer coffee, Father." Josh rubbed sleep from his eyes. "And food."

"As I have said, I cannot use the title 'Father' any longer, my friend." He busied himself with making tea and putting coffee into a pot. "Max's chef has provided us with a tray of pastries." He gestured to a tray on the table between the two chairs. "Help yourself while the coffee is brewing."

Josh sat down and grabbed an apple turnover. He bit into the fragrant, flaky pastry and his stomach growled. He hadn't eaten the evening before. "Any word on Jonathan?" He said anxiously.

"If so, Max would have let you know immediately, laddy." Caskey said over his shoulder. "How was your homework?"

A gnawing sensation hit his stomach from more than emptiness. The longer Jonathan was missing, the less the chance they would find him. He cleared his head. "I fell asleep around midnight. I read all the verses on demons as you asked." He finished the turnover and snagged a blueberry muffin. "And, no visions. Or dreams."

"Good." Caskey said. "Now, once we get settled, we will talk more about exorcism." He turned and leaned against the counter, pointing his cane at Josh. "You have to learn the proper way to deal with a demon possessed individual."

The tea kettle whistled and Caskey poured steaming water into his cup. He poured coffee into another cup and offered it to Josh. "Cream? Sugar?"

"Black." Josh hurried over and took the cup. He sipped the bitter, hot liquid. He needed the caffeine to stimulate his thinking. "Once this caffeine kicks in, my brain will work, so teach away."

Caskey motioned to Josh's chair. "Patience. Let me prepare my tea."

"Be patient! Just wait! Give us some time!" Josh growled. "We don't have that kind of time."

Caskey took a carton of milk from the refrigerator and poured a thin stream into his cup. "Have you ever considered what it takes to get you a cup of coffee? Or a cup of tea?" He spooned two heaps of sugar into his cup and stirred. He retrieved the tea bag and held it up, allowing the tea to drip into the sink. "Look at this tea bag."

"What about it?"

"Someone had to think up this device in order that tea making would be simpler. No more tea leaves to sift from your tea." He dropped the bag in a trash can. "And sugar. Refined. Where did it come from? Who discovered the process of turning sap from sugar cane into this beautiful white substance? And a simple carton of milk. Someone figured out how to take raw milk from their cow and deliver it safely without microbes to you and me in a paper carton without the carton leaking."

"Your point?"

Caskey settled into the opposite chair and leaned his cane against the table. "Preparation and planning, Josh. You cannot rush into these things and expect to get perfect results. We are talking about two thousand years of dealing with demonic beings. What you should have learned from your Bible reading is demonic presence peaked at the time of Jesus' ministry. That should not be surprising to consider that God was walking the earth. The church has developed tools and practices for dealing with demons. Centuries of trial and error. Dozens of prayers developed. If you want to deal with ANY demon under ANY circumstance, you must learn from the wisdom of the ages, Josh. You and Jonathan have been very fortunate in dealing with these powerful demons up until now. Mostly, that success is due to the intervention of angels from God. Tell me, have you ever faced off against a demon when an angel was not present?"

Josh opened his mouth to protest and then leaned back in the sofa. "Okay, I get it. There have been many times I found myself in a bad situation and wondering where Dude was."

"Dude, if I remember correctly, is your name for your guardian angel?" Caskey sipped some tea and sighed. "Ah, perfect Earl Grey."

"Yes, I first met Dude not far from here."

"And what did Dude do for you?"

Josh looked away and recalled his encounter with the angel at the edge of the bayou. "He saved my life. The Vitreomancers were going to kill me."

Caskey's scarred hands wrapped around his teacup as he sat forward. "God gives his messengers very specific tasks. You and I cannot change the mind of God. We cannot call up an angel at a moment's notice, Josh."

"So I have learned bro."

"But, a person in league with a demon, can do just that. Demons are eager to do our will, not God's! Remember that. As I told you earlier, a relationship with a demon is a legal contract. That agreement becomes more powerful and more difficult to undo the longer a person is under that influence."

"Fine. I get it. Be as patient as a demon and don't rely on God to bail you out when to do so would be against His will." Josh said harshly. "Did you talk to the exorcists?"

"I'm waiting to hear back from someone on the team." Caskey tapped his shirt pocket. "Should get a text any minute. Now, as I have said, exorcism requires a team approach. The lead exorcist, in my case, is a priest with extensive experience in exorcisms. The church has many definitive prescribed prayers which must be constantly prayed not only by the leader priest but every member of the team. At least two people are required to help with restraint."

"Restraint? You mentioned that earlier." Josh sat forward. Now it was getting interesting.

"Humans possessed by demons can manifest supernatural strength. They can hurt or harm members of the team. Remember this, Josh. A victim agrees to the process. A victim must at least want to change. And they must agree to restraint as this is never forced upon them. Another team member must be a physician, preferably with psychiatric training."

"So you said. Separate the crazies from the possessed." Josh sipped coffee. "Got it."

Caskey sighed. "Not that simple, my boy. Many manifestations of mental illness can mimic demon possession. Many times, individuals have faked demon possession for a number of reasons. Pro tip: if the victim uses the Lord's name in vain, they are not possessed. A demon cannot utter the name of Jesus Christ without pain and suffering on their part. Only a tiny percentage of possible possessions turn out to be true possessions."

Josh nodded. "Okay, noted. Although I've seen a demon in action, tell me the supernatural abilities of a demon?"

"Possessed individuals demonstrate unnatural abilities. They have forbidden or unknown knowledge they should never possess on their own and can speak in a foreign language they do not know of. Demons can manipulate the surrounding environment to a limited degree."

"I've seen one turn into a giant scorpion." Josh said, recalling his first encounter with the thirteenth demon.

Caskey paused, his mouth open. "What did you say?"

"The thirteenth demon manifested as a huge scorpion." Josh shuddered at the memory.

"That is incredible! I have never seen such a sight." He wiped his mouth and stood up, hobbled slowly around the chair. "One time, we were in the middle of an exorcism and the victim broke through their restraints, fell on the floor and undulated like a serpent." Caskey paused and pointed a crooked finger at Josh. "Like she had no bones in her body!"

"I saw one turn into a giant batlike creature." Josh said. "And some kind of chimera creature? And a giant blob thing."

Caskey paused and collapsed back into his chair. "Josh, you and your friends are very blessed you did not suffer from these extraordinary encounters."

Josh sipped his coffee and stared off, deep in thought. "These are the most powerful demons on the planet. The twelve chosen by Satan to counter the teachings of Jesus, according to Uncle Cephas."

Caskey nodded and sipped more tea. "Well, let me continue while I calm my nerves. The demon is summoned during intense prayers. Often, there is more than one demon available. The more powerful demon possessing a person may send forward a lesser demon to endure the prayers. This serves to wear down the exorcist. We get tired and the sessions can individually last for hours."

"What's the longest you've spent on an exorcism?"

"Three months."

Josh almost dropped his cup. "Three months?" He put his cup down on a table. "How long does it usually take?"

"Weeks. Rarely, days. It is a spiritual game of chess, Josh. The dominant demon sends forth lesser demons. The dominant demon gives the victim knowledge only they would know, often revealing secrets held by the members of the team. This weakens and intimates the team. Their greatest weakness is pride. Appeal to their proud nature and you will find their weakness."

"What is their weakness?"

Caskey rubbed his chin in deep thought. "Their victim's desire to be free. But, if the victim is unwilling to release the very thing that caused them to surrender to the demon in the first place, the exorcism can be pointless." He lifted his cane. "The other weakness can be a relic, like this cane."

"A relic?"

"An object. Sometimes it can be holy water. But if there is a relic from the past associated with an evil deed perpetuated by the demon against a saint, that object can carry powerful incentive to leave the victim. This cane, for instance, once belonged to my mentor."

Caskey blinked away moisture. "Father McCoy taught me everything he could about the Lord. He took me under his wing. He had a limp from a war injury and carried this cane. This seemingly innocuous piece of wood came from a banyan tree in Hawaii. Father McCoy served in a parish there after

World War II. He exorcised a demon from a former shaman of a pagan religion and the man took a root from the tree and carved this cane. It was a thank you gift."

Caskey looked away and his voice grew quiet and hoarse. "The shaman's followers were not so thankful. The successor to the man was possessed by the same demon and he led a gang of believers to ambush Father McCoy in a dark alleyway in Honolulu. They beat him to death with his own cane."

The air was still and cool. Josh swallowed hard and sipped his now cold coffee. "I'm sorry for your loss."

Caskey nodded and waited until the emotion passed. "A year later, I was summoned to prison to meet with the man who killed Father McCoy. He asked if I would take away the demon." Caskey glanced back at me, his eyes bright with tears. "Josh, you cannot imagine how difficult it was to face the man who had killed my friend and find forgiveness. You see, I had to forgive him before I could lead a team to exorcise the demon. Father McCoy was a saint, a child of God and I knew he would find it in his heart to forgive the man who had killed him. It took me weeks of prayer and intermittent fasting to find that level of forgiveness before I began."

He gulped his tea. "Three weeks into the exorcism, we were getting nowhere. The prison warden was impatient. His only reason for allowing us in was because he thought we could in some way influence this man to be less of a purveyor of chaos in his prison. We were at an impasse. And then, I remembered the cane. I wasn't disabled at the time. I kept it leaning in a corner of my office. I brought it to the next session and hid it behind my back. As I drew closer to the man, the demon went berserk, begging me to leave him alone. When I brought the cane into sight, the demon screamed and contorted the victim. All I had to do was touch the cane to his hand and the demon relented. The man was healed and the demon left him. He became a pastor in the prison. A man forgiven."

"I could never forgive a demon." Josh hissed.

"No, you cannot. Demons are irredeemable. But you can forgive the host. And unless you do that, you are wasting your time. An unrepentant and unforgiving heart fuels the strength of demons and their master. This is why I told you be prayed up, confessed up, and read up on the Scriptures." He tensed and pulled his cell phone from his pocket. He smiled. "Now I suggest you get cleaned up. The team is meeting this evening in Rockwall, Texas."

Josh straightened and grinned. "Now you're talking, bro." He paused and his heart sank. "Rockwall?"

"Yes, Rockwall."

Josh leaned against the table. He had lived in Rockwall until his adoption by Jonathan Steel. He had not been back since the encounter with the twelfth demon.

"Are you okay, my boy?" Caskey said.

Josh shook his head and tried to shrug it off. "Sorry. Jonathan was in prison in Rockwall. That's all." He clapped his hands and put on a false smile. No need to mention he used to live there. "Let' do this!"

Caskey placed his teacup on the table. "Don't get cocky, kid. Spend the next few hours in the presence of our Lord. What you are about to experience is nothing like you encounters with demons in the past. This encounter will be very personal." He looked away and a chill ran over Josh's spine. Personal? What did he mean? Did Caskey know he was from Rockwall? It didn't matter. All that matter was implementing his plan.

CHAPTER
TWENTY-ONE

Steel sat on his meager bed and waited. Neither Nanny nor Jeremiah had shown up to lock him in his room. Supper had not appeared. He hadn't eaten since breakfast time. His stomach growled and echoed in the silence. He waited some more. The green light with the woman's voice never came. Finally, he lay back on the bed and drifted off and awoke hours later with a jerk. Was it a dream? No, he had not dreamed. It was the fragrance of bacon and toast.

A tray of food sat on the floor inside the open door. He retrieved the tray and gobbled down the food, chasing it with acidic orange juice. Once finished, he changed clothes and stepped out into the hallway. Empty. Silent.

He returned to the Grimvox chamber and settled into his chair. Ila sat at the glowing device instead of Snake. A shadow passed over him and Jeremiah moved to his chair and sat.

"Why didn't you lock my door?" Steel said.

"I knew curiosity would keep you here." Jeremiah kept his gaze averted. Dark circles rimmed his eyes.

"More trouble sleeping?" Steel asked.

Jeremiah looked away. "Yes."

"It was hard seeing our mother, wasn't it?"

Jeremiah glanced at him and pulled the tablet from his coat pocket. His trembling finger hovered over the glowing window. "I ought to kill you now." He hissed.

"But you haven't done so," Steel said calmly pulling the metal disc from his pocket. "It's not on my chest anymore. Your tablet is useless." He tossed the disc on the table. It spun around a few times and finally fell flat. "You want my memories as much as I want yours."

Jeremiah licked his lips and his eyes glowed for a second with demonic power. "Put the tablet away, you fool!" His voice changed. His arms and hands stiffened in a battle of will and finally placed the tablet to the side. "We want his memories, remember?" He said to himself. His eyes faded to turquoise, and he slumped onto the table.

"Tough price to pay, brother?" Steel said.

Jeremiah lifted his head slowly and his eyes focused on Steel. "You called me brother."

"That's what we are, no matter how much either of us wants to admit it." Steel leaned forward and rested his arms on the table, one hand stretched toward the Grimvox. "You made the choice to consort with the second most powerful demon on the Council of Darkness. You're paying the price." He pointed one finger toward the Grimvox. "Before we sift through my memories, which are still a bit tumbled around in my head, let's review your memories. "

Jeremiah looked his way. "Why are you cooperating?"

"You give me no choice, brother. I might as well make the best of it. I want to understand you as much as you want my memories. Shall we begin?" He touched the Grimvox.

"My monkey has two heads." Jeremiah said. He held up the stuffed animal to Nanny.

Nanny towered over the four-year-old boy. "What have I told you about your animals?" She hissed.

"Nanny, I love my monkey." Jeremiah blinked away tears. "I don't want it to have a goat's head."

Nanny ripped the stuffed animal from the boy's hands. She grabbed one of the monkey heads and tore it away, hurling it across the room. Stuffing filled the air and Jeremiah sneezed. She handed the monkey back to Jeremiah.

"Now, I have shown you how to dismember your toys. And I have shown you how to mix and match different animal parts to make a chimera." She leaned over him and her black eyes glittered. "You want to know things, don't you?"

"Yes, Nanny." Jeremiah sniffed.

"Then stop crying, you little brat, and put the goat's head on your monkey. If you don't, I will put you in the cage again."

Jeremiah stepped back, his eyes wide in fear. "Please, Nanny. Not the cage."

"What is going on here?"

Nanny straightened and turned to face the man in the nursery doorway. "Mr. Lucas. I was just instructing the boy in the art of vivisection."

Lucas, his pale scalp glistening in the sunlight streaming in through the castle windows, moved gracefully across the room. Jeremiah stepped back, his eyes drawn to the tattoos visible on the man's neck just above his turtleneck collar. They moved!

Lucas' red eyes glittered with malice. "Nanny, your techniques are too harsh."

Nanny sniffed and crossed her arms over her chest. "I have carte blanche from Grandpoppa, Lucas. When the day comes, for the boy to receive his gift, you can take over. Until then, leave his education to me."

Lucas reached for the stuffed monkey and the tattoo of an insect writhed on his wrist. Jeremiah let the monkey go. He inspected the stuffed animal. "Your incisions are crooked, Jeremiah. And your sutures are spaced too far apart." Lucas glared at Nanny. "Perhaps Nanny needs lessons?"

Nanny's face paled, and she stepped back. "No! I will double my efforts. The boy will be ready. Now leave him to me."

Lucas thrust the monkey into her grasp. "Nine more years, Nanny. He must be ready." Lucas smiled at Jeremiah, running a very red tongue over his lips. "And you, Jeremiah, will one day have unsurpassable knowledge. One day, you will learn that knowledge is power." He turned and left the room.

CHAPTER

TWENTY-TWO

"My name is Jeremiah Stone." The boy said to his first-grade teacher.

Mrs. Sloan frowned as she towered over the boy's desk. Her gray hair was cut short around her lean face and her reading glasses hung around her neck on a golden chain. "I know your name, young man. You have a visitor in the principal's office."

Jeremiah studied the chain around Sloan's neck. If he grabbed it just right and twisted it, Mrs. Sloan would suffocate, and he wouldn't have to leave the classroom. His hands itched with the thought.

Mrs. Sloan looked away at the rest of the classroom. The other students were beginning to fidget. "I need to know your proper name before I can allow you to leave the classroom. It's standard procedure."

Jeremiah squirmed in his chair, his stomach suddenly uneasy. Was *she* here? He thought of the blood he had been made to drink for breakfast. "I don't want to see a visitor right now."

Mrs. Sloan motioned to the other woman in the room. "Fine! Teresa will take you to the office." She turned to her student teacher. "Make sure and ask for identification. I'm sure the office has already done so. But in view of past incidents, be sure."

Teresa was a short, plump woman with black hair pulled back in a ponytail. Her eyes filled with fear as she motioned to Jeremiah with a trembling hand. "Come along, Jeremiah."

Jeremiah stood up shakily and tried not to vomit. "I don't want to go." How he longed to grab the golden chain.

"You must." Mrs. Sloan said.

Teresa took his hand and pulled him toward the doorway. Jeremiah sighed. It was inevitable. If he didn't do as he was told, Teresa would suffer. Not that he minded. He just wanted to be the one to make her suffer. The fragrance of her fear was stronger than his own. He drew a deep breath as he walked ahead of Teresa toward the office. He had to marshal his strength and prepare his mind and soul for the encounter.

They entered the reception room of the school office, and she stood at the counter. She was remarkably short, but exuded a powerful sense of menace. Her gray hair was pulled back into a tight bun at the nape of her neck. She wore her usual dark gray skirt and matching jacket with a white ruffled blouse. She turned away from the counter and her blood red purse hung from her left elbow. Her intense gray eyes focused on him.

"Nanny." Jeremiah mumbled.

She pulled a clear plastic bag from her purse. It contained something cylindrical, hairy, and bloody. "What is this?" Her scratchy voice made him flinch.

Teresa gasped behind him. Jeremiah glanced over the counter, barely below the level of his eyesight at the secretary. Her face was pale and sweaty. Nanny had that effect on others.

"I don't know." Jeremiah managed.

Nanny gestured with her free hand toward Teresa, and she froze behind him. She motioned over her shoulder toward the secretary and she began to moan. Nanny had taken away their mouths.

"Do you want them to die?" Her eyes glowed with evil.

"I don't care." Jeremiah said fiercely. "I'm tired of you hurting others just to control me." He jerked the bag out of her bony hand and ripped it open. The contents hit the floor, spattering blood over Nanny's shoes. Bone and teeth shined through the hair from the head of chihuahua. The eyes were white in death and yet, the tongue began to move and it suddenly came to life. The jams locked on Nanny's black shoes.

Teresa tried to scream, but only a moan came from her closed mouth. The secretary fainted and fell out of her chair. Nanny gestured toward the inner door leading into the principal's office and it locked. Jeremiah could hear the pounding of the principal's fist on the door.

Nanny grabbed the dog's lean head by the jaws and clamped them shut. "Did you do this?"

Jeremiah lifted his jaws in defiance. "Yes."

Nanny's lips curled up, and she laughed. "I think not. Your supposed powers have not yet arrived or I would pass on my evil spirit to you. Only then would you inherit the power of the second demon, boy! I know who made this head animate and he will be punished."

Jeremiah chuckled. "Like you can punish Lucas."

"Lucas is meddling too much in your upbringing," Nanny hissed. She squeezed the dog's jaws, and the bone shattered, splattering blood and gore across Jeremiah's shirt. She stuffed the now motionless mass into the torn bag and tossed it into a nearby trashcan. "I told you not to kill another animal on my watch. It is messy and unnecessary. It is crude and pointless. It is the work of a future serial killer. You are above pointless violence." Nanny pulled a handkerchief from her purse. She wiped the blood from her hands. She gestured to Jeremiah's shirt, and the blood disappeared.

"I wanted to make it bark without the rest of the dog," Jeremiah said.

"Well, I have to give you credit for your response to me," Nanny said. "Now, come along. This will cost you three days in the cage."

Jeremiah's heart sank, but he hid his smile. He liked his time in the cage. Without the constant supervision of Dr. Santiago and his lab assistant, he could practice many skills. "Fine."

Nanny snapped her fingers, and Teresa slumped to the floor. "They will not remember what happened. I'll leave the dog's head in the trash for them to worry over."

Nanny grabbed his arm in a firm and painful grip and then they were no longer in the school, transported through the Void back toward the castle.

CHAPTER
TWENTY-THREE

Jeremiah stood next to the Bottomless Pit and waited for Sarah. Smoke and fire leapt from the depths of the pit. Most of the guests to the theme park would think the smoke and fire were clever effects. Jeremiah knew they were real.

He looked down Maimed Street toward the entrance to the park. When the Tragic Kingdom had opened, it had been a sensation. Jeremiah had been only two years old, but he had grown up in this theme park of the damned. Now, with attendance dwindling, the park would soon close after eleven years of operation. He saw Sarah as she separated herself from the crowd and ran to meet him.

Jeremiah's heart raced with anticipation. Oh, the things he longed to show Sarah! Maimed Street, the Hidden Kingdom, Dark Space! Just to name a few. Sarah's dark features glistened with a sheen of sweat. She had pulled her hair into multiple braids that projected from his head like the snakes of Medusa.

"Hey, Jeremiah." She gasped as she slid to a stop. "Thanks

for inviting me. I've been wanting to come here for ages, but my parents think this is all demonic."

"It is." Jeremiah said. Sarah laughed.

"Do you have a brother?" She said.

Jeremiah pushed away the thoughts of what he was about to do with Sarah and tilted his head. "No. Why do you ask?"

Sarah pointed to her phone. "We drove over to Disney World last week and I saw you there. I called out to you, but you looked right at me and acted like you didn't know me. I even took a selfie with you in the background. But it wasn't you. He had the same rad eyes, though."

Jeremiah took the phone from her hand and stared at the photo. Sarah's face filled half the image, and he zoomed in to the boy standing behind her. He could have been Jeremiah's twin. Reddish blonde hair. Turquoise eyes. Same body type. Both bordering on teenage years. Who was this? His stomach ached for a moment.

"I do not know who he is." He shoved the phone back into Sarah's hand.

"Great! What are we going to ride first?"

Jeremiah's thoughts were far away. He pointed to the "land" known as the Dark Space. "The asteroids."

The afternoon passed without incident. Jeremiah's plans for Sarah were gone in the face of the sudden revelation of this other person who looked alarmingly like him. After the fifth ride, he left Sarah in the girl's room and ran back to the castle. He took the side door accessible to staff and descended into the floor beneath known as the Dungeon. He could care less what Sarah would think now. He had to know about the other boy.

Jeremiah pushed his way through the workers moving in the tunnels beneath Maimed Street and the castle to his living quarters. He made his way down a narrow tunnel and took the small elevator at the back. He tapped his fingers impatiently as the elevator made its way to the upper floors of the castle. He stepped out of the elevator and into the foyer of his home. But, instead of moving into the living room, he took the secret doorway to his right into the laboratory.

Dr. Santiago oversaw the laboratory. It was here Jeremiah had learned to utilize the powers he possessed from his occasional demonic guest. Recently, he had been taken on some adventures with his demon. He moved through the counters filled with arcane instruments and he heard Santiago's deep tones in a heavy discussion with his assistant, Rhona Brack. Rhona was a small, hunched woman making her the caricature of the mad scientist's assistant. Jeremiah paused just out of sight and listened in on their conversation.

"When do we tell him?" Rhona said.

"When he turns thirteen, according to the boss." Santiago said.

"That only gives us two more days." Rhona said.

"He is ready. He's worked with five different demons and so far, he has controlled three. When he is ready, two will take up residence." Santiago said.

"But, will he manifest the gift when he turns thirteen?" Rhona said.

"His DNA will show if he does." Santiago said. "We will get a sample the minute he biologically turns thirteen. That is when he is supposed to change."

"And if he doesn't?" Rhona said.

"Don't even think that." Santiago said. "You know what the boss will do then? Start over. I performed the in vitro placement of the embryo and if he is not the one, the boss will find another surrogate." Santiago said.

"What about the other?"

Santiago cursed and slapped her across her face. She recoiled and simpered in misery. "Never mention him! If the boss hears you, he will gut you and skin you alive! The boy must never know."

Jeremiah peered through the eyes of an African mask hanging over the counter. Rhona straightened and leaned agains Santiago's desk. "I'm sorry. I have often heard there was another."

"I was there when he was born. Jeremiah is the only person who matters." Santiago straightened his lab coat and Rhona cringed. "Now go and prepare the chamber for day after tomorrow."

"What do you think?" A voice whispered in his ear. Jeremiah recognized the voice of his demon. It had returned.

"I don't know what to think." Jeremiah whispered. "Sarah said she saw someone who looks like me. And what is this talk of my DNA and the 'gift'? And there was another like me?"

The voice continued in his ear and he felt the demon move slowly into his mind. "Dr. Santiago hides many secrets even we are not aware of. Perhaps it is time for you to show them your 'gift'."

Jeremiah nodded in agreement. "They think I've been visited by three different demons. I haven't shown them many of my abilities just as you instructed. You will help me this time?"

"Of course." The voice whispered in his mind. "Both of them house minor demons. But I am more powerful. It will be a simple task to control them. Just think of what you would like for them to do to their hosts and I will make it happen."

Jeremiah held the mask against his face and stepped out from behind the counter. Rhona gasped at the sight of the African mask hovering in the air. She put a hand to her mouth. "He's here."

"I am here." Jeremiah said. "And I have a few questions."

He dropped the mask and reached toward her with his

right hand and made a fist. Rhona froze, paralyzed with fear. Santiago whirled and Jeremiah closed his other fist and thrust it at the man. He froze.

"Now, just a few questions and then we will have a party." Jeremiah said. "Who are my mother and father?"

Santiago tried to shake his head, his mouth wide open in shock. Drool ran down his chin and dripped on the floor.

"Silly of me." Jeremiah laughed and wiggled an index finger. Santiago's head jerked and twisted. "Now, you can talk."

"I can't tell you." Santiago whispered. "Nanny!"

"You think I have only meager abilities. What I am capable of doing is beyond your imagination. Your knowledge is limited by your pride." Jeremiah walked over and looked into the man's eyes. "Do not think that just because I am about to turn thirteen that I have the mind of a child? I have seen and experienced things no child has ever known, doctor. Some of those heinous acts were at your discretion, if you remember." Jeremiah glanced at Rhona. "And you helped."

"I can't tell you anything," Santiago said. "You have no idea what Nanny is capable of."

"You have made a fatal mistake thinking it matters to me what Nanny can do. She is a tool, a pawn. She is expendable. Now, my parents. Who were they? Was there another like me?"

Santiago shook his head. "I'd rather die than tell you anything."

"Your mother would have loved you." Rhona said. Jeremiah hurried to her side.

"You know who my mother is?"

"Rhona!" Santiago screamed. "Don't!"

"She is a kind woman."

"And taking care of my brother, right?" Jeremiah growled.

Rhona's face paled, and she shook her head. "I can't say any more."

Jeremiah looked back at Santiago. "My brother gets a normal family and I have to live in this hellhole? Why?"

"You are special, Jeremiah." Santiago said.

"Yes, I heard. On my thirteenth birthday, something happens. What?"

"You manifest." Rhona said.

"Manifest?" Jeremiah said.

"Stop!" Santiago shouted at Rhona.

"Why? He's going to kill us. He might as well know the truth." Rhona said.

"Jeremiah." Santiago said. "If you release me, I will show you. The program for the chamber is on that computer." He nodded toward the monitor screen on the nearby console. "I can show you what you can expect. On your birthday."

"It seems I'm manifesting right now."

"No! That is your demon. Not you." Santiago said.

Jeremiah squinted at him and gestured. Santiago slumped out of his paralysis and leaned over the keyboard. Suddenly, he lurched toward a nearby drawer, slid it open, and pulled out a pistol. He pointed it at Rhona, and before Jeremiah could react, pulled the trigger.

Blood spurted from Rhona's chest, and she collapsed. Jeremiah pointed at Santiago and he froze again. "Why did you do that?" He screamed.

"Death is better than what will happen if we tell you more." Santiago said. "I set off a silent alarm from the keyboard and security will be here momentarily." He smiled. "You can do your worst, but you can't subdue a dozen men. Now Nanny will reward me for silencing Rhona. I will be in her good graces, and you will be prepared for the chamber."

"It is time to go." The voice whispered in his head, "I can

help you find your brother. I can help you find the parents who abandoned you. But we must hurry. They are on their way."

Jeremiah glared at Santiago. "I already have a gift. It's called the second demon." Jeremiah walked slowly toward him. He gestured with his open hand. "Why wait until I'm thirteen?"

"No." Santiago said through rigid lips. "That is not the gift. You're supposed to have the third demon."

"It will have to do." Jeremiah stood inches from Santiago's face. He placed his hand on the man's chest. Santiago screamed in agony as an invisible vise closed around his heart.

"I have a brother. How?"

Santiago's face twisted in agony and Jeremiah released his grip. Santiago gasped for breath. "He was born first. He is nothing. You are the one. You have the gift."

"Where is he?"

Santiago shook his head. "I don't know."

Jeremiah nodded and motioned to Santiago's face. Blood poured from his nose. Crimson streams squirted from his ears. Jeremiah waved his hand toward the adjacent wall. The blood streamed through the air and formed letters on the wall. Santiago's eyes were growing dim. He moaned one last time and fell to the floor.

"You moved too quickly." The voice said.

Jeremiah stood over the man's lifeless body. "Nanny taught me much about death and torture and killing. But she never mentioned my brother. If I am to find him, then you will need to give me more instruction. And then I will find my brother."

He turned and walked out of the laboratory. The words on the wall ran with fresh blood: "I am on my own, Nanny. Don't come after me or you will die."

TWENTY-FOUR

"Are you going to take me back to Nanny?" Jeremiah ate another bite of his steak. "You're welcome to a bite of my steak. Very rare. The color matches your eyes."

Lucas Malson settled into a chair across the table from Jeremiah. "I'm very impressed, Jeremiah. You've been on your own for almost two years and you've managed to elude me."

Jeremiah chewed his steak and shrugged. "Easy when I've got a demon as my assistant."

"I'm sure it is the other way around." Lucas' red eyes glowed. "You are merely the host. A tool."

"As long as his interests align with mine, I get my way." Jeremiah drank some wine.

"You're too young to be drinking." Lucas said.

The server appeared at the table. "Would you like a menu, sir?" His eyes were wide and empty of life.

"Mind trick." Jeremiah chuckled. He motioned with his hand. "This is not the demon you're looking for."

"This is not the demon I'm looking for." The service said in a monotone.

"You will bring me more wine."

"I will bring you more wine." The server glanced at Jeremiah and forced a rigid smile. He walked away.

"One of the third demon's legion." Jeremiah finished the last bite of his steak. "Their minds are so weak."

Lucas placed a white hand on Jeremiah's hand. "Stop."

Jeremiah studied Lucas' hand and plunged his fork through the back of the hand. Lucas never flinched. Blood pooled around the fork tines and then disappeared.

"I heal very quickly." Lucas grabbed Jeremiah's hand and jerked the fork from his flesh. Jeremiah watched in amazement as the wounds closed and the blood disappeared. "You, on the other hand, are wasting your talents and skills."

Jeremiah jerked his hand from Lucas' grasp. "I was supposed to manifest, whatever that was supposed to be, when I turned thirteen."

"How would you know if you have any innate talents when you let the second demon do all your dirty work?" Lucas said. "He's using you, Jeremiah. You were intended for the third demon."

"Yeah, I know. Nanny told me. How is the old hag, by the way?" The servant appeared and poured more wine into Jeremiah's empty glass.

"Waiting patiently for me to find you. Along with the first demon. We have plans for you." Lucas said.

"How did you find me?" Jeremiah sipped more wine. For a moment, the reflection of his turquoise eyes stared back at him from the surface of the wine.

"You've been looking for your brother on the internet. We know where he is, and I have been tracking your tracking." Lucas said.

Jeremiah sniffed. "I thought I was being more careful."

"Jeremiah, just what are your long-term plans?" Lucas intertwined his long, white fingers.

"Find my brother." He pushed his plate away.

"And then, what?"

Jeremiah leaned over the table. "Kill him! Maybe! Probably! For abandoning me to you monsters."

Lucas sat very still, the visible tattoos at his neck and wrist suddenly still. "You cannot kill your brother. He is important to our long-term plans."

"Really?" Jeremiah's face warmed with anger. "Like me? Where did I fit in? What were you going to do with me when I didn't 'manifest'? Kill me?"

"This manifest event you refer to is very hypothetical. It may take longer to show up." Lucas said.

"And just what is going to manifest? Huh? Grow a new goat head or something? Turn into a vampire?"

"The circumstances of your manifestation are beyond my knowledge, Jeremiah. They are only known to the first demon." Lucas looked away and seemed deep in thought. "There is a possible trigger for your manifestation."

"And what is that?"

"Commit murder. Take another human's life." Lucas whispered.

Jeremiah sat back. "Is that all? Piece of cake."

"Not just any human, Jeremiah." Lucas' eyes fairly glowed with red fire. "It must be a parent."

Jeremiah froze, and his heart raced. "A parent? Like Nanny? Nothing would bring more pleasure."

"No, Jeremiah. Your mother or father." Lucas said quietly. "And you must do so before you turn sixteen."

Jeremiah studied the creature's red eyes and his pale skin.

Kill his mother or father? Could he do such a thing? "I don't know."

"The woman abandoned you to Nanny, Jeremiah. You could have had a loving father and mother, just like your brother. Instead, they gave you away to a fiend. Ask yourself why?"

"I have asked that question a thousand times." Jeremiah choked back emotion.

"I will let you know I was present on the day you and your brother were born. He came first and your mother claimed him as her own. You were an afterthought. She didn't even know she had a twin pregnancy. Imagine that! When you were born, she gave you immediately into the arms of Nanny. Told her to take you far away." Lucas leaned forward and his gaze burrowed into Jeremiah's skull. "Listen to that voice within. He knows. We all know the truth, Jeremiah. We see and hear everything. Your mother thought you were a product of a demonic gestation. She thought your brother was a natural conception."

"I don't understand." Jeremiah blinked away tears.

"I offered your father the bloodstone when your parents were trying to conceive. Place it nearby and a demon would enter your father and help foster conception. Imagine your mother's shock when she discovered there were two babies. One natural. The other unnatural."

Jeremiah's heart raced. "Am I? Unnatural?"

"Of course not." Lucas said. "Without your meddlesome second demon, you would be ordinary."

"Unless I manifest."

"Yes."

"And to do that, my mother must die at my hand?" Jeremiah whispered.

"Yes."

Jeremiah looked away. Across the restaurant, his server shook his head and looked around, free from influence. His power was waning. Why?

"Your server is free. You are growing weak."

"Why?" Jeremiah's thoughts were muddled.

"Because I found you and the second demon knows the best plan for you will be to kill your mother with the third demon's help."

"Third demon?"

"He is adept at despair and hopelessness. He thrives on death. You will learn much from him." Lucas smiled. "Power is something that has always eluded you. And now, your power is fading."

"Yes." Jeremiah felt the spirit fading. "I don't want to be alone. I want that power."

Lucas put a hand on Jeremiah's hand and the power seeped back in. "Power will be yours once you complete this mission, Jeremiah with the help of the third demon."

"How will I do this?" Jeremiah's resolve strengthened.

"You will have access to funds and people. I will find you a place to stay in Austin, Texas. There are mercenaries who will be at your disposal. Funds will be available. You must think through this carefully and plan your approach wisely. Your father will be out of the country most of the time, and your mother and brother will be vulnerable."

Could I do it? Jeremiah thought. Kill his own mother? What mother, a different voice hissed in the back of his mind. Slowly he felt his strength returning. Was this the third demon?

"Poor Jeremiah. Abandoned. Alone. Unloved." The voice droned in with unctuous tones. "What kind of mother leaves you in the hands of a monster like Lucas and Nanny? What kind of mother throws you to the wolves over your brother?"

Anger, unlike any he had ever felt, flooded his mind. His

heart raced and his breathing quickened. Yes, he could do this. He would take his time and plan this carefully. He looked up at Lucas and grinned. "If I kill my mother, can I frame my brother?"

A smile flickered on Lucas' lips, and he nodded. "Excellent plan."

TWENTY-FIVE

The images faded away, and Steel gasped for breath. He touched his chest where his heart raced and sweat soaked his clothes. He glared at Jeremiah. "You're a monster!"

"Surprised? You wanted to know my story." Jeremiah stood up and paced around the table, pausing behind Ila. "When you live with monsters, you become one. I never had our mother to take care of me. I had Nanny. And Lucas. Love was never an ingredient in my life." He took Ila's head in his hands, his wild eyes focused on the top of her head. "Instead, I learned how I could end a life with one swift twist of the head."

"Don't!" Steel stood up and put out his hand.

Jeremiah chuckled. "Of course I won't, brother. I need Ila to take care of the Grimvox. Just like I need Snake. My point is I could. Without hesitation. There is no moral imperative to stop me. I am free to do whatever I want."

Steel settled slowly back into his chair. "What about yesterday?"

Jeremiah blinked. "What?"

"When your true master took over. You're not free, Jeremiah. You've never been free. Can't you see the second demon has controlled you most of your life? He doesn't serve you! You serve him!" Steel shook his head. "You are far from free."

Jeremiah's eyes rolled back in his head and then down again. His eyes glowed with faint blue light to match the turquoise pigment of his irises. "Of course you are right, Jonathan Steel. Or JJ. Or, whatever your name is." He released Ila's head and leaned over and kissed her on the forehead. "Such sweet flesh. Oh, the things I have tasted."

He walked around the table toward Steel. "You know, we are noncorporeal beings in this realm. No body. No flesh. No senses." He squatted beside Steel and looked into his eyes. "To feel, JJ. To taste. To smell. These sensations are intoxicating. One reward of possession."

Jeremiah moved to his chair and sat. He reached toward the Grimvox. "I'll share a memory with you, JJ. Just touch the Grimvox."

"I don't want to."

Jeremiah's eyes glowed. "Yes, you do. You want to know more about me. Knowledge is my specialty." He touched the Grimvox. "The more you know about me, the more power you think you have over me, right?"

Steel calmed his racing heart. The creature was right. He had to know more. He touched the Grimvox.

"Noah, my friend, you have lost your mind." The giant said.

Noah glanced at the Nephilite. "I am not your friend, Golim. I have much to do before the Lord God sends a flood to destroy all of mankind."

Golim sat on the bench beside the hulking expanse of Noah's folly. The bench sagged beneath his weight. "Look around you, Noah. This valley is rich with life. We are flourishing. There is not enough water to cover this valley in a flood."

Noah continued filling the cracks between the beams with pitch. "Nothing is impossible for God, Golim." He dropped his brush in the bucket and wiped the pitch from his cheek. His long, white hair hung in sweaty strands over his shoulders. "I am 600 years old, Golim and a man of my age should never be able to build such a boat."

"A man of your age should be senile. Crazy?" Golim laughed and his deep voice echoed through the valley.

Noah sat beside him on the bench. "Look around you, Golim. There is nothing but evil. Our advanced age has allowed evil to grow and fester. You are an example of that."

Golim pointed a meaty finger at his enormous chest. "Me?"

"Yes, you. Offspring of a fallen angel and a human woman. I know a foul spirit inhabits your soul. What is your true name?"

Golim's black eyes focused on Noah. "Very well, old man. I have many names, but you can call me Abylon. We have taken control of the Creator's world. We are in control of this power and principality."

"And you seek to destroy what God has made."

Golim laughed. "I think it is the Creator who has decided to destroy his creation."

"Thanks to you and your evil kin." Noah stood up and spat in the dirt. "What have you given us?"

Golim stood up and motioned to the city in the valley. "Knowledge, Noah. Mankind has built a glowing city. Progress has occurred. Soon, we will spread beyond this valley to the rest of the world."

"And that is the problem." Noah pointed a finger at Golim. "The Lord God Jehovah commanded us to subdue and fill the earth. But your kind have tempted us to stay here in a cloistered *valley trying to recover the Garden of Eden. We were cast out of the garden because of our rebellion against God. We will not inherit that place again as long as Satan and his evil spawn continue to possess mankind. Yes, God has chosen to wipe out humanity, but he will preserve a remnant in my offspring. As for me and my household, we serve God and not Satan."*

Golim shook his head and laughed. "You are so deceived, Noah. This flood you predict will not kill all of humanity. There will be some who survive, thanks to the knowledge I have given them."

Noah stepped around the colossal figure. "You will see, Golim. With God, all things are possible. He does not have to cover the entire world in water, just the land occupied by man. And even if He desired, He could cover the entire world with water to the mountain tops. It does not matter that it cannot be done. With God, it will be done, and you and your arcane knowledge will be of no use when it happens."

Golim picked up Noah by the nap of neck and dangled him in the air. "You self righteous idiot! Let your God try and kill us! Let him send you on a fool's mission. You will see."

"Put me down! In the name of Jehovah God I rebuke you!" Noah growled.

Golim dropped him and blew on his hands. "Hot!"

"Even now, God has told me to go into the ark with all my family and the animals we will need to rebuild our community. Even now, my sons have finished that task and the final cracks have been pitched. Even now, the rain comes, Golim."

A drop of rain hit Golim in the forehead and he looked upward. Lightning lit up the sky and the thunder echoed through the valley.

"It will never happen." Golim said. "We will be waiting for you when this pitiful rain stops and you come out of your ark. We will show you who is master of this world."

"No, Golim or Abylon. God will be victorious. All your knowledge will not save you. For you have forgotten one thing. Knowledge is useless without wisdom. And a fallen angel has no wisdom or you would not be fallen."

More thunder rattled the walls of the ark and the rain fell harder. "Now, if you will excuse me, I will seal myself into my folly, as you call it, and I beg your human host to make peace with God before he drowns."

Golim looked down and water had already reached his ankles. He watched Noah climb up a rope ladder to the top of the ark. "Fine, Noah. If you survive, my kind will be waiting. This battle is over but the war is eternal." Inside Golim's mind, the human began to panic and scream in fear as Abylon sloshed through the water back toward the village.

"Shut up, human. Your torment is only beginning."

Steel gasped as the memory released him. "You failed."

Jeremiah leaned away from the Grimvox. "Did I? How many souls were harvested that day for the master? Imagine their sense of loss, of defeat as the waters rose. Imagine the shock and surprise when we left their bodies and minds to drown." Waves of evil washed over Steel from the thing inside Jeremiah. "I knew number three very well. Want to know what he enjoyed most while he possessed you?"

Steel stayed still, not daring to move. When he was a teenager, the third demon had possessed him and made him think he had killed his mother. He refused to give in to the creature's taunting. "I don't care."

"Oh, but you should. It was the pain of separation from your father. How desperately you yearned for his approval. And love. That deep-seated emotion of depression and loneliness was number three's addiction. It's why he focused on depression and despair for his victims. The ultimate high for him was total self destruction."

Steel swallowed hard and focused on the thing's eyes. "Why are you telling me this?"

"Things will not end well for you or your family. Matters are coming to a close. Your brother has no idea what I'm telling you now. I will see to his ultimate destruction and his journey into eternal pain and suffering. He is as doomed as the chattel of Noah's day. You can shorten his suffering, you know. All I need is a memory."

"Of what?"

"Oh, no. I'm not going to reveal that to you. Then you would hide it." He stood up. "You are still assimilating your recovered memories and with all you have been through, you would have no problem hiding it. No, if you want matters to come to close more quickly, then we need to get to your memories, not Jeremiah's."

The door behind Steel slid open. "But enough for now. Go to your room and rest and be prepared to share your past." Jeremiah disappeared down the long hallway behind him. Steel stood up shakily. Nanny appeared from the shadows, rolling the wheelchair with Snake.

Snake's head lolled helplessly on her neck, and Nanny made the exchange with Ila without making eye contact with Steel. Once Snake was back in place, Nanny rolled Ila away into shadows. Steel moved around the table and squatted beside Snake.

"I hope you can hear me. I see signs you are not totally under the control of the Grimvox. Fight it. Fight it for both of us."

Snake flinched, and for a second, her eyes focused on the table and not the Grimvox. She tried to turn her head, but the effort made her tremble. The effort failed and her gaze once again locked onto the light cascading from the opening of the Grimvox. Steel almost gazed into those depths, and he was somewhere else.

Snake wandered down a long, dark corridor. Ahead, a tiny, blue light pulsed in the darkness. Around her, the walls of her corridor were pebbly and dark green, like the skin of a dying reptile.

"Thanks for remembering me." A voice echoed from ahead. She hurried toward the voice. Who was it?

"Who are you?"

"You know me." Clearer now. The voice of a teenager.

The blue light intensified, drowning out the dark, pebbly surface around her. She moved into the light and stepped into a small room with a window looking out over snow-capped mountains. Moonlight reflected off the snow, poured through the window like a spotlight. Posters of skiers and photographs of soccer players covered the walls of his bedroom. To her left rumpled covers piled on a small bed. A young man sat on the bed reading a colored brochure. He looked up at her and the wan moonlight lit up his face.

"Pablo?" she gasped.

"Yes. You remembered me." He said. He held up the paper. "My dad wanted to ski the Alps. Here's the map of the ski resort." He held up the map, and she looked out the window at the snowy Alps.

"But you didn't make it, did you?" She said hoarsely.

"No. Our airplane crashed, and I woke up in the arms of Jesus." Pablo smiled and folded the map. "The mountains here are so much more beautiful than the Alps. And I've been skiing every day. I don't even fall."

Tears clouded Snake's eyes, and she wiped them away only then realizing the arm given to her by Jeremiah was missing. Pablo studied her arm.

"In heaven, you'll get your arm back. Don't you want to come to heaven?"

"I am the reason your airplane crashed. I am the reason you died."

"I know. You reached out to remember me and an angel let this happen so I could tell you I forgive you. That's what Daddy showed us. Forgiveness."

"Your Daddy is here?"

"Yes. But, I'm talking about Jesus. I call him Daddy. He's the ultimate Daddy." He tossed aside the map. "So, I'm supposed to ask you. What do you want to do?"

She wiped tears from her eyes and settled onto the bed beside him. "What do you mean?"

"You know. Stay here or go back. It's up to you. Staying here is great. Greater than great. Cooler than cool. Don't get me wrong. It would have been nice to grow up and all that. But when you look at it from here, I think I can live with eternity. It's awesome!"

Snake drew a deep breath and looked out the window at the distant glittering snow-capped mountains. "Why would I go back?"

"To help Jonathan."

She glanced at him and sighed. "Jonathan. Yes. That would be a good reason, wouldn't there?"

"His guardian angels told me you can still help him. Hey, you might find a way to forgive yourself. You know, Daddy has already forgiven you."

Snaked gasped and stifled a sob. "I guess I need to go back, then." It was then she noticed something under the skin of her good hand. She squinted as tiny, bright green particles swirled beneath her skin. The particles surfaced and drew stronger than receded and disappeared. What were these things? She gasped. Nannomemes! Max had laced her tea with Nannomemes to control her. Boone had designed them to erase memory. She had no idea what Max might have modified them to do. But they were there. For some reason, they were there.

Pablo picked up the ski resort map and tore away a photo of the mountain. He picked up a pen and wrote something on the back of the photograph. He handed it to her. "Put that in your pocket so you will remember me some more. I know it was hard to think about me, but it made a difference. To me. And all of us." He stood up and gestured behind him. Dozens of people appeared behind his now transparent wall. She recognized each face, each loss, each missing person from the flight. Their faces were no longer nameless and unimportant. She pointed to them one by one and said their names.

STEEL FELL BACK onto the floor, his head throbbing. His eyes finally focused on the back of Snake's head. Maybe she wasn't totally lost after all. More reason to stay. Shakily, he rose to his feet and, leaving her behind, made his way to his room.

TWENTY-SIX

Steel sat in his usual seat at the table. He had slept poorly through the night with disturbing dreams of things floating through the Void. No visitation from the woman in the green mist.

"I guess you really hate me now." Jeremiah said as he entered the chamber. He paused behind Snake and ran a hand through her wild red hair. "Snake seems to be holding up remarkably well. Ila, on the other hand, is failing, Jonathan. She lacks Snake's stamina. I'm afraid if we don't get on with exploring your memories, Ila will perish much sooner than expected."

Steel stared at his brother. "Fine, I want to know how you found me after you ran away."

Jeremiah leaned over and kissed Snake on the forehead. For a moment, her gaze shifted from the Grimvox to Steel and then back. Jeremiah did not seem to notice. "It didn't take me long, brother." Jeremiah sat in his chair. His turquoise eyes glittered with evil. The second demon returned.

"I used the demon network to locate your father. The

Captain traveled to South America quite a bit. Turns out you and your mother lived in that weird mansion with servants. Travel documents for international visits listed your father's home address. With the resources supplied by Lucas, Jeremiah was able to move into an apartment in Austin and begin surveillance of your mother."

"I'd rather hear it from my brother, not you." Steel hissed.

"Ah, hate the demon, not the host? Doesn't work that way. Sin is sin, JJ. Our sin is unforgivable and eternal. Jeremiah's is not as permanent. But don't worry. He will never turn to your side. I guarantee it. The longer they remain in our grasp, the further they move away from the influence of the creator. There is a line, JJ. Cross that line, and your master gives them over to our influence. It is a point of no return."

"The unforgivable sin," Steel said. "Yes, I'm familiar with it. Vivian tempted Josh with that fearful possibility." Steel leaned forward and smiled. "She failed. So will you."

Jeremiah raised an eyebrow. "Interesting. You seem to be growing soft on your hatred of your brother."

"And if I do, you lose influence over me. So whatever it is you have planned, get on with it. Right now, I am here voluntarily."

The light faded from Jeremiah's eyes, and he blinked. "Well, that was fascinating, brother. Kindling some kind of affection for me? We can end that pretty quickly. All I have to do is show you the memory of our mother's death."

"Wait!" Steel held up a hand. "I have a few questions."

Jeremiah leaned back in his chair and crossed his arms. "Okay. I'll bite."

"When I was a teenager, I found our grandfather's photo album in the garage. That is when things went south for me."

"Ah, the album." Jeremiah smiled. "I made sure you found

it. Sent one of the third demon's Legion demons into the album to tempt you."

"So a demon influenced me when I had those blackout episodes?"

"Oh, yes." Jeremiah sat forward and giggled. "It was so much fun pretending to be you. Getting into fights for which you would be blamed. Acting out to tarnish your reputation." He held up a finger. "And to convince everyone, including you, that you were losing your mind. That's one of the third demon's specialities."

"You didn't convince mother." Steel hissed. "She always believed in me."

Jeremiah frowned and looked away. "That was why I had to send that little mixen into your path."

"Mercedes?" Steel hissed. He had been only fifteen when he met Mercedes at a youth function. But they had not stayed and had driven away. "I don't recall anything that happened with Mercedes. I woke up in the car afterwards and threw the photo album off into the woods. Did you and Mercedes?"

"Oh, no, brother. That was all you. You gave into the temptation fully, JJ. However, I found the photo album and brought it back to Uncle Hampton. Here, let me remind you." Jeremiah touched the Grimvox and even though Steel's hands were clasped before him and he never moved to touch the thing, he was swallowed by a memory of the encounter with his father in the library when he was a teenager.

TWENTY-SEVEN

"Sit down." The Captain said as he took off his hat and hung it on a brass hat rack. His short reddish blonde hair was cut in a fierce crew cut. Spikes of gray glistened in his hair as he ran a hand through it. The Captain wore a white button-down shirt and dark pants. He paced in front of the fireplace and pulled his meerschaum pipe out of a pants pocket. He stopped in front of a humidor on the mantle and scooped tobacco into the pipe. He lit the pipe and puffed on it, expelling huge clouds of smoke into the chilly air.

"I suppose you've already heard the test results?" He glared. JJ squirmed on the couch and averted his eyes. "Mother told me. Everything was normal."

"Yes, normal. I've already chastised your mother about withholding this information from me." His father paced again. "Anything peculiar about your behavior is of utmost importance."

JJ looked up. "Why?"

The Captain paused and glared at him. "That doesn't concern you."

"Of course it concerns me!" Anger boiled up within him and he clenched his fists. "Why won't anyone just tell me what is going on with me? All these unanswered questions. All this subterfuge and mystery."

The Captain stopped and raised an eyebrow as he puffed on his pipe. "Good. You're angry. And, you haven't passed out. Yet."

"What is that supposed to mean?" He stood up.

"What do you think is happening to you?"

JJ drew a deep breath and walked across the room to the door. "That is happening to me. Grandfather went mad. He killed someone behind that door. Am I going crazy? Will I kill someone?"

The Captain stood silently on the other side of the room, pipe smoke drifting away toward the far ceiling. He blew a cloud of smoke and walked across the room. He placed a hand on the boy's shoulder.

"What happened in that chamber is of no concern to you. The lives that were taken that night were because of his poor choices. He was not insane. He was merely evil."

JJ slowly pulled away from his father's grasp. "But the stories of his ravings and his tantrums."

"All true. Of course, today he would have probably been diagnosed with multiple personality disorder. One moment, he was a loving, caring man. The next, he was a demon in flesh. Sometimes, he seemed to be speaking with another man's voice." The Captain turned away and walked back to the fireplace. "Or it could all have been an elaborate ruse?"

JJ studied the black door and shivered. "Multiple personalities? Father, what if that is what is wrong with me? What if, when I black out, I take on another personality?"

The Captain whirled around and his eyes danced with fire.

"Don't say that! You are who you are and no one else! Do you understand?"

JJ blinked. "But?"

The Captain raced across the room and grabbed his son with an iron grip, both hands squeezing his upper arms. "Listen to me, boy. You are who you are. You are a good person. You have your mother in you, not me. Not your grandfather, do you understand?"

JJ grimaced in pain under his father's grasp. "Father, you're hurting me."

The Captain's gaze broke, and he released him. "I'm sorry. You're just tired. Too much studying and too much stress at that school. Next year, you'll go away to a boarding school. There won't be any bullies or any thugs to threaten you. You are a good boy, understand? A good boy!"

JJ shook his head in confusion. "Go away? I don't want to go away."

The Captain's face stiffened, and he straightened. He walked over to the fireplace and tapped the spent tobacco out of his pipe. He tucked it into his pants pocket. "You don't have any choice. I've allowed your mother to be the dominant influence in your life. I wanted you to make the right choices. But now you must become a man and stand on your own two feet. I realize I have made a mistake not being more of an influence in your life. I know you will miss your mother, but there will be no discussion on this matter. You have two weeks of school left and then we will start looking for a prep school somewhere on the Eastern seaboard."

The Captain never turned around and walked over to the library doors. He opened them and motioned outside. "You may leave now."

JJ wanted to protest, to cry out in anger and frustration. He wanted to unleash the angry being within when he had the photograph album. Ah, the album! "I need to tell you something," JJ said.

The Captain's eyes filled with fiery anger. "I told you to leave."

"I found grandfather's journal."

The Captain froze, and for a second fear crossed his features. "Where is it?" He hissed.

"I threw it away. Into the woods behind the church. There was something in that journal. Something, I don't know, evil. Was it the spirit of grandfather?"

The Captain hurried across the room and looked into JJ's eyes. "You know where it is? Then, come on. We must get that journal back. How long ago was it?"

Something about the Captain's manner was deeply troubling. The man was scared, desperate. "Several weeks."

A servant appeared at the door. The Captain flinched at his arrival. "What is it, Hobbs?"

"You have a visitor and he insisted on meeting you, ahem, in the library."

The Captain's eyes blazed with anger. "Did you let him in the house?"

"Come, come, my good friend." A voice echoed in the hallway outside the library. "Since when am I not allowed to visit my own home?"

A man stepped into view, short and with a receding hairline. He was stocky and wore an outdated bowler hat. He carried a wrapped package beneath his arm. The Captain gasped and stepped back. "Nigel?"

The man must have been in his late sixties, and he glanced at the boy. "Your son, I presume. I believe he lost something. A stranger who noticed my name on the back cover found it and he contacted me.

Nigel moved past the Captain, who was paralyzed with

confusion and, yes, fear. Nigel placed the package on a table and tore at the wrapping. He motioned to the travel journal. "Young man, you really should take better care of family heirlooms."

"Who are you?" JJ asked.

"I am Dr. Nigel Hampton. I was your grandfather's benefactor and traveling companion. He allowed me to collect artifacts from all over the world." Dr. Hampton stepped closer to the boy and his pale blue eyes bored into the boy's eyes. "You are very special, JJ. Your grandfather left this journal for you." He glanced at the Captain. "And you alone! Please take better care of it."

"I didn't see your photo in the journal." JJ said.

"My dear boy, I was the photographer." Hampton smiled.

"The camera is not kind to my portly figure."

JJ glanced at his father, whose mouth was open and whose eyes were frozen in fear and indecision. Hampton but a hand on the Captain's shoulder. "Why haven't you told the boy about our special relationship, eh?" Hampton turned back to JJ. "I'm your grandfather's brother. I built this house along with your grandfather. These are my artifacts I have allowed to stay here in the states. I take it from my accent you have deduced I am not from the continent. I have put together a museum to display these artifacts. I could use an excellent assistant, JJ. You could come live with me in London." He glanced at the Captain. "Instead of a boarding school."

How had he known about the boarding school? Hampton smiled and tapped his bowler. "I will leave now. I think your father has a lot of explaining to do." He turned to the journal and tapped it with a finger. "Don't let this out of your sight, my boy. It will change your future for the better."

As the man let himself out of the library, passing the motionless and speechless Captain, JJ felt an unmistakable, yet familiar wave of evil pour out of the journal and over his mind and soul. A voice whispered in the back of his head.

"I'm back!"

~

Steel was back in the chamber. "How did you trigger that memory without my touching the Grimvox?"

"You wanted to share it, evidently." Jeremiah grinned.

Steel's heart raced. Could Jeremiah now access any of his memories without his touching the Grimvox? The thought was troublesome. He couldn't hide anything from his brother. "So, I am truly at your mercy."

"You always have been, JJ. Now, as to great uncle Nigel, you've had some experience with him."

"He's a Vitreomancer."

"I know. Sort of a double agent, if you will. I assure you his interests do not go beyond what benefits him the most. He will betray the Vitreomancers in a heartbeat if it benefits him. He brought the journal back to you and that set the stage for your fall."

"And so you began the setup for me to take the blame for our mother's death?" Steel said.

"Yes." Jeremiah looked away. "Time is growing short, JJ. I could share more memories with you. Suffice it to say, after the trial, I traded the second demon for the third demon in my plan to incriminate you. Once the trial was over, the third demon went wandering again. Legion is his name after all and the second demon came back home. I began my hunt for you and father. I had resources, thanks to Lucas." His gaze shifted back to Steel. "But the two of you were very clever. You had help from Yvonne, Sam, and Daniel. It wasn't until I saw you on the news from Switzerland I realized you were right in front of me the entire time. How did you stay so protected?"

"That's where my memories come in, isn't it?" Steel said. Daniel? Had Jeremiah referred to Daniel Brown, the man who had tortured him?

Jeremiah stiffened and the second demon returned. "Yes. Let's start with the day you tried to kill me right after the trial." Jeremiah reached for the Grimvox. "I can pull those memories if I want to, JJ. I have the power now that your brain has become attuned to the Grimvox." His turquoise eyes suddenly gleamed with evil light. "Let me show you, JJ." The voice of the second demon came from Jeremiah's lips. "Let me show you how easily I can influence even those most devoted to your creator. Here's one of my favorite memories."

Jerusalem

"I just don't understand, Japheth." Judas Iscariot drank more wine from his flagon. "I mean, here we are in Jerusalem for the Passover and he has the perfect opportunity to proclaim he is the Messiah! The people welcomed him with palm branches. He has an army at his disposal."

Japheth sat back in his chair and glanced around the inn. "My friend, you should be careful with your voice. There are not only Roman soldiers nearby, but Herod's guards as well. Remember what happened to Theudas? I should know. I was one of his lieutenants."

"And why did you not perish with the others? How many were killed? Four hundred?"

Japheth frowned. "There were some of us who escaped, Judas.

And, speaking of Judas, remember the man who came after Theudas?"

"Though he shared my name, he did not share my wisdom, Japheth. Are you telling me you joined his movement, too? If so, why didn't you die with his followers?"

"I tried to join them. I spoke with Judas and warned him about what could happen. He did not listen to the knowledge I shared with him. His followers were scattered after he was killed."

"But Jesus of Nazareth has performed miracles! He brought Lazarus back from the dead! I have watched him heal hundreds! He is not Theudas or Judas. He is the Messiah, Japheth."

"Judas, I have taught you many things when we once worked together. Surely, the knowledge I have given to you is worthy of our friendship. And so, I tell you, if you want your mentor, your leader, to become the Messiah, then he must do so unwillingly."

"Unwillingly?" Judas whispered and glanced around at the inn. A Roman soldier stood just inside the door and his dark eyes focused on Judas for only a moment before roving around the room. Two of Herod's guards sat at a table drinking and laughing with a woman, no doubt, of ill repute. Judas felt his heart swell in fear. "What are you suggesting?

"If your master is truly capable of these feats of magic, then if he were to be arrested, he would call down an army of angels to his defense." Japheth said quietly.

Judas swallowed more wine, building up his confidence. Could such a plan work? He looked at Japheth and for a moment, something dark and foreign filled the man's eyes and then was gone. Judas was not a stranger to the evil spirits his Master had cast out. He tried to clear his mind and feel with his spirit. Was his old friend evil? He looked away and let the possibilities play across his mind. Evil or not, the plan had merit. If Jesus of Nazareth were arrested, then his followers would rise up. The very people who had welcomed him into Jerusalem would become an unstoppable army!

"Yes!" Japheth said.

Judas jerked and glanced at the man. "What did you say?"

"I see the wheels are turning in your mind, Judas. The plan is coming together, is it not? Betray your Master to the Jewish authorities who are poised to kill him, and your Messiah will proclaim himself to the world. Is it not the very plan your master has in mind? You are merely helping him." Japheth leaned forward. "In fact, if your master is the Messiah, then this very idea may have been planted in your mind by supernatural forces. Your plan is the Creator's plan, Judas! What you will do is nothing more than fulfilling the plan of the Creator and his Messiah."

Judas swallowed hard. Could that be true? "I am not so sure." He whispered.

"Judas, you have been this group's treasurer. Have you been paid for your services? How often have you had to beg the group to be wise with the finances? Your job is not to count coins. You are here for one specific purpose. You can count the cost and you know the inevitable sum of that cost is your destiny. After all, with the knowledge you have of your master's movements, you can easily set up a time when he can be arrested before the Passover. His trial will become a spectacle. What do you think he will do then? Willingly die? I think not! If he is the Messiah and all knowledge points to that inevitability, then you are the person of history who will push him onto his throne." Japheth suddenly stiffened and sat back. His face contorted and, for a moment, sadness covered his features.

"No, Judas. Do not do this." His voice was different, pleading, strained. Then his facial muscles tightened, and Japheth shook his head. "Sorry for that. Perhaps it was my conscience speaking. Do not listen to my conscience, Judas. Listen to destiny."

Judas nodded and took one more swig from the flagon of wine. "Perhaps if I approach the Sanhedrin, they will agree to arrest

Jesus of Nazareth and not condemn him to death. The point is to bring about a trial in which the truth of his nature will come out."

"Yes!" Japheth's face contorted again, and he looked away. "You chose me, you pig!"

"What did you say?"

Japheth looked back at him and wiped sweat from his face. "Nothing. I was just thinking out loud. A trial would be a perfect public stage for your Messiah to proclaim himself." Japheth leaned toward him and his black eyes glittered. "And if you ask, I would imagine they would offer a fee for your services. You could fill your money bag. You would have funds to build this army of yours."

Judas blinked as he listened to the soothing, hypnotic voice. "Yes. I will think about this."

Japheth nodded and paused for a moment, as if listening to a faraway voice. He smiled. "Judas, when the time comes, you will find the strength to do this. Go now and make your plans. My spirit will be with you."

Judas hefted the money bag from the table and listened to the coins clink. There had been a time when the bag had been full. Perhaps it was time to fill it again!

STEEL BLINKED, and he was back in the chamber. The transition to the demon's memory had been seamless. And very disturbing. He realized Jeremiah could pluck any memory he wanted to from his mind. The light went out in Jeremiah's eyes and he looked around the chamber.

"Well, that was interesting." He said hoarsely. "Now, JJ, with no further delay, let's recall what happened to you the day you tried to kill me."

CHAPTER

TWENTY-EIGHT

The bailiff led me down the hallway to my holding cell. He locked me in and disappeared. My head ached with pain from the presence of the third demon. Before the demon had left me in a state of forgetfulness. The episodes in which he had used me to perform his evil deeds were lost to me. But this time, I recalled every moment of what just happened in the courtroom.

I had a brother? An evil creature who had killed our mother? My anger boiled and fury took me. I turned and pounded my hand against the cinderblock wall of the cell. I welcomed the pain. It helped me clear my mind. I would find my brother and I would kill him! If I was to face a murder trail it would be for a good reason.

"Son?"

I whirled. My father stood outside the cell door. The bailiff accompanied him and unlocked the door. He had a pile of clothing and a bag of my personal belongings.

"The judge has dismissed your case. Get out of those prison clothes. We're leaving."

I grabbed the jeans and the tank top from the bailiff and stripped down to my underwear. My father glared at the bailiff. "You were supposed to take him to Kevin, JJ's youth pastor."

"The Judge gave me other instructions." The bailiff said.

"Never trust a demon." My father said.

"When were you going to tell me?" I growled.

"I did not know. Honestly, son."

I pulled my clothes on and took my possession bag and removed my watch, my socks, my sandals, my wallet and my car keys. They were all crusted with rusty particles. It was only then I noticed the hard, dry clotted blood soaked into my clothes. I pulled my tank top away from my chest. "This is her blood, Dad! Hers! He killed her and yet you say you never knew he existed?"

My father motioned down the hall. "Not here. I've asked someone to meet us outside. I'll tell you more as we walk."

I followed my father down the hallway. But instead of taking me out the main entrance, he motioned to a service exit. "We're keeping a low profile. Your brother is very dangerous. Someone was supposed to have come and gotten you."

"Who?"

"Kevin."

"What is going on?" I stopped at the exit door. "Tell me now."

"We did not know your mother was having twins. Dr. Santiago hid that fact from us. You were born and there were no problems. Then your mother started having more pains and your brother was born. But he stopped breathing. Dr. Santiago took the body, and I never told your mother. As far as she knew, you were her only child. She almost died from bleeding, JJ. I never thought that your brother was alive."

"Who was Dr. Santiago?"

Something dark and foreboding crossed my father's turquoise eyes. "I never saw him again. I tried to track him down. He just disappeared. Now we know why. The demons orchestrated the entire incident."

"What?"

My father wiped his face and sighed. "We couldn't get pregnant. Your mother underwent embryo implantation. Two of them. Santiago always told us only one embryo survived. Now we know he lied."

The door opened suddenly, and a hand grabbed my arm and jerked me out into the shadows of an alleyway. The door slammed shut on my father.

"Listening to father's lies?" I looked into eyes that were turquoise and fiery. I looked at the ginger hair, the regal face. Dark circles rimmed my brother's eyes.

"You!" I hurtled into him, driving him back against the brick wall. He laughed as I pounded his head against the wall. He head butted me and I fell back onto the ground.

I was dizzy for a moment and Jeremiah leaned over me. He drew back his fist and pounded my face. Over and over until I felt the blood run down my throat. I had to fight back. This was the thing that had killed my mother!

I kicked his feet from under him and he fell on top of me, knocking the breath out of both of us. I crawled from underneath him gasping for breath and kicked him in the face for good measure. He grabbed my ankle and pulled me back toward him.

"I'm sick and tired." He gasped. "Of hiding because of you!"

I rolled over onto my back and tried to kick him in the face again. He dodged and caught my free foot and pulled himself on top of my legs. Blood dripped from his nose and his eyes were blood shot. "Where do you think you're going to go?" He said.

"Wherever I want after I kill you!" I finally had enough breath to scream.

Jeremiah crawled up my body, pushing me underneath him until his face was above mine. "I knew you had it in you. It took a while to get up the courage. I had help from our demon. Yes, the one we shared." His eyes were bright with insanity. "I videotaped the whole thing. I watch it every day to give me strength. I watch it to remind me what our father took me from. I never had a mother like you did. And if I couldn't have her, neither could you. She abandoned me and kept you! And after I take care of you, I will go after Father!"

"Go ahead." I spit in his face. "You'll have to wait in line for him." I shoved my knee into his groin, and he groaned and rolled away. Stumbling to my feet, I wiped blood from my face. Jeremiah rolled in pain on the pavement. One kick and I could cave his face in!

"JJ! Stop!"

I froze with my foot drawn back and glanced up at Kevin hurrying toward me.

"What are you doing here? Go away. I have to finish this."

Jeremiah gagged and then giggled and slid up against a wall. "Don't listen to him! Go ahead. Pound my head in! Slam my skull against the brick wall! Finish what you started."

"JJ, don't let his evil taint you any longer. That's not your brother talking. That is an evil spirit." Kevin said.

I looked at Jeremiah, my heart pounding. I wanted this. I wanted to end this creature who had taken my mother from me. "Kevin, go away!"

Kevin drew closer and for a moment I saw fear in Jeremiah's eyes. I blinked. What? Why was he afraid of Kevin?

"JJ, Yvonne called me. She asked me to come get you and take you to my church. Your father wanted me to talk to you about your spiritual condition."

I froze and shook my head. "My father did that?"

"Don't listen to him, JJ." Jeremiah said.

"Shut up you spawn of hell." Kevin said in a thundering voice. "Or I will send you back into a herd of pigs."

Jeremiah scooted away from Kevin. He licked his lips, and I saw him for what he was. A meat puppet. A pawn in the hands of an evil power that had destroyed my mother and ruined my life. I relaxed my clenched fists and lowered my foot. He slid away from Kevin, keeping his back against the wall.

I knelt in a pool of blood. Our blood. My head pounded and painful spasms racked my body. The pain cleared, and the fury and the violence slowly faded. Kevin squatted before me. He glanced once more at Jeremiah, slowly moving down the alleyway. The righteous anger gleaming in Kevin's eyes should have made the third demon tremble. Then he turned those eyes on me and they were filled with a brotherly, divine love as deep as the sea.

"Hey, man, I've come to get you. You need to come on home. Your friends and family love you. It's time to walk away from all of this. Would you like for me to help you?"

Down the alley Jeremiah glanced once over his shoulder and the look of utter defeat in his face almost made me want to cheer. But that look was a mirror of what I had been for the past few months. I was no better off than my brother. I had given in to the evil spirit within me. I did not want to be my brother any longer. I turned my gaze back to Kevin. He held hope in his hands. "I don't want to go on like this. Will you help me?"

"I promise." Kevin said.

"Stop!" Jeremiah screamed.

Steel's memory faded around him like watercolors washed away by rain. Jeremiah stood from his chair, his hands clasped to his head.

"Don't even think about your conversion." Jeremiah's eyes were wide in fear.

"You wanted my memories. This is one of the most powerful. You can't be choosy." Steel said.

"Oh, yes, I can! I want to know where you went afterwards. What happened when you totally disappeared?" Jeremiah hurried over to Snake and put his hands on the side of her head. "I don't need her, JJ. Cooperate, or she goes and Ila returns."

Steel held up his hands. "Fine! We'll skip my encounter with Jesus."

"Don't say that name!" Jeremiah's eyes filled with demonic fire. "Or I'll snap her neck like a twig."

"I'll cooperate. Just sit back down."

Jeremiah's eyes faded to normal, and his breathing slowed. He ran his hands through his hair and then straightened his shirt. He returned to his seat. "Now, what happened?"

"You almost killed me. You pounded my head into the wall, remember?" Steel said. "My father was in such a rush to get out of the area, he never realized I went into a coma on the airplane. Not only did I have a concussion, I had a subdural hematoma, a blood clot around the surface of my brain."

Steel ran a finger along the right side of his head. "I once had an incision right here from the surgery. But the scar healed up."

"Surgery? I didn't think to check hospitals." Jeremiah said.

"It wouldn't have done you any good. I didn't have the

surgery in the hospital. I had it somewhere else. Off the grid." Steel pointed to the Grimvox. "Want to see?"

Jeremiah hesitated before touching the Grimvox. "No tricks, brother."

"No tricks."

CHAPTER
TWENTY-NINE

I woke up to the roar of waves pounding on a beach. My head pounded along with the waves. I sat up and opened my eyes to blinding, painful sunlight glittering off gray ocean waves.

"Where am I?"

"Napier." A voice thick with phlegm said. I looked at the man sitting in a beach chair beside me. He was hunched over with a bile green sweater over his huge chest. One eye was slightly lower than the other. His wispy brown hair stirred in the breeze.

"Who are you?"

"Daniel Brown." He held out his hand with short, stubby fingers. "We haven't formally met."

A shadow fell over us and my father appeared. "Good, he's awake. I told you the sunshine and fresh air would do him some good."

Brown stood up, and it was painfully obvious he had a deformed back. "The cerebral edema hasn't resolved completely. He needs to be inside, where I can monitor him."

The Captain puffed away on his pipe. He wore his ever present Panama hat and a beige shirt over jeans. "Then take him back inside. Now that he is awake, we'll be leaving anyway."

I tried to stand up and fell back into the chair when the vertigo hit me. My mouth tasted like snail slime. "Dad, what happened?"

"We ran."

"But I was at church with Kevin." After we left the courthouse, I had gone with Kevin, my youth minister, back to his office at his church. There, I had prayed earnestly to receive the forgiveness and power of Jesus Christ. The change had been profound and instantaneous. Now, I no longer had to fear demon possession.

"I got you on the airplane to Mexico and you passed out. I just thought you were tired. But when we landed in Mexico City, you had a seizure." The Captain sat in Brown's chair and pointed behind. "Go get your stuff together, Toady. We leave in a couple of hours."

"Don't call me that!" Brown said through his thick lips.

"If you don't like the way I speak to you, I can take you back to the states where you can finish your prison sentence." The Captain said icily. "Now go."

Brown glanced once at me and then hobbled away toward a small house on the beach. I rubbed my head and tried to stifle the pain. "What happened to me?"

"Your brother. When he slammed your head against something in the alleyway, it tore veins around your brain. Toady, that is, Dr. Brown, said you had a hemorrhage around your brain. Feel the right side of your head."

I ran a finger along my right temple, and pain lanced into my jaw. Bristly stitches protruded from an incision. "Who operated on me?"

"Dr. Brown." The Captain blew smoke out toward the ocean. The surf picked up and washed almost to our chairs. Behind us, the sun lowered on the western horizon. "I found him through some contacts in Mexico City. We were there when you were born and I made sure I had contacts in case Santiago bailed on us. Brown is a fugitive from the states. He's a board certified neurosurgeon who operated on a politician in Texas while under the influence. The politician died. He went to jail. During a drug cartel jail break, he ran and ended up in Mexico."

I tried to look over my shoulder at the retreating figure of Dr. Daniel Brown, but the movement made my head swim. "You let an escaped convict operate on me?"

"If I hadn't, you would be dead, JJ." The Captain said. "I knew of some off the books concierge medical clinics with pristine conditions and the right kind of help for Dr. Brown. He may look like a squashed toad, but he knows what he is doing."

"As long as he's sober, right?" I looked back out at the surf. The heaving waves made me nauseous. "Where is Napier?"

"New Zealand." The Captain stood up and helped me to my feet. "I have several identities and this seemed the farthest away from the states for now. We're leaving tonight for the south island. I have an associate with a huge farm where we can stay while you recuperate, now that you're awake."

He held my arm as we walked toward the house. "What about Jeremiah?"

He froze and looked over his shoulder. "Never say that name again. We are now in hiding, JJ."

"Hiding? Why? Jeremiah is the criminal. He killed my mother." I stumbled through the sand.

"And my wife." The Captain said quietly. The wind caught his hat, and it flew off his head. He didn't bother going after it.

"We both lost her, son. And, for a while, I thought you killed her."

"I didn't. I wouldn't." I said hoarsely, and it all came crashing in on me. The bloody body of my mother on the altar. The blood on my hands. The knife that had killed her. The jail cell. The courtroom. I collapsed in the sand, dragging my father down with me, and the tears came. I sobbed and my head pulsed with pain. I heard someone else crying. It was my father. I had never seen or heard him cry.

"JJ, we are in trouble. Jeremiah represents something horrible and evil. There are forces I know nothing about that brought on this calamity. Sam and Yvonne knew this and they are in hiding." He said hoarsely as he knelt in the sand.

I wiped snot from my nose. "Where were you?" I glared at him.

"What?"

"Where were you when mother was killed? You were always running after something. Now you're telling me you're running away from something. Was that what you were always doing? Running from me. Running from mother?"

Anger flared in my father's eyes. Tears still glittered on his cheeks. "There is much I haven't told you about our heritage. Your grandparents, for instance."

"Who are both dead. Murder suicide, right?"

The Captain averted his gaze. "Yes. In the same chamber where your mother died."

"So who is after us, father? Why must we run and hide? I deserve to know that."

"Dr. Santiago? Maybe. Or the person he represents."

"Who is Santiago?"

"The doctor who delivered you in Mexico. After you were born, there was another fetus we never knew about. Your mother almost bled to death after delivering a second boy. Dr.

Santiago took the boy and said he had died. Your mother didn't know this for years." He balled his fists and pounded the sand. "I believed Santiago! Jeremiah, your bother did not die. Santiago took him away and gave him to someone. That someone raised your brother to be a monster."

I drew a deep breath. "The third demon?"

"Demons! Supernatural forces! These are infestations in our family tree, JJ. Your grandfather dabbled in the occult. My uncle Nigel is obsessed with it. He's building some kind of museum in London dedicated to the macabre. And Santiago, wherever he is and whoever he works for, has much to answer for." He stood up again and brushed sand from his jeans. "We have to find a safe place until I can gather my resources and informants and begin the process of finding the truth." My father looked down at me and the setting sun painted his face in red light. "You can hate me later, JJ. Right now, we have your mother's death to avenge and we need to avoid another disaster."

"What disaster?"

"You."

I stood up. "I'm a disaster?"

"Someone went to a lot of trouble to frame you for your mother's death. A lot of trouble. Jeremiah might have done that, but why? What was his motivation? Why did he kill his own mother and then blame you for it? Why not just be done with a murder and disappear? He was your age and yet he had resources at his disposal no teenage should have had." He finished searching our surroundings with his anxiety filled gaze. "We are on the other side of the world from Austin, Texas. I have changed our identities to hide from whatever is behind this. Someone tried to kill Yvonne and Sam before the trial, no doubt Jeremiah. But how does a teenager have access to trained assassins? No, son, I must put our differences aside and protect you from whatever is out there. Here, living in obscurity, I will train you in the art of self-defense. I will teach you how to kill silently if need be. I will show you how to disappear in a crowd in a heartbeat. You will become a trained marksman. Without these skills, Jeremiah and his forces will track you down and kill you."

I drew a deep breath and brushed sand from my hands. "At least you could have let me tell Clay goodbye."

The Captain helped me to my feet and focused his intense turquoise eyes on mine. "JJ, as of right now, you have no friends. You are totally alone and isolated from the world. If you even think about contacting anyone back in Austin, Jeremiah will use his resources to track you down and kill you. You are no longer JJ Stone. You are someone else and you need to embrace that right now or it will get us both killed. Yvonne and Sam are looking into Jeremiah and trying to learn what they can. When they find out something useful, they have ways of contacting me. Until then, we are off the grid. No phones, no internet, no credit cards. As of right now, JJ Stone no longer exists."

CHAPTER

THIRTY

"It's so strange not to see the Big Dipper." I tossed another piece of wood on the fire.

"The Southern Cross takes its place." Daniel Brown leaned sideways on the log. "Nice thing about being down under is no light contamination."

The gentle sound of a cow's bell echoed down the hill. Behind me, the red deer herd moved along the hill's ridge. My father's friend owned over four hundred head of red stag and a hundred head of cattle. Not a sheep in sight.

"Dr. Brown, I'm feeling much better over the past few weeks. My father said I should start my training soon. But I have a strange question."

Brown nodded toward the fire. "Turn the meat over before it burns."

I took tongs and turned the red stag filets over on the pan sitting on the embers. Foil wrapped purple sweet potatoes filled a pot on the fire. "I'll turn the potatoes too."

Brown rubbed his thick lips and ran a hand through his unruly hair. "Now, what was your question?"

"You. What's wrong with you?"

Brown sniffed. "Neurofibromatosis. I'm fortunate to not have as many cutaneous manifestations. But it caused my scoliosis and my difficulty with walking. It's what got me interested in neurology."

"I've heard the neurosurgeon tract is pretty tough."

"Yeah, it is. I was blessed. A special program in South America was looking for a resident with neurological problems. Part of some kind of government angle. Trust me, I had lots of experience in the surgery area." Brown motioned to the filets. "They should be done. I'll call your father."

I took the filets from the pan and put each on a plate sitting on the picnic basket. Next, I used the tongs to put a potato on each of the three plates. Brown dialed his burner phone and spoke quietly. I heard my father approaching down the hill and the fragrance of his pipe smoke wafted on the night breeze.

"No one in sight." He settled onto the log beside me. "Just bovines and stags."

"I would hope no one could find us here." I cut into my filet and popped it into my mouth. The meat was succulent and so tender it almost melted in my mouth. "Now, this is a filet."

The Captain tapped the tobacco from his pipe and slid it into the pocket of his jacket. The air was growing cooler around us. My back felt cold while my front warmed from the fire. He ate his filet and dug into his potato. "Dr. Brown, I have a proposal for you."

Brown drank from a bottle of water. "I was hoping you would let me head back to Mexico. It's been almost nine months and JJ is doing just fine. I can medically clear him for your training."

"I want you to hang around." The Captain said.

"Why?"

"In case JJ has another accident."

I paused. "How hard will this training be?"

The Captain's turquoise eyes caught the flickering light of the campfire. "Much harder than you can imagine. I want you prepared for anything. Physically, emotionally, and spiritually."

"Spiritually?" I paused.

"Dr. Brown, didn't you start out at a seminary before you went to medical school?"

Brown froze, and his dark eyes filled with sorrow. "I'd rather not talk about that time."

"I understand from some of your classmates you were rather disillusioned." The Captain said.

Brown glared at him. "My classmates? Who did you talk to?"

"Brenda." The Captain poked at his potato.

Brown almost dropped his bottle of water. "That's it. I'm out of here." He stood up shakily.

"We're in the middle of nowhere on the southern island of New Zealand, Daniel." The Captain placed his plate slowly on the picnic basket. "You're not going anywhere. Tell JJ about Brenda. Go ahead after you sit down and accept your fate."

"You're a monster." Brown collapsed on the log and almost fell backwards. He stared into the fire.

"Dad, maybe we should just call it a night."

"Nonsense. I brought the three of us out here for a reason. It's two miles back to the camp house by ATV. It's dark on these hills. Dr. Brown would never make it by foot. And, if he did, it would take hours to reach Christchurch. I have his passport hidden away." The Captain tossed his food into the fire. "Lesson one, JJ. People are tools. You use them for your own purposes as long as they allow themselves to be tools. Dr. Brown traded his independence for a shot in the arm. He's no longer free. He sold his soul to the next hit, and I picked up the tab."

Silence descended, broken only by the mournful sound of cowbells in the distance. "What do you want from me?" Brown whispered.

"JJ became a Christian before we left the states. I insisted on that to protect him from these demon forces we ran into. I want you to make sure his spiritual state strengthens."

I glanced at my father. "You act like this is some kind of business transaction."

"In my mind, it is a necessary step to protect you from Jeremiah and his plans. In truth, this is more like a military action. Trust me, son. I've seen way too many people claim to have a 'come to Jesus moment' only to walk away from it when times got tough."

"Have you had a 'come to Jesus' moment?" I said.

The Captain stared at me, his face inscrutable. "This isn't about me, JJ. It's about you. It's about being prepared for any eventuality. Brown spent time at seminary before Brenda broke his heart. Maybe one day he'll tell you about it. I couldn't care less about the details. He's the closest thing we have around here to a pastor."

Brown stood up slowly and glared at my father. "If nothing else but to prepare JJ to handle fiends like you, I will take care of it. Now, can we go back to the camp house? My bones ache." He walked away toward the ATVs.

I threw the rest of my food into the fire. "What is wrong with you? People are not pawns on a chessboard."

"Yes, they are, JJ. You need to understand that." The Captain stood up and motioned toward the ATVs. "The sooner the better. This world is out to get you and right now, you are hiding away from those forces. One day, they will find us and when they do, I want you prepared. If you don't like it, too bad." He started up the hill and paused to turn back toward me. "If for no other reason than in the memory of your mother. Make sure THEY don't win." He moved into the darkness and left me alone beneath the distant stars and the cold darkness of night.

THIRTY-ONE

Snow fell from a leaden sky and made the rocky path treacherous. The pack on my back weighted almost 30 pounds. Somewhere in the fog and snow ahead, my father waited for me to finish the run up the mountainside to the glacier. Occasionally, I would round a curve in the mountainside and meet hikers coming down from the glacier. But in the winter months, hiking up the path was foolish. I would have to agree. We had been in New Zealand for almost a year. Summer had arrived in the United States. Winter had arrived at the bottom of the world.

The blow caught me in the side and I slid sideways across the path and tumbled down the slope toward the river below. I scrabbled for a handhold as I slid through the bushes and rocks until I rolled off a rocky shelf and fell six feet into the frigid water flowing from the melting glacier. The cold water took my breath away and something splashed by my head, followed by the "thunk" of a silenced pistol report. I gasped for breath from the blow of the bullet to my bullet proof vest. He should have gone for a head shot, I thought. That was my father talking!

I dove into the freezing water and swam toward the near shoreline. More bullets hissed through the water around me and the current tore at my backpack. I slipped out of it and let it rush away. Through the surprisingly clear water, I watched bullets tear into the backpack as it tumbled away.

I found a handhold on slippery rocks and pushed my face slowly out of the water. The rocks hid me from view and I sucked in sweet, cold air. Who was shooting at me? I moved cautiously as the water robbed me of the feeling in my feet and hands so that I could look up through a crack between two rocks. A man in a gray and white jumpsuit stepped into view. Just moments before, I had avoided him hiking down the path. He lifted a pistol with a scope on the top and pointed it at my face. Before I could duck out of view, blood gushed from the man's neck and he fell down the hillside toward me. My father pocketed the knife he had just used on the man and ran down the slope toward me.

I climbed shakily out of the river, shivering uncontrollably. The dead man's body had rolled to within a foot of the rocks. My father, dressed all in white with a ski cap over his head, knelt beside the man. He searched the man's pockets and then took the pistol and stuck it in his parka.

"You okay?"

"Just freezing." I said through chattering teeth.

"You'll live." He shoved me back into the water. "Retrieve your backpack and meet me in the parking lot."

I sputtered and coughed and cursed him. He rolled the man's body in after me. "You want to live? This is only the first attempt out of many. We've been discovered. We have to move. Now, go. Get the backpack and I'll cover our retreat."

I FOUND my backpack snared in rocks not far downstream and crawled out of the water. I ran down the path, hoping my running would generate some heat. My father had the SUV started and the side door open. I jumped in and closed the door behind me. The interior was warm.

"Get out of those wet clothes." He growled as he pulled slowly out of the parking lot. "There's a blanket behind the back seat.

Teeth chattering and every muscle quaking, I removed all my clothes pausing to pull the bullet slug from the vest. I leaned over the back seat and retrieved a wool blanket. I wrapped it around me and embraced the warmth. "Who was trying to kill me?"

"Don't know. I'll have the pistol analyzed. We can't go back on the ferry. I'll have to call in a boat rescue once we get to Stahl." The past few months had passed in a painful blur. And now, sitting cold and exposed in the back of an SUV on the southern island of New Zealand, the true extent of the danger we were in hit home. Nausea gripped me and I retch and vomited my breakfast onto my wet clothes.

"NAME?"

"Jason Pennington." I handed my passport to the customs official.

The uniformed man with skin the color of an eggplant studied my photo and then looked back at me. "What is wrong with your right eye?"

"What?"

"Your eye?"

I glanced at my reflection in the plexiglass enclosure around the man. My right eye was turquoise. My left eye was brown. I had lost one of my contacts. "Oh, it doesn't show up well in the photo by I have scientific name for it."

My father stepped up beside me and slid something through the opening at the base of the plexiglass. The customs official glanced at the bills folded into a small wad and quickly snared them and tucked them beneath the desk. He stamped my passport and nodded.

"Everything appears to be in order, Mr. Pennington."

"The third." My father said handing him his passport. "I'm the second."

Dr. Daniel Brown hobbled to the desk and presented his passport. "Mason Dixon." He said. I smiled and almost laughed. Brown glanced at me and smiled. The official stamped the passport without a word.

"WHY BERMUDA?" I sat on the edge of the rocking boat.

The Captain wore only his swimsuit and a ball cap. "Lots of boats. Lots of tourists. We can pass anonymously through these waters for a while. This boat was cheap."

"I know. The head isn't much larger than the commode."

"At least we're warm."

I pulled off my tank top and dove into the warm water. Our boat was anchored along the southern shore in an area of active coral reef. I marveled at the sight of tropical fish and colorful coral. I had taken off the contacts and my normal turquoise eyes adjusted to the salt water quickly. I swam under the boat and made my way to the nearby rocky shore. The beach was small and covered with the famous pink sand. No tourists in sight on this isolated beach.

My father emerged from the waters. "You shouldn't be seen without your contacts."

I collapsed on the sand. We might as well have been back in New Zealand except the water was emerald and warm. For the past almost two years we had traveled through several destinations. At a compound in the states, my father had taught me to be an excellent marksman. At first, I had resisted the training and my father and I fought physically more than once. Sometimes it was because of his drinking. But one look at Dr. Brown and my father sobered pretty fast. We had heard nothing from Sam and Yvonne about the whereabouts of Jeremiah. No one had tried to kill me since we had left New Zealand. Maybe it was time for me to relax and accept life on an island in the deep blue sea. But, I couldn't do that. Already, I was checking out the nearby boats and their occupants and scanning the beach for any approaching person. Next to me, Daniel Brown reclined in a beach chair.

"I hate the sun." He said. He wore a wide brimmed straw hat and a long sleeve shirt and long pants.

"Aren't you burning up?"

"I'm fine, JJ." He held up a tablet. "Time for your lesson."

I groaned. "Really? Are we still in Daniel?"

"My namesake. He was quite the prophet. Predicted falling empires and defeated kings." Daniel tapped the tablet and handed it to me. "Finish reading the book of Daniel."

I took the tablet and read. For the past few months, Daniel had been taking me through the Bible chronologically. I had read bits and pieces of the Bible when my mother was alive. We were CEOs, that is Christmas, Easter and occasionally when it came to church attendance. But reading the Bible chronologically really brought it alive. We had finished most of the New Testament and Dr. Brown had taken us back to Daniel to read prophesies before we jumped into Revelation. I had to confess that some passages I had been reading were tedious, like Lamentations and Numbers. But it all seemed to fit together.

"Like my training." My father collapsed on the sand beside me, water streaming from his chest.

"What?"

"I know what you were thinking. Why should I waste time reading the Bible?"

"My training kept me alive in New Zealand." I said.

"Just don't pay any attention to the 'turn the other cheek' nonsense." The Captain said.

"Sir, that passage does not mean Christians are cowards." Dr. Brown said.

"Oh, yeah? Then why turn the other cheek?"

"To do the unexpected." Dr. Brown sat forward and his floppy hat almost blew off his head. He grabbed it with a stubby hand. "In that time period, when a person was to be insulted, you slapped him across the cheek with the back of your hand. It was not a sign of fighting. It was a sign of humiliation and disrespect. To turn the other cheek meant to accept your differences from that person and to celebrate it by presenting the other cheek. To refuse to compromise and give in to the person's point of view. It meant to be unique, as the followers of Christ certainly were."

My father grunted. "Be that as it may, turning the other cheek never achieved anything with me and my endeavors. One must be prepared to strike both cheeks and to do so with force and malice."

He belched and I smelled the alcohol on his breath. I glared at him. "You've been drinking again."

He ignored me. "You have one more round of intense training. Put you in an isolated area with no resources and see how long you last. I'm thinking the Negev desert in Israel."

"You're going to drop me in the desert?" I sat forward.

"Naked and alone." He nodded. "Yep. That will show him."

"Show who? Jeremiah? Are you trying to kill me?"

"That man in New Zealand messed up. You weren't supposed to see him."

"What? Wait a minute. You sent that man after me?"

"The bullets were real, JJ. Had to be. Part of your training." My father glared at me with blood shot eyes. "He could have hit your vest a couple of more times without killing you."

"You killed him." I stood up.

"He survived. But, he deserved to die. A hood from down under."

"I can't believe this."

My father stood up and motioned to the boat. "Tomorrow, we leave. Get your stuff packed tonight. A private airplane will pick us up at the main harbor at 6 AM."

I handed the tablet back to Daniel. "Dad, I'm done. I need a break! You need a break more than I do. You almost killed an innocent man just to teach me a lesson?"

"He was far from innocent, JJ. He was a crack head like Brown over here. I plucked him out of a slum in Christchurch and gave him a chance to live. He blew it. You have to take this seriously. Jeremiah is after you and he won't be aiming for the bullet proof vest." He shoved me back into the chair and walked off into the surf to swim back to the boat.

I struggled out of the chair and followed him into the water. My face burning with anger. When I reached the boat, I pulled on my fins and my mask and snorkel. Dr. Brown struggled with his dinghy as he rowed back toward the boat.

"What are you doing?" My father drank from an insulated water bottle.

I was sure it had more than water. "I'm going snorkeling one last time before I die in the dessert at your hands. If you want to stop me, shoot me." Before he could say anything I dove on the far side of the boat toward the coral reef.

I swam through the schools of brightly colored fish for almost an hour. The coral was beautiful but receding according to the locals. Sad but true. Nothing was as it seemed! As I floated face down in the warm waters, the anger let up. Nothing my father did should have surprised me. My heart still ached when I thought of my mother, but time heals. Unfortunately, time had not dulled my hatred of my brother. What would I do if he were right here, right now? My hands gripped tightly in anger. I would NOT turn the other cheek.

Something pricked my right leg, and I flinched. Could it be a jellyfish? I looked down and saw the small dart sticking out of my leg just as the sedation hit me. I gasped for breath, glad my snorkel was above the water as oblivion took me.

THIRTY-TWO

"Yes, I have him." The voice carried a heavy Eastern European accent. I blinked in confusion as consciousness returned. Water pooled in the back of my throat, and I resisted the urge to cough. Keep still, father had taught me. Don't let them know you have recovered consciousness. I never thought I would need to heed those words of wisdom.

I opened the eye opposite the side from which the voice could be heard. Rusty metal ceiling above me dripped water on my legs. At least I could feel them. My mouth tasted of salt water and vomit. I swallowed it gently to keep from coughing and inhaled slowly. Fish smell. Human body odor and not mine! I sensed the gentle rocking of the floor beneath me. We were on a boat and not the one we had been living on.

"I will prepare him for transport." The man said. "Yes, he is breathing and not yet awake. Good bye."

Clomping footsteps approached me, and I closed my eye. Rough hands grabbed me under the shoulders and started dragging me across the wet floor. Now was the time to act. I reached up and grabbed the man's head and heaved him toward my legs, raising my feet up to catch him mid body and throw him across the room. I rolled and lurched to my feet. Dizziness hit me, and I stumbled right and left as I ran away from the man. I did not know where I was running to, but it had to be away from him. He grunted and shouted behind me.

Stairs led up to light. I ran up the steps, lurching from side to side, and emerged on the deck of some kind of commercial boat. A half-dozen men working on the deck froze and turned toward the shouting coming from the stairs. I didn't even think, just ran to the edge of the boat and jumped.

What was I thinking? I hit the water hard and dove deeply to keep out of sight. The bottom was surprisingly close here, and I swam into the rocks and waited. The boat plowed on above me thanks to momentum. My head was beginning to hurt and darkness closing in. I had to resurface and breath. They would be looking for me. What to do?

I swam up quickly, shoved my head above water, and hyperventilated. The boat had moved over a hundred yards away. Men stood on the stern, pointing in my direction. I turned and looked around. The shore was a good two hundred yards away. I had to make it before they could get a smaller boat into the water. I swam as hard as I could, remembering my father's instructions.

To their credit, they never fired a gun in my direction. They wanted me alive. And they knew once I reached the island, there would be nowhere to go. More shouting behind me as the boat turned and moved in my direction. I swam harder, my heart racing and my lungs burning. I finally touched bottom and stood up, running through the surf toward the beach. Low-lying trees grew close to the shore, and I disappeared into the overgrowth of scrubby trees and rocks. The rocks and roots tore at my bare feet, but I couldn't let up. I had to keep moving. I came out of the trees onto a two-lane dirt road. Where was I?

I had to be in Bermuda. There were no other islands close by unless I had been transported to the Caribbean hundreds of miles away. The boat I had been on did not move quickly, so it made no sense to keep me on such a boat if I had been moved that far. They would have moved me by airplane.

A roaring sound came from my left and one of the small electric vehicles used by tourists came into sight. I waved it down. The car stopped and a woman's head popped out of the driver's side.

"I need help." I shouted. "Can you give me a ride into town?"

Her eyes widened in fear at the sight of my bleeding feet. I wore only my swimsuit. "I don't know."

"Please. Just give me a quick ride to the nearest store. I promise I won't hurt you."

She motioned to the only other seat in the car. "Okay. But if you try anything, I know taekwondo."

"So do I." I slid in beside her. Her skin was a deep copper hue, and the wind had blown around her blonde hair. She wore a halter top and shorts. She started down the road and I glanced back over my shoulder. No one in sight yet.

"So, what kind of trouble are you in?" She asked, her voice shaking.

"I was kidnapped." I blurted out. She glanced at me with fear in her eyes. "Human trafficking."

Her gaze softened, and she nodded. "I lost my sister to that. I hate them." She stepped on the accelerator and drove faster. "We'll get you to the police."

"No!" I blurted out.

She glanced at me. "Why not?"

"Uh, just get me somewhere to call my father. I don't have any identification. I don't even know what island I'm on."

"We're in Nassau in the Bahamas." She said.

Nassau? My heart sank. I had been on the boat longer than I thought. They must have put me on an airplane and then transferred me to the boat. I should have recognized the vegetation. It differed from that in Bermuda.

"I was in Bermuda." I said.

We came into the outskirts of a town with low-lying, brightly colored buildings. People moved up and down the road and she pulled into an alleyway. She stopped the vehicle. "Look, you need help. What is your name?"

"Jason." I remembered to use my new name. "You've been very helpful. But the people who took me will hurt you if they find out you helped me. It's best if I leave now and get in touch with my father and leave you out of this. Thank you for your help."

She grabbed my arm as I tried to get out of the car. "Jason, my name is Bethany. I'm at the Grayson Condominiums if you need me."

"Thanks for helping me, Bethany." I hopped out of the car on painful feet and ran down the alleyway. I glanced once more over my shoulder at the sight of her pulling away down the street.

Above me on the second floor of a pink house, clothes hung out to dry. I hated to do this, but my survival instinct kicked in. I painfully climbed a fire exit ladder and jerked a shirt and shorts off the line. A line of sandals sat out to dry and I grabbed a pair.

An hour later, I sat in the lobby of Grayson Condominiums. Keeping an eye on everyone around me, I had not seen any of the members from the boat. I sat with my back to the security cameras and waited patiently. Bethany appeared from the elevator with a coverup over her swimsuit. She wore a floppy hat and carried a beach bag. Two other teenage girls accompanied her. I followed them down to the beach and waited until the other two girls headed off into the surf.

Bethany reclined in a rental chair, eyes glue to her cell phone. I eased up beside her and sat in the chair next to her. She looked at me over her sunglasses.

"I wondered when you would show up. Did you get a hold of your father?"

I scanned the people milling around us. "I don't have a cell phone." And there was the remote chance my father had set all of this up. Although sending me to the Bahamas seemed like overkill.

She glanced out over the water at her two friends splashing each other. "I'm not alone. Don't try anything."

I smiled and made sure she saw my eyes. Girls always seemed to like my eyes. "I'm not going to stalk you, Bethany. I just wanted to thank you for helping me. I know it's a stretch but if you could lend me some cash that is all I ask. My kidnappers are still looking for me and I have to figure out how to get off this island."

"Go to the police." She said.

"Yeah, I think they might have had something to do with this. After all, this is Nassau."

She nodded in understanding. "Look, uh, Jason, right?"

"Yes."

"You seem like a straightforward guy. Surely you understand my cautious nature."

"Yeah, especially if you lost a sister to human trafficking. Did she, uh, pass?" I asked.

Bethany took her sunglasses off. "No. We found her. But she was never the same afterwards. Counseling and therapy aren't helping." She looked out at the beach. "She's in a facility for special people."

"I'm sorry. I have a brother who tried to kill me." I said before I thought.

Bethany gasped and looked at me. "What?"

"Sorry, no need to burden you with my history. Thanks for listening. I've gotta keep on the move." I stood up and she put a hand on my arm.

"Wait! This will sound strange, but I think God wants me to help you."

I froze. "God?"

"Yeah, I know it sounds freaky. I'm a Christian and when I saw you on the road, something inside of me said I needed to help you. After what happened to my sister, I try to live by the motto of being a helper in the time of need."

"Good Samaritan." I nodded. "I'm a Christian, too. Look, Bethany helping me could be dangerous. I think it's best I just walk away."

"No!" She stood up. "My friends will understand if we go for a walk. Let's talk. At least out here on the beach you are surrounded by lots of people. Whoever is looking for you won't try anything, right?"

I followed her through the beach crowd. My feet had stopped bleeding but the sandals weren't exactly smooth against the cuts on my feet. We made our way down the beach.

"Chelsea was into drugs. Messed around with the wrong gang in high school. Loved to party." She said, pushing her wild hair back under her floppy hat. "We tried all kinds of interventions without success. We're from Mobile, Alabama. Dad is a financial advisor so we have money."

"Probably shouldn't tell people that." I said as I scanned the people around us.

"You're right. He, uh, owns that condos we are staying in."

"Oh! Definitely shouldn't mention that."

She laughed. "Sorry! I need to be more careful. Chelsea

went to a party put on by an investor in my father's firm. Turns out he was with a cartel in Mexico. He took fifteen teenage girls and disappeared with them." She stopped and put a hand under her sunglasses to wipe at her eyes. "I don't know why I'm telling you this." She turned to walk back toward the condos.

I nodded and wanted to reach out to comfort her. But touching her was out of the question. She noticed and smiled. "Thank you for your restraint."

"I didn't want to trigger taekwondo."

Bethany laughed. "We found her after almost a year. A professional tracker, a Christian, located her in Aruba. Fifteen girls had been taken. She was the only survivor. And she was just that, a survivor. Not the Chelsea I had grown up with. So you see I have no love lost for kidnappers."

We had reached the beach in front of the condominiums and she motioned to the pool. "Let's get something to eat and drink at the pool bar." I followed her across the sand to stairs leading up to the pool. "Burger and fries?"

My stomach growled. "Sounds lovely."

She went to the bar and ordered while I scanned the small crowd of people around the pool. I looked out over the beach. No surly fishermen or boat people among the tanned crowd. Maybe one day, I would live on a beach. Now, I had to decide what to do.

Bethany returned to the table and put a bottle of water in front of me. "Water okay?"

"Yes." I said suddenly parched. I drank half the bottle in one gulp and my nose wrinkled. "Thanks. And I stink. Haven't had a shower since I escaped. Sorry."

Bethany shrugged. "So you can't tell me about your brother?"

"Let's just say he committed a crime for which I was framed."

I drank more water. The cuts on my feet hurt. "My father and I are running from him. He has resources, you might say."

"Like those of a cartel?"

"Yeah! My brother wants to kill me like he did, my —" I paused. "Again, I don't want to endanger you."

"What is your plan, Jason?"

"If I can get off the island, my father has some resources hidden away." I finished the water and a server brought us two plates with burgers and fries. My mouth salivated.

"Hidden away?" Bethany reached for a fry and stopped. "Okay, so you have to know, I pray before I eat."

"Good idea. I need all the prayer I can get." I bowed my head.

Bethany whispered a prayer in a voice so low I had a hard time hearing the words. I did catch my name during the prayer. She looked up and I smiled.

"You prayed for me. Thanks." I grabbed the burger and bit into it. Wonderful! Succulent! I didn't care. It filled me up.

"So, your father is some kind of spy?" Bethany ate a fry.

"He was in the military. He has connections around the world." I mumbled around the burger.

"You know, if I didn't know better, I'd think you were making this up."

"It sounds pretty wild, doesn't it?" I ate some fries. "I wish it was fiction. But I'm living it."

Bethany looked past me out over the beach and put a hand on mine. I flinched at the touch of her hand but I followed her gaze. Her two friends were coming down the beach pointing at the condominium. I recognized the man from the boat.

"I think I believe you." Bethany said.

"That's the man from the boat. The one who kidnapped me." I swallowed hard.

Bethany grabbed my hand and pulled me up from the table. I followed her behind the bar and into the foyer of the condominium. "I don't have my beach bag or I would give you money. You have to get out of here."

"How did they find me?" I blurted, hobbling after her on my damaged feet.

Bethany led me out front and motioned to a man standing next to a car. He was short and stocky with a crew cut and dark skin. "Phillipe?" She called.

Phillipe smiled and hurried over. "Miss Bethany. How are you?"

"I'm fine, Phillipe. I need a favor. Mr. Jason here needs a ride."

Phillipe raised an eyebrow as he gave me the once over. "Miss Bethany, are you sure?"

"Yes. Take him to the pier to the Saint Marie."

"I don't want to get you into any trouble." I kept looking over my shoulder at the foyer.

"Phillipe is one of our drivers for the condominium. You can trust him." She looked at Phillipe. "Jason is a victim of trafficking, Phillipe."

Phillipe's demeanor changed. "Like Miss Chelsea?"

"Yes. He needs to get off the island so he can contact his father. Take him to the boat and tell Michaela to call me. Hurry."

Phillipe nodded and took me by the arm. He pushed me into the back seat of his SUV before I could say anymore to Bethany. I cast one last look at her as Phillipe pulled away from the condominium.

Phillipe never said a word and drove to the nearby marina. He motioned to the pier leading out among dozens of sailboats and yachts. "The Saint Marie is docked at number 32. Forgive me if I do not accompany you. I want to get back and make sure Bethany is okay."

I nodded. "Please do that. And give her my thanks." I paused. "Tell her I'm praying for Chelsea."

I got out of the car and he tore out of the parking lot. Michaela was an older woman with skin like tanned leather. The Saint Marie was a small luxury boat for rental. She had little to say to me other than she had been very close to Chelsea. Her instructions were short and sweet. She would take me to a small cruise ship looking to hire workers. Bethany's family had connections with the captain of the vessel to aid and abet anyone trying to escape human trafficking.

Michaela delivered me to the ship and the captain ushered me down into the depths of the vessel. I was given an identity card and a job working in the laundry. I spent three months on the ship, working my way around the Caribbean. At each island, I was forbidden to leave the ship as I did not have a passport. When we arrived in Puerto Rico, the captain allowed me to leave when I told him there was a safe house owned by my father and it was time to let him know I had escaped.

I made it to the safe house in Puerto Rico. I had let my hair and beard grow out. In the months toiling away in the ship's laundry I did a lot of thinking. Should I return to my father? What if he set up the kidnapping to "train me"? I was tired of that. By the time I reached Puerto Rico, I was a week short of my eighteenth birthday.

The safe house sat high on a hill overlooking the ocean. Entry was through a combination lock on the back door. The interior was musty, and I opened windows to let the sea breeze clear out the mustiness. The hidden cache of supplies beneath the bathroom tile was still there. Four passports with my photo from two years before would still work. Various currencies from around the world gave me plenty of cash. I kept an eye on the security feed to make sure my father wasn't waiting for me. I wouldn't be here for long.

I found tins of beans and meat and made a passible meal. I sat on the balcony overlooking the white sands of the beach and the surf. The setting sun painted the sky a deep red orange. Below me, a family with three kids played in the waves. What I wouldn't give to have a normal family! Instead, I had a father who had nearly killed me during my training and a brother who wanted to kidnap me for reasons I could never fathom.

Now, what to do? It was time for me to move on. I had done well over the last few months on my own. Maybe it was time to put into play my training, both spiritual and physical. If I could track down Jeremiah and turn the tables on him, I could find out more about why he was looking for me. I would need a new name, for sure.

I looked through the passports. "John Steele." I studied the photo of myself with my ginger hair and turquoise eyes. "Good cover name. John Steele it is."

I stood up and looked once more out of the ocean and nodded. "Jeremiah, I'm coming for you. It's time I put a stop to you!"

THE ISLAND FADED AROUND STEEL, and he was back in the chamber. He blinked and glanced at Jeremiah. "No need to keep reliving memories, Jeremiah. I started my search for you. I tracked your movements all over the globe. I suspected you were the mercenary I encountered the night we tried to apprehend the children of the bloodstone."

Jeremiah released the Grimvox and sat back. "I was. And it wasn't until I saw your video in Switzerland that I realized I had been right there beside you. You're like Clark Kent hiding in plain sight."

"Did you kidnap me in Bermuda?"

"That wasn't me." He looked away.

"Then, who was it? It couldn't have been our father."

"Later." He glanced back at me. "So how did you end up as Jonathan Steel?"

Steel told him about the night his father had thrown him from the boat into the ocean and erased his memory.

"Implants? The man is more ruthless than I thought. I have to say I admire him more than I would ever have. I suppose he was torturing you to find out if you had located me?"

"Yes." Steel said.

"And your seminary trained neurosurgeon tortured you?"

"He had no choice. My father controlled him absolutely."

"Would you kill father if he were here?" Jeremiah smiled.

"No. We met after my encounter with the twelfth demon. I have forgiven him. He did what he had to do to survive. I understand now."

Jeremiah stood up. "Let's take a lunch break and continue afterwards."

"Didn't get the memory you needed?" Steel asked.

Jeremiah glared at him. "We'll get there. I need to hear about your trips to Africa and the Middle East."

Steel tried not to react. "Fine." He pushed back from the table. "I'll be in my room. Have Nanny bring me lunch. I'm starving." He walked out of the chamber like he was in charge.

THIRTY-THREE

"Can we stop at Buc-ee's?"

Josh glanced at Father James Caskey in the passenger seat of his truck. "Really?"

"I need some taffy." That morning, Caskey had instructed Josh to pack a couple of days of clothing and head to Rockwall, Texas, to 'engage' the exorcist team. The two of them had hardly spoken during the two and half hour drive from Shreveport, Louisiana to the Dallas, Texas area. Josh had expected a lengthy lecture on exorcism, but the man had been eerily silent. He had napped off and on with a fine drop of drool almost on his black turtleneck shirt.

"You've hardly spoken a word since we left." Josh took the exit for Buc-ee's. "Dude, are you mad at me? Or just napping?"

"Hardly, my boy. I have been in prayer the entire time. I am praying for our upcoming encounter with this team as well as the recovery of Jonathan Steel. And I have been in prayer for you."

"For me?"

"If you are allowed to witness an exorcism, it will be potentially dangerous for you. I am praying for your spiritual condition."

Josh resisted the urge to curse and damage his "spiritual condition" as he wove his way through lines of trucks and cars jockeying for a parking place around the enormous store. Dozens of gas pumps held dozens of vehicles waiting to pull in for the cheaper gas.

Josh parked near a door and Caskey slid out of the car. He leaned over and fixed his rheumy eyes on Josh. "Don't you want to come in?"

Josh's heart raced, and he shook his head. "I'm fine."

"Clean restrooms." Caskey said as he leaned on his cane.

That was true, and Josh needed to use the facilities. Reluctantly, he turned the truck off and followed the man into the vast store. People milled about like ants in a disturbed ant bed. Josh made straight for the restrooms and tried his best to ignore the fragrance of baked goods, barbecue and coffee from the wall of coffee machines on either side of the restroom doors. He hurried inside and found a vacant stall. Inside, he leaned against the wall and fought hyperventilation. He slowed his heart race and took care of his business. At the sink, he washed his face and stared at his reflection. He really needed to shave, and his hair was uneven and unkempt. He looked into his blood-shot eyes. "Dude, you gotta get yourself together. You're about to face another demon."

When he left the restroom, Caskey was waiting for him. "Josh, you're white as a ghost. Motion sickness?"

"No." He moved away from the coffee. "I'm sorry, James. My mother would bring me to this place for a special treat. She liked the coffee. I liked the roasted nuts and the sandwiches." He slowed his breathing. "I haven't been back here since she died."

Caskey touched his arm. "I am sorry, Josh. We never should have stopped."

"Bro, it's okay. I have to deal with this."

"Well, let me get my taffy and check out. If you want to wait in the truck, I won't be long."

Josh nodded and went out to the truck and started the engine. Movement among the people caught his eye and his mother walked along the sidewalk. Her ginger hair was just as he remembered it and her jade green eyes glittered in the cold February sunlight. She paused in front of the truck and smiled at him. Josh closed his eyes and shook his head in confusion. When he reopened them, the Crimson Snake stood where his mother had been.

"Help me." She mouthed.

Josh jumped out of the truck and hurried to the sidewalk. The Snake was gone. So was the apparition of his mother. Father Caskey emerged from the store tapping his cane along the sidewalk and carrying a large bag filled with taffy.

"Josh, are you okay?"

Josh motioned to the truck. "Get in. I'm losing my mind."

Caskey sat silently by Josh as he drove out of the parking lot. "Sorry, James. I thought I saw my mother in the crowd. Then she turned into the Crimson Snake."

"The Crimson Snake?" Caskey said. "Josh, if she is tethered to the Grimvox, she must be trying to communicate with you. You are prone to visions. The scriptures talk of young men and their visions." He rubbed the scar on his neck as he thought. "In the book of Joel, he wrote: *'I will pour out my Spirit on all people. Your sons and daughters will prophesy, your old men will dream dreams, your young men will see visions. Even on my servants, both men and women, I will pour out my Spirit in those days.'* You, my son, have been touched in a special way by the Holy Spirit. Because of that, somehow, Snake can connect to you spiritually." Caskey sat toward me and smiled. "And, if she is with the Grimvox, then she is also most likely with Jonathan."

"She asked me to help her. If she is under the influence of Jeremiah and the Grimvox, it is unlikely she even knows where she is." Josh said as he took the road leading to Rockwall.

"She may be our only hope," Caskey said as he popped a piece of peppermint taffy into his mouth. "Don't discount these visions and dreams. But don't fall asleep on the road."

With his heart racing as he neared his meeting with the exorcists, sleep was the last thing on his mind. He had another plan more promising than a connection with an assassin!

"Where are we headed to?" Josh asked.

Caskey glanced around at the town of Rockwall. "Primo's Tex-Mex restaurant. It's on the lake."

"I know where it is." Josh said. "Tourist trap. Ernesto's is better."

"Ernesto's doesn't have a meeting room, my boy."

"Meeting room? Wait! Your exorcists are at a Tex-Mex restaurant?"

Caskey glanced at his wristwatch. "Yes, it is happy hour. They always eat Tex-Mex after a session."

They stopped at a stop light and Josh laughed. "Really!"

"Josh, after an encounter with a host and their demon, the exorcist team needs something ordinary, grounded. They need time to decompress. This team likes Primo's. There is an outside room on the second level overlooking the lake. This time of the year it is enclosed with one of those propane heaters."

"You can imagine what people would think if they overheard a raucous conversation about the behavior of a demon. It is best if the team can be away from the crowd. But still close to the crowd. Make sense, my boy?"

"Sort of, bro." He pulled into the parking lot of the large restaurant and turned off the truck. "What can I expect?"

Caskey sighed. "We will not be welcome, I can tell you that."

"They don't know we're coming?"

"Absolutely not! If they did, they would go where I can't find them." He cleared his throat. "I am not on the best of terms with them. Let's go."

Josh followed Caskey into the restaurant. A heavily tattooed woman met them at the podium. Loud music filled the crowded restaurant. "There's a 45 minute wait." She said brusquely.

"We're here with Father Valdez." Caskey said.

The woman eyed him up and down and then glanced at Josh. "You know where they usually meet?"

"Yes."

"You need menus?"

"Nope." Caskey said at the same time Josh said, "Yes."

Josh glanced at Caskey. "I'm hungry."

"A teenager is always hungry." Caskey took a menu and handed it to Josh. They made their way through packed booths and tables to the outside patio. Lake Ray Hubbard stretched into the distance, dotted with sailboats and motorboats. A cold, stiff wind blew in over the water. Caskey climbed a set of stairs and Josh grabbed his arm.

"Let me help you."

"Thank you, my boy." Caskey said as they made their way

up the stairs. To their left a covered hallway led to another outside seating area enclosed in clear plastic. Laughter and loud voices echoed down the hallway. A server shouldered his way past them and paused long enough to glance at Josh.

"What are you having?"

"Chicken quesadillas and cola."

Caskey paused at the end of the hallway. "When we get inside, don't say a word. Let me do the talking or they will have us both thrown out." His rheumy eyes glittered with what could only be fear. "Understand?"

"Yes." Josh said.

Caskey hobbled out of the hallway. One lone table sat in the center, and the assembled people at the table were talking animatedly and loudly. Here, the music was much quieter.

The man sitting at the head of the table made eye contact with Caskey and all the talking ceased. He stood up slowly. "James?"

"Jesse." Caskey leaned on his cane. Jesse wore a white turtleneck shirt. His salt and pepper hair hung around his lean face. He pushed the hair on the right side of his face over his ear and Josh stifled a gasp. The right side of his face was pale compared to his dark skin, obviously a skin graft. His eyebrows arched over his dark brown eyes.

"Before the assembled group picks up stones to hurl against your unwanted presence, I will give you a moment to depart peacefully." Jesse said. He crossed his arms.

"I need to speak with your group, Jesse."

"Father Valdez told you to leave." A tall, black-skinned man stood up from his seat. His emerald green eyes glittered with anger. He wore a brightly patterned robe most likely of African origin. A red fez sat on his bare scalp. "You are not welcome here among serious exorcists."

"We've heard all about your escapades, James." A woman

turned to look at them. She wore a totally white blouse and white pants. She spoke with a northern New England accent.

"What Sister Jo is saying, pater, is get out!" A portly man with a comb-over motioned toward the door. His pot belly hung over his polyester pants.

"Just a minute." Caskey raised his hands in protest. "This is not about me. It is about this young man and his missing father."

A thin Asian woman rose from her chair and walked toward them. Her black hair draped across her shoulders. She wore a gray blouse beneath a dark blazer over jeans and boots. "I know this young man." She paused before Josh. "You were in Transylvania."

Josh's mouth fell open. "Yes, I was."

"Dr. Jiah Moon." She extended a hand. "You are more welcome than this outcast."

"You wound me, Jiah." Caskey said quietly.

"I believe we have made our position clear." Father Jesse said from the table.

"I believe this young man is familiar with your latest victim." Caskey said.

Josh stiffened. "What?"

"How would you know who we are currently helping?" The tall African said in a heavy accent. "Why am I surprised? You do not value confidentiality, and that was your undoing."

Caskey shook his head. "I learned of your victim's name from an anonymous source. I also understand you are making little progress in, how long? Three months?"

"You know these things can take longer." Father Valdez said.

"Father Caskey, you didn't tell me about this." Josh said.

"He's not a father anymore." Sister Jo said tersely.

Another man hunched over the table with his back to

them. He turned slowly and his slightly off centered face paled. Josh looked away from the deformed man. A strange mixture of familiarity and revulsion came over him. He drew a deep breath and crossed his arms. Glaring at the man in the fez, he let his anger take him.

"Look, I don't care about your animosity and your hatred for this man. My father, Jonathan Steel, is missing, and he has been taken by the second demon. James tells me I must be prepared to deal with the second demon. I asked him to let me sit in on an exorcism so I can be ready to deal with the demon and his host who has taken my father. So put your stupid prejudices aside and help us."

Valdez's arms fell to his side, and he glanced at the others at the table. "Did you say Jonathan Steel is your father?"

"Yes, my adopted father."

Dr. Moon turned and faced the table. "I told you I recognized him. This is Joshua Knight. He was possessed by the thirteenth demon and then taken prisoner by the twelfth demon."

The African man massaged his chin and nodded. "Then we owe him an audience. Not so James Caskey."

Josh's gaze shifted to the deformed man. His eyes were averted and his face pale. "I think we should help him."

"Thanks." Josh said. "Now, if you want to talk to me, Father Caskey stays. I think he has more than paid the price for his failures. Now can we get on with this?"

Moon motioned to a chair. "Please, sit. I'll introduce us."

Josh moved to an empty chair and Caskey slid into the one next to it. Moon nodded toward him as she sat. "I am a psychiatrist. My job is to make certain we are not dealing with true mental illness before we proceed with an exorcism."

Moon pointed to the African. "Amobi Osondu from Nigeria."

Moon pointed to the portly man. "Reverend Chuck Wesley."

"I'm a Pentecostal pastor, Josh." He shook Josh's hand but ignored Caskey. "I've heard quite a bit about you and your mentor."

Moon pointed to the other woman. "Sister Josephine Thompkins."

"Call me Sister Jo." She nodded toward him. "From the look on your face, I will answer your unspoken question. I am a nun."

Two twenty something guys sat at another smaller table, eyes glued to their cell phones. "That's the twins, Timothy and Thomas from Haiti. Our restrainers." Moon said.

They looked up in unison and nodded then back at the phones. Dark skin and short black hair with necks thick as a rhino.

"I hope they don't have to restrain me."

Moon motioned to the deformed man. "Dr. Donald Black our resident physician."

He nodded at Josh. "To assess the possible presence of organic causes for the appearance of demonic possession."

He looked away and struggled to drink some of his water. Something about the man disturbed Josh but he moved past the feeling. He had to be firm and aggressive with these people. Jonathan's life was at stake.

Moon motioned to Father Valdez. "Our lead exorcist, Father Jesse Valdez."

Valdez sat at the head of the table. "You need to know that we are giving you a large portion of grace. Father Caskey has been excommunicated, defrocked, exiled from our church."

"I don't care." Josh said. "He told me to be quiet but I'm tired of being quiet. I need your help."

A waiter appeared, carrying a large tray of food. He placed

steaming plates of food before each person and handed out drinks.

"You'll have to forgive us. We are very hungry at the end of one of our sessions." Valdez started digging into his food.

"Why here?" Josh said.

"It's loud." Sister Jo said. "The things we talk about when we debrief would disturb most people. But I would assume you are used to such talk."

"I don't debrief." Josh said. "I live with it twenty-four seven. I was possessed by the thirteenth demon. Then, I was kidnapped by the twelfth demon who planned to sacrifice me in exchange for my blood to feed his arm of vampires. Then the eleventh demon and the Vitreomancers came along and I almost died at the hand of their white-eyed assassins. My real father showed up no longer dead, as I was told, and I ended up on the tenth demon's spaceship and almost became a crispy critter. I was lucky to dodge the ninth demon, not so Jonathan. And then the eighth demon sucked us into a virtual reality that almost killed us all. The seventh, sixth, and fifth demons were the unholy triad, and I was infected with a virus that made me a zombie. Jonathan got arrested for murder and was put on trial by the fourth demon and I had to face off against the third demon. They both ended up in a courtroom where Jonathan discovered he had a brother he never knew who was behind the murder of their mother. And now, Jonathan has been abducted by his brother, Jeremiah, who is working with the second demon. If anyone at this table needs a drink, it's me!"

"You're a minor." Caskey said. "I told you to let me do the talking."

"Then talk!" Josh shouted. He drew a deep breath.

Caskey pointed to Josh's quesadillas. "You're hangry. Eat. Then we'll talk."

THIRTY-FOUR

The conversation became muted as Josh wolfed down his food. Caskey asked for a glass of sweet tea and ate some tortilla chips. Father Valdez kept looking at him and he felt the relentless gaze of Osondu. He finally spoke.

"Mr. Knight, what is it you want from us?" Osondu said.

Josh wiped his mouth with a napkin. "I want to attend a session."

"I'm afraid that is not possible." Sister Jo said. "Confidentiality issues are involved."

"Not to mention trust issues." Wesley said as he bit into his taco. "We're working hard to build trust with the person."

"That kind of trust is paramount to enable the human host to begin to reject the claims of the demon." Moon said.

Josh nodded and glanced at Black. He had spoken up for Josh's involvement. "Dr. Black, what do you think?"

Black looked up from his plate and his uneven eyes focused on Josh. "Under most circumstances, I would agree with my colleagues. But you are unique, Joshua. You have extensive experience with demons. Real life experience, not just activity during an exorcism, but actions taken out in the real world."

"Donald!" Father Valdez interrupted him. "How can you say this? He's a total stranger and his presence in the process could set us back weeks. James has made it clear Josh has connections with our client. Or maybe the demon. What does the demon would know about Mr. Knight's previous interactions? It could use that knowledge against us." He placed his knife on the table and glared at Josh.

Josh looked at Caskey. He so desperately wanted to know about his connection with the 'client.'

"I am the head of this team, even though Jesse is the lead exorcist." Osondu shouted. "I put this team together and I say unless it's unanimous, you will not be allowed to attend our sessions."

"I agree." Wesley said.

"My vote is no." Moon nodded.

"Me, too." Sister Jo said.

"I guess I'm outnumbered." Dr. Black said. "Unless you have some kind of supernatural connection that trumps us all."

Josh blinked in confusion as the other members of the group glanced in shock at Dr. Black.

"What?" Valdez said.

A light flashed from a reflection down on the water, and Josh squinted. The other members felt it, too. Then he felt the warmth of light and goodness behind him. He stood up and turned and Dude, his guardian angel, leaned against the wall.

"Josh, you must talk to Amobi Osondu alone." His voice was gently lapping waves on a beach.

"Where have you been? Just when I need you most to find Jonathan, you are gone!" Josh said.

"Who are you talking to?" Valdez said, rubbing his eyes.

Josh glanced over his shoulder. "Just a minute. I'm talking to Dude."

"Dude?" Sister Jo said.

"My guardian angel."

Silence fell behind him. He turned. "Look, Dude is his name, and he has been there for me." He glanced back at the angel. "Most of the time. Give us a minute."

"Guardian angel? Please!" Moon said.

"Says the psychologist who takes part in demon exorcism." Caskey grinned. "Give the boy a moment."

Josh's cheeks warmed with anger. "He's right. You talk to demons every day and you can't believe I talk to angels? You guys are unreal. Now, shut up for a moment."

"You shouldn't talk that way to them." Dude said.

Josh closed the distance between them. The angel wore the familiar green surgical scrubs and his green eyes glowed. "I asked you where you've been."

"Right where you need me, Josh. We don't have time for your pride. God has instructed me to help you with this one thing. Osondu is the key. You must be present at tomorrow's exorcism. Ask him about Abeni Oni."

Josh blinked and tried to calm his racing heart. "Okay. But we need to talk."

Dude smiled and disappeared. Josh turned back to the table and looked at the assembled exorcism team and their skeptical faces. "Father Caskey?"

"Yes, son?"

"Do you believe me?"

"Yes."

Josh retrieved a napkin from the table and found a pen on the nearby serving tray. He wrote the name, "Abeni Oni" on the napkin and walked around the table to Amobi Osondu. He placed the napkin on the table. "Dude told me to ask you about this name." He tapped the napkin. "Tell everyone to leave so we can talk. Now."

Osondu froze and slowly picked up the napkin. "How did you know about this?"

"Dude told me."

Osondu stood up slowly and glared at Caskey. "You brought this on us."

"No, don't look at James. He has nothing to do with this." Josh tapped the napkin. "I take it neither does anyone else. We need to talk. Alone. Now."

"You are an impertinent young man!" Osondu hissed.

"I'm tired of your games. I've faced the most powerful demons on the planet and helped best them. This demon you're dealing with is low hanging fruit and I need help."

Osondu wiped his mouth and nodded. His hands shook as he picked up the napkin. "I think it best we convene for the evening." He motioned to the others around the table.

"But we can't possibly allow him to be present!" Valdez said.

Osondu tapped the napkin with a finger. "This changes everything. You will have to trust me. Besides, an angel has spoken."

They muttered among themselves and then slowly trickled from the room. Dr. Black stood up, his crooked frame almost knocking over his chair. He winked at Josh and followed the others down the hallway.

Osondu pointed to Caskey. "You, too, James."

Josh nodded. "It's okay, Father. I've got this."

"I believe you do, my boy. Forgive me for doubting you." Caskey stood painfully and shuffled from the room. "I'll wait outside."

Osondu slowly collapsed into his chair, his gaze drawn to the napkin.

"Want to tell me about Abeni Oni?" Josh settled in a chair next to him.

"The name says it all. Abeni means 'we prayed, and we received'. Oni means 'someone born on a holy ground.'" He groaned and tears filled his eyes. "She was a beautiful child of six. Huge, brown eyes and a mane of black hair. Her skin was flawless for such a poor child born in Nigeria's Central Plateau." Osondu's gaze shifted to Josh. "What do you know about Nigeria?"

"Not much. But you're going to tell me what I need to know," Josh said.

"Slightly less than half of the population is Christian, mostly in the South. The other half Muslim. Some Muslims are radicalized by Boko Haram, a jihadist group bent on genocide. Thousands and thousands of Christians have been killed since 2009. For sport. For jihad."

Osondu leaned forward in obvious pain. He placed his head in his hands and wept. For a moment Josh almost relented, but there was too much at stake. Osondu lifted his tear-stained cheeks and leaned back in the chair. "Want to know what my name means? My first name, Amobi, means one who knows the heart of man." He laughed and shook his head in dismay. "Ironic, considering my last name. Osondu means running for life."

"Were you part of the Boko Haram?"

"No." Osondu whispered. "I wanted to be. I was small and skinny and could barely carry a rifle. They laughed at me and told me to go back to my mother's breasts. But, no, I had to prove myself." Osondu stood up and walked to the plastic screen and pulled it aside. Cold lake air filled the room. "I took Abeni from her family and dragged her to the Boko Haram gathering. I was so proud. I wanted them to recognize me as a full fledged member. There I was, a skinny fourteen year old boy who thought he was a man."

The sun had lowered along the western horizon and bright orange and red clouds hovered over the distant lake. "They laughed at me. They told me I was too young and a fool. I ran away into the underbrush ashamed of what I had done."

He returned to his chair. "I hid among the trees and cried and cursed and tried to come up with a plan. I wanted significance in a world where human life meant nothing, Josh. Night fell and as I shivered in the cold, a light appeared in the trees." His dark brown eyes filled with tears. "The most beautiful light I have ever seen. A warm breeze stirred, and the light moved and settled near my feet. A figure appeared in the light. Fear gripped me. I fell on my face in shock because somehow I knew the light was good and I was evil."

Osondu grabbed a glass of water and sipped it. "In that light I saw my Savior, Josh. Jesus appeared to me, his eyes filled with compassion and love. One thought filled my head. Love your enemy. Do not return hatred with hatred. When I looked up, the light was gone. I ran back to the Boko Haram gathering. What I had done with Abeni was wrong and I needed to take her back to her family."

Osundo fell silent and his face stiffened. "A fighter met me at the edge of the clearing. He grabbed me and shook me until my teeth rattled. I told him I had seen Jesus and I had to take Abeni back to her family. He laughed at me and said his spirit had given him power over me."

Osondu looked up at Josh. "His spirit, Josh. A demon! I don't know how I knew, but I said the name of Jesus Christ and he released me. He looked at me with fear. I tried to push him aside, and he backed away in fear. As I headed toward the clearing, he laughed."

"You're too late, traitor. They have taken her as their prize. There is no Abeni left for you to rescue."

Osondu drank more water. "I screamed to the top of my lungs and he laughed and laughed. I knew if I stayed, they would take me and kill me. I had to do something. I did not know what to do, so I ran and ran and ran."

Osondu drew a shuddering breath. "I almost died in the bush until a hunter found me and took me back to his camp where I met one of his friends. She was the wife of a missionary. She took me in and adopted me, Josh. She taught me how to follow my Jesus. I vowed if I ever left Nigeria, I would never forget the name Abeni Oni. It has become my mission to defeat these demons wherever I can." He looked at me and frowned. "I'm not Catholic. I cannot be a part of formal exorcisms. Jesse approached me once I came to the states when I tried to cast out a demon on Bourbon Street in New Orleans. He took me under his wing and brought me into this group. Since he cannot sanction formal exorcisms with other denominations, he made me the leader of this group."

"Amobi, I am also adopted. Not adopted just by Jonathan Steel, but into the family of God." Josh drew a deep, shuddering breath. "My mother faced a demon. I lost her because she sacrificed herself to defeat a man possessed by the thirteenth demon." I looked at the man's dark features and his moist green eyes. "I have a plan, Amobi. All I want to do is watch an exorcism. But when the time comes, there is something I will do and you must not stop me."

Osondu looked at the napkin. "Dude, huh?"

Josh laughed. "Yeah, I used to say dude a lot. I guess he liked the name. You know, he saved me once by making me jump out of a moving airplane on the tarmac at Heathrow Airport."

Osondu raised an eyebrow. "Now that's a story I'd like to hear."

"After the exorcism, Osondu. We don't have much time."

Osondu nodded. "Then meet us at the prison in the morning at 8 A.M."

"Prison?"

"Sounds to me like James Caskey knows more than you think he does about our client." Osondu stood up and put out a hand. "Glad to meet you, Joshua Knight. Welcome to the team."

Josh shook the man's hand and wondered if he had bitten off more than he could chew. A prison? The only prison he knew of was Rockwall Detention center where Jonathan had been held after being arrested. And if he knew Jonathan, there would be a few enemies he had made while in jail.

CHAPTER

THIRTY-FIVE

Nanny delivered a sandwich, fruit, and bottled water and never said a word as she walked out of the room. Steel ate the meager lunch and waited for the call to return to the room. Why was Jeremiah interested in his trips to Africa and the Middle East? Since the return of his memories, Steel had yet to assimilate all of them. Did the Captain send him on missions to these places? In an African prison, Steel had his implants placed, but he had told Jeremiah about that incident. Where else had he been in Africa and the Middle East?

He relaxed on his bed and studied the stained acoustic tiles above him. Jeremiah asked for a specific memory. Steel wanted to know how his mother died. Could he make a bargain? Memory for memory? What then? Would Jeremiah release him? What would happen to the mysterious woman appearing in his room? Or Snake, for that matter? He couldn't leave them both behind.

"Oh, Snake what should I do?"

"Jonathan!"

Steel sat bolt upright on his bed. A green light played across the far wall and a figure appeared in the center of the wall, coalescing from the green light. A ghostly image of the Crimson Snake stepped out of the light and stood not a meter away from him.

"Snake?"

"Quiet. I have worked very hard to break through the rift in the Void to speak to you. Don't alert Jeremiah." Her left arm was missing.

"The Void?"

"I don't have much time. It is hard to break free from the constraints of the Grimvox. When I am reattached, I have learned to focus on the names of the dead from Max's notebook. It keeps my mind clear for a few moments before the two of you come into the room." She wiped a green tear from her cheek. "I can't hold out much longer, Jonathan. Soon, I will be lost in the maddening currents of evil. But before I am, I have to know something." She paused and grimaced. "This is hard for me to say. How do I become like you? I mean, how do I give myself over to your Christ?"

Steel stood up slowly. "You're kidding."

"I am not kidding, honey. Look, I asked Max for help. She told me to memorize the names of those I had killed. I did. Now, in the chaos of the Void I see their faces and when I do, I cling to them. They are my lifelines that keep me from being sucked down into madness. I will die, Jonathan. I know it. It is inevitable. And when I do, I do not want to serve the second demon and his master. Now tell me. What must I do?"

Steel couldn't believe his ears. Snake wanted forgiveness? She was willing to repent? But he had never shared the method of turning one's life over to Christ. Lord, what should I do?

"All I can tell you, Snake."

"Rebecca. My name is Rebecca Reynolds. I had a terrible

childhood and ended up in an abusive home. I killed the men who abused me, Jonathan. I was only fourteen. They had chained me in their auto repair garage. After I killed them, still in chains, one of them did one last deed before he died. He had me elevated by the chains to the ceiling. I hung there for hours. It was the weekend. No one came to check on me. I still had the knife I had used on one of them." Snake, that is, Rebecca, closed her eyes as she spoke. "Well, you can guess what I had to do to escape." She held up the stump of her left arm. "Bleeding to death, I almost died when he showed up."

"Who?"

"A pale man with living tattoos. Would you like to see?"

Before Steel could answer, he found himself in a darkened garage.

THE ODOR of death filled her nostrils as Rebecca slashed at her left arm. With one last swipe of the knife, her upper arm was free from the chain and she fell ten feet to the floor. Blood poured from her arm despite the temporary tourniquet she had fashioned from her belt before using the knife. She tried to tighten it more, but the blood kept leaking from her arm. Weak from over twenty-four hours hanging from the chain, she couldn't sit upright much longer. She slumped over onto the garage floor, her head on its side. She focused on the empty eyes of one of the stooges lying in a pool of blood a couple of feet from her. She would die here despite having her revenge. "Somebody help me." She whispered. "I'll do anything. Just help me."

Rebecca blinked as something appeared in the shadows. A sinuous form lifted into view from the open pit in which she had crushed one of her assailants with the hydraulic lift. The form writhed into the meager light, a giant snake with glittering red eyes and stark white scales. It slumped forward onto the floor and coiled in upon itself in the pool of blood before her. The mound of white flesh moved and pulsed and from the puddle of blood it arose into the figure of a man. His skin was snowy white and stained with the blood of one of the dead men. He had no hair on his body and his eyes glowed with red fire. He wiped his hands across his chest and blood flowed down his body. Behind the wiping motion, pants appeared on his torso, leaving his chest uncovered. Tattoos appeared on his bare chest. Snake blinked in confusion as they moved.

"Rebecca, you called for help?" He said.

"Who are you?" She whispered.

"I am your savior. If you accept my help, I will heal you."

Rebecca swallowed hard. "What's the catch?"

"You are wise beyond your years. I see you have acquired valuable skills." He motioned to the two dead bodies before her and then behind him to the third body in the pit. "I can make use of your skills. You can bring this vengeance on any and all who deserve it. I can empower you." He licked his lips with a very red tongue. His eyes glowed.

"I don't have much choice, do I?"

"You always have a choice." He tilted his head like a lizard examining an insect.

"You mean live or die?" She tried to sit up and her good hand slid in the blood pooling around her.

"My name is Lucas. Join with me in this endeavor and you will find a new life filled with purpose. You can bring justice to those who deserve it."

"Fine. Get on with it."

❧

"He stopped the bleeding and in the coming years, trained me to be an assassin. I never knew about the demons, Jonathan, until later. I never accepted one. I was already a puppet of the highest bidder. At least with them, I could walk away."

Steel stood up and approached her image. "Then you must realize you can't possibly be good all the time. God is goodness and we cannot abide in His presence. In order to do that, we must receive his forgiveness for our brokenness. I wanted to kill my brother but chose a different path. Would you like to know what I did?"

"Yes. Please."

I sat in Kevin's office at his church. My mind was reeling with what I had just experienced. I had a brother! He killed our mother! He worked with a demon. I had been possessed by that demon!

My heart raced and my mouth was dry. I wanted to scream. I wanted to cry.

"Dude, calm down." Kevin said.

"I wanted to kill him, Kevin." I blurted out. "He killed Mother and he deserves to die."

"No one deserves to die." Kevin said calmly.

"Yes, they do!" I opened and closed my fists.

"Who is telling you that? God or Satan?" Kevin said.

I glared at him. "I don't care. I find out I have a brother and he is the one who killed our mother and you want me to do what? Forgive him?"

"No, I want you to find forgiveness for yourself." Kevin said.

I put my face in my hands and screamed. Kevin touched my shoulder, and I shrugged it away.

"JJ, what was it like to be controlled by a demon?" Kevin asked.

"I don't remember much. Just wanting to get out of my cage. He had me locked away in my mind. I was doing things I wanted to do, but I *didn't* want to do. He was controlling me. But deep inside, I wanted to do some of those things." I focused on Kevin. "I don't understand, bro. What's happening to me?"

Kevin nodded and retrieved a Bible from his desk. "Paul had the same problem. Can I read you a few verses?"

"Why not? It won't change anything!"

"Romans 7:14-20. *'We know that the law is spiritual; but I am unspiritual, sold as a slave to sin. I do not understand what I do. For what I want to do I do not do, but what I hate I do. And if I do what I do not want to do, I agree that the law is good. As it is, it is no longer I myself who do it, but it is sin living in me. For I know that good itself does not dwell in me, that is, in my sinful nature. For I have the desire to do what is good, but I cannot carry it out. For I do not do the good I want to do, but the evil I do not want to do—this I keep on doing. Now if I do what I do not want to do, it is no longer I who do it, but it is sin living in me that does it.'* Sounds confusing, doesn't it?"

"Bro, it sounds like what's going through my mind right now."

"JJ, there is only one thing that will replace the pain and emptiness and guilt and shame and terror in your heart and mind. It is making Jesus Christ the center of your life. If you don't, I fear another demon will find you empty and move back in."

Tears filled my eyes. "Then help me, Kevin."

Kevin leaned toward me and motioned around us. "JJ, we see beauty, purpose, and evidence of God's design around us. The Bible tells us that God originally planned a world that worked perfectly where everything and everyone fit together in harmony. God made each of us with a purpose: to worship Him and walk with Him. In Genesis 1:31, it says, *'God saw all that He made, and it was very good.'* And then in Psalm 19:1, it says, *'The heavens declare the glory of God, and the sky proclaims the work of His hands.'* But life doesn't work when we ignore God and His original design for our lives. We selfishly insist on doing things our own way. The Bible calls this sin. We all sin and distort the original design. The consequences of our sin is separation from God, in this life and for all of eternity."

"Bro, I got that part down pretty good." I said.

Kevin nodded. "In Romans 3:23 it says, *'All have sinned and fall short of the glory of God.'* And Romans 6:23 says *'for the wages of sin is death.'* Sin leads to a place of brokenness. We see this all around us and in our own lives as well. When we realize life is not working, we begin to look for a way out. We tend to go in many directions, trying different things to figure it out on our own. Brokenness leads to a place of realizing a need for something greater. Romans 1:25 says, *'They exchanged the truth of God for a lie, and worshipped and served something created instead of the Creator.'"*

"At this point, we need a remedy – some good news. Because of His love, God did not leave us in our brokenness. Jesus, God in human flesh, came to us and lived perfectly according to God's design. Jesus came to rescue us – to do for us what we could not do for ourselves. He took our sin and shame to the cross, paying the penalty of our sin by His death. Jesus was then raised from the dead – to provide the only way for us to be rescued and restored to a relationship with God. You know John 3:16, *'For God so loved the world in this way: He gave His One and only Son. And whoever believes Him will not perish but will have eternal live.'* And in Colossians 2:14 *'He erased the certificate of debt and has taken it out of the way by nailing it to the cross.'"*

"I think I understand, Kevin. I know what evil feels like. I lived with it and I don't want it to control me anymore. What happens next?" I said.

"Well, simply hearing this Good News is not enough. We must admit our sinful brokenness and stop trusting ourselves. We don't have the power to escape the brokenness on our own. We need to be rescued. We must ask God to forgive us and turn from sin to trust ONLY in Jesus. This is what it means to repent and believe. Believing, we receive new life through Jesus and God turns our lives in a new direction. Mark 1:15 says *'Repent and believe in the good news.'* Ephesians 2:8-9 says *'For you are saved by grace through faith, and this is not from yourselves, it is God's gift, not from works, so that no one can boast.'* And Romans 10:9 tells us *'If you confess with your mouth, Jesus is Lord, and believe in your heart that God raised Him from the death, you will be saved.'"*

Kevin reached out and put a hand on mine. "JJ, now that you have heard this Good News, God wants you to respond to Him. You can talk to Him using these words: 'My life is broken. I recognize it's because of my sin I need you. I believe Christ came to live, die and was raised from the dead, to rescue me from my sin. Forgive me. I turn from my selfish ways and put my trust in You. I know that Jesus is Lord of all, and I will follow Him.'"

"I can do that right now?"

"Right now! Just repeat after me." Kevin repeated the prayer and I let the words echo in my mind as I spoke them out loud. A wall crumbled around my heart. Light chased away the dark shadows of my mind. I felt something warm and stable fill my heart and my mind. A voice echoed within my emptiness and filled it with love. Jesus Christ through his Holy Spirit moved into the shattered rooms of my house and filled me with love and light and forgave me. Yes, forgave me. I felt it and I knew it.

I laughed and clasped Kevin by the shoulders. "Bro, I'm changed. I feel so different."

"It's a start, JJ. But you have to grow deeper. Read your Bible. Let me or other Christians guide you as you grow. You're not in this alone."

I nodded and then frowned as the realization hit me. "But I still can't find it within me to forgive Jeremiah."

"I never said this would be easy." Kevin said. "Anything that is worth something will always come with a cost. You will have to eventually find a way to release this hatred toward your brother. Until then, it will cost you every time you think on him and wish him to come to harm."

The door to Kevin's office opened and the Captain stepped in. "Did he do it?" He looked at Kevin.

"Yes." Kevin stood up. "JJ just surrendered his life to Christ."

I stood up. "Wait! He knew what we were doing?"

"Son, I counted on it. It's the only way to protect you against these demons." The Captain said. He glared at Kevin. "And there is no turning for me. I have to keep my options open. This is war and sympathizing Christians can't fight the kind of war we are about to find ourselves in."

I glanced at Kevin. "You agreed to this?"

"JJ, I agreed to share the Gospel with you. I agreed to help you because I care about you. I don't care about what your father's motives are. This was about you. Not him." Kevin looked at the Captain. "And what's to keep you from succumbing to demons?"

"My hatred for my other son." The Captain nodded toward the open door. "We have to go. Now!"

"I'm not going anywhere with you." I said.

The Captain pulled a pistol from his back belt and fired it at me. A dart imbedded itself in my upper chest. "Yes, you are. Willingly or not."

THE MEMORY FADED, and Steel gasped. Reliving his moment of redemption filled him with new meaning, new purpose, new hope. He smiled. "I had almost forgotten the most important moment in my life. Thank you, Rebecca."

Tears rolled down Snake's cheeks. "I can find that kind of forgiveness despite all I have done?"

"Rebecca, I did terrible things at the command of my father. At the time, I could not remember all my past. But through all those terrible days and horrible deeds, the Spirit of God stayed with me and kept me from becoming a monster. In the middle of my amnesia, I had one memory as my anchor, and it was the moment I prayed with Kevin to make Jesus the Lord of my life. It hasn't been easy reconciling who I had become with what I need to be. But God's grace is sufficient. You've heard the story of Saul on the road to Damascus?"

Rebecca nodded. "I was dragged to church many times."

"Saul killed Christians. He led others to stone Jesus' followers. And one day, he had a one-on-one encounter with the risen Christ and it not only changed his life, it shaped the early church. All part of God's plan. We can't understand why you and I have lived a life hurting people. We can't understand why God allowed people like my father or Lucas to hurt us. There is only one thing I am certain of, and it is the redemptive power of Jesus Christ. You just experienced one of my most powerful memories. I remember every word of that prayer. You pray it with me and you will be changed." Steel said.

Where was this coming from? The words seemed to pour out of his mouth. The only time such a thing had happened was when Joshua Knight asked him how to become a Christian. Even though he had been steeped in anger and resentment toward the thirteenth demon, he had been able to recount this one memory to Josh. It had made a difference in Josh's life. Much had happened since then. Reaching out to Rebecca seemed so natural. "You want to try?"

"Yes." She whispered.

Steel repeated the prayer and Rebecca echoed each word. As she softly spoke, her face relaxed and tears streamed down her cheeks. When they finished, she opened her tear-filled eyes.

"Oh my! It is so beautiful! I see him, Jonathan. I see my Lord." Her eyes focused beyond him. "Yes. I will." She looked at Steel and laughed. "He spoke to me, Jonathan. I will help you escape, eventually, Jonathan. But He says you must find forgiveness."

"For Jeremiah?"

"Yes. And yourself. I will go now. I have much to do. I'll be at the table. Thank you, love." She faded into the green light.

Before Steel could assimilate all that had just happened, the door screeched open behind him and Nanny stood on the threshold. He turned and wiped tears from his eyes.

"It stinks in here!" She hissed. "What are you crying about?"

"Another one has escaped your grasp. Can we get on with this?" Before she could react, he slid past her and headed for the conference room. If Rebecca could find forgiveness, could he find a way to forgive his brother? God help me, he prayed.

THIRTY-SIX

Snake hovered over the Grimvox and Jeremiah sat in his chair. He wore a plaid flannel shirt and his hair was in disarray. Steel avoided eye contact with Snake. He couldn't let Jeremiah know they had communicated.

"You don't look so good." Steel settled into his chair. "I have a proposition for you."

Jeremiah frowned. "You are in no position to bargain."

"I think I am. I told you I was willing to stay. I want to speak to the second demon. Now."

Jeremiah laughed. "You can't make a demand of me." He froze, and the demonic presence seemed to climb up his back and over his head. His hair stood on end and his face stiffened and changed. His turquoise eyes glowed with power.

"What do you want?" the second demon growled.

"A bargain. I know who is really in charge."

"Do you?" Jeremiah's hand drifted toward the Grimvox. "Let me show you what happens to those who oppose me. Touch the Grimvox."

Steel hesitated, and the second demon frowned. "If you desire a bargain, then you need this memory, JJ."

Steel touched the Grimvox, and he was somewhere else.

Shameal hurried down the alleyway, with Topas by his side. "I tell you we are on the edge of a knife."

Topas nodded. "I understand, Shameal. Peter has preached to Gentiles."

"Blasphemy!" Shameal hissed. "Come, we must hurry before Peter has a chance to weave his lies."

Topas grabbed Shameal by the arm and jerked him to a stop. "Shameal! You cannot call Peter a liar!"

Shameal rolled his eyes. "He had dinner with an officer of the Roman army, Topas! The very people who crucified Jesus! They have deceived him, I fear. We must confront this deception before the others are also deceived." Shameal pulled his arm out of Topas' grasp and rushed down the alleyway toward the house where the believers waited.

The room was hot and humid, and the odor of sweat filled the air. Shameal paused and listened to the small voice in the back of his head. "Be strong," it said. "You alone have knowledge of the ways of Jehovah God. You alone see the truth." Yes, he thought. I must be strong and listen to my spirit.

The believers sat around an opening in the center as Peter appeared. Before anyone could speak, Shameal felt the prodding of his inner voice to speak. "Peter, you entered the home of a Gentile and even ate with him." Shameal shouted as he stood up.

Murmurs ran around the room. Other voices joined his. Yes, he thought. They see the truth as I do. This man must be stopped. "Peter, we cannot allow Gentiles into the church. They defile God's ways."

Peter raised a hand, and the room grew silent. "I was in the city of Joppa praying, and in a trance, I saw a vision. I saw something like a large sheet being let down from heaven by its four corners, and it came down to where I was," Peter said.

"A dream?" Shameal said. "You speak of a dream? How much wine had you drunk before you slept?" Some in the crowd laughed. Shameal's heart soared. They were on his side, on the side of truth!

Peter ignored the laughter, his intense gaze focusing on Shameal. "I looked into the sheet and saw four-footed animals of the earth, wild beasts, reptiles and birds."

"Unclean animals?" Shameal said sternly. "Perhaps Lord God Jehovah was showing you what you must not eat."

Peter shook his head, his long gray hair falling across his shoulders. He smoothed out his beard and continued. "Then I heard a voice telling me, 'Get up, Peter. Kill and eat.'

"I replied, 'Surely not, Lord! Nothing impure or unclean has ever entered my mouth.'"

"Yes!" Shameal said. "And yet, you still ate with Gentiles? Did you not heed your own words?"

Peter raised a hand to silence Shameal. "The voice spoke from heaven a second time, 'Do not call anything impure that God has made clean.' This happened three times, and then it was all pulled up to heaven again."

Murmurs filled the room. Shameal groaned and pulled at his robe. "Blasphemy, Peter! You are defying God's laws."

Peter raised his hands, and the room grew silent. "Right then, three men who had been sent to me from Caesarea stopped at the house where I was staying. The Spirit told me to have no hesitation about going with them. These six brothers also went with me, and we entered Cornelius' house. He told us how he had seen an angel appear in his house and say, 'Send to Joppa for Simon, who is called Peter. He will bring you a message through which you and all your household will be saved.'"

Peter paused and looked around the room. "Brothers and sisters, as I began to speak, the Holy Spirit came on them as he had come on us at the beginning. Then I remembered what the Lord had said: 'John baptized with water, but you will be baptized with the Holy Spirit.'"

Shameal groaned again and tore his robe. "Peter, you defy God!"

Peter paused and the room fell silent. His gaze fell on Shameal and something inside of him writhed and groaned. He grimaced and touched his chest as pain blossomed within him. What was happening? Was not the same Holy Spirit within him that Peter spoke of? The thing inside of him spun and writhed and he hurried from the room. He stopped in the hallway.

"What is happening?" He hissed.

"You asked me in." A voice spoke in his head. "I gave you the knowledge of your own scriptures to defy Peter. And you have failed. This day, your soul will find its way to Hades and eternal punishment."

"No!" Shameal collapsed against the wall and the last words he would ever hear on earth echoed down the hallway.

"So if God gave them the same gift he gave us who believed in the Lord Jesus Christ, who was I to think that I could stand in God's way?" Peter said.

THE MEMORY FADED and Steel collapsed back in astonishment. He had just witnessed scripture brought to life. Why had it not affected the second demon?

"You may wonder why I showed you such a powerful memory, JJ? Imagine that Jeremiah is Shameal. He has asked me in, and he has given himself to me fully. There is nothing you can say or do or promise that will allow me to free him. His fate is sealed just as Shameal's."

Steel drew a deep breath. He had to believe otherwise. "Here is what I offer. I want to talk to Jeremiah and I have two questions. He will answer each question from his memory. And when he has, I will gladly and freely give you the memory you desire. This I promise. And I never break my promise."

The second demon studied him, head tilted and eyes glowing. "Two questions?"

"And Jeremiah must answer them truthfully by showing me his memories."

The second demon crossed his arms and leaned back in his chair. "It is done. You realize any deal made with a demon has the strength of a legal contract?"

"I have made such a contract before, if you recall."

"With the fifth, sixth, and seventh demon. Yes, I remember. You also turned that agreement around on them."

"I did. But this agreement is fairly simple. Can you bring Jeremiah back?"

The second demon pursed his lips and shrugged. "Fine."

Jeremiah's face relaxed and he blinked. He glared at me. "What did you do?"

"I spoke to your boss. We made a deal. You will keep it."

Jeremiah cursed loudly. "Two questions? You can't ask where we are."

"I don't care, right now, Jeremiah. I only want answers to two very important questions. You can only answer these questions by giving me your memories. In exchange, I'll give you any memory you desire. First question: How did you meet the second demon?"

Jeremiah ran a hand through his hair and stood up. "Fine! But tomorrow. I need to rest and so do you." He walked out of the room.

Steel stood up slowly and walked around the table to stand behind Snake. Rebecca, he corrected himself. Her eyes were open and empty, fixed on the swirling clouds within the opening of the Grimvox. He tried to focus on the interior of the Grimvox and for a moment, the face of a teenage boy appeared.

"Go to you room!"

Steel flinched and Nanny appeared with her wheelchair bearing Ila. "I'm taking Snake back to rest. Now, go!"

Steel cast one last glimpse at Snake and returned to his room. He spent a restless evening sifting through the events of the past couple of days. Patiently, he waited for Rebecca or the mysterious woman to appear. Nothing happened and he finally fell into a dreamless sleep.

CHAPTER

THIRTY-SEVEN

"Are you sure Jason is safe?" Ruth paced around the conference room table at the cabin compound.

"He'll be fine." Yvonne said. "He's with Sam." Yvonne had returned to the cabin compound at Max's request.

"Did Jason learn anything new from the Captain's recordings?" Max said.

"Not really. A little more insight into the Captain's motives. Maybe. The man is inscrutable." Yvonne said. "They were going to check out JJ's house."

"I understand you've been in that chamber under the library." Max sat at the head of the table in a snow white blouse and matching slacks. Her eyes were dark and her hair slightly askew. The stress was getting to Max, Yvonne thought. If it were her, she would be a basket case by now.

Yvonne shivered and nodded. "Yes, I was there with Sam's ex-partner right after they had removed the body."

Ruth settled at the table beside her. "That must have been horrible."

"Beyond horrible, Ruth." Yvonne's gaze focused on the far wall. "The smell of death! And old blood."

"Let's move on from that, shall we?" Max interrupted her horror-stricken moment of reverie. "You asked about a theme park in Florida? You must realize there are dozens of such parks in central Florida."

Yvonne placed a shaky hand on her laptop keyboard before her. "We saw something, Max." She turned the screen toward Max. "This is the moment we were watching the Captain's recording when it happened."

Max leaned forward, all attention focused on the laptop. The Captain's moving lips froze, and the screen glitched and pixelated. An image appeared from the vantage point of someone walking down "Maimed Street" toward an arcane castle in the distance. The point of view shifted to show the young girl walking beside the observer. The image faded back into the Captain's monolog.

"I have seen the Captain's video before and do not recall what you have just shown me." Max said.

Yvonne frowned. "I figured as much. You've got your fingers in everything."

"Whatever it takes, my dear." Max said. "That brief image of a theme park was not in the original recording."

Yvonne nodded. "Exactly! We were watching the video footage, and I was transferring the video to Jason's cell phone so he would have a copy. That way I didn't have to worry about transferring a digital copy that might end up in some hacker's cloud account. Whatever just happened occurred in real time as we were watching the video."

Ruth sat back and sighed. "How is this helping us find Jonathan?"

Max stood up and paced behind her chair. "There is one

object that could conceivably contain such images. Recordings of memories of the host of a demon. We have spoken of this before."

"The Grimvox?" Yvonne said.

"The what?" Ruth asked.

"An arcane object capable of storing the memories of demons, my dear." Max leaned on the back of her chair. "Somehow that object keeps surfacing in our discussions. Although I cannot explain how a snippet of a demon's memory could have transferred to that video. Were there any other such snippets?"

Yvonne shook her head. "No. Just that one."

Ruth had her own laptop open and tapped away at the keyboard. "Can we find this theme park?"

Max sat back down and motioned to a monitor. Gamma, her every present assistant appeared on the screen. "Madam, I have searched the archives and there was indeed a theme park in central Florida with a 'Maimed Street'. I'm sending the information to Ruth's laptop."

Ruth nodded and air played her screen back to the monitor. A faded brochure in PDF format opened on the screen. In big, scary letters, the name of the theme park covered the top of the front of the brochure.

"Tragic Kingdom?" Yvonne said, turning to survey the monitor mounted on the wall behind her. "Really?"

"Looks like it opened in 1989 about the time of Disney MGM Studios and Universal Studios Orlando." Gamma said over the audio feed. "Maimed Street is the main thoroughfare leading into the park. Several 'lands' patterned on scary notions. Stayed open about twenty years or so before going out of business."

"Who would want to go to this horror show?" Ruth paged through the document on her laptop.

Yvonne had turned back to her laptop. "Gamma can you share those links with me?"

"Sure."

Yvonne opened links that appeared in her messages and scanned the pages. "It did well for about fifteen years until Harry Potter became really big. Seems the Tragic Kingdom couldn't compete with magical wizards and the park suffered low attendance for years before closing about five years ago."

Max watched the brochure page by on the monitor. "That castle. What did Vivian say? She met with the Dark Council in an abandoned theme park castle!" Max stood up. "Gamma, get me Vivian, please. I sent her and Raven to Snake's island for reconnaissance."

"Yes, madam."

Yvonne studied the screen of her laptop. "The question, Max, is who built this thing? This took millions to build and millions to maintain."

A video chat appeared on the screen. Vivian looked a little worse for wear. "Didn't finish my beauty sleep, Max. Twenty hours with no sleep."

"Have you found anything on the island?"

Vivian held up an insect like object. "A micro-drone shaped like a dragonfly. We think that is how Jeremiah got past security."

Raven appeared behind Vivian. "And how he knew Snake was here."

"He left it on the table in the house along with Snake's notebook."

Max drew a deep breath. "I have underestimated that fiend."

"What notebook?" Ruth asked.

"The Crimson Snake asked for a path to redemption. I tasked her with memorizing the face and names of every individual who died on the Swiss flight she sabotaged. I was hoping to awaken her conscience." Max stood up. "Perhaps we can backtrack the drone's connection with Jeremiah."

Raven shook her head. "It's fried. Self destruct mechanism took out the insides." She squeezed it between her hands and the insect like drone crumbled into dust.

Max swore and Ruth tensed at the words. Max sat slowly back into her chair and fought for composure. "I have another task for you. We found a connection. Does the name Tragic Kingdom ring a bell, Vivian?"

Vivian froze. "Yes. The castle where the council meets in an abandoned theme park called the Tragic Kingdom."

"And you never thought to mention this?" Max said tersely.

Vivian blanched. "There's a lot I haven't mentioned, Max. Mostly because I know so much. The park is abandoned, a wreck. They met there because of the atmosphere. Ghoulish delight, you might say."

Raven sat beside Vivian. "What does this have to do with Jonathan?"

"It's a long story. Gamma will get you a flight to central Florida. Birdsong and Ross are on another assignment. Go to the park, Raven. Vivian, you're the tour guide. Make sure Jeremiah isn't hiding Jonathan in that castle."

Vivian sat back away from the camera view. "Maybe I can grab a nap on the way."

RAVEN ENDED the chat and turned in her chair to face Vivian. "Tragic Kingdom?"

Vivian stood up and paced around the small house on the island. "I met with the Council there at least twice. They liked the spooky atmosphere. But, I also met with them once in

Dubai. I doubt this abandoned theme park is their permanent residence."

"Spooky?"

Vivian paused and laughed. "Yeah, Maimed Street. And Malignant Mouse will eat you. Let's get going."

THIRTY-EIGHT

Josh drove south on highway 175. Traffic was horrendous, and he had been driving for almost an hour to a facility just eleven miles southeast of downtown Dallas. The snow storm settling over northwest Louisiana had passed through the area leaving behind a stiff, icy wind.

"Seagoville Correctional Institute, right?" He glanced at Father Caskey in the passenger seat. "I'm glad we're not going to the Rockwall Detention center."

"If Jonathan had not been released, he would have been transferred to Seagoville from the Rockwall Detention Center." Caskey said. He wore his black turtleneck shirt and a black jacket and matching pants. His white hair was combed smoothly and his face shown red from his recent shave. "The client was at Rockwall until yesterday. He was transferred this morning to Seagoville."

"You clean up pretty good," Josh said. Father James Caskey wore a pressed black shirt buttoned to the neck beneath a black blazer and black pants. All that was missing was his white clerical collar. Josh wore a flannel shirt and jeans to offset the biting cold air.

"I have to be spotless for the team, Josh. The least imperfection will give the demon something to focus on."

"What about me?"

Caskey patted his arm. "You will not be seeing the client today, Josh. We cannot introduce you on the first day. It will disrupt weeks of progress."

"What?" Josh said. "James, time is running out to find Jonathan."

"And when we find him, you will be prepared to face the second demon. Isn't that what you wanted from this encounter?"

Josh's face warmed with anger, and he avoided glancing at Caskey. "Of course." But I will speak to the demon before the day is over, he thought. "Tell me about this place."

"Seagoville Federal Correction Institute is a prison facility is located on an 830-acre tract. The facility includes a detention center for male offenders and an adjacent satellite prison camp that houses minimum security-male offenders. We will go to a special conference room in the satellite camp."

"So, this person is a prisoner, right?"

"Yes. He agreed to share information about his former criminal associates if the prison would arrange for an exorcism." Caskey said. He leaned toward Josh. "It seems his defense attorney's claims he was not guilty because he was demon possessed fell on deaf ears. But the attorney was sharp enough to arrange a plea bargain for less jail time at a minimal security facility with an 'appropriate' response to the prisoner's religious requests."

"What did this guy do?" Josh saw the exit with the sign for the prison and pulled onto the off ramp.

"Attempted murder, among many other federal charges. You can park in the visitor lot."

Josh pulled into a parking space. Red brick comprised the main building, and it looked for all the world like an elementary school. Outbuildings dotted the expanse of open land surrounded by razor wire fences beginning behind the main building.

"We'll have to walk to the main entrance. Osondu will meet us there."

"James, yesterday, you claimed the client knew me. I assume he ran into Jonathan while they were both at Rockwall, and that is the connection." Josh said.

Caskey refused to meet his gaze. "Excellent deduction. It is a good thing," he pointed upward. "And a God thing the man was moved from that facility. I understand Jonathan made quite a few enemies during his brief incarceration. If we had stayed at Rockwall, my boy, it is likely harm might have come your way. Now, let's get on with this, shall we?"

Caskey climbed out of the truck. Josh followed him around a circular drive and through an open brick wall with two yellow traffic poles to prevent a vehicle from approaching the main building.

Inside the main 'welcome center', two guards stood beside metal detectors. After being searched, Josh and Caskey spied Osondu at the reception kiosk.

"James. Josh." He said with just a bit of tension in his voice. "You'll have to sign some papers and show your I.D. and then I'll take us to the conference room."

The exhaustive screening process demanded everything but a blood sample. Josh and Caskey were given visitor passes and Osondu led them out of the main building. The wind whipped around them as he led them across an open courtyard and toward long brick outbuildings. A guard met them at the entrance and, after checking their passes, allowed them through an electronic lock up into a long hallway.

Osondu stopped before a doorway and motioned inside. "This is a meeting room, Josh. If you and James will wait here, I will have Father Valdez come and give you some orientation as to what will happen. So far, our client has agreed to have two visitors present. Frankly, I think the demons are looking forward to fresh meat."

"Demons? There's more than one?" Josh asked.

Osondu nodded. "The main demon often sends lesser demons to obfuscate and frustrate us. Over the past few weeks, we have seen glimpses of the main demon as we are wearing out the lesser demons." He frowned. "Of course, now that the two of you are here, it will set us back a few days. Now sit."

Caskey sat at a table in the small room and Josh paced around the periphery. Barred windows looked out over a facility that looked far more welcome than any prison should. "Who is the client?" Josh said.

"I can't divulge any information until Father Valdez allows me to." Caskey leaned on his cane with two hands gripped at the top. "You must be patient, Josh. Patience is the most important trait a successful exorcist must develop. It takes time to tease out the secrets of why a person opened themselves to demonic influence."

"Like playing chess." Josh said. "I never liked chess. I prefer video games. Fast-paced."

"In an exorcism, there is no reset, Josh. But battling the demon is much like getting bested by the big villain and having to try new strategies until you find the proper way to get to the next level." Caskey sighed. "And with exorcisms there can be many levels."

The door opened, and Father Valdez entered. He had pulled

his long hair back into a ponytail. The skin graft on his face was clearly visible.

"How did you get that?" Josh pointed to his face. "If you don't mind me asking."

Valdez held a folder to his chest. "I was in an accident at midnight on New Year's Eve. Someone had left an empty trailer on the side of a back road. The wind had blown it into the center of the road. I hit it going about seventy and my truck turned sideways. My head was caught between the cab and the road. I lost my left ear and most of my skull on that side. They said my brain was exposed when they found me on the side of the road."

He sat down and his vision focused on something far, far away. "The policeman said someone had cleared my airway and turned me on my side or I would have died." He looked back at Josh with moist eyes. "Problem was, the officer was alone. There was no one with me. We were surrounded by open fields north of Abilene, Texas. Hill country dominated by windmills." His voice grew husky, and he cleared his throat. "I went to heaven and saw Jesus. He told me my time was not up, and I had to go back and fight the forces of evil. I woke up six weeks later after brain surgery and skin grafts. I became a priest." He smiled. "I have a guardian angel also, Josh. I just don't know his name. He only showed up once and that was when I needed him most."

"Now, let's get on with this." He placed a brown folder on the table. He handed Josh a set of ear buds. "These are for you, Josh. James can come in and sit in the back of the room. But I want you to hear the proceedings before you enter the room."

"Why not video it?"

"We don't use video, Josh." Caskey stood up. "The demons don't need encouragement. These are private and confidential proceedings. No recording of any kind."

"He's right, Josh." Valdez rubbed the side of his face with the skin graft. "You'll hear what we pick up on a cell phone with no audio recording. Once you've heard our proceedings, then you can observe."

"When?"

"Maybe tomorrow." Valdez stood up and turned to leave the room.

Josh collapsed into a chair. "Patience, dude. I have to have patience." He put the ear buds in and watched Caskey follow Valdez out the door. The door closed and silence descended. In a moment, he heard whispering.

"Josh, this is James. I'm sitting in the rear of the room with the cell phone and I'll give you a running comment on the proceedings. They are bringing him into the room now. You will hear Father Valdez address the host and the demon. The others will begin a series of prayers. These prayers have been used for centuries. It will sound chaotic but it is very deliberate. Timothy and Thomas are checking his restraints."

Josh heard people jostling around, the clinking of manacles and a chair sliding on the floor.

"I guess there's no question a demon could break those manacles." Josh said.

A distant voice echoed and he could not understand the words. Valdez's voice overrode the other voice. Multiple voices drowned out Valdez as Moon, Wesley, and Black began to pray. The only thing Josh could hear were the prayers until suddenly a harsh, guttural voice cut through them all.

"Why is *he* here? Why is the fallen priest here? Has he come to relive his sins? I can help him."

"The demon is trying to divert attention by referring to me." Caskey's voice sounded much louder than the demon's voice. "I shouldn't be in the room."

"No! It is good you are here!" The demon's voice shouted.

Valdez raised his voice commanding the demon to back down. The prayers increased in volume. Two more voices joined in with prayer, no doubt Thomas and Timothy.

"She is not gone, Father Caskey." The demon shouted above the others. "She is in eternal limbo. She suffers and suffers and it is because of you."

"You will not address James." Valdez said loudly.

"I will address whomever I wish." And then, with a loud groan, the voice was gone. The prayers continued, but Josh heard another sound. Sobbing and gasping. Caskey was crying.

A new voice rose above the others. Normal in cadence and timber, the new voice sounded normal. "He has allowed me to speak. I want to talk to Josh. Now!"

Josh shot to his feet. That voice? It sounded so familiar.

"Tell him Armando wants to see him again." The voice said and the man's laughter drowned out the prayers.

JOSH BENT over as the cold wind jostled him. A fine misting rain was falling outside the building but he didn't care. Caskey appeared beside him. He glared at the old man.

"Why didn't you tell me it was Armando?"

"I did not know who Armando was," Caskey said. "The man's name is Winston Poole." He looked into the cold wind and his eyes watered. "I inquired through Dr. Black. He is the most accessible person on the team. I merely asked if they could allow us to observe. He was the one who said the client was familiar with you. He was my anonymous contact."

"Yeah, Winny the Poo we called him. He was the head of the vampire clan that kidnaped me and took me to Transylvania." Josh's heart raced. "He tried to kill me. Tried to impale me with spears. That's how Moon knew I was in Transylvania. She knew I had a connection to Armando."

Caskey put a hand on his arm. "I'm so sorry. We couldn't let you know the man's name. Confidentiality."

"How did he know I was here?"

"The demon network, Josh." Caskey said. "I never should have brought you here. It is my fault, my boy, for agreeing to your request. We will go back to Shreveport this evening."

"No! I want to talk to him."

"Out of the question!" Caskey said. "They will never allow it."

Josh whirled on the old man. "Oh yeah? What happens now it knows I am here? What little progress they have made just vanished, and I wasn't even in the room. You were."

Caskey's hair blew in the cold, wet wind and he shivered. "I shouldn't have been there. He taunted me with the past."

"Yeah, she is in limbo. Who is she?"

Caskey blinked against the cold wind. "I can only assume Mary, Max's daughter. She died when she was sucked into the black hole battling the eleventh demon."

"And Cephas said she had given her heart to Christ." Josh tried to calm down. "I'm sorry I reacted this way. She can't be in limbo. She is with Him, James."

Caskey nodded and tears trickled down his face. He wiped them angrily away. "They lie. Their master is the father of lies. They say whatever it takes to bring chaos and confusion."

"I think he was talking about the Crimson Snake." Josh said. Which meant, he thought, Armando knew where Snake was. And if he knew where Snack was, he knew where Jonathan was.

Josh's anger cooled. Father James Caskey had suffered so much more than he had for his poor decisions. He took the man by the arm. "Let's get you back inside where it is warm."

THE TEAM SAT in the room around the small table. Valdez glared at Josh when they came back in.

"I hope your guardian angel is proud, Josh. We just lost months of progress."

"What do we do now?" Sister Jo crossed her arms over her chest. "Start over?"

"He made a deal," Moon said. "If he backs out now, he gets solitary and a much worse prison than Seagoville. He'll have to cooperate."

"The demon will delay things as long as it can." Wesley ran a hand across his comb-over. "It doesn't care if we go back in time three months and start this all over again."

Dr. Black raised his hand as if asking permission. "I say let Josh talk to him."

"What?" Valdez said.

"I agree." Osondu stood in the corner. He turned around. "The angel told Josh to come here after revealing a secret only I would know. Josh is here for a reason."

Dr. Black glanced at Josh. "Do you know who I am?"

Josh nodded slowly. "I figured it out after James said you were the one who told him I would know your client. Dr. Black? Donald? Why don't you tell them your real name?"

The members of the team all looked at Black. He drew a deep breath and his large chest expanded. "I was responsible for helping the man known as Jonathan Steel learn the Bible. When he was injured after confronting his brother, I operated on him and removed the blood from around his brain."

"You also tortured him at the demands of his father." Josh said.

"That is true. I hated it. I only oversaw the torture. But I made sure JJ would survive being thrown in the ocean after his father removed his memory."

Osondu approached the table and looked down at the man. "Who are you?"

"Dr. Daniel Brown. The man known as the Captain created a new identity for me so I could return to the United States. I asked to be a part of this team so I could make restitution for the wrongs of my past."

"Then we are indeed at an impasse." Moon said. "Are you even a doctor?"

"A neurosurgeon." Brown said. He turned in his chair toward Josh. "Josh, you must speak to this man. He may have some information about Jonathan."

"My plan exactly." Josh said.

"Wait a minute!" Caskey stood up. "Your plan?"

"I'm sorry, James. I didn't tell you. Your demon network. Whatever demon has taken possession of Armando, I mean, Winston, can find out where the second demon has taken him."

"No! You're not having this conversation with a demon." Valdez slapped the table top. "This is not why we exist."

"Then what are you trying to do?" Josh said hotly.

"Save a man's soul." Osondu put a hand on Josh's shoulder. "Winston has deep regrets for his past but cannot ask for our Lord's forgiveness while he is a slave to a demon. Our job is to facilitate his freedom."

"And salvation." Wesley said.

"Well, I'm here to save my father's life and if I can do that by talking to a demon, you have to let me speak to it."

"Making a deal with the devil?" Sister Jo said. She looked down at her hands. "I can understand that. I sold my body into the sex trafficking trade at the urgings of a demon's voice. I made may own deals. But my Savior forgave me and gave me a new life. A new purpose.”

“And I sold my soul to the health and wealth industry. Fake healings. Selling handkerchiefs soaked with my holy sweat.” Wesley said. “Until one day, my own estranged son showed up paralyzed from the waist down from a bomb in Iraq. He begged me to heal him.” Wesley swallowed hard. “I couldn’t because my faith was in myself and not my God. I walked away from all of that until I hit bottom and God gave me a new purpose.” He tapped the table. “This team.”

“I’m sure you each have a moving story about how you got here.” Josh said as he made eye contact with each of them. “I’m sure Father Valdez has told you why he has that skin graft.”

“And I had a patient who committed suicide because I was more interested in getting to an opera engagement than paying attention to his pleas for help,” Moon said.

“Well, I am right there in desperate straits like all of you were. My father is missing and has been kidnapped by the second most powerful demon on the planet. I will speak to Armando with or without you. He said he wants to talk to me and I’m sure I can get an audience with him after all of you go back to Rockwall and drowned your sorrows in beer and chips. So go. Get out of here and repurpose or reboot your next exorcism. Armando is mine!”

Josh sat nervously at the table. The team had agreed to wait in the other room in prayer. Father James Caskey sat beside Josh, his face haggard and drawn. The door opened, and a guard ushered in Winston Poole. The last time Josh had seen him, Winston, aka Armando, his hair was down to his shoulders. His eyes had been maroon thanks to the influence of his demons. Since then, he had cut his hair to less than a half an inch and his brown eyes seemed totally ordinary. The guard shackled his manacles to a metal ring on the table. The guard stepped outside the door and the room was silent.

Winston looked around. "Where's Frick and Frack?"

"Timothy and Thomas will not be needed." Caskey said. "At your request, Josh is here."

"I don't want to talk to you, old man." Winston said.

"Too bad. If you want to talk to me, he stays." Josh said with a hint of nervousness in his voice.

Winston stared at Josh and finally smiled. "Well, Josh, you're looking well. How is your chest?"

Josh blinked and before he realized it, rubbed his chest. "I still have the scars."

"A reminder from me."

"You wanted to talk to me?" Josh said, his voice breaking. He swallowed away his nervousness.

Winston studied him for a moment and tilted his head. "Vivian sent her demons into me and forced me to take the fall. I got blamed for so many things she actually did. And now I understand she has received a get out of jail for free card." He leaned toward Josh. "I want you and your broken padre over here to understand I want the same thing. I was used and I want out of here."

"You will never be free as long as you have your demon," Caskey said.

Winston glared at him. "I wasn't talking to you!"

"Like I said. You want to talk to me, Father Caskey stays." Josh said, as his confidence grew. He breathed prayers under his breath. "This is not about me, Armando."

"Armando" leaned back. "Okay, we will go with that name. I know why you're here."

"Enlighten me, dude." Josh said.

"You want to find her."

Josh tried not to flinch. "Yes."

Armando laughed. "No one can rescue her, bro. She's gone."

Caskey tapped the tabletop. "Just to be sure, who are you referring to?"

Armando glanced at him and then back at Josh. "Wait a minute. This isn't about *her*? Someone else is missing. Who is it?" He sat silently for a moment and then grinned. "You know Ila is missing."

Josh drew a deep breath. "Ila? Last I heard, she and her mother had made up."

"No, bro. She went back to the clan. At least what's left of it." Armando raised an eyebrow. "I know where she is."

Josh's heart raced. Could Ila and Jonathan be in the same place? "She's with the second demon." Josh said, trying his best to keep the shakes out of his voice.

Armando shrugged and looked away. "Could be."

"Let me speak to your demon," Josh said.

"So you can send it off to hell?"

"You know it isn't that easy." Josh said. "You've been trying to be rid of it for months. Or have you? Are you really committed to finding redemption? Or is that all a ruse to keep you in this rather sedate prison, dude? This place is like a summer retreat."

Armando frowned. He tried to scratch his face and his hand was brought up short by the manacles. "I don't want you to talk to it." Suddenly his head lurched back and something seemed to overcome him as if crawling up his neck. He shook his head and his face melted into a tense mask of anger. His eyes glowed.

"Fine! I'm here." His voice changed. He rattled off something indecipherable.

"You know that is anatomically impossible." Caskey said. He turned to Josh. "He's speaking Aramaic."

Armando laughed. "What do you pitiful mortals want with me?"

"Which one of Vivian's low hanging fruit demons are you? The bat? The shark? The ameba?" Josh said. "Or are you a slime worm?"

Armando growled and hissed at them. "You think you can insult me? I've dealt with humans for thousands and thousands of years."

Caskey placed his cell phone on the table. "I'm using a translator app, demon. No matter what you say, we will understand it. And we don't have time for you. We would like to speak to the main demon. Your boss."

"What makes you think I need a boss?" Armando growled.

Josh stood up. "Let's go, James. I don't think he really wanted to talk to me. He's wasting our time. Let him go back to his cell and soon they can transfer him to a maximum security cell."

"Wait!" Armando's demon said. "I could care less where this creature rots but I have to answer to a higher authority."

"Ah, the boss?" Caskey said.

Armando glared at him. "Fine. He's coming. And when he gets here, you will regret it."

"I think we can handle it." Josh sat back down.

Armando's face relaxed and his head fell forward limply onto his chest. He looked up, his eyes filled with fear. "Josh? I need help! Please! I don't want this thing in me anymore."

Josh glanced at Caskey. "The team is here to help you, Armando."

"Winston, my name is Winston." Armando looked around wildly. "If Vivian can find forgiveness, so can I. Will you help me?"

"Yes."

Armando shook his head. "I mean it, Josh. No matter what it says, you have to promise to help me. No matter what it takes. Do you promise?"

Josh looked at Caskey. "I can't help you, my boy. It's up to you."

He looked into Winston's fear filled eyes. "Yes, I promise."

Armando smiled and then tensed. "Oh my God. He's here!" His head fell down again and the short hair stood up on his scalp. Static electricity filled the air and sparks popped around Josh's fingers. He jerked his hands up off the table.

Slowly, Winston Poole lifted his head so that his gaze bored relentlessly into Josh. He smiled and slowly, oh so slowly, a dark spiral formed around his right eye. "Hello, Josh. It's been a while."

Josh gasped and stood up. The thirteenth demon had returned.

～

JOSH RAN from the room and out into the cold afternoon air. Caskey hobbled after him.

"Josh! What's wrong?" Caskey stumbled after him.

Josh hyperventilated and fought for control. Caskey took him by the arm, his chest heaving with the exertion. "Josh?"

"The spiral around the eye? It's the thirteenth demon!" Josh whirled on the man. "How? Vivian cast him into Tartarus while we were in Numinocity."

"The false reality?" Caskey's breathing slowed. His breath steamed in the cold air. "Josh, you were in a virtual reality. It's possible the thirteenth demon fooled you into thinking it was being taken away."

"No!" Josh's eyes filled with moisture. "I can't face it again. It was in my head. It is why my mother is dead. It's supposed to be gone into eternal punishment."

Caskey tugged him back toward the building. "Let's go back inside. Talk to the team, my boy. See what they think."

The rest of the team waited in the meeting room. Josh plopped down at the table and put his hands on his head.

"What happened?" Osondu asked.

"The main demon manifested." Caskey leaned against this cane and straightened his unruly white hair. "The thirteenth demon."

Moon gasped and Sister Jo cursed. Valdez turned away in shock and paced across the room to the windows. "This is bad!"

"One of the most powerful demons." Wesley drawled.

Daniel Brown stood up from the table. "What is wrong with all of you? Have you not forgotten that our Lord is greater and more powerful than the most powerful of Satan's minions?"

Josh looked up at Brown. "You worked with the thirteenth demon, bro."

Brown shook his head. "I worked for Ketrick. He knew about my past and threatened to turn me into the authorities if I did not help him with his plans. I had no idea a demon was involved until later and that was when I disappeared."

"Leaving Thomas Parker and his wife in the hands of Ketrick." Josh said.

Brown slumped into his chair. "Granted, you are correct. I am ashamed of much I have done in my life. It is why I joined this team to defeat the demons in this world, Josh. I am trying to make restitution."

Valdez returned from the windows. "Brown is right about

one thing. This thing is just another demon. We will deal with it through the power of our Lord Jesus Christ." He sat beside Josh. "But Josh, you must first deal with this thing. It will use you in the coming exorcism. You must be present or it will disappear and leave lesser demons as place holders. Do you have the strength to deal with the thirteenth demon?"

Josh sat back. Memories of his many encounters with the thirteenth demon played in his memory. He was under the demon's influence right up until his mother took Ketrick into the incinerator. He blinked away tears. Anger, hot and fiery, filled his heart. There was no place for anger in encounters with other humans. Jesus had been clear he should love his enemy. But Jesus had exhibited righteous anger and now was the time to channel that anger. He had to become Jonathan Steel!

"Let me talk to it. Now." He stood up. "No one but me. Give me a few moments with the thing."

ARMANDO SAT PATIENTLY at the table, the black spiral pulsing around his right eye. Josh sat across the table from him and waited. Armando's eyes filled with fire and he tilted his head like a bird examining its prey.

"You are probably wondering why I'm still here in the mortal realm." Armando said.

"Numinocity was a virtual reality. You didn't really get hauled off to hell," Josh said. "I get it. You fooled us. Again."

"I told all of you I would still be left standing when your father finishes with the Dark Council. Once they are gone, along with the Vitreomancers, I will ascend to become the most powerful demon under my master." Armando shrugged. "What can I say? I'm patient."

"Where is Jonathan?"

Armando blinked. "What?"

"Where did the second demon take him?" Josh asked.

Armando sat back and the spiral almost disappeared. Armando's voice returned. "That threw it for a loop, Josh. He's trying to recover."

"Winston, if you want to be free, renounce the thirteenth demon and his minions. Now! While he is distracted."

Armando opened his mouth to speak and cringed, shutting his eyes tightly. "No! Don't come back now! Not yet!" He opened his eyes, wild with fear. "I told you I would help if you will take these demons away. I want to be free, Josh. You promised."

"Then you will help me?"

Before Armando could speak, the spiral sharpened and spun around his right eye. His eyes filled with demonic influence. "Now, let's get back to our bargain."

"I'm not making a bargain with you, Huizilopochtli."

Armando raised an eyebrow. "Nice! You remembered my adopted name."

"Drenched in blood. I remember our encounter on the pyramid in my mind. If you recall, I won that battle."

"Thanks to your late mother showing up as a butterfly." Armando leaned across the table. "But she is gone, Josh. You are alone. Helpless. If you want to save the man known as Jonathan Steel, we need to make a deal."

"What kind of deal?" Josh said tentatively.

"The second demon wants something from your father's memory. I think you may have access to that answer as well. If you give it to me before your father shares that memory with his brother, I can defeat the second demon and free Jonathan."

"Why would you do that?"

"Jonathan Steel has almost single-handedly dismantled

the Council of Darkness. Our endgame is the same. He needs to be free to take down the first demon. And, soon." Armando sat back and tried to cross his arms. The manacles raked across the tabletop, stopping his arms in mid motion. "You know, I could break these chains in a human heartbeat."

Josh stood up. "I'll be back in the morning after I consider your proposal. I'll see you then."

Before Armando could speak, Josh walked out of the room and returned to the meeting room. Caskey stood up and leaned against his cane.

"How did it go?"

"The hubris of these demons!" Josh said. "The thirteenth demon told me something I didn't know. Jeremiah wants a memory from Jonathan Steel. Something specific. That means as long as Jonathan holds out, he's safe. Jeremiah will not kill him."

"Why is that important?" Osondu asked.

"It means I have some time. I know Jonathan and he is a stubborn man. He will not yield up his memory easily." Josh paced around the room and glanced at Caskey's cane. "James, let's head back to the hotel. I need sleep and rest and I need to make a call."

"A call?"

"Yes. Tonight. Father Valdez, I suggest your team get ready to face the thirteenth demon tomorrow. I spoke to Winston, and he wants to be free."

"But the thirteenth demon's presence changes everything." Valdez said.

Josh smiled. "You let me take care of thirteen. By this time tomorrow he'll be roasting in Tartarus and your job will be much easier. I promised Winston I would help deliver him, and that is exactly what I'm going to do."

As they walked across the cold, open courtyard of the prison, Caskey struggled to keep up with Josh. "Josh, what is your plan?"

Josh led them through the welcome center, back out into the parking lot. "First, it's afternoon and I'm starving." He paused and pointed a finger at Caskey. "But we're going to Ernesto's for a late lunch. Remember, I used to live in Rockwall and I know the good places."

He climbed into the truck and Caskey struggled into the passenger seat. "And then?"

"Then, I'm giving Dr. Elizabeth Washington a call." He smiled. "It's time we finish the thirteenth demon for all of eternity."

～

"Mama Liz."

"Josh! I hope you're calling to give me good news." Dr. Washington's amber eyes glistened with unshed tears. Josh tilted the iPad screen away for a moment to stifle his own tears.

"Not yet, Mama Liz." He swallowed hard and returned the screen to show his face to Washington.

"Honey child, you never need be embarrassed by your tears." Washington smiled. "We will find Jonathan. He has been through worse."

"I don't know about that." Should he tell her what he planned? Best not to. "I need something that might help. An artifact recovered from the church."

Washington raised her eyebrows. "An artifact? How will that help?"

"I can't go into details. Things might be listening."

Washington sighed. "I see. If you are talking about the objects found beneath the altar of the spiral eye, both objects are now on display in the new museum built in the annex of the old church. Thomas Parker has moved his congregation to a new site while the new church is being built. Can't say I blame him. Fresh start and all. He gave the state permission to use the annex as a museum for the history behind the church site."

Josh recalled the long discussions about the church built on a mound. The ancient civilization in the area centered on the mound and the worship of a false god from the Aztec and Inca civilizations until the entire ancient civilization had perished from smallpox.

"Jabbo Suyu and Phillip?" Josh asked.

"Yes, son. Their stories are told in a multimedia presentation. We have dozens of artifacts unearthed from the church site. The museum isn't slated to open until June but I have a small team working on the manifest and backstories." She smiled and a twinkle filled her eyes. "How is Olivia?"

"I just checked on her. She is up and walking around. A slight headache but so far no seizures. They are letting her leave the hospital tomorrow and Dr. Monarch has leased a house in Houston for her to stay while she recovers. If my plan works, I may be able to visit her in a couple of days."

Washington nodded. "What do I need to do?"

"I'll need them by tomorrow morning at Seagoville prison. I can text you the address. Maybe you can overnight them."

Washington smiled. "You'll have it by tomorrow morning. I guarantee it." She leaned into the image window. "Josh, be careful. I sense whatever plan you have is dangerous."

Josh nodded. "Very dangerous, Mama Liz. But I have a wonderful adopted grandmother who will pray for me and for Jonathan. I'm not the same kid you met for the first time."

"No, you're not. I haven't heard one 'bro' or 'dude'." She sat back. "One other thing, Josh. Pray for me. I have been having some disturbing dreams of late. I fear something big is coming and Jonathan's kidnapping is only the beginning."

A chill ran up his spine. "I think the same thing, Mama Liz. Love you."

CHAPTER

THIRTY-NINE

It was déjà vu all over again. Vivian drove through the debris and wreckage of the parking lot toward the main gates. She had ignored the 'no trespassing' sign on the fence surrounding the 'Tragic Kingdom'. Max had supplied them with an SUV capable of driving over anything and she had needed it.

The sky was a dull metal gray and leaked chilly rain. Vivian parked the SUV with its headlights directed toward the entry gates. Lightning spiked in the distance and thunder rumbled.

"Nothing as cold as a cold rain in Florida in February." Raven said. "Remnants of the storm that came through Texas and Louisiana."

They both wore heavy rain parkas. Despite the heaviness, the icy rain leached the heat from Vivian's exposed hands and face. She led the way over broken pavement and decaying palm trees through the entry gates to the head of Maimed Street.

Maimed Street stretched into the distance, a combination of upheaved, broken concrete and weeds. Even the weeds seemed to bend beneath the oppressive nature of the place.

They passed by the shops advertising palm reading and blood letting and potions.

They reached the open "hub" in front of the castle. A black hole opened into the earth and steam rose from its depths. The air was tainted with the odor of decay and rotten eggs.

"What is this?" Raven leaned against a rusty rail to peer into the depths.

"The Bottomless Pit." Vivian said. "A fountain once spewed blood colored water in a show coordinated with music."

"How ghastly." Raven said. "You came here by yourself?" Raven said. "You're braver than I thought."

"I had a few demons to bolster my courage at the time." Vivian said.

"Well, now we have someone more powerful than demons at our disposal." Raven said.

They stood in the shadow of the huge, deformed castle. Its decaying edifice slumped and oozed with moss and mold. Turrets hung at odd angles, as if melted by hellish heat. Broken stained glass windows opened into darkness. The rain had picked up and rivulets of silver gray water poured off the castle. Vivian suppressed a shiver, and she was back in time on the last night she stood here after her then Master, Satan, had given her specific mission instructions.

Vivian stepped back and her Master straightened. His laughter echoed down the tunnel as he faded from sight, swirling in a cloud of red light and mist. She walked to the end of the tunnel. Bile waited beside the limousine. The night cleared as the storm receded. She studied Bile's face, the pulsing tattoo of the thirteenth demon around his right eye.

"I take you heard all of that?"

Bile was speechless for a moment. "It would seem you have the upper hand for the moment."

"I agree." She slapped him hard across the face. The tattoo pulsed and fury filled the man's eyes. He swallowed and rubbed the red spot on his cheek. "Now, Bile and number thirteen, from now on, you do as I say." Vivian hissed.

"You are mistaken, sweetie." Someone said behind her. She whirled in surprise. A figure paused, and a match flared. He held the match up to the bowl of a Meerschaum pipe and for a second the flaring flame illuminated his Panama Hat. "The Master instructed me to continue with a plan I started twenty years ago. Together, we will bring down the Council."

"And just who are you?"

"To some I would appear to the Captain." He waved a hand across his face and his features morphed into those of a dark-haired man with eyes of different color. Again, his hand passed over his face and he had the green eyes and high cheekbones of Robert Ketrick.

"Or you can call me many names. I can be whoever I please, my dear. The Council knows me as the first demon."

Now, the Captain claimed he had never been to the park. Who was the person she had met at the gates to this castle on that night? Was the man lying again or could someone be impersonating him?

"I thought I had met people who were truly insane but this takes the cake, Vivian. How many lives were ruined by attending this park? How many children and families fell into despair because of this place?" Ruth shivered.

"Thank God it failed and closed." Vivian said. "Now, down the dark tunnel into the abyss."

Writing figures carved into the walls depicted various forms of human suffering. Open mouths dripped slime and fungus. Vivian averted her gaze, afraid some of the hideous creatures would come to life. At the end of the tunnel, gigantic wooden doors hung askew on their hinges. Vivian led Raven into the chamber of the Council of Darkness. The ballroom had once housed a bright and charming dining hall complete with floating candles and roaring fireplaces. It had been the one bright and happy spot in the entire park.

Now, pale light from the gloomy outside came through holes in the roof. Water streamed through the gaps and pooled on the old, moldy carpet. Vivian moved to the center of the chamber.

"There were tables here arranged in a pentagram. All twelve members sat in individual chairs with curtains covering their forms." She motioned to the periphery. "Servers brought in carts with food and drink. Now, it's all gone."

She paused and walked over to a large, wooden table at the side of the chamber. The table was covered with carvings of demons and monsters and snakes. "It's gone."

"What's gone?" Raven followed her.

Vivian threw back the hood of her parka and ran a hand over the wet surface of the table. "It sat right here with the Tomemaster and his Keeper. The Grimvox."

"There's that word again." Raven said.

"It's a mysterious object. The Council claims it stores all the memories of demons from the beginning of time until now." Vivian sighed and leaned against the table as she faced Raven. "But the Grimvox requires a human interface. The presence of a living human brain serves as the conduit into the inner workings of the Grimvox." Vivian stepped away from the table and hugged herself as she shivered. "And the 'keepers' don't last long. It burns out their brains."

"Where is the Grimvox now?" Raven said.

"It is missing." A voice echoed across the chamber.

Vivian stiffened at the sound of the voice. From across the chamber he appeared from the shadows. Lucas walked through the waterfalls and the water parted at his gesture. He seemed to hover over the ruined floor.

"Lucas!" Vivian hissed.

"My dear Vivian. How far you have fallen." He paused in the center of the chamber.

"I have not fallen, Lucas. I have ascended." Vivian said.

Raven appeared at her side. "Lucas Malson. We thought you were dead."

"I have died many times." Lucas shrugged. "I can die but until it is the time for my appointed death, I will live."

"That makes no sense." Vivian said.

"It is appointed men once to die and after the judgment." Lucas said moving closer. "I have met judgment once before and deemed to walk this earth until the time of my punishment arrives. Living long is overrated, my dear Vivian."

"Then perhaps we can arrange another temporary death." Vivian hissed.

Lucas laughed exposing his bright red tongue. "You cannot harm me, Vivian. As of now, I am protected for a time until I achieve my goals. I found redemption with the master since I last saw you in the," He paused and looked around the chamber, "ironically abandoned theme park in Great Britain." Vivian had been held prisoner by Lucas in that park in Great Britain.

Lucas wore black pants and a dark overcoat, exposing his bare chest. Tattoos writhed on his skin.

"You no longer bleed." Vivian said.

"No." Lucas said. "I am restored as I search for something and it is fortuitous you have arrived."

"The Grimvox?" Raven said.

Lucas crossed his arms and shrugged again. "Well, that arcane apparatus is important. But, I'm looking for something else."

"The Grimvox is missing, then?" Vivian smiled.

Lucas frowned. "Yes."

"But you don't know who or where, do you?" Raven said.

"Jeremiah has taken the Crimson Snake. Has he also taken the Grimvox." Vivian said moving toward him. He moved away from her. "The Grimvox goes wherever the Council meets. It could have been anywhere."

"You have just confirmed where it is. With Jeremiah. I suspected as much." He smiled. "I had to be sure by checking all of its previous locations."

"Why are you backing away from me?" Vivian stepped closer.

"It is because you have crossed over to the vile side of the Other," Lucas hissed.

"Then join us," Vivian said. "Turn your back on your master and come into the arms of our Master."

Lucas' laughter echoed throughout the chamber. "I am afraid my soul was damned long ago, Vivian. I am beyond redemption by my choice."

"You can never be beyond redemption." Raven stepped up beside Vivian. "I thought I was, and I'm sure Vivian thought so as well."

Lucas backed up some more, and both women moved to the center of the chamber. He gestured toward the floor. "Beneath this chamber is another meeting room. Would you like to see it?" He flicked his hand, and the floor dropped out from beneath Vivian and Raven.

They tumbled down a sloping floor into a dark, dank chamber. Water dripped down moldy walls. Vivian rolled through muck and stood up sputtering and cursing.

Raven tucked and rolled into a defensive posture. "He wasn't backing away, was he?"

Vivian wrung the water from her clothes and looked around. "No! He was playing us all along. Where are we?"

"Dungeon? Like the tunnels underneath the Magic Kingdom." Raven looked around them.

They stood in a hallway with rough hewn walls of stone. Ahead down the tunnel pale green light flickered. Raven looked above them at the ceiling. The floor had opened and pivoted down as a ramp and had now retracted into the ceiling. "Well, we're not going that way."

Vivian headed down the tunnel toward the light. The tunnel ended in a large chamber whose walls were sculpted out of the rocky base. Water trickled down the walls and an inch of rancid water covered the floor. In the center of the chamber, a five-sided stone slab sat. On the walls, pale green fire flickered from torches. Lucas lay on his side in the center of the slab.

"Welcome to the altar, milady's." He stood up. "Oh, the sacrifices that have been made on this sacred stone. Blood cries from its cervices." He closed his eyes and moaned in pleasure. He licked his lips.

"Oh, stop it. Don't be such a drama queen." Vivian growled.

Lucas shrugged. "Life can be so boring, Viv." He climbed off the altar onto the wet floor. "Now, on this altar, the first and second demon meet regularly to plan the future of the master's domination over mankind."

"Yeah, well, I think one person, Jonathan Steel, has decimated your precious council." Raven said, crossing her arms.

"Precisely!" Lucas said. He pointed a ghostly white finger at her. "Which is why there is now division among the two remaining members. Jeremiah steals the Grimvox for reasons I can only imagine." He paused and blinked a few times and placed a finger on his lips. "No, I can't. What has gotten into the man's mind?" He shrugged. "Doesn't matter to me. I know what he is seeking." He stepped closer. "And, guess what?" He looked to his right and left and then whispered. "It's the same thing number one is looking for. But, they are both looking in the wrong direction."

He moved within arm's reach of them. "You see, the Master has tasked me to acquire this unique object, and I know exactly where to find it. And when I do, then guess who will be in charge of a new Council?" He smiled and raised his hands in triumph. "Moi!"

"Until your appointed time to die?" Vivian said.

Lucas lurched forward, his smile replaced with a grimace. "Honey, better to rule in hell than serve in heaven, right? I will go out with a bang." He smiled and snapped his fingers and disappeared. The air popped where he had stood.

"Where did he go?" Raven looked around.

"Teleported." Vivian hissed.

Around them, the air grew stale and quiet. Water ceased to run down the walls. Slowly, oh so slowly, the torches faded. Complete darkness fell, and Vivian reached out and touched Raven's arm.

"I hate Lucas." She said.

FORTY

S am stood at the top of the spiral staircase. His heart pounded, and he fought down panic. Years before, he had descended into the hell that had awaited him in the chamber below. Birdsong appeared beside him.

"You okay, Sam?"

Sam nodded. "Terrible memories."

"There's no body down there now, Sam."

Sam turned haunted eyes on Birdsong. "We don't know that."

Birdsong sighed. "Well, let's find out." He started down the stairs. His flashlight chased the darkness away. His footfalls echoed in the chamber. Sam nodded and said a quiet prayer. He followed Birdsong down the stairs.

The chamber below was just as he remembered it. Only no body lay across the five-sided altar in the center of the chamber.

"Where do these doors go?" Birdsong pointed around him.

"I have no idea." Sam said. "From the investigative report, the doors wouldn't open."

Birdsong walked around the chamber, pointing his flashlight at the doors. Their pebbly surface was slick, as if wet. He touched the stone. Dry as a bone. "Well, Jeremiah and Jonathan are not down here." He examined the rest of the chamber. "No evidence anyone has been in here since Hampton disappeared through the doors upstairs." Nigel Hampton had escaped from the library through the doors to his chamber after Jonathan defeated the fifth, sixth, and seventh demons.

Sam moved from door to door, examining each with his own flashlight. "Could they be behind one of these doors?"

"Would you like to find out?"

They both spun at the sound of the man's voice. A short figure stood at the base of the stairs. He wore a khaki jacket, white shirt and jodhpurs. A Panama hat sat on his head. White hair leaked from under the edges of his hat. His turquoise eyes glittered in the flashlight beam.

"The Captain?" Birdsong said.

"Look again, son." He took off the Panama hat and let it dangle by his side. When he put it back on, it had become a pith helmet. His face was similar to the Captain's. But older. More severe.

"He was right." Sam said. "You have been impersonating him."

"Easy to do when I am his father." The man said.

Birdsong froze. "What? He said his father was dead."

"The rumors of my demise are much exaggerated." The man stepped toward them. "I am terribly sorry the two of you have been pulled into this monumental enterprise."

"Where is Jonathan?" Sam said.

"Sam, right? You have been his protector for years and now you have lost him? It's a wonder we didn't find him before now."

"We? Meaning you and Jeremiah?" Birdsong said.

"Yes, my grandson."

Sam nodded his head slowly. "You don't know where they are, do you? You came here looking for them?"

The man paused and frowned. "Your deductive instincts are good, Jason Birdsong."

"What did Jeremiah do?" Sam asked. "Take the Grimvox and Jonathan?"

The man tensed and took the pith helmet from his head. His eyes burned with anger. "The workings of the Council are none of your business."

"I'd say they are exactly our business." Birdsong said. "Jonathan and his friends have been dismantling the Council of Darkness one by one. Which one are you? Number two?"

The man studied them silently as if making up his mind. He put his helmet back on. "I am the first demon."

"What has Jeremiah done?" Sam said. "Taken the Grimvox in an effort to supplant you? There is no honor among demons?"

The man looked away and then gestured with his right hand. The grating sound took them by surprise. Sam whirled as one door slid aside and bright sunlight filled the chamber. A force took them and shoved him through the door.

Sam and Birdsong moved through a silver wall, a mirror that reflected their very souls. Around them stars spun and galaxies collided. In the distance voices moaned and screeching in agony and then they tumbled onto a tile floor. The door grated shut behind him.

Sam stood painfully to his feet. They were in an office with windows that looked out over a desert. A woman sat behind a desk to their right. Her long, black hair draped over her shoulders. Her scarlet robe covered her figure as she stood up.

"Her eyes." Birdsong said.

No pupils marred the total white expanse of her eyes. To the right of the desk Nigel Hampton stood quietly, his bowler hat in his hands. His eyes glowed white.

"Good morning, gentlemen. This is quite the surprise."

"You!" Birdsong hissed. "What is going on?"

"We teleported." Sam said. "Or something like that."

"You moved through the Void." The woman walked gracefully around the desk. "I'm Dr. Sno."

"Vitreomancers." Sam said. "I've run into your kind over the years."

"Rivals to the Council, right?" Birdsong said.

Sno paused at the side of her desk. She glanced toward the wall that had once held an open door to the altar chamber.

"He cannot hear us." Hampton said.

Sno threw Hampton a sideways glance. "Are you sure?"

"He's too busy looking for the artifact." Hampton said. "What did he do? Surprise the two of you in the bloody chamber beneath the library?"

"We were looking for Jeremiah and Jonathan." Sam said.

"Yes, my dear Sam. I understand Jeremiah has absconded with Jonathan and the Grimvox." Hampton said.

"Enough!" Sno said. He studied them with her empty white eyes. She pursed her lips and sighed. "Very well. Yes, there is much at stake here. Grandpoppa, as he is known, is seeking something that will help him replenish the Council."

"What?" Birdsong said.

Sno glanced at Hampton. "We don't know."

"But, in spite of making a temporary truce with the man, Dr. Sno and I have concluded the best that we can do is to thwart the man's plans and see that your precious Jonathan completes his task of destroying the Council."

"So you can take its place?" Sam said. "I've read about your rivalry. How many demons are dancing on the ends of your puppet strings?"

Sno lifted her head in defiance. "Enough. Our plans are long and we are patient. Once the Council is gone, we will rise to the top and the master will reward our efforts."

"All we have to do is insure that the two of us end up on the Penticle." Hampton said.

Sno erupted in foul cursing. "You fool! Shut up!"

Hampton grinned and raised an eyebrow. "If they are to help us, they should know what is at stake."

"What makes you think we are going to help you?" Birdsong said.

"Because you have someone at your disposal that can defeat the first demon. He is not aware of it yet." Sno moved toward Birdsong. "Destiny is a force beyond human control. It is in the hands of the Creator. We humans moved and dance within the shadow of that destiny. There are those of us who choose to weave the threads of destiny in a slightly different direction. The end is set. But the third act can still be rewritten ahead of the ending, and as reluctant as I am to do so, you and your friend are the key to an ending that Dr. Hampton and I desire."

"My friend?" Birdsong said.

"And once you are members of this Penticle?" Sam said.

"World affairs can be determined that will benefit us. Microscopic changes. Our hope is not in the ending that awaits but in the interim. If I am to be damned for all eternity, I will insure that the last few years of my life will be molded to fit my plans."

"I have no intention of helping you," Birdsong said. "What does my friend have to do with this?"

"Oh, but you will help us, Jason," Sno said. She pointed to the wall and the grating sound filled the room. The doorway opened, filled with a fluid, pulsating mirrored surface. The surface cleared, revealing a room beyond.

"Go ahead. Sam and Jason, step through that doorway and you will see inevitably, you will help me."

Sam looked at Birdsong, but his eyes were focused on the doorway. He stepped through. Sam followed. They emerged in a hospital room. The smell of antiseptic filled the air. A bed sat in the dark room with only a night light giving scant illumination. Birdsong hurried to the bedside, and a figure emerged from the darkness. He gasped.

"Faye?"

His fiancé, Faye looked up at him with tear stained eyes. "Jason? Where did you come from? I've been trying to reach you. They called me about Cassie."

Birdsong looked down at the woman covered by a sheet. Her blonde hair was greasy and draped around her head. Her face was as white as snow and her eyes sunken.

Sam placed a hand on his arm. "Cassandra Holmes?"

"Yes." Faye came around the bed and they embraced. She tilted her head to look up into his eyes. "She's dying, Jason. The doctors have no idea why. I came from Dallas as soon as Monty called me."

Sam stepped back. Cassandra Holmes had married Dr. Montana Holmes at Christmas. Cassie was well known for her online show about Biblical artifacts. Monty was known for his knowledge of Biblical history and Christian apologetics.

So this was the temptation? This was Sno's gambit? What would Jason do? He turned and looked at the wall behind him. For a moment it faded into the doorway and he saw Sno and Hampton standing in the office on the other side of the world. Help Cassie and help the devil himself? What would Jason do?

FORTY-ONE

After arriving back at the hotel, Josh contacted Max. No progress in finding Jonathan. He tossed and turned in his bed that night, his dreams filled with recollections of his encounter with the thirteenth demon. He woke up before dawn and dressed. He went outside and sat in the cold beside the covered pool and prayed.

After breakfast, they drove to the prison and Josh had little to say to Caskey. He just sat quietly in the seat beside him and mouthed prayers. When he pulled into the parking space, the door to a car beside them opened up. Pastor Thomas Parker got out of the car.

Josh's eyes widened at the sight of the man and he jumped out of the truck. "Thomas? I mean Reverend Parker?"

Thomas Parker had gained back some of his weight since the affair with the thirteenth demon taking over his church. Josh rushed over to him and grabbed him in an embrace.

Parker stiffened and then finally relaxed. Josh stepped back and Parker smiled. "Well, that was a far better hello than the last time you said goodbye."

"I was pretty sullen, wasn't I?" Josh said. "In fact, I was a jerk."

"I understand you've become a Christian?"

"Yes." Josh patted the man on his arm. "You look so good. How's Emile?"

"Great, and Claire is doing well."

Josh froze and blinked tears. Thomas and Emile had named their baby after his mother. He looked away and blinked away tears. Father Caskey introduced himself and motioned to the greeting center. "Are you here to help with the exorcism?"

Parker nodded. "I hope so. Dr. Washington called and wanted me to find something for Josh and ship it overnight. I thought it would be better to drive over." He went back to the car and took a leather pouch from the car. He handed it to Josh. "Is this what you wanted?"

Jos took the pouch and unzipped the top. He glanced inside. "Yes. Perfect."

"Great! I guess I'll head back."

"Thomas!" Josh gripped the pouch. "We could use you. You have experience with demons. A few of your prayers would be welcomed."

Parker glanced at Caskey. "I've never attended an exorcism."

"All you have to do is pray." Caskey said. "There's been quite enough chaos introduced into the process already, so another man of the cloth will only make things better."

Josh led them to the welcome center and through the check-in process. A guard took the pouch and glanced inside. "What's this?"

"We need it for the exorcism." Josh said. The man raised an eyebrow.

"Well, I've already let the others in with a keg of holy water." He handed the pouch to Josh. "May God be with you."

They walked into the reception room. Josh introduced all the team, and Parker stiffened when he met Dr. Black.

"You're Dr. Brown." He said.

Brown nodded and bowed his head. "I am, Thomas."

"You know each other?" Osondu said.

"I administered the in vitro fertilization to Reverend Parker's wife."

"And you were in on Ketrick's plan." Parker said.

"Forgive me, Thomas. I did not fulfill Ketrick's plans. I could not. I understand you have a healthy daughter?"

Parker blinked and pushed his glasses up on his nose. "Yes, we do."

"Can you ever forgive me?"

Parker nodded slowly. "In time. But I'm still working on it."

Brown nodded and wiped his knobby face with his stubby hands. "You need to know something, Thomas. The demon we are dealing with is the thirteenth demon."

Parker gasped and took a step back. "What?"

"I forgot to tell you." Josh said. "I thought Liz would have mentioned it."

Parker turned away and paced across the room. He sighed and nodded. "She asked me to take care of this for a reason." He looked up at Josh. "I was supposed to be here, Josh. It is time I finish this. It is time I face the thirteenth demon and end him."

Josh smiled. "You may be the key to making this happen." He placed the pouch on the table. "But, I need to go in first and talk to Winston."

Osondu glanced at the pouch. "What is this?"

"My insurance policy."

"What is it?" Valdez said.

"I have a relic, Father. All I am asking is to let me walk alone into the room with the relic hidden behind me. I want to see how Winston reacts. Is that too much to ask? If things go south, you're literally a few feet away."

"I say give him ten minutes." Sister Jo said. "Ten minutes and no matter what, we come through the door."

Timothy and Thomas sat in the corner and stood up at the same time. "We'll be ready to intervene."

"We got your back, dude." Timothy said.

Valdez interrupted. "Ten minutes, Josh. That's it. The guard has already brought him to the table."

Josh grabbed the door handle and winced. It was ice cold. He twisted the handle and stepped into the room. Winston sat at the table. "Hello, Josh." He whispered. No spiral. Just Winston. "Are you alone?"

"Yes. Looks like you are alone, too." Josh calmed his racing heart and closed the door behind him. "I have ten minutes and they'll come in. Ten minutes between you and me."

"What did you bring me? Something behind your back?"

"You know what it is." Josh hoped he was correct. If not, he had lost his only advantage. "Can you sense it? Can you feel the pain, the suffering, the loss that accompanied it?"

Winston blinked and focused on Josh's middle. His face twisted and he frowned. "No! It can't be."

"It is." He took a step closer. "Do you feel it now? Feel the goodness, the righteousness soaked into it by the ones you killed?"

Winston shook his head and blinked furiously. "I didn't kill them."

"How do you know who I'm talking about?"

Winston glared at him. "Stop! You talk about goodness and yet you come here to torture me and this poor mortal." He cursed and spit ran down his face.

Josh's heart threatened to burst from his chest. He took another step and Winston screamed in agony. "Come no closer!" More cursing and now his body shook and writhed in pain.

"Talk to me. Now! Stop pretending to be Winston. I know you're in control." Josh stepped closer.

Winston froze and the spiral formed around his right eye. He shook some more and spit ran down his chin. "Get it out of here! Get it away from me!"

Josh reached into the leather sack behind his back and retrieved the object within. He held up the jeweled cross of Jabo Suyu. "You mean this?"

"No!!!!" Winston's head turned almost completely around. His shoulders dislocated. The chair levitated off the ground tethered only by the manacles. Josh stepped closer.

"Silence, you fiend! In the name of my Savior Jesus Christ I command you to be silent or I will place this relic against your heart."

"And the mortal perishes." Winston hissed.

"Do I look like I care? He gave himself to you. He knew the consequences. He would welcome the release. Now, you will be still and you will be silent until you answer one question. One question only and I will take this relic away and release you. Do you understand?"

More cursing filled the air and Josh reached forward and touched the tip of the cross to the back of Winston's hand. His unearthly screams filled the room.

Josh pulled back the cross. "Ten minutes will seem like an eternity, Huizilopochtli. You have lost control and I can do this all day. Consent to answer one question. Now! Or your suffering will only have begun."

"You call yourself righteous!" He shouted. "You are no better than me."

"Oh, I have one advantage." Josh raised the cross. "I am redeemed, forgiven, and a host of the Holy Spirit."

"Fine!" Winston stopped shaking, and the chair settled down. With a shrug, Winson popped his shoulders back into joint. His eyes focused on Josh. "One question."

Josh stepped within inches of Winston and held the cross just in front of the thing's face. The spiral pulsed. "Where is Jonathan Steel?"

FORTY-TWO

Jeremiah's unruly hair and body odor testified to his lack of sleep when Steel sat at the table. "Looks like you had trouble sleeping."

"You want to know how I met the second demon? Then shut up and touch the Grimvox."

Steel cast one hopeful glance at Rebecca, but her eyes were focused on the Grimvox. He touched the Grimvox with his left hand, hiding the glow in his palm from Jeremiah.

JEREMIAH RUBBED the bruises on his face. His backend ached from his beating. One bruise next to his right cheekbone had swollen and was very tender. He settled slowly and painfully on his bed and felt tears trickled along his jaw. He hated crying! He hated losing control. The room fell into more darkness as the sun disappeared over the horizon and the one window looking out over Maimed Street became a black, cold rectangle.

"I hate you." He whispered. "I will kill you one day."

"Who are you going to kill?" A voice whispered.

Jeremiah froze and peered toward the window. Who was there? His heart skipped a beat at the possibility *she* was listening. He swallowed hard and wiped tears from his face, wincing at the pain.

"Who is there?"

"I asked you a simple question, boy." The voice strengthened.

"I will kill whoever stands in my way." He said hoarsely.

"How old are you?"

"I am eleven."

"An eleven-year-old assassin? You are a child and totally powerless, boy."

Jeremiah's face warmed with anger. "If you don't leave, I'll kill you."

"Now, that is more like it." The black window changed color. A pale green light came from outside. The light filled the room with an eerie green cast and a shadow appeared in the window. A figure coalesced from the green light and stepped through the glass of the window into the room. The shadow figure had no features, just a flat empty plane of darkness, a stick figure filled with night.

"I can give you that power, boy."

Jeremiah sat up slowly, pressing his back against the head of his bed. His bruises ached at the touch and he stifled a moan of pain. "Who are you?"

"I do not have to tell you my name unless you want me to be a part of your life." The dark figure shifted from right to left as if drifting on a breeze.

"What kind of power?" Jeremiah asked.

"Knowledge."

Jeremiah laughed. "What? Are you some kind of school-teacher?"

"Do not laugh, boy. Knowledge is power." The figure drifted toward his bed and he tried to push himself further into the wall without success. "Let me give you an example. When you show up for breakfast in the morning and Nanny scolds, you merely say the name Sheldon."

"What?"

"Try it, boy. You'll see what I mean." The figure drifted back to the window and faded into the green light. The light lessened until nothing remained but the dark, empty room.

THE NEXT MORNING, Jeremiah sat at the breakfast table waiting for Nanny to deliver his food. Was the shadowy man real? Had he really seen a stick figure drifting around his room? And what had he meant about 'knowledge is power'? Nanny scowled at him as she put a bowl of oatmeal on the table.

"Eat up. You have chores after."

Jeremiah watched something move under the surface of his oatmeal. "What is in this oatmeal? I saw something move."

"Fresh protein. Probably a roach. I thought the microwave would have killed it. Now eat." Her lips curled up in a slight smile and she crossed her arms across her severe chest.

Jeremiah glanced at her and thought of the name. Would it work? "I'm not eating this garbage. I'm not eating a roach."

She raised an eyebrow and leaned toward him. "Then you'll do your chores on an empty stomach. Now eat."

Jeremiah grit his teeth and shook his head. "Who was Sheldon?"

Nanny jerked as if slapped. Her eyes widened and her arms dropped by her side. "What did you say?"

"Who was Sheldon? A brother? A son?" He paused as something blossomed and swelled within him. "A lover?"

The slap caught him by surprise and he tasted blood. Red drops dribbled into the oatmeal and the roach surfaced. Its feelers danced over the blood drops.

"Where did you hear that name?"

"I'll never tell you." Power grew within him. True power. He stood up and pushed past her. He went to the cookie jar and pulled out a cookie. "I'll have cookies and milk for breakfast."

Nanny's claw like hand closed on his arm. "You will not, Jeremiah."

Jeremiah looked at the hand and jerked it out of her grasp. He took a bite of the cookie and spit it in her face. She stumbled back and fell over the kitchen chair. She sprawled clumsily on the floor. Jeremiah stepped over her spindly legs and reached the door. He turned back.

"I know a lot about Sheldon." He lied. "And knowledge is power. For lunch, I want a grilled cheese sandwich. Without a roach."

THE BEATINGS WERE NOT QUITE a severe as the day before. Jeremiah licked his swollen lip and waited impatiently for the setting sun. He focused on the window and waited as the darkness fell. The green light came again and the shadow man appeared. He moved into Jeremiah's room. Rather than having thin margins, his silhouette seemed sharper.

"Beaten again, boy? Such a wimp, you are." The voice echoed around the room.

"I asked her about Sheldon." Jeremiah lisped through his swollen lip.

The shadow man moved closer and Jeremiah began to

make out contours of the man's face. "Good! So you now understand the power of knowledge?"

"It would have helped to know more about Sheldon."

"Well, you can know that. And much more. I have access to almost infinite knowledge. All you have to do is invite me into your mind and I will fill in the blanks." Glowing green eyes appeared in the shadow man's face.

Jeremiah licked his lips again and swallowed hard. "What does it mean to invite you into my mind? Will you control it? I don't want to be controlled. Nanny is already trying to do that."

"Idiot!" The eyes filled with red flames. "Do you want to be powerful, or not?"

Jeremiah flinched and tried to calm his thudding heart. "Of course. But it seems everyone has a plan for me. No one cares what I want for myself."

The flaming eyes faded back to green and the man's hand came up to his face. "Yes. I see where that could work for us. You realize that with power, you can have anything you want. In time, you can make others do whatever you WANT them to do. You can turn this entire situation upside down."

"I need some time to think." Jeremiah said.

"Sheldon was her boyfriend. He drowned trying to save Nanny from a sinking sailboat. Now, decide quickly, boy. I will not wait forever." And with that, the shadow popped out of existence, leaving the room cold and dark. Jeremiah gasped and fought back tears. Had he acted rashly? Maybe he should have taken the shadow man's advice.

THE NEXT DAY, Nanny doubled up on her cruelty. The end of the day found Jeremiah exhausted from silly, repetitive "chores". Only once did she get the strap for a beating.

"Why were you on the sailboat?"

Nanny flinched and put her hands on her hips. "What did you say?"

"Why did he have to swim out to save you?" Jeremiah thought fiercely. There had to be a reason. "Were you trying to get him to save you? Maybe he was paying attention to another girl?"

Nanny's face paled and she dropped the strap. "How do you know?"

"I have great knowledge." Jeremiah grinned.

Nanny turned her back and left the room and Jeremiah was spared a beating. It wasn't just enough to have knowledge. He had to know how to use it! As night fell again, he sat on the edge of his bed, his mind made up.

"Shadow man, are you there?" He said.

The shadow man appeared as suddenly as he had vanished. "Yes, boy?"

"I want you to know something. I will invite you in. But, when it is time for you to go, you will listen to me and you will obey. Once I have learned enough knowledge to wield power, I will make you go. Understand?"

The shadow man laughed and his open mouth revealed glowing stars. His chest solidified into a window onto the infinite. Galaxies and nebulous clouds bright with color filled his silhouette. He pointed to his figure.

"I am all of the knowledge of the universe, Jeremiah. With my help, you can know anything."

"Who are you?"

"You cannot pronounce my name. To try and do so would annihilate you. I am known as the second angel. If you want knowledge and power all you have to do is place you hand on my heart and break the plane of your pitiful, mortal existence."

Jeremiah reached forward with a trembling finger. The dark silhouette of the man leaned toward him and he felt the pull of the worlds beyond. His flesh broke the barrier between this world and another, and he was sucked into the darkness. Tumbling through vacuum, his chest exploding, his head pounded until he landed on white sand. Bright light surrounded him. Something clicked and scratched through the sand behind him. He whirled and an insect-like figure towered over him resembling a praying mantis. The thing's enormous eyes focused on him and before he could move the articulated jaws closed on his head and something hot and fluid flowed into his mind and heart.

THE MEMORY FADED and Steel pulled his hand from the Grimvox. Nausea gripped him and he fought vertigo.

"I'm sorry you were surrounded by monsters." Steel whispered.

Jeremiah stiffened. "I don't want your pity. Besides, I *am* a monster."

"No, you're not." Steel said softly. "You couldn't even murder our mother."

Jeremiah glared at him and slowly collapsed into his chair. "How did you know?"

"The third demon told me as Drake was dying. The second demon told me while I was here. If you didn't kill our mother, who did? And how did you end up working with the third demon?"

Jeremiah's breathing quickened and his eyes filled with tears. "I wanted to know my mother, JJ. I wanted to see her.

The third demon said he would set it up. He said I could come and see her. He called her and she agreed to meet me."

"Who called her?"

Jeremiah shook his head as he closed his eyes. Tears trickled down his cheeks. "No! I can't tell you. That is not why you are here!"

"Jeremiah, this is my second question. You must answer it. Tell me what happened the day you were supposed to kill our mother."

Jeremiah glared at him and nodded, moisture filling his eyes. He reached forward and touched the Grimvox.

CHAPTER

FORTY-THREE

Jeremiah parked his car in front of the enormous mansion. His cell phone dinged, and he studied the text message. His mother had sent the servants home. She was alone. His hands shook as he put the cell phone in his jacket pocket. He looked at himself in the rearview mirror. Bright turquoise eyes clearly focused on one objective. The end of the life of the mother who had rejected him!

"You can do this." The voice whispered in the back of his mind. Which one was it? Between the third demon's itinerant nature and the powerful voice of the second demon, his mind became confused and fuzzy when both were present.

"Who is here?"

"Silly boy. I am here." The image of the third demon appeared superimposed on the reflection of his face. He felt himself slipping down the slope into the darkness of his mind.

"No! If you want this done properly, leave me in control!" he said. The slipping ceased and the third demon faded away as another voice echoed in his head.

"Back off!" The voice of the second demon said. "He has to do this under his own power. Only then will he manifest!"

Manifest! Yes, there was that word again. Since he had run away two years before at the urgings of the second demon, he had tried to understand what it meant. Manifest what? How? The voices in his head were silent. He was on his own.

Jeremiah left his car and walked up the bizarre entrance to the Stone mansion, carrying the bag with the video camera and tripod. He started to knock on the door, but instead opened it and walked confidently into the foyer.

She stepped into view in the living room beyond. He gasped at the sight of his mother. Her ginger hair matched his own. Her green eyes glittered with tears as she opened her arms.

"Is it really you?" Christine Stone said.

Jeremiah hesitated and leaned the tripod and attached camera against a sofa. He moved into her arms. She hugged him tightly, the fragrance of lavender and roses engulfed him. Her body convulsed with sobs. He placed his arms around her and returned the hug. She finally pushed him gently away and studied him with tear-filled eyes.

"Jeremiah, right? That's what they named you?"

"Yes." He whispered. Emotion coarsened his voice. He blinked away tears and wiped at his face. "You must be my mother." What a banal statement! The voice in his head echoed. He closed his eyes and chastised the demons. Keep quiet, he thought. You promised.

"Why did you bring a video camera?" She glanced at the tripod and camera.

"I want to keep a permanent record of our reunion." He said nervously, grabbing the tripod.

"Come into the library and we'll have some tea and tea cakes." She took his hand and pulled him toward the library. "I sent the servants home, just as you suggested. I made the tea cakes myself. An old family recipe."

She gestured to a chair, and Jeremiah settled into the cold leather surface. He studied the room filled with books and arcane artifacts. "What a strange collection."

"Yes, my husband, uh, your father collects artifacts from around the world." She poured him a cup of tea. "And some of them were collected by his father."

"Grandpoppa?"

His mother paused in the pouring of her cup of tea. "Well, that's not what JJ called him. But if you want to call him that, it would be fine." She set the tea kettle down. "Of course, he is no longer with us. He passed away when JJ was very young."

"JJ?" Jeremiah sipped his tea with a shaky hand. How was he going to harm this person? She was wonderful. Warm. Loving.

"Your brother." She sipped her tea. "My but you could be twins!"

Jeremiah glanced over at the black doors leading to the underground chamber. He had to get her down the stairs into that chamber. "What is behind those doors?"

His mother's face stiffened and she shook her head. "We don't speak of it. That is where your grandfather died. Along with others."

"What?" Jeremiah almost choked on his tea. He had not been told this information. They wanted her to die in the exact same place as his grandfather?

"He was holding some kind of seance or ceremony. We're not sure. Four other people were with him in the chamber at the bottom of a spiral staircase." She shivered. "I don't want to talk about this, Jeremiah. I want to get to know you. I can't wait for JJ to meet you." She pointed to the cameras. "You can set that up whenever you like. I'd like JJ to see the video if possible."

"I can't wait to meet him." Jeremiah lied. "Here, let me pour you some more tea."

He reached for the tea kettle and her cup. "What is the most bizarre artifact in this room?"

His mother turned and pointed over her shoulder. It gave him time to drop the tablet into her cup and then fill it with tea. "Well, that collection of pipes is rather interesting. It's how I met your father." She turned back to him and he handed her the tea cup.

"I'd like to hear that story."

She started talking, sipping her tea and crunching on a tea cake. Halfway through the cup she paused and blinked slowly. She looked over at him and alarm filled her face.

"What did you do to me?"

"Sorry, mother." He said raspily. Three had taken over. "It's time for us to descend into the private hell hole of the Stones."

STEEL MOANED in agony as he watched Jeremiah toss their mother over his shoulder and carry her through the arcane doors and down the spiral staircase. In a surreal experience, he followed along as if he had been in the same room.

Jeremiah placed their mother's limp body on the five-sided stone platform at the base of the stairs. Jonathan suppressed his surging emotions at being in this room once again. The last time had been when he had found his dead mother on this very stone platform. Five stone doors sat in the walls of the five sided stone chamber. He placed the tripod between two of the doors and pointed the camera at his mother. He started recording and shuddered. "What have I done, mother?" He whispered.

"What is required."

One of the stone doors had merely dissolved into thin air and the man stepped into the room from a darkened corridor. The door reformed behind him. A pith helmet sat on his white hair and his turquoise eyes glittered with malice. He wore brown jodhpurs and a khaki jacket straight from an old time jungle movie. He took off his helmet.

"Why are you hesitant, son?"

Jeremiah froze. "Grandpoppa?"

Even though he was not really present, Steel felt the evil roll off the man and he drew a deep breath. His grandfather had died in this very chamber. How could he be alive?

"Are you prepared to take your mother's life?"

Jeremiah knelt beside the stone slab and reached a shaking hand to his mother's face. "Must I?"

"She abandoned you, son. She hated you. She wanted you dead, remember? She chose the other son, not you." Grandpoppa hissed.

Jeremiah blinked and Steel wanted to stop this, to end this replaying memory, but he found himself frozen in place. He had to endure this unspeakable event.

"I don't know." Jeremiah pulled back his hand and slowly stood up. "Now that I see her. Now that I am with her, I don't feel the hate."

"You need some help, son." Grandpoppa said. Another door behind him slid aside revealing blinding sunlight. Lucas Malson stepped into the chamber. His bare chest gleamed whitely and the tattoos writhed on his skin.

"Jeremiah, remember what I promised you." Lucas paused beside Grandpoppa. His red eyes gleamed with power. "The third demon desires to have you once again."

Jeremiah blinked and glanced at Lucas. "I was promised the second."

"In due time," Lucas said. "Three has asked to sift you like sand. He has resided in you before."

"Yes, he comes and goes." Jeremiah licked his lips, his gaze fixed on his mother's motionless body. "They are both here now." He put his hands to his head. "I am lost between them. I can't think."

Grandpoppa reached out and placed a hand on Jeremiah's arm. Jeremiah jumped in surprise. "Son, the third demon will help you with this. But it must be you who performs this deed. Only then will you manifest. The choice to do so must be yours. Uncoerced." He glanced at Lucas and nodded.

Lucas held out his hand. "Number two will leave you now." Something dark and pebbly gushed from his mouth and nose as he exhaled. Spots played before his eyes as the oxygen in his blood plummeted. The particles coalesced into a black silhouette of a man with stars in his open chest. Lucas placed the tattoo on his chest.

Steel tried to cry out a warning. Stop this! Don't do this! But he knew this event was in the past. It could not be changed. Jeremiah looked over his shoulder at Steel, and their eyes met.

JEREMIAH DREW a deep breath as the memory replay paused. "You see, don't you?" He said to Steel. "I had no choice. They made me. The third demon made me."

Steel's control returned. "No, this was your choice, Jeremiah. You chose to follow through with this. There is always a choice."

"You will see." Jeremiah said. "You will see what happened and you will understand."

Jeremiah grabbed his head. "My head hurts."

"I told you two demons might be too much." Lucas said.

Grandpoppa snorted. "You know nothing, Lucas. Be quiet. If he is who he is supposed to be, then carrying two demons would be no problem."

The slap caught Jeremiah by surprise. Grandpoppa's backhand tossed him up against the wall. He tasted blood on his lips. Lucas backed up against the tripod with the small video camera and it almost toppled over. He grabbed the tripod and stabilized it.

"Let me give you more persuasion." Grandpoppa's eyes filled with fire. He gestured to one of the doors and it swung outward. The man who stepped into the room was a total stranger.

"Robert Ketrick?" Steel whispered to himself.

"Who are you?" Jeremiah climbed to his feet and leaned against the wall. The man crossed the room. His long, black hair hung about his shoulders like a mantle. His intense green eyes glittered with hatred.

"I am your worst nightmare, boy." Ketrick smiled, revealing bright teeth. He wore some kind of ancient central American tunic and a grass skirt. His tall cheekbones bore bright color slashes.

"Are you some kind of Pocahontas?" Jeremiah tried to smile.

Ketrick extended a bony finger and touched the blood trickling from Jeremiah's nose. He studied the drop of blood beaded on the tip of his index finger. He popped the finger into his mouth and closed his eyes in ecstasy.

"Ah, such precious blood."

Jeremiah wiped the blood from his face. "You're a sicko."

Ketrick smiled, blood outlining his teeth. "You have no idea."

"Get on with it, Ketrick." Grandpoppa growled. "Do you have the knife?"

Ketrick's eyes widened in anticipation. "The knife. Yes, the knife. It has taken the hearts of thousands and thousands. Its soul is stained with so much blood. Some of it innocent." He reached into the folds of his tunic and took out a stone knife.

Once again, Steel gasped behind him. Jeremiah whirled and everyone froze. "Would you stop interrupting?"

Steel stepped forward. "Robert Ketrick was there the night we were born, Jeremiah. He is under the influence of the most vile demon on Earth. And that knife was used in human sacrifices for thousands of years. Braxton used it to kill April Pierce."

Jeremiah nodded. "I know now. I didn't then. Just stop interrupting and pay close attention. We are almost done."

Jeremiah turned back to Ketrick and reached out a hand. "Give me the knife."

"Oh, no." Ketrick held it back. "Not until you're under the control of number three. I don't relish the idea of having my heart cut out." He leaned forward, cutting his eyes toward Grandpoppa. "There is another plan in place, Jerry. Let three take over and you will see."

"They said I had to do it alone." Jeremiah whispered.

Ketrick's eyes gleamed. "Three has his own plan. Let him take over."

Jeremiah swallowed and the third demon moved in the back of his mind. "Let me take over, idiot." It said.

Jeremiah surrendered control and the dark, dangerous

shroud of evil enveloped him. He fell into darkness and landed on a hard, stone floor. He looked upward as if in a deep well at the distant light of life and good and hope. He was trapped again in his mind by the third demon.

"Now, before we go on," the third demon appeared next to him. He assumed the shape of a man with dark hair and eyes of two different colors.

"Who are you supposed to be?" Jeremiah said.

"One of my newest companions, a serial killer." He smiled. "Ready to kill your mother?"

Jeremiah stood up slowly. "No. I've changed my mind. I let you in so I could beg you. Don't make me do it. Please."

"I wasn't going to. New plan. Ketrick can take care of your mother. What you need to do is run. Grab the tripod and camera and run up the staircase and make sure that woman hiding in the bushes outside sees you. She'll think you are your brother!"

"What?"

"I don't care about who gets killed, Jeremiah. I only care who gets blamed. Your precious brother is on his way here and when he comes down into this killing chamber, he will be blamed for his mother's death. There is a second knife I will leave behind for the police to find. The special knife stays with Ketrick after it has killed." He held up the stone knife and his eyes glowed with evil. "No one knows you exist and we need to keep it that way for now."

Jeremiah sighed. "We?"

"There are forces on the Dark Council who want to undermine the other demons. We are constantly battling among ourselves. I want number two and number one to fail. Do you understand?"

"What happens when two returns?" Jeremiah said.

"You invited *me* in, Jeremiah. You don't need number two.

We can do so much together! You want your power returned, don't you? You left to be on your own so you could find your 'Manifestation'? These controlling idiots can't help you. But, I will. I have a plan and you are a part of it. I have others under my influence who will make sure your brother takes the fall for this, not you. So, basically, run!"

FORTY-FOUR

Steel gasped as he was thrown back by his severed connection with the Grimvox. Jeremiah sat wide eyed and still in his seat. His anger took him and Steel bound across the table and landed full on Jeremiah's chest, driving him and the chair backwards onto the floor. They rolled across the cold concrete floor.

"Do you know what they did to her?" Steel screamed as he grabbed Jeremiah by the head. "I was there. I held her in my lap. I looked into her lifeless eyes. You could have saved her!"

"I know." Jeremiah sobbed. "I was a coward. I ran and left her to them, JJ. I know. I know." His eyes filled with tears and his body wracked with sobs. Steel rolled off him and lay on the cold floor beside him.

"They blamed me for it, Jeremiah."

"I know. All of that happened after the third demon took over. His plan!" Jeremiah said. "JJ, I finally found my mother and then she was gone. Gone!"

Steel sat up. "She wasn't the monster they told you she was. She thought you had died at birth, Jeremiah. She would have looked for you if she thought you were alive. You know that."

"Now I do. I didn't then. I was a teenager. I was stupid." He sat up and wiped tears from his face.

"And Ketrick had the knife. Who actually killed her?"

"I don't know. It could have been any of the three of them."

"It's time to let me go, Jeremiah. I'm tired of this game of yours."

"You are pathetic. What a wasted life." A voice echoed from the shadows.

Steel stood up slowly. A figure stepped out of the shadows carrying a Tazer. The man's turquoise eyes burned with fire. Jeremiah sat up.

"Grandpoppa?"

"You didn't think I could find you? Stupid boy." He shot the Tazer in their direction and the darts hit Steel in the chest. Sparks danced across Steel's chest. He collapsed.

STEEL AWOKE to a pounding headache and found himself once again strapped to his chair in only his pants. A sudden gush of cold water hit him and took his breath away.

"Wake up, you ninny," Nanny said. She tossed the empty bucket away. Steel looked around the table. Snake sat at her end, hands on the Grimvox. Jeremiah sat in his chair, drenched with cold water, his bare chest heaving with each deep breath. He stared at Steel with widened eyes.

"I thought he had killed you!" He said.

"Nonsense." Grandpoppa appeared from the shadows of the chamber. He wore a khaki shirt and matching pants with boots almost up to his knees. A green pith helmet sat on his head. He took the pith helmet off and smoothed down snowy white hair. His appearance was identical to the figure Steel had seen in Hampton's museum. But that man had been a long ago ancestor of the Stone family. This man claimed to be his deceased grandfather. He tossed his pith helmet on the table. "That will be all, Nanny. Take the other Grimvox keeper and dispose of her."

"No!" Steel lurched against his restraints. "Not Ila."

"She gave herself to us, my boy. Her fate is in my hands." Grandpoppa motioned to Nanny. "Do your job. Get on with it."

Nanny nodded and disappeared into the shadows. Grandpoppa took a seat opposite Jeremiah and smiled. "Look at this lovely family reunion."

Jeremiah surged against his restraints. "Let me go."

"So you can betray me again? What made you think you could get away with taking the Grimvox?"

"I was trying to reawaken his memory. We need that knowledge. You were dragging your feet working with the Sno woman and Hamilton."

"Nigel?" Steel said. "And Dr. Sno?"

"Vitreomancers." Grandpoppa shrugged. "Amateurs. For centuries. Wannabe demon masters."

"And I suppose you are a master of demons? Is that how you possessed me with your photo album?" Steel said.

"The third demon was quite useful back then. Roamed about. Loved to move from host to host. You shared that demon with your brother." Grandpoppa said.

"How could you do this to your own grandson?" Steel said.

Grandpoppa shrugged, his turquoise eyes glittering in the green light of the Grimvox. "I've had many grandsons. Most were disposable. Except for one of you." He tapped the table. "One of you is the pinnacle of my work."

Steel glanced at Jeremiah. "What is he talking about?"

"One of us was supposed to manifest. Whatever that

meant." Jeremiah growled. He leaned forward toward the table. "Grandpoppa, I was only doing what is in the best interest of the Council."

"Where is the second demon?" Grandpoppa asked. "I need to speak to him."

"What about?" Steel said.

Grandpoppa crossed his arms. "Well, if you must know, son, I need to finalize my plans with Joshua Knight."

"What?"

Jeremiah laughed. "The Pandora stone was a conduit like the Grimvox. He let Hampton take it and use it to supposedly perfect his Elixir of Life. But in reality it was there to stimulate and collect memories."

"He's right, JJ. Josh and I had a very nice conversation at the end of that failed process. I say failed for Hampton. But not for me." Grandpoppa smiled.

"He promised to give us the memory." Jeremiah nodded toward Steel.

"Really?" Grandpoppa smirked. "Let me guess. You never break a promise, right?"

"What memory are you looking for?"

Grandpoppa leaned toward him. "The Ark of the Covenant. You found it. You saw it. I need to know where it is."

Steel drew a deep breath. "I promised the monk I would never tell."

Grandpoppa gestured toward the Grimvox. "Now that I am here, I can control what you remember. Thank you for bringing up the monk. Let's see what happened, shall we?"

Steel stood in the heat and sunlight of Axum, Ethiopia. He had journeyed there with Cassie Sebastian in search of the throne used

by Anthony Cobalt and the tenth demon. There, he had met a robed man claiming to be a keeper of the Ark of the Covenant.

The man led Steel across the road into a flat expanse of stone and trees. A domed church sat in the center of the space. "This is the Church of Our Lady Mary of Zion." The man said. "It is the most holy church in the Ethiopian Orthodox Church. I will not allow the unworthy to violate the grounds of this church."

"Why am I so special?"

"Your angel told me you were coming." The man said quietly. "I want to show you something. I am the Guardian Monk of the chapel." He pointed to a square stone building sitting in the back corner of the property. It was beautifully constructed and surrounded by a red wrought-iron fence with arrows pointing outward at the top of each spire. The guardian monk opened a gate in the fence and led Steel up the stairs into a domed entrance. The interior was adorned with murals depicting a woman, most likely Mary, in various moments of her life. But whatever was in the center of the chapel was obscured by a huge, red curtain.

The man pointed to the corner of the room. There, another red curtain stirred in a breeze that seemed to come out of the very wall. "Your journey is only beginning, son. God has chosen you for an important task."

Steel's anger built, and his face warmed. "I don't care about a task. I'm here to find the Fallen Throne, so I can save my friends."

The man nodded. He placed a gnarled hand on Steel's chest. It was hot and the touch of the hand on his skin brought comfort. Steel's anger abated. Calm came over him.

"You have a good heart. You are a man who has the righteous anger of God at your disposal. Always make sure you unleash that anger on those who deserve it. A great loss is coming, and you must be strong in the time of tribulation. You must keep your eyes focused on the task. Cassandra Sebastian is not to be trusted now,

but in the future, you will have to trust her. God is not finished with her yet."

Steel swallowed. "I don't know."

"You have a great hatred in you, my son. Defeat it or it will destroy those whom you love." He withdrew his hand and Steel gasped as the warmth and comfort receded. The holy man pointed to the curtain. "You must now pierce the Veil. Another awaits you to show you to your fate."

He gestured to the curtain. Steel hurried across the room and paused as he looked at the center of the chapel. "Is that the Ark?"

The holy man smiled. "There are many things man cannot look upon and live." He moved to the center where the red curtains hung motionless. He reached inside and through the slit Steel saw a wooden chest; flashing gold, an angel's wing. The holy man pulled out a long leather-bound object with a sling from behind the curtains. He handed it to Steel. "You will need this."

Steel took the elongated canvas bag and felt something thin and flat within. "What is this?"

"When the time comes, you will know to open the container. The object within will be necessary and you alone must be the guardian of this object. Ask no further questions." The holy man said."

Steel nodded slung the bag over his back and nodded. "Thank you. I think." He turned and stepped through the billowing curtain and was some when else. The room was not there and was there. He floated and walked and flew. The air was thick with incense, and he was not of this world. A priest stood over a dying lamb. The priest had colorful stones on his chest and incense filled the Holy of Holies and the great purple veil hid all from the world and it tore, serrated from top to bottom obliterating the priest and there on the ceiling was the cross with the God man. His eyes were deeper and more powerful and more loving than was infinitely possible and He looked at Steel as blood ran and he said, "Father forgive them." A drop of blood fell from the crown of thorns and hit Jonathan between the eyes burning like molten gold, eating through his skull to his brain and igniting a fire that consumed his entire body and he was falling through darkness and ashes and light and death and life as the fire coursed through him to his heart and made it beat slowly then quickly and the thing he carried, the thing in the bag on his back glowed with holy light and he knew. He knew why he was but not who he was. The who was no longer as important as the why.

Steel stepped through the curtains and out into bright sunlight. He blinked even as the vision or journey or whatever he had just experienced began to fade leaving behind only the conviction. He had to stop Cobalt. He had to save Josh and Cephas and Theo. A holy man like the other stepped into view and Steel saw they were at the bottom of a narrow trough carved into the stone.

"Welcome, avenger, to Lalibela."

STEEL SHOOK AWAY THE MEMORY. Jeremiah slumped over the table. Granpoppa was motionless, mouth open and eyes empty. What had just happened?

Jeremiah shook his head and looked around. "JJ? What is happening? Where are we?"

Grandpoppa sighed and sat forward, drool running from his mouth. Jeremiah lurched and grinned. Grandpoppa sat up, his eyes clear. Something in his memory had interrupted his control.

"We're back." Jeremiah said. "That memory was a bit troublesome."

"You had to flee in the face of the Savior." Steel whispered.

"Not for long." Grandpoppa cleared his throat. "As the

monk said, you are still powerless because of your anger and hatred."

Steel glanced at Jeremiah. "Strangely, I understand why Jeremiah is the way he is. Your influence. And the demons. What did Jesus say from the cross?"

Grandpoppa slammed his hand on the table. "Do not say that name."

"Father forgive them, for they know not what they do." Steel said.

Jeremiah shook his head violently. "Stop it or I will hurt him." The second demon's voice came from Jeremiah's mouth. "What is the plan, master demon?"

"Now that we know where to find the ark, we can secure the artifact. It will take some doing, but it is not impossible. I will deal with the monk." He stood up slowly and picked up his pith helmet. "As always, I have a Plan B. When I spoke with Josh, I found all I needed to know." Grandpoppa donned the pith helmet. "I no longer need either of you for my plans. Josh will be far more useful." A cruel and guttural utterance came from his mouth, and Jeremiah stiffened.

"No! You cannot!" The second demon said.

"I bind you to your host. When he dies and his soul is taken to Tartarus, you will go with him. I no longer need you!"

"No! Stop! I can still help you." The second demon pleaded and slowly, oh so slowly, his power faded from Jeremiah's face leaving the man in control.

"What did you do?" Jeremiah screeched.

"Bound the two of you together, Jeremiah. He cannot leave you unless you die. And when you die, he goes with your soul to his, and your, eternal damnation." Grandpoppa pushed his chair carefully under the table. "I and the first demon will leave the two of you to the energies of the Grimvox. You see, it not only stores memories, it can remove them. It can suck your mind dry. Once it has established a connection, with your permission, of course, I can send it into overdrive and empty your mind of everything. It pains me to say goodbye to both of my grandsons. I have a new adopted great grandson, Josh Knight, to attend to. He will manifest soon and take your places at my side. Goodbye."

JOSH PUSHED the truck to its limits as he sped down the interstate. The thunderstorm had worsened and now, pellets of sleet bounced off the windshield. He drove into the backend of a winter storm moving east into the Shreveport area.

"Josh, slow down!" Caskey held onto the sides of his seat. "The road is icing up."

"Call Max. Now!" He swerved around a huge eighteen wheeler and for a moment, the truck's wheels slid on the growing ice. He righted the truck and rushed ahead.

Caskey dialed his cell phone and put it on the truck speaker. "Josh? I hope you have news." Max's voice came over the speaker.

"Max, I found out where Jeremiah is keeping Jonathan." Josh shouted as he sped around another large truck. "They're in the cabin's basement. Somewhere in the basement."

"What?" Max said. "That's impossible. Nothing is there."

"I'm telling you, the thirteenth demon revealed their location. I don't know how, but they are there somewhere."

"Thirteenth demon?" Max said.

"It keeps coming back." Caskey said. "Can you get Sister Mary Margaret to check on the basement?"

"Every time they have tried to go into the basement, something terrible happens." Max said. "But I'll see what we can do."

The line went dead and Caskey grabbed the dash as Josh sped around cars. "What did Winston say?"

"He said Jonathan was where we all began. The circle of death, he said. They're in the cabin's basement." Josh swallowed bile. Jonathan and Jeremiah had been only yards away from them the entire time.

"If that is true, we may not be able to reach them. You heard what Sister Mary Margaret said. Anyone who tries to breach the field around the basement disappears."

"We have guardian angels and hopefully they will help, Father Caskey."

"They seem to only help you when they want to." Caskey said.

"More like when God lets them." Josh swerved around a huge truck and prayed for their safety.

FORTY-FIVE

Jeremiah searched the misty darkness around him. Where was he? He wore only his pants and his chest and face were covered in sweat. He placed his hand on his chest. The metal disc was now on him! Where was the second demon? Deep within his heart was a tiny hard stone. The demon somehow had been imprisoned within him. For the first time in years, he was completely on his own. No knowledge. No power! What had Grandpoppa said? The Grimvox would destroy his mind?

"Anyone there?" He screamed. "Help me."

STEEL TURNED over on the cold, hard surface. He wore only his pants and a chill ran over him from the cold water still soaked into his skin. He slowly sat up and looked around at the vague, empty darkness. He felt the cold metal disc on his chest. Where was he? Nearby, he heard a voice calling for help. He slowly stood up and stumbled toward the voice.

THE BLOW TOOK Jeremiah by surprise knocking him to his knees. Another kick caught him in the kidneys and he fell forward onto his face.

"You did this to me!"

He rolled over and gasped. The teenage girl standing before him wore torn jeans and a bloody tee shirt. Bruises covered her face. Her eyes were surrounded by black rings and leaked bloody tears. Black goo dripped from her mouth. "Sarah?" He mumbled.

She kicked his leg and her foot came loose and flew into the darkness. She stumbled as she stood on the stump. "You let me fall into the bottomless pit. I died there surrounded by ever burning flames, Jeremiah. No one came to help me. I cried out until my tongue was so swollen I choked on it." She lurched toward him again and tried to kick him with her other foot.

Jeremiah crawled backwards as the lurching figure of Sarah pursued him. "Leave me alone." He screamed and he ran into another pair of legs. He looked up at Jonathan Steel.

"JJ? Help me." He pointed to the darkness. Sarah had disappeared.

Steel helped him to his feet. "Who are you pointing at?"

"A girl. I liked her and took her to the theme park." Jeremiah hung onto Steel's arm. "She must have died in the pit. I had no idea."

"Jeremiah, I don't believe you. What kind of plans did you have for her?"

Jeremiah looked at his brother. "Okay. So they weren't good for her. I wasn't going to kill her, though. I promise."

"Where are we, Jeremiah?"

"In the depths of the Grimvox. You heard what Grandpoppa said. It's sucking our minds into the matrix of its memories. If we don't break out, we will die at that table."

Steel looked around at the darkness. "We are not alone."

"Tell me about it." Jeremiah's voice filled with panic.

"Without your demon, you feel powerless, don't you?" Steel said.

"Now is not the time to gloat."

"I'm not gloating. Just stating a fact."

Jeremiah glared at him. "I guess this is where you tell me more about your Savior?"

"Not now. As long as you hang onto the second demon, it would do no good. Give it up first."

Jeremiah shoved Steel away. "Did you hear Grandpoppa? I'm bound to the second demon. It can't leave even if I wanted it to. It's trapped within me."

"And demons lie, Jeremiah."

"Well, in this case, Grandpoppa wasn't lying. I can feel the second demon like some worthless lump of rock."

"Then throw it away." Steel said.

Jeremiah glared at him. "Don't you think I would if I could?"

"Jeremiah, you've relied on the presence of a demon for so long, you don't know yourself. Now you know what it is like to be just Jeremiah." Steel said.

"We don't have time for self help lectures, brother. We have to figure out how to escape from the Grimvox."

"Or you die and go to hell," Steel said. "Your choice, remember?"

Jeremiah screamed and launched himself at Steel. They tumbled back onto the hard surface. Jeremiah rained down blow after blow to Steel's face. Steel blinked as each blow tried to land, but there was never any contact with his face. Jeremiah cursed and stood up, studying his fist. "What the?"

"The Grimvox won't allow you to do what you want the most. Kill me," Steel said as he climbed to his feet. "Where's your power now?"

Jeremiah cursed some more, stood up, and turned away. "Shut up."

"If we want to get out of this, we have to work together." Steel said.

Jeremiah glared at him. "Brotherly love? You no longer want to bash my head in?"

"I wouldn't go that far," Steel said. "The harsh reality is we have to put all that aside or die in this place. And I have to find Ila and keep Grandpoppa from doing all of this to Josh!"

"I'll die before I help you." Jeremiah hissed. He turned and headed off into the darkness. He hadn't covered a few yards before something hideous and ghostly appeared in front of him. The figure resembled Nanny only with hair that writhed like Medusa and purple tentacles growing from her back.

"You wretched boy! It's time for your beating." She screamed.

Her tentacles wrapped around his bare arms and lifted him from the ground. Her gray hair snapped and whipped in the air like snakes. The tablet appeared in her grasp. She smiled and touched a tentacle tip to the tablet. Arcs of white electricity burst from the disc. Jeremiah screamed in agony as, over and over, she touched the tablet.

Before Steel could move, the smell hit him hard, and he retched. The memory of that stench overtook him and he fell backwards onto the hard floor, his muscles paralyzed. From above him, the appendages with articulated eyes appeared. The thing from Cobalt's ship descended out of the darkness, all red and oozing with body appendages protruding from obscene angles out of the blob of reddish flesh.

"There you are." A mouth burbled on a stalk. "It is time to finish your examination."

The memory of the horror of those moments engulfed Steel. His heart raced and bile filled the back of his throat. He was on the metal table in Cobalt's ship once more as the thing above him lowered bone saws and shining scalpels on jointed pink arms.

"No! I destroyed you in the underground cave!" He said, but the fear continued to build. With the horrifying memory of that fear came another memory when he had recalled he did not belong to this creature. Such an abomination came from Satan's side of the spiritual war. He belonged to Someone else. And all he had to do was to give in, to allow the thing to actually touch him.

He hyperventilated as the bone saw lowered to the level of his right check. "Let's start with the right eye globe." Another mouth burbled. The saw barely creased the skin of his cheek and it suddenly disintegrated into goo. The hot liquid ran across Steel's cheek and the disintegration ran up the appendage.

The thing's mouths screamed in agony and Steel bounded up from the floor. He tore the disc from his chest and shoved it onto the creature's flesh. The disc ignited with energy intended to keep Steel from removing it. Instead, the electric sparks roved over the thing's flesh. It seethed and writhed as its skin ruptured in purulent pustules and it retreated into the darkness.

"Just memories." Steel said. He ran to Jeremiah. "They're not real, Jeremiah. Just your memories. You can deny them. Just push back."

Jeremiah's arched painfully from the electricity playing over his chest. "No! It's too real!"

Nanny turned her dark eyes on him. "Leave him to his fate."

"No!" Steel reached out and grabbed one of her tentacles. "Resist the devil and he will flee. Leave now!" He shoved the tentacle up against Jeremiah's sparking disc.

Nanny's eyes widened in shock and her tentacle dissolved into purple goo, splashing onto the floor. She released the tablet and screamed.

"You can't do this forever!" Nanny screamed. "Soon, your mind will be emptied and his soul will belong to us!" She pulled back into the darkness.

Steel helped Jeremiah to his feet. "Why did you help me?"

"Really? You don't know by now? It's what I do."

"A helper in the time of need. Yes, I know." Jeremiah rubbed his aching chest. "You just can't help yourself."

"Would you have rather I left you to her?"

"No." He glanced at Steel. "Thank you. What now?"

"There is someone here who can help us. We just have to find her."

"Her?"

"Snake." Steel walked into the darkness.

FORTY-SIX

The darkness faded around them, and the wind hit Steel like an icy razor. He glanced up and down the obscene street around him, shivering in the icy wind. "Where are we?"

"Maimed Street." Jeremiah said. "Welcome to the Tragic Kingdom." He pointed to the deformed castle at the head of the street. "I grew up living in that castle."

"Vivian said she met the Dark Council here."

"They used the park after it closed. Fits their macabre style."

"So, why are we here, Jeremiah?"

"This is where most of my bad memories came from. Beatings from Nanny. Harassment from Lucas. Experiments at the hands of Dr. Santiago. I ran away from this private hell." Jeremiah hugged his arms around his chest.

"How can we be experiencing this?" Steel asked, moving from the middle of the street into the meager protection of a sidewalk overhang.

"You've been to Numinocity? Augmented reality boosted by

demonic power. Well, the Grimvox is Numinocity with warp speed. Thousands and thousands of years of memories from humans possessed by demons." He pounded his chest. "Like the traitor inside me."

Lightning spiked, and rain poured from the leaden sky. The overhang protecting the sidewalk poured water like a sieve. Thunder rattled the broken windows up and down Maimed Street. Dizziness gripped Steel, and he leaned against the scabby wall. He pushed back on the nausea. "Did you feel that?"

Jeremiah leaned against a lamppost. "Yeah. It's affecting our brains. Sucking the memories, the life force, from us. It's what happens to the Keepers. Only accelerated."

"How do we stop it?"

"If we can release the Grimvox from our grasp and break the connection, we can get out of here. But the longer we stay, the more we are connected to the Grimvox and the greater our chance of dying from severing the connection abruptly." Jeremiah's breath steamed into the cold air.

The sound of footsteps came down the street. Steel leaned away from the wall and squinted through the rain. A dozen individuals appeared, all wearing black clothing. The rain plastered their long hair against their white skin. Red eyes gleamed with evil power. Each man and woman's mouth gaped open, revealing fangs.

"Great! The twelfth demon's vampires. We have to get out of the open."

Jeremiah pointed down the street. "There are tunnels under the castle. Run!"

Steel followed Jeremiah out into the street and they ran toward the castle over broken concrete and huge cracks. A shadow passed over them and the vampires appeared in the air on bat-like wings. Steel slid to a halt. "Keep going. I can handle these things."

Jeremiah ran on toward the castle. Steel stood in the pouring rain as the vampires landed in a circle around him. The lead vampire stepped forward, his long hair matted to his face. His red eyes gleamed.

"Miss your fangs, Steel?" Bile, the fangmaster who had fashioned false fangs for Steel, lisped through his pointed teeth.

"You're dead, Jerome." Steel said. "Vivian said you died on Boone's island."

"Hah, man of steel. I will always live in your memories. Remember the rain at Wulf's Bloodfest?" He snapped his fingers and the cold, wet rain turned hot. Blood fell from the skies. The coppery scent filled the air. The vampires turned their open mouths up to the rain.

Steel wiped blood from his eyes and stepped closer to Bile. "You are nothing but an echo of your evil master. I have one thing to say to you."

"What is that?" Bile smiled and blood ran over his face and into his open mouth. He licked it away from his lips.

Steel leaned close to Bile's ear. "I'm not afraid of you. But you should be afraid of my savior, Jesus."

Bile's screech echoed down Maimed Street, and the vampires crumpled onto the concrete. They writhed and clawed at their ears. The blood changed back to rain and washed the crimson away from their cold, pale bodies. Slowly, they dissolved like soap bubbles. Bile's fangs were the last to disappear. The Librarian had been right. Steel did not belong here!

Steel hurried down the street toward the castle. The turrets of the castle towered into the rainy sky. Instead of masterful architecture, the turrets looked like melting candles. The moat beneath the bridge into the castle reeked of decay. Things moved beneath the dark water. Steel paused inside the archway leading into the castle. The walls were covered with carvings of human beings in various stages of pain and suffering. An open doorway to his left led into darkness. The tunnels, he realized. Inside, the open door, stairs led down into darkness.

Steel walked into the hot, muggy air as he descended the stairs. The spiral staircase led down into darkness that opened onto a balcony with ancient chairs. From beyond the balcony, pale green light filled the chamber. Steel reached the balcony edge and looked down into an old style surgical amphitheater. Three rows of chairs descended step wise down to a central stage. The array of creatures seated in the chairs were the substance of the worst nightmares. Demons of all types moved and murmured as they pointed and gestured toward the central stage.

A tall man in a bloodstained white lab coat hovered over a surgical table. His hair stood on end, and a surgical mask covered his mouth and nose. His bright green eyes glowed with malice. Stretched out on the table, Jeremiah struggled against his restraints. Arms and legs spread out from his torso, he writhed and moaned against an oxygen mask shoved over his mouth. His eyes widened as he spotted Steel.

"Now, my most esteemed guests." The man shouted, holding up a syringe with a huge needle. "We shall force upon our victim the process we have waited years to occur." He giggled and laughed. A raucous cacophony of obscene sounds came from the demons.

"It is time for Jeremiah's manifestation! If it will not arise spontaneously, then I, Dr. Santiago, we will force it!" He whirled and held the syringe above his head like a knife. With one quick plunge, he drove the needle into Jeremiah's chest.

Jeremiah's scream blew the oxygen mask away from his mouth.

Before Steel could react something happened right beneath him. A demon in the last row popped out of existence. In its place an ordinary man in a three piece suit appeared. The demons stood and a collective cry of alarm rose above Jeremiah's screaming. More demons disappeared and were replaced by ordinary human beings. Men, women, and children filled the empty seats. Dr. Santiago pulled down his mask and surveyed the growing chaos.

"What is this?"

"Time for you to lose your medical license." A woman's voice filled the chamber. The Crimson Snake descended from the ceiling on a rope. Her copper hued artificial arm held a glowing, golden sword.

She landed on the surgical table one foot on either side of Jeremiah. She wore a one piece red jumpsuit and her wild, carrot colored hair surrounded her face like a lion's mane.

"Hello, sweetie." She said to Jeremiah, and with one quick move, she jerked the syringe from his chest. She somersaulted sideways and landed in front of Dr. Santiago. All around her, the demons had been replaced with people. One teenager stood up and smiled.

"Thank you, Rebecca. You have redeemed us."

"You're welcome, Pablo." She said. "You saved me." She glanced up at Steel. "You and Jonathan Steel." She turned back to Santiago.

"Now, you piece of Hades reeking demon dung, I hold in my hand the Sword of the Spirit, the only offensive weapon allowed to a follower of my new Master."

Santiago's eyes widened, and he stumbled back into the surgical table. Jeremiah sat up and grabbed him from behind. "Not going anywhere, doc." He said.

"Let me show you something I found just a few moments ago floating around in the memory of a person who died on a certain airplane crash I was responsible for." She held up a piece of paper. Steel could see the image of snow-covered mountains.

"My friend Pablo gave me this picture of the mountains, knowing there was something on the other side. A scripture, a verse from the Bible. Shall I read it to you?"

"No!" Santiago screamed.

"Finally, be strong in the Lord and in his mighty power. Put on the full armor of God, so that you can take your stand against the devil's schemes. For our struggle is not against flesh and blood, but against the rulers, against the authorities, against the powers of this dark world and against the spiritual forces of evil in the heavenly realms. Therefore put on the full armor of God, so that when the day of evil comes, you may be able to stand your ground, and after you have done everything, to stand. Stand firm then, with the belt of truth buckled around your waist, with the breastplate of righteousness in place, and with your feet fitted with the readiness that comes from the gospel of peace. In addition to all this, take up the shield of faith, with which you can extinguish all the flaming arrows of the evil one. Take the helmet of salvation and the sword of the Spirit, which is the word of God. And pray in the Spirit on all occasions with all kinds of prayers and requests. With this in mind, be alert and always keep on praying for all the Lord's people. Pray also for me, that whenever I speak, words may be given me so that I will fearlessly make known the mystery of the gospel, for which I am an ambassador in chains. Pray that I may declare it fearlessly, as I should."

Santiago trembled, and the chamber shook. "Jeremiah did not know when he attached me to the Grimvox that I would one day stand before him unshaken and filled with a new Spirit." She raised the sword above her head. "But the spiritual connection isn't enough to destroy this thing. I also need something very physical." Green dots swirled along her good arm.

"Nannomemes!" Steel gasped.

"Yes!" Snake smiled. "Jeremiah thought he chose me to merge with the Grimvox because I could be manipulated by restoring my arm. But, Jonathan, it was God's design I be the one. It is the reason I was chosen. I will end this. Now!' She turned to face Santiago and Jeremiah.

"Guardian spirit of the Grimvox, I resist your fiery darts, I embrace the mystery of the gospel, and I claim not only the forgiveness of those assembled whose lives I took but the forgiveness of Jesus Christ!"

Snake plunged the sword into Santiago's chest. The green particles swarmed along her arm, crawling down the shaft of the sword and into Santiago's chest. They began to spread everywhere.

"Nannomemes designed to erase memory!" Snake shouted. "And what is the Grimvox but memories from demons?"

Green particles flowed onto every surface in the amphitheater and outlined every seemingly real object. Suddenly, green fire erupted from the Santiago's torso, engulfing them all in wave after wave of green light and mist. The waves threw Steel backwards, and he landed hard on his back, knocking the breath out of him.

He stumbled to his feet and discovered he was back in the chamber. Jeremiah sat slumped over the table. Snake sat at the other end of the table, her good hand touching the Grimvox. The thing shook and vibrated, a high-pitched whine issuing from within. The green particles now swarmed up her arm and dropped like dust onto the table, moving across its surface like fire ants on steroids. Snake drew a deep breath and looked right at Steel.

"I can't let go. Get him and run! Now!" Steel grabbed Jeremiah's slumped, unconscious figure and threw him over his shoulder. The vibrations from the Grimvox had spread across the table and the entire chamber trembled with its releasing energy and swarming nannomemes.

"Snake! Rebecca!"

"I can't let go, Jonathan." She shouted. "If I do, it wins. Thank you. Get out of here. Now!"

With tears filling his eyes, Steel carried Jeremiah and ran out into the corridor. He hurried past his cell door and found a set of stairs at the end of the dark corridor. Suddenly, the nagging familiarity of the hallway brought back the memory of Theo King and Steel trapped in a basement cell confronted by the Vitreomancer Agent Cornelius.

But before she could pull the trigger, the room shook. The concrete ceiling crumbled and then tore apart.

Theo grabbed me by the arm and wrapped his other one around the doorframe. "Hang on, Chief! I don't know what's happening."

The crumbling ceiling was sucked upward and away from us, pulled by some unfathomable force. Wind whirled around us, carrying the bloody bones of Ketrick's forgotten victim. The bones pummeled Cornelius, and she tried to dodge them as she shot up into the open space above. A whirlwind of fire and crumbled stone and splintered wood hung against the pale blue sky. Cornelius screamed as she flew into the vortex and disappeared.

They were in the basement of Ketrick's cabin! The surrounding walls shook and dust and bits of stone fell from the crumbling ceiling. He hurried up the stairs into a stone chamber. Light leaked from above and he looked upward into a chimney. A fireplace? He shoved against the stone wall before him and the wall fell open. He rushed out into the open. Behind him, the fireplace collapsed, stones tumbling down into the lower chamber.

"Dad!"

Steel turned and Josh Knight rushed toward him. Steel motioned at Josh. "Wait! The floor is collapsing! Get back!"

Steel ran toward Josh as the remnants of the fireplace fell into a growing hole. Green light poured from the hole. The entire basement, visible beneath its misty green energy field filled with green fire. Steel grabbed Josh by the arm and pulled him toward an opening in the side of what appeared to be a giant tent like enclosure. Max and two people he did not recognize fell back as the entire foundation of the old cabin trembled.

Standing in the opening of a tunnel leading away from the cabin foundation, Steel lowered Jeremiah to the shaking ground. The green fire boiled up from beneath the energy field and for a moment someone appeared in the fire. A woman stepped forward onto the solid ground around the foundation. Her long hair rested on her shoulders. Her dress tattered and burned.

"Mary?" Max stepped forward. "My Lord, it's Mary!"

"Mother!" Mary reached for her. An elderly man in a black turtleneck held onto Max's arm as she walked across the shaking ground toward the image of Mary Lynn Alba, once possessed by the eleventh demon.

"Max, you can't!" The man said.

"James, it's my daughter. She's come out of the black hole

and the energy field!" Max tried to shrug off the man's grasp and he stumbled back, leaning for support on a cane.

Just as Max's hand almost touched Mary's hand another figure shot up out of the green fire. Flaming red hair and green eyes surrounded a face twisted in anger. White eyes glowed with evil.

"Not so fast!"

"Agent Cornelius!" Steel said in astonishment.

Agent Cornelius wrapped arms around Mary from the back and heaved backward. The two tumbled backward into the energy field. James grabbed Max's arm and pulled her away from the opening in the earth as the fire blasted against the tent fabric and blew it away.

Snow and cold wind blew across the now empty, lifeless basement and knocked them all to their feet. Steel stood up and walked into the blowing snow to the edge of the basement. The green energy field was gone. Down in the basement, crumbled cinder blocks filled the open area. No sign of Mary Alba or Agent Cornelius. No sign of the Grimvox chamber or the Grimvox. No sign of Rebecca, once known as the Crimson Snake.

FORTY-SEVEN

Steel sat Jeremiah up and shook him. "Jeremiah, wake up."

Jeremiah's eyes fluttered open and he jerked away from Steel. "What? Am I dead?"

"Not yet. Ila! Where did Nanny take Ila?"

Josh rushed to Steel's side. "Ila is here?"

"Rebecca and Ila were Keepers of the Grimvox." Steel glanced at Josh.

"Who is Rebecca?" Josh said.

"Snake." Steel shook Jeremiah some more. "Where did Nanny take her? Tell me now or I'll throw you back into the basement."

Jeremiah blinked and rubbed his head. "My head hurts, bro. Give me a minute. There's a tunnel that runs underground from beneath the fireplace to the barn. Then a path to the dock on the bayou."

"I know where that path is!" Josh said. "I'll go."

"Wait!" Steel said as Josh ran out of the tent tunnel into the blowing snow. Steel glanced once at Ruth Martinez and stood up. "I have to go help him."

"I know. Go. We'll watch Jeremiah."

Steel cast one glance at Max, shoulders heaving with sobs and took off after Josh.

JOSH SLID across the ground and almost fell into a long trench stretching from the collapsed fireplace toward the barn. The tunnel collapsed! Was Ila trapped? He heard a voice raised in anger coming from the far side of the barn. He ran through the snow and past the barn. The tracks of a wheelchair and footprints led into the woods.

Steel bounded up next to him. "Wait for me, Josh. We do this together."

Josh nodded and hurried into the woods. "The path to the bluff overlooking the bayou is right over here. The Vitreomancers took me down the path to the bayou." He gasped for breath as he hurried through the pine trees. Snow cascaded from accumulation in the branches and ran down his shirt.

"Here!" He pointed to more wheelchair tracks along the path. More cursing came from ahead and a scream.

They rushed down the path and emerged into a small clearing overlooking the bayou. An empty wheelchair sat at the edge of the bluff. Ila stood by the wheelchair, screaming.

"Ila!" Josh grabbed her and turned her around. Her eyes were wide and empty.

"Where am I? What happened?"

"It's me. Josh. You're fine. You're okay."

Steel put a hand on the wheelchair and leaned over the edge of the bluff. Twenty feet below, Nanny's body lay sprawled on the boat dock. Her empty eyes focused on something unthinkable, unimaginable, and far away.

"What happened?" Josh said.

"I woke up in the chair and that woman was pulling me toward the water and said she was going to throw me in and I pushed her to get away and she fell and where am I? What is happening?"

Josh crushed her to his chest. "It's going to be okay, Ila. We got you."

MAX STOOD at the edge of the old cabin basement. The energy field had returned. Waves of green and blue energy lapped at her feet. The snow had stopped and an icy wind blew from the surrounding trees. Whenever a leaf or a snow flake touched the surface of the energy pool, they merely disappeared.

Through the translucent energy, she could see the broken cinderblocks and empty rooms once used by Robert Ketrick and his kin for imprisonment and torture. More than likely the chamber in which Jonathan had been imprisoned lay under the collapsed fireplace. Sister Mary Margaret eased up beside her.

Max glanced at Sister Mary Margaret's severe facial features and her tight hair pulled back under a black headpiece. She wore a black one piece jumpsuit. A large golden cross hung on a chain around her neck. "I never should have underestimated you." Max said.

"You never estimated me." Margaret's gaze was riveted on the basement. "You dismissed my efforts as unimportant. I tried to warn you and you wouldn't listen." She turned her piercing gaze on Max. "I thought you were much wiser than that."

"You knew Jonathan Steel and Jeremiah were in the basement the entire time, didn't you?"

Margaret nodded. "I did."

"Why didn't you tell me?"

"Max, you assume you have the world's best interest at heart. You have taken up the mantle of combatting evil that once belonged to Cephas Lawrence, one of your old love interests." She stepped closer to Max. "And yet, your motivations are far from altruistic. You long to know what happened to your daughter. Where had she gone? Was she truly dead? Your heart ached for vengeance against these foul creatures who took her from you. Need I remind you 'vengeance is mine saith the Lord'? You are not doing God's work, Max. You are doing Max's work."

Sister Mary Margaret turned her attention back to the basement and gestured a hand toward the glowing pools of energy. "Here is a mystery only God can understand, Max. I knew there was some grand plan in place and you couldn't see it. God's ways are not our ways. God's thoughts are not our thoughts. We had to let that plan play out as it did. There are chess pieces on God's board whose moves in the far future are predetermined. God will be victorious. Despite your meddling."

"Meddling?" Max hissed. "You self righteous, pretentious!" She paused and closed her eyes in anger.

"Max, think about what has transpired. Jeremiah is now apprehended. Jonathan has taken pity for his brother and perhaps will find some measure of caring for his damaged sibling. Jeremiah may yet be saved! And Snake was redeemed, as you had hoped. The endgame nears. We know more now than ever, and it is because I chose not to interfere."

"You are playing God." Max said.

"Coming from you, how ironic." Sister Mary Margaret

crossed her arms and gazed into the basement. "Turing. You remember the man who deciphered the German code during World War II?"

"What of him?"

"He did his job and broke the code. But, when he urged his superiors to use the code to prevent attacks, a difficult decision was made. The British decided if they intervened on upcoming attacks against their ships, the Germans would realize they had broken the code." Sister Mary Margaret looked back at Max. "Turing was stunned to learn that some attacks were allowed to proceed. Sailors and soldiers died who need not have died. But the small sacrifice of their lives was more important in order to defeat a horrible evil in the coming future. The strategy worked and Germany was eventually defeated."

"You're saying I'm Turing?"

"Yes. And I will let God's plans unfold untouched by my bias."

"At what cost?" Max said.

Sister Mary Margaret looked away. "I am aware of the cost, Max. But remember the most horrendous deed in human history, killing God on a cross, brought about the greatest good mankind will ever know."

"My friends are not God." Max said. "Raven and Vivian are missing. Sam and Jason Birdsong are missing. Are we to sacrifice their lives for the greater good? Is that what you are saying?"

Sister Mary Margaret was silent, her face illuminated by the energies in the basement. "Max, there is a microscopic black hole somewhere in that basement. It is being used by supernatural forces to fulfill the will of Satan. If that black hole were released, it would consume the Earth. All life would die in hours. It would eventually obliterate our solar system. My team is trying to decipher how to control that black hole."

"The Turing Machine?" Max hissed. "For what purpose? To protect earth? Or to use as a weapon?"

Sister Mary Margaret looked at Max, her grim features answering the question. "We are in a spiritual battle against the powers of the air, Max. I will do whatever it takes to defeat Satan and aid God's plan."

"Well, I'm glad God is on your side, Sister Mary Margaret. He desperately needs your help, doesn't he?" Max stepped up to the very edge of the energy pool and pulled herself into a regal posture. "I want my daughter back. You have carte blanche."

STEEL HUGGED a blanket around his cold shoulders. He sipped water and waited patiently for Max to return. Josh sat across the table from him and had barely taken his eyes off Steel.

"Ross has taken Jeremiah?" Josh said.

"Yes."

"No sign of the Crimson Snake?"

"Rebecca." Steel looked at him. "Her name was Rebecca."

Josh nodded. "I found out where Jeremiah had you from Armando."

Steel tensed. "What?"

"He's at Seagoville prison in Dallas. Father Caskey and I met the exorcists, and I talked to Armando." Josh said.

Steel stood up slowly. "You did what? You went and confronted Armando?"

"Chill." He motioned for Steel to sit down. "I'm not some helpless teenager anymore, Dad."

Steel blinked at the sound of the word "Dad" and slowly sat down. "Sorry. I'm still in my protective mode."

"There's something else," Josh said.

"What?"

"The thirteenth demon possesses Armando."

Steel stood up again. "Not possible."

"It fooled us in Numinocity, Dad. It's still active. It has a plan to replace the second and the first demon. Which possesses my supposedly dead grandfather?"

Steel sat again. "Yeah, we've had it all wrong, Josh. My father is not the enemy. His father is. He claims to be in league with the first demon." His mind reeled with this new information. He slapped the tabletop. "We fight and we fight and we think we're getting ahead and it's all one step forward and three steps back!"

Hands touched his tense shoulders. He looked over his shoulder into the eyes of Ruth Martinez. His heart melted, and he stood up. Again. He turned and took her in his arms. Tears came into his eyes.

"Oh, baby, it's going to be okay." She whispered.

His lips touched hers and he looked into her eyes. "At least you were safe this time."

"No mechanical dinosaurs after me. But you were close to dying, weren't you? You could have left long before it all blew up in your face, couldn't you?" She held his face in her hands.

"Yes. Mary reached out to me, although I didn't realize it was her. And Rebecca, that is, the Crimson Snake. I had to stay and help them escape."

Max came through the outer doors. Her face flushed red with the cold. Or was it emotion? Sister Mary Margaret followed and ignored them, passing the kitchen area by to return to her laboratory.

Max motioned to the table and sat down. "Let's talk, shall we?"

Ruth settled beside Steel. Steel glanced at Josh's grinning face. "What?"

"Baby?" Josh grinned.

"What does Olivia call you?"

"Babe." Josh beamed. "Ain't love grand?"

Max cleared her throat. Steel took Ruth's hand under the table.

"We have several situations, of course. We have yet to hear from Sam and Jason. I sent them to investigate your old home, Jonathan. And I have yet to hear from Raven and Vivian. They are investigating the Tragic Kingdom."

"All of this looking for me?" Steel said.

"Yes. And the entire time you were right under our noses."

"I'll go to Austin and find Jason and Sam. Where's Yvonne?"

"She's on her way to this Tragic Kingdom with Gamma. I think your house with that ghastly death room off the library would be too much for them." Max said.

"The first demon is looking for the Ark of the Covenant." Steel said. "Not sure why. My memory of its location was what Jeremiah wanted." He looked at Josh. "You, my son, are the first demon's next target. He says you are instrumental to his plans."

Josh's mouth fell open. "Me? Why?"

"I wish I knew. You're staying right here with Max."

"No, I'm not." Josh said.

Steel's face heated. "Yes, you are!"

Josh stood up. "Dad, I made a promise. What did you say about promises? You always keep them. I promised Armando, I mean, Winston I wouldn't abandon him to the thirteenth demon. Father Caskey and I are going to the prison tonight and tomorrow, the exorcist team will start over with Winston. I have to be there."

Steel felt Ruth squeeze his hand. He glanced at her and his anger lessened.

"Jonathan, I'll go with Josh. He'll be safe surrounded by a half dozen exorcists, don't you think?" The look in her eyes cooled Steel's anger.

"Thank you, Ruth. Of should I call you Mom?" Josh said.

Steel flushed, and Ruth laughed. "We're not there yet, Josh."

He grinned and sat down. "Besides, Olivia is doing better and her mother said she would bring her to meet me in Dallas. I really need to see her."

Steel nodded. "Very well. Max, can you get a hold of Ishido?"

Max's eyes widened. "Excellent idea, Jonathan. I'm sure he can be in Dallas by the morning, wherever he is."

"Then, Josh, you can go as long as Ishido is with you. And Ruth." Ishido was an ex-assassin saved by Max who had helped Jonathan with the eighth demon. His skills were unparalleled.

"Fine, Dad. And I have another plan."

"You do?"

"Yeah, but I'm still working on it. I'll tell you about it later."

Max tapped the table with her fingertip. "Then it is decided. I am going to reach out to the Captain for an update. It would seem his father, alive and well, has been masquerading as his son to wreak havoc. And I will remain here while Sister Mary Margaret tries her best to locate Mary."

Steel reached over and took her hand. "I will pray she is successful. And be careful with my father. I still don't trust him."

Max patted his hand. "Neither do I."

Steel stood up. "I'll go find Jason and Sam. Time to return to my old home."

~

Josh waited nervously. He had only just met Jeremiah. The guard brought him into the room and shackled him to the table.

"Joshua Knight." Jeremiah said.

Josh almost gasped at the eerie similarity between Jeremiah and his brother. He had the same ginger hair and turquoise eyes. Only Jeremiah's eyes were filled with something far deadlier than Jonathan's. "To what do I owe this honor?"

Josh cleared his throat. "I understand your grandfather wants me for something special. Any idea?"

Jeremiah raised an eyebrow and shrugged. "If I knew, why would I tell you?"

"You want to be rid of it, don't you?"

Jeremiah squirmed a little and then looked away. "It will never go away. It's dormant. Trapped. Like a rock in my gut."

"But if you could get rid of the second demon, would you?"

"What is this all about? I told Ross I would cooperate, okay?" Jeremiah avoided answering the question.

"Which is why you're here in this conference room at Seagoville and not solitary somewhere else. Ross worked out a deal. But we have to deal with something first."

"Number two, right?" Jeremiah sat back. "I told Jonathan I wanted him to go. I'm tired of being a puppet. But you didn't hear what Grandpoppa said. The only way I can be rid of him and the only way you can send him to Tartarus is if I die." He paused and looked away. "Maybe it's time to end all of this."

"No. I have a solution." Josh said quietly.

Jeremiah glanced back at him. "I'm sensing another deal."

"Why am I so important?" Josh asked.

Jeremiah leaned forward. "Grandpoppa said he had talked to you when you were influenced by the Pandora Stone. I have no idea what he told you. But he pretty much made it clear that once I and JJ were out of the picture, you would take our place and 'manifest' whatever that is."

"Manifest?" Josh's brow wrinkled in puzzlement. "What does that mean?"

"I've been trying to figure that out since I was thirteen. Speaking of thirteen. I hear he's back."

Josh tensed. No need keeping it secret. "How did you know?"

"I saw Winny the Poo in the dining room this morning. He knows who I am, and he told me." He leaned over the table. "So, what are you after? A twofer?"

Josh nodded. "As a matter of fact, I am." He stood up and crossed to the door. He opened it and Father Caskey entered, followed by Father Valdez and Osondu.

"Jeremiah, meet the team that will bring you freedom in Christ."

EPILOGUE

Fine snow blew up into Rebecca's face and she laughed. Pablo stopped right in front of her on his snowboard.

"You've decided it's time to join us?" His thousand watt smile lit up the slopes around her.

"Yes. My work is done." She looked around her at the snow covered mountains. The sky glowed with a blue so bright and deep it defied human definition. Pablo stepped out of his snow boots and slung the snowboard over his shoulder.

"Come into the restaurant and have the best hot chocolate you've ever tasted." He led her across the snow toward a towering glass and dark wood alpine style building. Funny, but the snow wasn't that cold. It was just right.

Pablo opened the door and the fragrance of vanilla and baked bread and cinnamon and coffee caressed her senses. She raised her hands and marveled that both arms were intact. Natural. Warm.

Rebecca looked down at the white snow suit she wore. Pablo motioned toward the open door. "He's waiting for you."

A joy and anticipation unlike anything she had ever known filled her heart, washing away such mundane notions as regret and guilt and shame. In the face of the wonder around her, all earthly thought faded into a joy and peace she had sought her entire life.

Rebecca walked into the building and all around her, faces she recognized turned in her direction. Smiles, not frowns. No pain. No tears. No suffering. All was joy and, yes, understanding!

A man stood with his back to her. He wore a dark green snowsuit and his long hair hung over his shoulders. He turned and smiled at her. Eyes filled with eternity and today and tomorrow and forever and joy and love and light brighter than any human understanding pierced to her soul and she felt . . . love! She drew closer and He extended his hand.

Rebecca, once known as the Crimson Snake, reached out with her renewed hand and placed it in the man's hand. She looked down through tear filled eyes at her perfect hand and saw the scars in the man's palm and wrist. They were there for her. They were the marks of love and forgiveness. They were the only scars in heaven.

AFTERWORD

I know what it is like to be in the presence of evil. While working as an intern in the emergency room I encountered a young woman with supernatural strength. I am convinced she was possessed by a demon. I recently had a conversation with a young man interning in our church. He expressed skepticism about demons. This alarmed me and I realized that Wormwood had learned his lesson!

In "The Screwtape Letters" demons discuss the best strategy. It is one of apathy. Do not make your presence well known. Operate from obscurity. In today's culture we are obsessed with monsters and fantasy but find it hard to believe in the devil.

In the past few months I discovered an excellent resource, a podcast called "The Exorcist Files" with Father Carlos Martins. Each episode contains a dramatic recreation of one of his exorcisms. The sessions alone are worth listening to although I would not recommend doing so late at night. However, the true value lies in Father Martins' continual reassurance of the power of Christ in our world and in one's life. It is such a God honoring podcast. I recommend it although it may change you from a standpoint of apathy to one of becoming a warrior for Christ. Website: exorcistfiles.tv.

Two books are worth reading:

Begone, Satan! By Father Carl Vogl

Demonic Foes By Richard Gallagher, M.D.

To learn more about the plan of salvation used by Kevin check out https://www.namb.net/evangelism/3circles/

My fervent prayer is that this book and this story will do two things regarding your relationship with Christ.

First, I hope it will inspire you to revisit that moment Christ came into your life. It is the most important decision you have ever made.

Second, if you have not considered surrendering to Christ, go back and read that section when Kevin introduced Christ to a young JJ. Or go to the above website and watch the videos. It will become the most important decision of your life!

Bruce Hennigan

December 12, 2024

About the Author

Bruce Hennigan grew up in Northwest Louisiana and became a physician practicing in the field of radiology. He was a church drama director for 15 years and wrote over 150 plays. He is a certified apologist, or one who defends the truthfulness of the Christian faith with Reasons to Believe and with the North American Mission Board in the role of a Certified Apologetic Instructor. He speaks on this topic on a regular basis. Bruce is also the author of nine books in the supernatural thriller series, "The Chronicles of Jonathan Steel" as well as "Death by Darwin", "The Homecoming Tree", "Our Darkness, His Light", and, with Mark Sutton, "Hope Again: A Lifetime Plan for Conquering Depression" and "Shadow Merchant: A Jack Merchant Medical Mystery".

Together with Mark Sutton, he participates in a seminar based on the book entitled, "Conquering Depression". For more information on the book and tool, "LifeFilters" go to www.conqueringdepression.com.

Bruce is married to the most incredible woman in the world, Sherry. They have two adult children and they live in Shreveport, Louisiana. Bruce and Sherry along with their daughter, Casey, are strong advocates of support for epilepsy patients and their caregivers.

For more information on books: hopeagainbooks.com